A WHITE FEATHER

The old way was over.

She knew that, yet something in her soul still screamed in denial.

She was Comanche, after all. She did not know how to give up.

Then she saw it. A nock feather, torn free from the shaft of an arrow . . . bleached, delicate, broken, the feather of a white bird.

Had he known she would come? Yes, she thought, yes. From the moment their eyes had first met, he had known her soul.

Storm Trail knelt painfully and closed her hand over the feather. A ragged gasp tore from her throat as she felt him again, even stronger now.

She had hated him forever, and had loved him twice that long. She could not forgive him and she could not forget him. She smiled bitterly and let herself fall back into all the old memories.

So be it, White Raven. I will find you.

WALK
INTO THE
NIGHT

BEVERLY
BIRD

PINNACLE BOOKS
KENSINGTON PUBLISHING CORP.

PINNACLE BOOKS are published by

Kensington Publishing Corp.
850 Third Avenue
New York, NY 10022

First Pinnacle Books Printing: January, 1996

Printed in the United States of America

Prologue

1873

The Comanche wind moaned with a pain all its own. It whipped her hair and tore at her doeskin as Storm Trail lifted one leg stiffly over the back of her pony and dropped to the ground. The old bullet wound near her hip throbbed from sitting so long astride, and something in the small of her back squirmed nastily. Ah, she was old, and he was all of her memories.

She jerked at the unbidden thought of him. Why should she think of him now, after so many seasons? Then as she turned slowly to look out at the abandoned camp, she understood.

She felt him. He had been here. The lingering ghost of his presence was still in the air, and she had always been able to sense it.

She forced herself to walk, picking her way slowly through the hundreds of burned-out fire pits. Dog-ravaged carcasses of antelope circled the place where the warriors had danced. The earth was packed hard there, and if she closed her eyes, she could almost hear their moccasins stomping in desperate urgency.

The Nermenuh, the once-mighty Comanche, had flocked here so that Eeshatai The Prophet might give them hope again with his *puha,* his medicine. Eeshatai had promised that a fire-star would blaze across the night sky, and that there would then come a period of drought. He had told the Nermenuh when it happened they should perform a Sun Dance and grow strong again. Then they would enter upon one last great war of extermination against the *tejanos,* those brazen, indefatigable Tex-us white men who had slowly destroyed them.

Storm Trail's Penateka band had not come to Eeshatai's Sun Dance. Kills In The Dark had spoken against it in council. Though many despised him, and she herself no longer trusted him, she believed he was right this time. The Nerm were beaten. The old way was over.

She knew that, yet something in her soul still screamed in denial.

She was Comanche, after all. She did not know how to give up. She had seen The Prophet's fire streak across the sky, and she had watched Mother Earth wither in thirst. A faint thready hope had moved stubbornly in her breast, and she had left her Penateka to come here to find Eeshatai herself. She had come to look into his eyes, to *know,* but she was too late. The Prophet and the Nermenuh had been here and they had gone on.

Raven would not have danced, she thought. He would have stood back, watching with that trace of wariness, with that half smile of superiority. Her breath snagged as she remembered how he could look.

Defeated, she started to turn back to her pony, and then she saw it. Her feet carried her toward it even as everything inside her cringed. She stood over it and began trembling. A nock feather, torn free from the shaft of an arrow . . . bleached, delicate, broken—the feather of a white bird.

Had he known she would come? Yes, she thought, yes. From the moment their eyes had first met, he had known her soul.

Storm Trail knelt painfully and closed her hand over the feather. A ragged gasp tore from her throat as she felt him again, even stronger now.

She had hated him forever, and had loved him twice that long. She could not forgive him and she could not forget him. Her need for him was still an endless ache in her heart. She had come here to see the truth in Eeshatai's eyes, so she might finally stop believing, but now she knew she would have to see Raven one last time.

She smiled bitterly and let herself fall back into all the old memories.

So be it, White Raven. I will find you.

Part One

The Beginning

One

"This is how the boys do it."

Yellow Fawn and She Smiles pressed closer to watch the grasshoppers that Storm Trail had tied together with a piece of sinew, but Turns Her Eyes Down rocked back on her heels. That was all right. Eyes Down wasn't really one of them—her father was a very poor hunter, and her mother was known to be lazy. But Yellow Fawn's uncle and She Smiles's father were so respected they sat on the council, and Storm Trail's father was the second most important chief of all.

"How do you know what the boys do?" Eyes Down demanded.

"Kills In The Dark showed me."

Yellow Fawn hooted the Nerm love call, and She Smiles launched herself upon Storm Trail to tickle her, but Eyes Down still held back. "He did not."

"He did!" gasped Storm Trail.

"Prove it."

It was a bald challenge. "Yes," Storm Trail decided. "I will."

She stood up, hitching her breechclout up over her skinny hips. She ran her palms over her bare chest, wishing more than anything that she had breasts. Then Kills In The Dark would come to her. But she had seen only ten snows, and she did not have breasts yet, so she ran back to the camp to find the warrior in question.

The Penateka band's lodges were crowded into a timber break beside a full, tumbling river. They trickled out over the grasslands, toward the great escarpment far to the east that guarded Nermenuh land. Some small rocky hills sat closer to the south, studded with scrubby cedar. Cottonwoods tangled near the water, and thickets of plum and grapes were wild there.

Storm Trail passed through the outlying tipis, heading for the ones in the center. The more respected a man was, the closer he camped to the arbor. Storm Trail found Kills In The Dark there, at her brother's lodge, bending over to peer through the open, weighted door flap.

"Wolf Dream is with my father," she called out, running to him.

Kills In The Dark looked back at her, frowning. "Where?"

"Paya-yuca's lodge." Paya-yuca was the Penateka's most important chief.

Kills In The Dark turned away. "Wait!" she cried. The footsteps of the other girls sounded close behind her. "Tell how you showed me the grasshopper game."

"I did what?"

"The grasshopper game." She begged him with her eyes to lie for her.

Kills In The Dark grunted a sound of disgust and went to Paya-yuca's lodge.

Her heart squirmed warmly as she watched him move away. His black hair was twisted neatly into braids, and it shined in the sun. He wore both a breechclout and leggings, and the fringes down the outside seams danced as he walked. He had strong golden-red shoulders and short sturdy legs. His nose was sharp and it gave him a haughty look. His eyes were small and very black.

It was true that he had probably seen fifteen more snows than she had, but Storm Trail already knew she would marry someone much older than herself. She was Black Paint's only daughter. Storm Trail guessed that a man would probably have to be thirty-two, maybe even as old as thirty-three before he could collect all the presents that Black Paint would demand to let her go. She thought that by the time Kills In The Dark was ready, she would finally have breasts.

She sighed and dropped down to sit in the dust of the path. Yellow Fawn squatted beside her. "You lied," her friend said dejectedly.

Storm Trail glanced at her. "Did he say that?"

Yellow Fawn scowled, considering. "No, not truly, I guess."

"There. He was just too much in a hurry to tell about it."

Then abruptly all thoughts of Kills In The Dark vanished from her mind. Suddenly she wondered why everyone was gathering in Paya-yuca's tipi instead of beneath the cool arbor when the sun was so mercilessly hot.

She shot to her feet.

"Where are you going?" asked Yellow Fawn.

Storm Trail didn't answer. Her eyes were intent on the chief's lodge as she moved in that direction.

"She is going to get punished again," She Smiles muttered.

Yellow Fawn nodded glumly. Nothing was very much fun when Storm Trail wasn't allowed to play.

Storm Trail circled around to the back of Paya-yuca's lodge. The big outer hide was rolled up, but the inner dew cloth was down, even though it hadn't rained for many suns and a breeze should have been welcomed. She moved closer, but they were talking quietly inside, and she couldn't hear what was being said.

She squatted down, scratching impatiently at an insect bite on her thigh. She could hear better now, though not very well. Their voices were murmurs, wordless. She sat back on her heels, chewing her lip, then she poked tentatively at the dew cloth.

Her fingers met something solid. There was bedding or maybe some storage parfleches on the other side.

She lay down and carefully tugged the liner out from beneath whatever it was. Bedding! She began wriggling into the robes. Now she could hear her father's voice perfectly.

"They were found in Wichita country."

Storm Trail peeked around a grass-stuffed, rabbit fur pillow and saw Paya-yuca nod solemnly.

"They left all the other white-eyes near that big water and rode inland to the *Tohapt Pahehona,* the Blue Water River, to live by themselves. Buffalo Piss told how they fell off their horses in the fighting. They did not shoot their guns very well. They tore down the trees and built walls of the wood to put their lodges inside as though that would protect them, but then they left the doors wide open. Buffalo Piss said his warriors rode in and asked them for one of those strange little buffalo they keep, those cat-tul. One of the white-eyes came to meet them without even carrying a weapon, and then he told them no, they would not give any presents!"

"What kind of men dare to live so near our country?" Storm Trail heard Lost Coyote ask. He was her cousin. Her father had claimed his mother for a wife after her own husband was killed in the Pawnee war.

"The Mex-ee-cans call them *tejanos,* because they call that Wichita land 'Tex-us,' " Paya-yuca was muttering. "And if what Buffalo Piss says is true, then they are infesting it now like maggots."

There was a murmur of voices. "Did Buffalo Piss bring any captives?" her brother, Wolf Dream, demanded. "I would see some of these people."

"His Quohadi band has them. They took a woman for a slave and some children to be adopted."

"Only crazy-brave men would crawl right up to our country alone without fear," said Paya-yuca, still dwelling on what troubled him most. "I do not think their women and children will make very good captives if they are not afraid of anything. How would you train them? Probably by the time we see the

Quohadi, they will all be dead. Those warriors will kill them rather than fuss with them."

"Then we should go east and get some of our own," Wolf Dream insisted.

"They sound easy to kill and steal from," Kills In The Dark suggested.

The younger men began talking loudly. They would go, Storm Trail decided. People who offered up their property and their lives without caution or fear could not be ignored when there were coups to be gained and ponies to be stolen.

She began to wriggle out again, eager to tell Yellow Fawn and She Smiles about the strange new captives they would be getting. She had never seen a crazy person before, unless you counted Turtle Dancing, the Quohadi medicine man. She thought the way he talked when no one was there was pretty strange.

She was almost out when something hard and heavy came down on her hand. She started to yowl and bit the sound back, but not quickly enough.

"What was that?" her father asked sharply.

"I think there are vermin in your bedding, Paya-yuca," her brother answered too mildly. "You should talk to your wives."

The pressure left her hand. Storm Trail wiggled her fingers. They throbbed, but suddenly, her belly hurt worse.

She was in trouble again. Her brother was not covering up for her—he was simply not disrupting the council. He would tell her mother later what she had done.

The sun climbed higher, bleaching the sky, filling the air with a dusty, baked smell. Storm Trail's sleek shoulder-length hair was damp with sweat, and grime clung to her sticky skin. In pairs and in threes, the other children raced past her mother's lodge, heading for the spot where the river deepened enough to be bathed in.

Storm Trail was still squatting over a buffalo cowhide

pegged out on the ground. On the bright side these spring cows were thin. There weren't as many clumps of fat to scrape off, so she could work faster. On the bad side these were the best hides for lodge covers, and it took many hides to make a new lodge.

Storm Trail looked glumly at the pile beside her. Then she brightened as she saw She Smiles, Yellow Fawn, and Eyes Down coming back from the water.

She glanced quickly over her shoulder. Loses Something, her mother, and Star Line, her aunt and her father's second wife, were busy at the fire pit. She waved her friends over furtively.

"I found out something," she whispered when they reached her. She told them about the new, crazy white-eyes in Wichita country.

Yellow Fawn and She Smiles listened avidly, but Eyes Down only scowled. "You are lying again."

Storm Trail straightened indignantly. "I heard them say it!"

"Are their eyes really white?" She Smiles wondered. "Do they have no centers, no black parts?"

Storm Trail nodded sagely. "They are like the snow all the way through."

"You never saw one," scoffed Eyes Down.

"I heard about them."

"Where?"

"In the council."

"When will they go get them? It is almost time for another hunt."

"Right after that, I think."

Eyes Down leaned closer. "That is one way to get Kills In The Dark to notice you."

"He notices me now." Storm Trail began scraping again, just in case her mother or Star Line looked over. But then she looked up from her work, her curiosity overcoming her pride. "How?"

"Capture your own crazy white-eyes."

Yellow Fawn's jaw dropped. She Smiles laughed. Storm Trail clapped a hand over her mouth before she could draw her mother's attention.

"I could do that," she muttered, "if I wanted to."

"No!" gasped Yellow Fawn.

"How?" pressed She Smiles, prying her friend's fingers from her face so she could talk.

"Go on the raid," Eyes Down suggested.

"They would never let her."

Storm Trail thought about it. "I could dress like a boy. How would they know?"

"You have no braids!" The Nerm women wore their hair cropped at their shoulders. They did not have time to fuss with it like their men did, greasing and plaiting it into braids.

Storm Trail looked out at the distant pony herd, her eyes narrowing. "I could take hairs from their tails and make some."

Yellow Fawn's face blanched. "Oh, if they catch you they will feed you to Piamempits, to Cannibal Owl!"

Storm Trail considered that evil creature. He lived in a cave on the south side of the Wichita Mountains. She had never actually seen the cave, but her brother said he had spotted it once on a raiding trip. Cannibal Owl ate the children who were sent to him when they did something very, very bad.

"I think maybe there is no Cannibal Owl," she said finally. The others gasped.

"Well, I think he would have eaten me by now." Still she couldn't be sure. "No," she decided. Even if Piamempits didn't exist, she couldn't begin to imagine how many hides she would have to scrape if she got caught.

"I dare you," whispered Eyes Down.

"Oh," groaned Yellow Fawn. "Now you've done it."

But Storm Trail shook her head. "No," she said again.

Except it *would* get Kills In The Dark to notice her. Maybe he would be so impressed he would try to buy her right away. Black Paint would say no, of course. Kills In The Dark would be turned away for a few more seasons, until she got breasts. She shivered a little as she imagined him pining for her.

And the stories she could tell when she got back! Eyes Down could never say they were lies.

Storm Trail looked at the pony herd again, considering.

Two

The war band left camp four sleeps later.

Storm Trail lay rigidly beside Yellow Fawn in her friend's lodge, her heart beating so hard she felt dizzy without even lifting her head from the fur pillow they shared. Finally she heard the swish of moccasin fringes in the dirt outside as the men moved about. She sat up, and Yellow Fawn rolled over, mumbling in her sleep.

She dug the braids she had made from beneath their bedding and scowled at them in the dark. One was good, but the other was skinny and scrawny. Getting the hairs had been surprisingly time-consuming, and she had had to do it when no one was paying attention.

She slicked her hair down with some buffalo grease, knotting the horsehair braids into it at each side. Finally she shrugged into one of Yellow Fawn's brother's fringed shirts so she would look like a boy. Swallowing dryly, she ducked outside and hurried away from the lodges.

She slipped into the herd, caught her breath and looked back at the camp. She could just make out the arbor from here. The war band had gathered in front of it, but even as she watched, the men dispersed.

Storm Trail scowled as she realized there were not many of them. That changed everything. If it had been a big war band, one more boy would not be noticed. But she counted only twenty warriors—and an extra one would surely raise eyebrows.

She could not go. She could not dare it. But Eyes Down would mock her if she didn't! She couldn't let that happen.

She whinnied the signal her father used to call his horses. When a gelding trotted up, she grabbed a handful of his mane and pulled herself astride. She would just have to stay so far behind them that they would not know she was there.

She gave the war band time to get ahead of her, then she closed her eyes and took a deep breath. She hoped there was no Cannibal Owl.

Their horses were lathered and blowing by the time Wolf Dream reined his mount in on a hill on the fringes of Wichita land. His cousin came up beside him. Lost Coyote made a small grunting noise when he saw.

Nestled into the bottom of an oak-studded valley was a tiny white-eyes encampment.

"It is true then," Lost Coyote said, bemused.

It was true, Wolf Dream thought, all of it. These *tejano* white-eyes were far from their water. They had raped the trees and had built the logs all around in a square. Inside were strange lodges, squat and ugly, built of more of the wood. Off to one side of the stockade, Mother Earth had been savaged. Her dirt showed through in neat rows between thrusting ears of corn. A woman in a long cumbersome dress worked there along with a young man. Wolf Dream could see five more men toiling inside over gun barrels and horses.

Suddenly the woman in the corn looked up and saw them. Her screams sliced the air. She tried to run, but she took only a few steps before her long dress tripped her. She landed face-down in the dirt, and the boy-man had to stop to haul her to her feet again.

Wolf Dream shook his head in disgust and wonder. "Kill the men. Take that woman and any children you can find."

* * *

Lucas Mazur was more startled than anything else when the preacher's wife began howling. Then he looked up at the oak-scrubbed crests above the cornfield and he saw the Indians.

Finally.

Adrenaline sang through him, exploding into his blood. He dropped the hoe he had been holding and almost leaped with joy. This was exactly the kind of excitement that had been calling to him all his sixteen years. He recognized the exhilaration of danger as intimately as he might have known a lover, if he had ever gotten lucky enough to have one. He couldn't really count the whore in Saint Louis. She'd smelled like other men and besides, he didn't figure that a lover was somebody you had to pay.

She hadn't turned out to be what he had been searching for when he'd left Philadelphia last year, running away from home with all of two dollars rolled into the toe of his shoe. Not that he couldn't have taken more. His father—The Banker—wouldn't have missed it, but it was the principle of the thing. He had left Miss Myra's Christian Home in Saint Louis on principle, too, when the old lady had tried to save his wandering, delinquent soul. He'd relieved her of a healthy chunk of her savings before he'd left, but not all of it. Miss Myra was the one of the few genuinely nice people he could ever remember encountering.

Lucas just hadn't wanted his soul saved. He'd wanted . . . *something.* So he'd drifted to Texas, and now here it was—at least twenty 'Manches sitting on a hill. Fighting Injuns on the raw, new frontier was *definitely* something.

Except it didn't appear as though Abigail Rust was going to give him the opportunity. Abby was still wailing, and at the rate she was going, she'd get them both scalped long before he found the gun he'd left somewhere in this cornfield. Lucas dragged hard on her hand, trying to pull her toward the fort walls.

"Come *on!*" he shouted. She finally took two running steps

after him, then she tripped on her skirt, going down into the dirt with an unladylike grunt.

"Jesus Christ on a mule!" He stopped and hauled her to her feet again. Her face was beet red, and after a moment he realized that it wasn't just the Injuns that had her breathing so hard.

"Lucas, don't use the Lord's name that way!" she gasped.

Oh, bugger the Lord's name. He almost said it aloud, but he hadn't gotten from Philadelphia to the Texas plains by being stupid. Such a comment would freeze her up for sure.

"Miz Abby, you've got to run now," he cajoled.

She looked up at the hills instead. Lucas groaned. Once, in Missouri, he'd seen a doe look just like that when he had trained his shotgun on her, just before he'd pulled the trigger.

He snatched a handful of Abby's skirt hem and tore at it with all his strength. It ripped away almost to her hips and he gave it another sharp tug, pulling the last piece free where it clung to her waistband. Now the blood drained from her face, and her eyes started to go glassy with shock. He shook her hard enough to make her teeth click together.

"No disrespect intended, Miz Abby, but you've got to listen to me. That fort gate is about a hundred yards away, and you've got to be able to run fast to make it. I'm not looking at anything I've not seen before, but if those Injuns get you, they sure will be. Do you know what they do to white women?" He shook her again, jarring her.

A horrible understanding began to replace the dull glaze in Abigail's eyes. Up on the crest one of the 'Manches gave another ungodly howl. Abigail took a few staggering steps backward, her throat working. "I'd rather . . . die."

"You might get that chance, too, if you don't start moving." She moved.

Lucas watched her dainty bare feet fly down the cultivated row, then he moved off in search of his weapon. A fresh crescendo of screams came as the Injuns finally attacked, and Lucas felt his blood sluice down to his toes. Regret rolled briefly in his belly as he considered that unless they got those fort doors closed, the Rust clan was probably all going to die with their good Lord God watching on, just as the Parkers had done a few weeks ago.

He shoved his way through the next tangle of stalks and finally found his rifle. It was as long as a man's body and more than capable of taking down everyone in that buzzing horde. The 'Manche yipping and screaming sounded distant now—Lucas thought they were probably inside the fort. If he could find an angle looking back there, he could brace the gun and pick the savages off as they came out again.

His face split into a grin that would have made Abigail blanch.

When Storm Trail dismounted behind a canebreak on the other side of the fort, her legs gave out.

She felt as though someone had stuffed a bunch of fur between her ears. The sounds around her seemed thick and muffled and distant. It hurt to sit on her pony, and it had hurt to get off. She was pretty sure she was going to die. Nothing but dying could feel this terrible.

She might even have cried and not cared too much because there was nobody to see it, except she didn't think there was any water left in her to cry with. Oh, why had she thought this was a good idea? She hadn't had anything to drink since they had left the camp five whole suns ago. She felt dry and parched—as if she would crumble into dust and blow away if the wind blew too hard.

She was definitely going to die unless she found water, she thought. She staggered to her feet again and peeked out of the cane, and her eyes went huge.

Directly in front of her were the most bizarre plants she had ever seen in her life. What could make them grow in such perfect lines like that? She thought this was probably something she would want to tell Yellow Fawn and She Smiles and

Eyes Down about. A dizzying rush of excitement filled her so that she didn't feel quite so sick anymore.

The warriors were inside those wooden walls, fighting. She had plenty of time. She pushed through the cane and darted across the grass, into the strange plants. She skidded into the first row, appalled at the way the big sprawling leaves seemed to tangle about her.

Storm Trail fought off the leaves and pushed her way deeper into the corn. Then a scream stuck in her dry throat. She moved into a cleared path and a *tejano* looked right back at her.

She had found one!

Her blood rushed in her ears with a strange *thump-swoosh*. She wondered what to do now, and then she saw his gun—right there on the ground like the men had said in council. The crazy white-eyes had already dropped it!

She looked at him to see if he was closer to it than she was. His eyes burned right back into hers.

They *weren't* white all the way through. Oh, how she hated being wrong! They were a dark gray-blue, the color of a storm sky. In a shattering instant she knew he wasn't crazy at all. There was something reckless in his eyes, but it was only the same kind of feeling that was always getting her in trouble.

She looked at the gun and she looked at him again, then she dove for the weapon. It was so heavy! She gave a tiny cry of protest and squeezed her eyes shut. The gun pulled her down, down . . . down—and she collapsed, rifle and all.

Storm Trail hit the ground with a swooning, graceless thud, and she never heard the weapon go off.

The air exploded with a crack of close gunfire just as Wolf Dream galloped past the cornfield. He reined in hard and fast, and a moment later there came another shot. This time his beloved war stallion lurched and fell.

He leaped free of it and pulled an arrow from his quiver, holding it ready as he plunged into the corn. He pushed through a row of the plants, then he came up short, his breath snagging.

There was his sister. His *sister?*

The boy-man in the field had her. Wolf Dream knew her delicate features immediately, though her strange, lopsided braids gave him pause. She was unconscious, and the *tejano* had one arm cocked around her throat, pinning her drooping form against his side. The boy-man's gun was at his feet, but he had a knife, and it was pressed to the sweet spot on Storm Trail's midriff, the place where her rib cage came together.

"Hold up right there, Injun," Lucas gasped, not giving a tinker's damn if the savage understood him or not. The meaning of his knife was clear enough. "One more step and the boy dies."

The Comanche stopped in his tracks. Lucas grinned, pleased, then his bowels went hot and watery.

Oh, Jesus Christ on a mule.

The kid was one thing. This guy was something else again. The 'skin's expression was hard as stone. Red paint slashed his cheeks and his chin, and a cylindrical earring hung from his left lobe. Just beneath it a long livid scar started and ran down across his collarbone.

Lucas stared at it in sick fascination. It finally occurred to him that he was probably going to die here. He was going to die very badly.

All the things he had heard about Parker Fort flashed into his mind again. Somebody had said that the old Baptist elder there had been pinned to the ground and his privates and hair had been cut off because he wouldn't give the heathens a cow. Lucas thought he would give them just about anything they asked for, but the buck only started circling him slowly.

Lucas moved with him, inching around, keeping his eyes on him. "Come on, Injun, come on," he muttered. "Stay put where I can see you."

The 'Manche notched the arrow he had been holding and aimed it at Lucas's head. Lucas tensed. Without intending to, he dug the knife a little deeper into the kid's midriff. The kid groaned and the buck's eyes shot to him.

"So you care what happens to him, huh? That's good to know. I guess as long as I've got him, then I've got you, too." He took a deep breath and a careful step backward.

"Tell you what. I won't cut if you don't shoot. I'll just take this kid and head over to the fort and see if you've left any horses standing. Just let me get out of range, and I'll dump him off someplace—"

Lucas broke off suddenly, the hairs on his nape lifting, as a whispery sound of movement came from behind him.

Too late he realized that the screams and the howls back at the fort had fallen silent. He wondered if the entire Rust clan was dead. He wondered if they had managed to take any Injuns out with them. If not, there were nineteen of them waiting behind him for his scalp and his balls.

The buck in front of him erupted in an explosive rush of Comanche. He made a sharp, cutting gesture and Lucas thought he understood. He was holding his boys off.

"Smart move, Injun. Now would you care to tell them to get out of my way so I can go?"

Nobody moved.

Lucas opened his mouth to try again when the kid stirred with a little gagging sound. His arm was notched hard at the boy's throat. He shifted his elbow instinctively to allow him some more air just as the bucks began to surround him.

A bad sign there.

Suddenly the kid let loose with a terrifying howl. His elbow caught Lucas hard in the ribs. Lucas slammed his arms down reflexively, catching the boy around the waist and pinning him against him. The kid was small and wiry and fought like a demon from hell. If he got away from him, Lucas knew he was as good as dead.

And *that* pissed him off.

He'd had one lousy whore who'd stunk like a pig! It wasn't fair, and he wasn't ready to die—and if these 'Manches wanted his balls, then they were damned well going to have to cut his heart out first. For some reason that struck him as funny. He gave a cackling laugh, and a few of the bucks jumped back warily.

The kid's legs were flailing now. Lucas pinned the knife against his hip with one hand and grabbed one of his braids with the other. It was slick as bear shit, and he wondered crazily if that was what was on it, then the damned thing came free in his hand.

What the hell?

The kid wrenched away, running. For one lethal moment Lucas stared down at the braid. A body punched into him from behind, and he felt the cold blade of a knife at the side of his own throat as he went down. He ate dirt and tried to spit it out. He rolled over halfway and came up hard with his knee.

The blow drove the buck forward, over Lucas's shoulder. Lucas laughed again, crazily, and the Injun scrambled away to crouch and watch him. Lucas roared and lunged for him, cracking the buck solidly in the jaw. He felt bone splinter and he cackled again, and the 'skin went crazy.

Well, I'll be damned, Lucas thought. He's as scared as I am.

It gave him a preposterous, unexpected edge. He was smart enough to know it, but there was no time to figure out how to use it. A hard sinewy arm came around Lucas's neck from behind. Another buck dumped him in the dirt, and the first one wrestled with his legs until he had them in a deadlock.

The Injun at his head drew his knife in a slow circle around his neck. Lucas flinched but blood only trickled. The cut had been oddly gentle, nothing more than a threat.

Suddenly he understood that they weren't going to kill him. Not yet, anyway. They sure as hell hadn't wasted this much time on the Rusts. The first brave made a motion to the one at his head. Together they yanked him upright. The second buck pinned his arms behind his back, and the first pointed an arrow at his chest.

It was a deadly situation, and maybe he was wrong about

them letting him keep everything he'd been born with, but Lucas's attention was diverted from them as that blasted kid was dragged back into the cornfield.

A big 'Manche had him, one whose rolls of fat seemed to slide downward in waves until they reached the hide flap he wore over his privates. The kid shrieked and twisted. Suddenly his mannerisms and voice left no doubt as to his gender.

Christ on a mule! *He* was a *girl!*

Too Much finally hoisted her completely off the ground. He held her effortlessly in front of him so her feet couldn't connect with his shins anymore.

"Tie her on," snapped Wolf Dream.

Too Much carried Storm Trail to her horse. Falls Into The Water had found it and was leading it into the corn.

"What of the *tejano?*" Too Much asked.

Wolf Dream hesitated. "Tie him on behind her."

"He could hurt her."

"Good," Wolf Dream snarled.

Too Much heaved Storm Trail up onto the horse. He caught her ankle. Someone else caught her other one—and before she knew it, they had lashed them together, the rope looped beneath the pony's belly.

They were treating her no better than a captive!

Lost Coyote began pushing the *tejano* toward her. The crazy white-eyes jerked free of him and Storm Trail screamed again. Too Much and the other warriors hurried to catch him, but the *tejano* only fought off their grip and moved toward her pony on his own. He spoke in his twangy white-eyes tongue.

"As long as you're willing to let me keep my testicles, I'm willing to do this your way."

The warriors stared at him. The *tejano* grabbed hold of the pony's mane and pulled himself clumsily astride behind her.

Storm Trail twisted around to gape at him. Oh, yes, he was

a crazy person! And now his odor was wafting to her over her shoulder. He *smelled*.

Wolf Dream shouted for someone to get the horses. He grabbed the most likely looking prospect of the white-eyes sorry bunch and swung astride.

"Ride out!" he ordered.

Storm Trail thought she'd better not ask what had happened to his stallion.

Three

It didn't take Lucas long to decide that going with the 'Manches hadn't been such a great idea after all.

He tried to shift his weight on the bony spine of the horse beneath him. His ankles were tied, his hands were lashed together behind his back, and there was a noose around his neck. The other end of it was held by the first buck he had encountered in the cornfield, the one who was in charge.

They had been galloping since they had left Rust Fort, but somehow, impossibly, the brat tied in front of him managed to sleep. Her head had dropped forward some time ago, and now her breathing was slow and even. Lucas was in too much pain to relax. The insides of his trousers were wearing thin where they rubbed against the horse's hide. Blood matted his skin to the torn buckskin, tugging at the hairs with each of the pony's strides. Balance was a constant, excruciating struggle. Every once in a while the rope around his neck pulled tight as the 'Manche horse got too far ahead or his own mount lagged behind. Then pain would shoot, hot and tingling, down his chest. That sizzling feeling was the only sensation he had in his arms now.

He knew without being told that he was in a deeper part of Texas than any white man had ever seen, and there was something exhilarating about that, something staggering about the land. In spite of his pain, it called to that instinct he had long lived with and had never quite named.

Hell, yes, he thought, this was something.

The war party had passed up onto the huge Balcones Escarpment, and now there was only a breathtaking sea of grass that reached belly-high to the horses. There was no sign of water. The sky was blinding, almost white where the sun climbed into it. The grass waved on and on without break or boundaries. The wind blew with a sullen sound, making his eyes tear and his skin feel cracked and dry.

When the sun was straight above his head, Lucas finally noticed something different on the horizon, a knot of darkness. The war band headed that way, and after a time he realized that he was seeing trees, a deep green stretch of pecans. When they reached the river hidden behind them, the Rust horse that the first buck had been riding finally collapsed.

Lucas looked at the water. His tongue was so dry it felt permanently cleaved to the roof of his mouth. He was eternally grateful that they had stopped moving, but unfortunately it woke the kid. He worked himself backward, away from her, grunting with the effort. The rolling gait of the horse had urged his weight forward so that he was crammed against her. That had been all right while she was sleeping, but he knew what was coming now that she was awake.

He wasn't quick enough. Her hands were lashed behind her like his were, but not as tightly. She was able to swivel her wrists. He looked down, watching helplessly as her fingers squirmed. She finally found his thigh, the tender part on the inside where the shredded buckskin was ground into his raw flesh. He bit down on his lip and closed his eyes as she pinched hard.

When he didn't cry out, she worked at it more determinedly, just as she had been doing off and on since they'd left the fort. *Damn her to hell.* He knew what she was aiming for. She wanted him to complain. And if she wanted it that badly, then doing it would probably get him killed.

She got in an especially savage twist and Lucas groaned silently. He'd had enough.

"All right, weasel, your turn."

He leaned forward and sank his teeth into the muscle along the top of her shoulder. She howled and bucked, but he hung on. The 'Manches rushed for them. If they killed him now, Lucas thought, it might almost be worth it.

But the one who had caught him only grabbed a handful of his hair and yanked his head back. He growled something abusive and angry at the kid. He worked at the ropes around her ankles and finally dragged her down off the horse. She wobbled a little when her feet hit the ground, then her legs gave out beneath her. Lucas laughed. He watched her struggle to her knees again. When she gained her feet, she swayed off unsteadily toward the water.

In spite of himself Lucas was impressed. She managed to flick her hair back as though telling them all to kiss her ass.

The buck untied the knots around his own numb feet and tried to pull him off as well. Lucas snapped at him.

"Hold up there. I'm coming." He slid down the side of the pony and held on nonchalantly, one arm looped over the spine that had felt like the Appalachian crest when he had been sitting on it. He was disgruntled to see that from this angle it looked harmless.

His legs tingled and burned, then his feet started throbbing. The Injuns gathered around to stare at him. The first one motioned angrily at the water.

"Yeah, I get your drift. Just a minute." He eased his weight off the horse. So far so good. It hurt abominably to walk, but he managed it, finally heading off toward the river.

He got a good clear look at the kid for the first time. She had washed some of the grime off her face. Her hair was short and otter-sleek with the water. She had something of an aristocratic look about her, what his mother—The Queen—would have called the mark of good blood. She had high cheekbones and perfectly arched brows. Her features were strong without losing their delicacy.

They let him guzzle a handful of water and relieve himself. When he turned away from the stream, he saw that the girl had gone back to the horses. She was pawing through a buckskin sack thrown over the back of one of the Injun ponies, then she began jamming food hungrily and greedily into her mouth.

The other 'Manches noticed this at the same time as Lucas. The one in charge bellowed something and the girl froze in midchew, her eyes flashing to him. Then she gulped defiantly, pushing in another mouthful, and Lucas gave a bark of laughter in spite of himself.

It was his last good moment for quite a while. They mounted again and began galloping. Pain screamed along his inner thighs as they scraped and rubbed, scraped and rubbed. He slid back into the kid and her pincer fingers began fidgeting, reaching.

The closer they got to home, the less Storm Trail worried about the *tejano*. She became very preoccupied with Cannibal Owl.

Her imagination flew like the hawk gliding by overhead. She would be very, very brave when they sent her away. All the Penateka would talk about it long after she was gone. Her banishment would cause as much of a stir as riding in with her own captured white-eyes would have. Kills In The Dark would be sorry he had ignored her on this ride home.

Would he come rescue her? Storm Trail decided that if he tried, she wouldn't let him. On some distant sun she would come back on her own, and the band would be amazed by that, too. Maybe she would wait a few seasons until she had breasts. Then *all* the best warriors would try to buy her. She would let Kills In The Dark suffer just a little bit before she begged her father to accept his offer from among all the others.

Of course she would have to escape Cannibal Owl first. Storm Trail scowled because she really could not think how she might do that. She couldn't even imagine what Piamempits looked like—she did not think anyone had ever said. She thought he must have a lot of sharp teeth to eat children, and she had heard that he was huge. She thought of Paya-yuca, the biggest man she knew. Paya-yuca was not very fast. If that was the case with Cannibal Owl, then she could probably dodge and run and wriggle just enough that he would not be able to hook his talons around her—

Her pony stopped suddenly and the crazy *tejano* slid into her again from behind. She twisted around angrily, then the wind blew the distant smell of the camp to her.

Relief flooded her, followed by a skitter of alarm. The horrible ride was over, but now she would have to face her father.

Storm Trail watched worriedly as the warriors began to repaint their faces. They spit on the feathers on their lances and shields and rubbed them until they were perfect and smooth again and they shined. Then they began to scrub down their ponies with handfuls of grass. More feathers were slipped carefully from their *tunawos,* the special buckskin pouches on their breechclouts. These were woven into the animals' tails and manes.

Storm Trail fidgeted, waiting for someone to come and untie her. Finally Lost Coyote passed close to her, and she grinned at him appealingly. Then her eyes went huge, following him as he went right past her.

"Wait! Help me!"

Her cousin looked back at her. "If you are not quiet," he warned, "I do not know what Wolf Dream might do to you. It could be worse."

"Worse than what?" This ride had been horrifying! Then she understood. Wolf Dream was going to carry her into camp like a captive.

Panic made her pulse gallop. She fought her restraints desperately, bucking to thump her legs against her pony. But the lazy beast just stood there, pulling up grass with its long yellow teeth. Storm Trail twisted around again to look at the crazy *tejano.*

"Do something!"

He was watching the warriors prepare to ride in, his strange eyes rapt. She knew he would not help her—not unless he thought he was saving his own maggot-ridden hide.

"You stupid coyote-breath!" she cried. "They will kill you if you do not run now! Make the pony run!"

His legs were longer than hers. He could do it! But he didn't do anything, and the warriors began moving.

"No!" she howled. She squeezed her eyes shut and felt her skin burn with humiliation.

Someone came up behind her pony and swatted it on the rump. It began a shambling trot toward the camp. Storm Trail choked, thinking of Eyes Down's reaction to this.

The warriors began whooping. Storm Trail peeked and saw them raise their lances. Fresh hair streamed from them. Her pony lunged wearily into a run. Storm Trail closed her eyes again.

The camp smells came at her more strongly. There was the tangy odor of torn grass and the heavier scent of manure as they raced past the pony herd. Then she caught the smells of fresh hides and buffalo-chip smoke as they reached the outskirts of the camp. Her nose told her that someone was roasting pecans, and someone else was boiling meat to make it soft for one of the old ones who had no teeth. But Storm Trail knew the people would all stop what they were doing to watch the warriors and hoot at them as they came in, to stare at *her*.

Her skin itched with the feeling of all their eyes. Then they surrounded her, making her pony stop because it was too much effort to press through all the bodies. Finally Storm Trail could stand it no more. Her eyes flew open, and she drew in her breath angrily, but no one was even looking at her!

The children were pulling at the *tejano*'s strange droopy leggings. The women were tugging at his hair, pinching him curiously to see if he would cry out. Storm Trail could have told them that he was practically as pain-dead as a tree stump, but no one asked her learned opinion.

Then suddenly the *tejano* began fighting back. His teeth flashed like a horse's as he snapped at them and started yelling.

Storm Trail shrieked. *"Help me!* Somebody help me! He would kill me!"

Her brother strode to her and she snapped her jaw shut again, eyeing him warily. He untied her, and she slid down the far side of her pony. She waited for the feeling to come back to her legs, then she began inching away.

She would go to her mother's lodge, she decided. She would hide there and soon everyone would forget about her. She turned about to hurry and bumped squarely into her mother.

Loses Something looked sad. "Oh, little one, why do you do these things?"

Storm Trail dropped her eyes. Her mother's sorrow was worse to bear than all her brother's fury.

"Your father would see you right away."

"Where?" Storm Trail managed.

"The council arbor."

Her heart plunged clear down to her toes.

Storm Trail went to the arbor, her legs wooden with dread. All the important elders were there, as well as Wolf Dream's war band. Other warriors were pressed close behind them, and a few children peeked around their legs to listen and see as well.

She dropped down to sit behind her father, trying to get lost in his shadow. Maybe they would start talking about the raid and forget about her if they could not see her. But finally she could not stand it anymore. She peeked around Black Paint to find out what they done with that crazy *tejano*.

She found him over by the fire. He lay facedown, his hands

and feet still tied. His left cheek rested in the dirt as he watched the council. Then he saw her looking at him and he grinned back at her.

Storm Trail jolted. He knew! He knew she was going to be punished in front of everyone, and he was laughing at her!

Rage made her wild. She bolted to her feet again, then her father looked up at her in a silent, quelling warning. She sat again, seething.

Wolf Dream cleared his throat and accepted the pipe that was passed to him. He drew in smoke, then he exhaled and watched it dissipate on the wind before he spoke.

"There was only one woman among them." His voice was filled with just the right amount of shame and disgust. "She was either courageous enough or stupid enough to die by her own hand rather than let me take her. But I do not think she was stupid. Her eyes were sharp and clear."

Lost Coyote told what had happened inside the fort. "They all stood together, watching us. We asked for presents, the same as Buffalo Piss did. One of their men shouted at us as though he would rather die than give anything. Then he put his arms up—" Lost Coyote demonstrated "—and looked at the sky. He talked loudly, so I killed him first. I think he was calling for his spirit-protectors, and I did not want to give them a chance to answer. We killed them all except the one we brought home."

"Why did you bring that one?" Crooked Nose asked finally, looking over at the *tejano*. Crooked Nose was Yellow Fawn's uncle.

Wolf Dream hesitated. "After the woman died, he was the only one left worth taking. All the others were men. If he is not suitable, then we can kill him. I will go back and look for a woman. I will probably do that anyway."

"He fought well?" asked Paya-yuca.

Lost Coyote shrugged. "He hurt Kills In The Dark." That

warrior gave a sound of anger and abruptly left the council. "And he had the girl for a hostage," Lost Coyote went on.

Storm Trail winced.

"I could not kill him right away because he held her. That gave me time to consider him," Wolf Dream explained. "I think he is a good example of these *tejanos*. He showed no fear, not even when we surrounded him." He paused, then told the most disturbing thing. "After we got him, he seemed to come with us willingly."

There were grunts and murmurs.

She Smiles's father, His Horses Cross The Water, finally scowled. "What will we do with him? He is not young enough to be adopted."

Wolf Dream could not tell how old this white-eyes was. Clearly these people aged differently. This one acted like a man, but his skin was not scarred. There was nothing to indicate that he had been through anything like the Nermenuh trials of manhood. He could not even shoot well, if his attempt with that gun was any indication, and he certainly could not ride.

It was not uncommon for the Nerm to spare enemies who fought well, but this one had merely been brave. Of course, he had not had much of a chance to fight, Wolf Dream allowed, and what he had done, he had done well enough. He remembered Kills In The Dark's sorry face.

Black Paint finally cleared his throat. "I would like to buy him. I need a slave. That would be a good thing to do with him."

Wolf Dream raised a shoulder in half a shrug. "One pony," he said. "I do not know how you will make him work. He knows no fear."

"Ah, but you miss his true value." Black Paint's gaze moved to Paya-yuca. "Have you got any of that sinew that your wives braid together to strengthen your travois when we move?"

Paya-yuca bellowed for Sweet Water, his youngest wife.

Storm Trail watched her father warily. Her tummy began to feel sick.

"Daughter," he said. Storm Trail jumped. "I would like to know why you went after the war band. What could make a girl do such a thing?"

"She wanted a crazy *tejano!*" Eyes Down called from outside the council circle.

"And you caught one," Black Paint observed. "I think that is a good reason to keep him. I would not want all your efforts wasted on a captive who dies."

"He can die," Storm Trail replied magnanimously. "I do not mind." Oh, to be free of the embarrassment of him! If he lived, she would have to see him around camp every single sun. If her father claimed him, he would be nearby all the time. Whenever she looked at him, she would remember how terribly awry her glorious plan had gone.

Black Paint *knew* that! She gave him a heartsick look.

"You should know the price of success, daughter. I would teach you to think carefully of all the ramifications of what you want before you set out to get it." He caught her wrist. She did not dare fight him. She choked back a sob.

Ah, how it hurt him to strip her of her jaunty pride! Such spirit was good in a child, Black Paint thought, although it usually manifested itself in a boy. Still, if this girl would have it, then he would see her earn the right to it.

"Bring me this *tejano* I have claimed," he went on quietly. "Since you led the war band to this boy-man and got what you wanted, you should have him with you every moment. When he works, you should work beside him. When you eat, he will eat with you. He will bed down just on the other side of the lodge wall across from you."

Wolf Dream got the *tejano* and pushed him beneath the arbor. The crazy white-eyes boy-man looked down at them curiously. Black Paint motioned for his wrist. He tied the two of them together.

He kept the knot on his daughter's arm so the *tejano* would

not be able to escape without Storm Trail's assistance—unless
of course he killed her—but Black Paint would be watching
them closely. Nor would the white-eyes be able to steal their
horses or kill any of them in their sleep unless he did so with
his daughter's cooperation.

Black Paint sat back, finally shooing them away. When they
were gone, he smiled.

Compared to some of the things they might have done with
him, Lucas decided he could live with this just fine. The kid
tugged and hauled at him by way of the rope, trying to get
him to go toward the tipis. He decided that the first order of
business was to establish some ground rules.

He stopped dead in his tracks and jerked his arm back. Her
feet flew out from beneath her and she landed hard on her
bottom. She looked back at him, stunned, then she started
howling.

She scrambled back to her feet and barreled into him. Her
small fists pummeled him, then she started trying to claw his
eyes out. Lucas twisted sharply and finally managed to pin
her beneath him.

"Rule number one," he panted. "I'm bigger and stronger."

She twisted her neck around and sank her sharp little teeth
into his wrist.

"Jesus—ouch!"

Suddenly a pair of leather-shod feet appeared in his line of
vision. The moccasins were pretty and cleaner than he might
have expected, with blue beads of some sort stuck in fringe
that ran down the outside seams. Lucas heard a woman's soft
voice above him, guttural like the rest of their accents, but
softer and feminine even as it scolded.

"Daughter! You act like an animal!"

The brat went still, craning her head back to look up at the woman. Lucas took his eyes off her for a second to risk a peek himself.

He felt immediate shame squirm in his gut. Until four days ago, he had thought these 'Manches were all uncouth animals. But if this squaw ever walked into a saloon in Saint Louis, an awful lot of throats would go dry. When she bent over them he got a whiff of something like flowers and smoke, not at all unpleasant. She motioned that he should get off the girl.

Lucas eased himself off the kid. The woman put a surprisingly strong hand on his arm. He looked down at it, grimacing. The teeth marks were deep. The brat had broken his skin.

"You ought to live in a cave somewhere," he muttered, then he stepped back quickly when she looked like she was going to throw herself at him again.

The squaw nudged them into movement. They started off toward the tipis and stopped in front of one of the first tent shelters they came to. Lucas was curious to see what was inside, but they were led around to the side. The girl dropped down onto her haunches, pulling him with her.

The bottom edges of the tipi were rolled up, held in place with thick leather thongs. The kid scooted underneath. Lucas started to follow her. Why the hell didn't they use the door?

The woman held him back, motioning that he should lie down right where he squatted. Lucas sat. The woman kept gesturing, speaking to him now as well.

"There will be food for both of you tomorrow. Not now. Her father and brother are still very angry with her."

As soon as she put her hand to her mouth and mimed chewing, Lucas's belly cramped. She left and he waited for her to come back with something to eat. What exactly *did* they eat? It didn't matter. He was ravenous enough to swallow anything.

Then again, maybe not.

When she returned, she brought a little sack of something putrid. He couldn't decide if it was animal or vegetable, but he sure as hell wasn't putting it in his mouth. Then she took his arm and smeared the stuff on his bite wound. He couldn't decide if he was relieved or appalled that it wasn't food.

He watched her go again. Suddenly now that he was alone, the sky above him seemed black as death.

The ever-present wind was broken some by the tipis, but it still teased dirt and debris into his face. Lucas rolled over to try to shield his eyes—then beyond exhaustion, he slept.

Four

Something sharp, a pebble maybe, was lodged beneath Lucas's right hip. It woke him what seemed like a heartbeat later.

The wind had let up a little. He rolled onto his back again to look at the sky. It seemed lighter. The leafy-roofed thing where the men had been sitting earlier was deserted now, and the 'Manche village was quiet.

Lucas yawned, then he pulled his arm back sharply. There was a sleepy groan from inside, and the thin inner hide snapped up. The kid's angry black eyes peered out at him.

"G'morning."

She yanked the liner back into place. Lucas watched the sky. It was definitely turning gray. He waited until he could no longer see the stars, then he tugged again.

The kid didn't respond this time. He thought about it for a moment, then he smiled to himself. He twisted his wrist ever so delicately, as if he didn't want her to feel it. Sure enough, she poked her nose past the inner hide again.

"Just testing," he told her.

He figured she wanted him to escape with all the hope in her nasty little heart—and if he did, her father would no doubt whale her hide for it. He had noticed the way the man had tied their rope. The connecting part was on her side. So if he got loose, the big guy would know she had helped him.

Lucas waited until he figured she had had a chance to fall asleep again, then he stood up, pulling her outside with him. She came spilling out onto the ground, her arm angled upward.

"I've got to go."

This time he motioned with his free arm to make sure she got his meaning. He watched her nasty temper blaze back into her eyes, but she seemed to gulp back her anger.

"Keemah," she muttered. "Come. I will show you where to do it."

Keemah. Lucas repeated the word silently. He wasn't sure how long they intended to keep him here, how long it would be before he could escape, but one thing was for sure—while he was here, it was in his best interest to know what they were saying.

Later in the morning they were sent to the river to do laundry. No shirt or leggings were considered serviceable until they had been scrubbed with sand and some kind of goop that turned sudsy when it got wet. The clothes weren't even particularly soiled, Lucas thought, although a smell of smoke and tallow seemed to cling to them even when they were clean.

Almost as soon as he got into the rhythm of the work, the woman called out to them from the camp. The kid tossed the shirt they had been working on back onto the pile of dirty stuff and dragged him up the bank. They went to the tipi, and as soon as Lucas realized what was happening, he almost staggered.

Thank Christ. They were finally going to feed him.

By now he really didn't care what they used for food. They sat outside the tent door, and the woman brought them a piece of hide with some little cakes heaped upon it. She gave them an animal horn, too. He peered into it and saw a cloudy liquid inside.

The kid grabbed one of the cakes, scooped it in the horn, and crammed the whole thing into her mouth. Lucas did the same but a lot more cautiously. Then he coughed, his eyes widening. The liquid was honey, and the cake was delicious. He tasted fruit and nuts and meat.

"Tara-hyapa," the woman said. "Pemmican."

He eyed the brat for a while, waiting until she had a hunk of the stuff up to her gaping mouth. Then he jerked at the rope that held them together. Her teeth snapped down on air.

Lucas laughed, and she wriggled her bottom around to kick viciously at his shins. She tried to transfer the cake to her free hand, but he stretched, keeping her off balance. There was no more on the hide. If she was going to be a pig, then it would have to be with that last cake she held.

She finally leaped to her feet with a shriek. His arm jolted upward, then she landed on top of him, scratching and biting. Lucas brought up his free hand to defend himself, but suddenly she went very still. She slid back off him carefully, keeping her knees pressed tightly together.

Lucas scowled at her, then his jaw dropped and he laughed again, so hard he thought he would upchuck everything he had finally eaten. When she had shown him where to relieve himself that morning, she hadn't done anything herself. Christ on a mule, he thought, she must be ready to burst by now!

She managed to stand, tugging on him impatiently, and when he got up she led him to the water again. She went right back to work. They washed and scrubbed almost through the afternoon, her mouth tightening gradually. Once or twice he thought he saw her eyes tear, but when he looked closer he decided he was wrong.

Her stubborn determination finally gave out when the laundry pile was almost finished. She stood with a regal toss of her head. Even The Queen would have been impressed.

"Ready now, huh?" he asked, amused.

She pulled him downstream, then she drew an imperious circle in the air with her finger.

"Nah. I've been waiting too long for this."

She motioned again, more furiously. He guessed she figured he didn't understand that she wanted him to turn around. He shook his head so as to leave no doubt that he did.

She shoved at him angrily. He shoved back. She went down

hard in the murky water. She started to leap up again, then she realized that she was in precisely the situation she needed to be in, splayed in water up to her hips. Her eyes closed for a second in an almost blissful expression, then she stood.

He thought maybe, just maybe, she had invented pride. Damn it if he wasn't starting to like her a little.

Storm Trail woke the next dawn to the sound of Bear Wound chanting and singing. The elder-crier's voice was deep and resonant as he worked his way along the trampled paths between the lodges. Sometimes it reached a strident pitch that made her shiver with excitement. He was telling where Paya-yuca and the council had decided the band would go next.

She pushed her bedding aside. She was on her feet, headed for the door, when the *tejano*'s clumsy weight at the other end of the sinew snapped her arm backward and dropped her again. For a single sweet moment she had forgotten about him. He had not awakened her last night. Maybe he was dead.

She lifted the dew cloth and peered out. The crazy white-eyes looked back at her, very much alive.

She climbed over him, deliberately gouging him with her knees. She put her face close to his and thrust her jaw out, defying him to hurt her. Oh, if only he would hit her! Then her father would have to untie them.

He only got up and headed toward the water. Storm Trail started toward the pony herd. They both came up short.

She tugged frantically at the rope. This crazy *tejano* was so stupid! All over the camp women were beginning to bustle about—the air echoed with the *thump-swish* of lodge covers coming down. Didn't he see what was happening? Storm Trail was so appalled that for a moment she let him drag her without even making a fuss.

Her mother came out of the lodge, carrying some parfleches. Loses Something stopped short when she saw them.

"What is this?" she scolded. "Hurry. We will be late to join Mountain and Too Many Relatives and Sweet Water."

They were Paya-yuca's wives, and that was exactly what Storm Trail was worried about. "Tell this coyote-breath *tejano!*" she cried. "He will not let me get the ponies. We will be so far back in the line, we will have to ride with the old men and the lowest warriors! When we get to the new camp, we will have to put our lodges near the waste water!"

Loses Something looked at the boy-man and shook her head. "He will hurry once he understands what is happening."

She motioned them closer and hunkered down to draw in the dirt. "Lodges," she said, pointing at the one behind her. The crazy white-eyes scowled and nodded.

She drew again. "We are going now. We have *oyo'ts,* parfleches, and other things to pack. We need ponies to carry all of it to the new place." She gestured at the herd. "You must bring them back so we can load them."

The *tejano* finally grinned and headed for the herd. Storm Trail sighed heavily, dragging along behind him. She couldn't imagine why she had ever thought it was a good idea to capture one of these people.

She managed to skip ahead of him until she was pulling him. Lucas dragged back deliberately and looked around. For the first time since they had brought him here two days ago, he was far enough outside the camp to really see it. Tipis stretched along the water for what he guessed was a couple of miles. There had to be four hundred of them.

The runt tugged at him impatiently. She was trying to cut some ponies out of the huge herd. There were thousands of horses, Lucas realized.

The idea of camping somewhere new appealed to him tremendously. It had been purely wanderlust that had taken him from Philadelphia to Saint Louis to Texas. But he was a little concerned about the huge amount of work it would entail. It had finally occurred to him that he was a slave to these folks, so he guessed they would expect him to do it.

"Hey," he called out, helping her chase a handful of ponies in the direction of the camp. "What's your name?"

The girl's face only reddened with temper. He punched his chest with his thumb. "Lucas."

"Loo-cus?"

"Yeah!" Then he realized that it wasn't the kid who had spoken, but another girl who had inched up shyly behind her.

Lucas eyed the newcomer and grinned widely. This Injun business was getting better all the time.

She was older than the runt, and she wore a dress. The skirt seemed to be made from the hide of a deer, or probably two or three of them. The legs of the animals hung down to make an uneven hem. The skirt was laced to the top with hide thongs, and the top was like a poncho with a slit for a neck hole. It was decorated with beads like those he had noticed on the kid's mother's moccasins. This girl was barefoot.

She filled out the top of her dress nicely with small high breasts. Her hair was shoulder-length like that of all the other women, ebony-black and parted neatly in the middle. She tucked a strand behind her ear and laughed nervously at his scrutiny.

The runt spat something at her. She colored and her smile faltered. Lucas acted quickly. He pointed to her with a question in his eyes.

"She Smiles," she said. She pointed to her mouth, then to herself, grinning, and repeated the whole routine a second time. Lucas nodded. It suited her.

He gestured toward the brat. This, he thought, ought to be interesting.

She Smiles motioned at the sky, then pantomimed rain. She hugged herself, shivering, then blew a sound like the wind moaning.

"Storm?"

She bent down and drew a line in the grass, then marched her fingers along it. Storm Moving? Storm Going?

It was a start, Lucas thought. He let the brat drag him away into the herd again. They finally got all the ponies and turned around to go back to the lodge. Lucas's jaw dropped hard.

They had been in the herd all of five minutes, but the camp was gone. All that remained were a bunch of heavily laden ponies, some already moving out onto the prairie.

Storm Trail never cried—but, oh, how she hated this wretched *tejano!*

He flopped around behind her again on one of her mother's ponies. But this time her hands weren't tied together, and she was able to elbow him hard.

A very long line of Penateka ponies plodded along ahead of them. Paya-yuca's travois was so far in the distance he looked like an ant crawling through the grass. And here she was, stuck in the back of the line with this lump of coyote droppings behind her.

At least Yellow Fawn and She Smiles and Eyes Down stayed back to keep her company, although Eyes Downs's father was so poorly acknowledged, she always rode here anyway.

"What did he say to you?" she demanded of She Smiles.

"He wanted to know my name. Yours, too. He is Loo-cus."

"It probably means Smelly And Crazy," she muttered.

She Smiles darted a look at him. He caught her eye and smiled coaxingly, and she felt herself blushing.

"I think it is just his leggings that smell bad," she ventured. "They are not tanned right. And I do not think he is so crazy. He has not done anything strange so far."

Storm Trail opened her mouth to argue, but the truth of the matter was that he hadn't. He hadn't done anything particularly bizarre on the ride here, either. Of course She Smiles did not know that.

A slow grin spread across Storm Trail's face.

"He is not crazy all the time. It comes in bursts. Sometimes, when we were riding home, he would just . . ." She trailed off, shivering.

"He what?" gasped She Smiles.

Storm Trail thought fast. "I found him in some plants. They grew in very neat, straight lines." She drew a picture in the air to illustrate and got just the reaction she knew she would. Their eyes widened.

"What makes them do that?" asked Yellow Fawn.

"White *puha.*"

"What was he doing in there?" Eyes Down demanded.

"Making them grow in such a way." She remembered what Lost Coyote had said in the council after the raid. "He had his hands up as though to catch the sun and he yelled, even though no one else was there to hear him."

"*You* were there," Eyes Down pointed out critically.

"But he did not see me yet. I was hiding in the plants."

"What did he do next?" Yellow Fawn breathed.

Wasn't that enough? "He sat down in the dirt and . . . and he ate it."

"Ugh."

"Worms and all," she added. "Then he was fine for a while, just like he is now."

"How long was he normal?"

"I think it was about two suns. He was all right until we got him here. But then do you remember how he howled and bit when the women tried to touch his hair?"

She Smiles shot a quick, uncertain look at him. "I thought they were hurting him."

Storm Trail shook her head. "White-eyes do not feel pain."

"How do you know?" sneered Eyes Down.

"Because I pinched him all the way home." He *had* bitten her back, but she decided to skip that part.

"That was brave," She Smiles murmured, and Yellow Fawn nodded hard. Storm Trail's chest swelled with pride.

"He has been here two suns now," she pointed out, "so I think he is about to get crazy again at any moment. I hope he does not kill me when it happens. If he gets loose, I do not know what he might do to the rest of you."

* * *

Lucas knew they were talking about him. He tried to catch She Smiles's eye again, but now she studiously avoided looking at him. He stared at the back of the weasel's scrawny neck. Oh, to have his other hand free so he could choke her!

Suddenly the pony they were riding stopped in its tracks. It dropped its head and began grazing as Lucas slid up against the runt again. But this time she didn't turn around to spit and hiss at him. Something was happening.

The long line of people ahead of them began to break up. The men began returning—they had spent most of the ride out of sight. The traveling line had been comprised almost entirely of women and kids and old folks.

Storm Whatever began gouging their pony with her heels to get it to move again. They followed the others to a spot where the land rolled gently downward. Before they began their descent, Lucas saw a glint of silver in the distance—a river, he realized.

Before the canyon narrowed there was ample grass even for so many horses. In fact, the 'Manches left the unencumbered part of their herd there. Then they moved down toward the water where the tracks of a plenitude of deer showed in the muddy sand along the creek. No one would be going hungry, Lucas thought. There was water, wood for their fires . . . and the sky for a ceiling.

As they had approached this place, he had seen nothing but the ever-present grass undulating in the wind. Hundreds upon hundreds of people would effectively be hidden here from the casual observer, he realized. It both intrigued him and left a hollow feeling in his chest. If retaliation was coming for the Rust attack, then he didn't see how anyone could possibly find them here.

But Lucas didn't honestly believe that retaliation would be coming. For one thing, except for a few women who seemed to be squabbling over where they would put their tipis, the

'Manches showed absolutely no concern. He thought that if they were hiding from pursuit, there would be some amount of furtiveness, some panic.

The other reason he didn't think anyone was coming was because he was pretty sure only he and the Parker captives had ever made it this far. For the first time he wondered where they were. The Parkers were towheaded and blue-eyed, from what he had heard, and he thought he probably would have noticed them if they were around here.

He slid down from his pony, dragging the kid with him, and went to find the woman he had decided was her mother. That squaw's tent was now a skeleton close to the water, twenty or so poles spread out at the bottom and lashed together at the top. Lucas studied it a moment, then touched the woman's sleeve to get her attention.

"I am Loses Something," she said. She took up a parfleche and demonstrated the concept. "You should call me that."

Lucas nodded. "Why did we come here?" he asked—then in a burst of inspiration he dropped down onto his haunches to draw in the dirt as she had done earlier. "Why?"

Loses Something shrugged. Lucas came back to his feet, frustrated, but then she waved a hand around the canyon.

"Toquet," she said quietly.

"Toquet?"

"It is good. We came just because it is here, because it is good."

A slow smile spread across Lucas's face. Damned if he didn't like these people.

Five

As the days passed, Lucas realized that he was losing track of time. Sunrise until sundown seemed to define no cycle here. The bucks, at least, were as apt to smoke and talk the moon to bed as they were to doze all through the night and the next day besides.

Then on what felt like his seventh or eighth day of captivity, he awakened one dawn to utter pandemonium. He was still groggy when the buck who had captured him came bursting out of the next tipi. By the time Lucas jolted fully awake, men were running all over the village. Kids shouted and streamed toward the pony herd. The squaws bustled and tore down their lodges. It seemed like chaos, but Lucas got the feeling they all had a purpose.

The ground began to tremble beneath him. It moved gently at first, then harder. From somewhere outside the camp, up on the grasslands, there grew a tremendous roar.

What the hell was going on?

Suddenly his arm was wrenched painfully. The kid pulled him half into the tipi before she remembered she was tied to him. She screeched in frustration and began dragging him toward the door.

Lucas scrambled to his feet. He wanted to look around, but he had no time. She was going outside come hell or high water.

They tumbled through the hole in the front of the tipi. He had to duck fast to get through, but he managed to skim his free hand along the piece of hide that was pegged back outside. It was hard and stiff, weighted down with rocks hanging in little braided twine sacks from the bottom.

He bumped into the weasel's back as Loses Something planted herself squarely in their path.

"You know your father will not permit you to go. You must stay here and help me pack. He says we will all follow the herd this time. Something has scared them. They are moving fast, and he does not know how far they might go before they stop. We will move camp."

Lucas looked past both of them, up toward the grasslands. The ground was still trembling, but the roar was more muted now.

Loses Something sighed and relented. "You may go as far as the pony herd to look at them," she allowed. "Bring my packhorses back with you."

The kid began running. Lucas broke into a jog beside her, too curious to provoke her by holding back.

They went through the valley where the horses grazed. Children and women streamed past them, but the men all seemed to have vanished. Then they reached the prairie, and Lucas's pulse stumbled in awe and surprise.

The land they had crossed to get here was marked now by an immense swath. The endless grass did not sway there. It was trampled and crushed, and the air was sharp with its pungent tang. He looked along the swath.

Buffalo.

He had heard of them but had never actually seen one, had never made it far enough west to encounter any. Now a huge churning mass of buffalo thundered away, a million strong. He scrubbed a hand over his eyes and looked again. He would never have been able to grasp their numbers if he were not seeing them, feeling them roar their way across the earth with his own senses.

He glanced down at the kid. Even her eyes were wide, and she wore a silly grin.

"Yeah," he said, and he smiled with her.

Some carcasses began to litter the herd's wake. The bucks were all out there, Lucas realized. He saw their heads now, bobbing occasionally along the flanks of the mass. A nearly painful ache yearned in him to be among them.

The kid began pulling him the other way. *"Keemah,* come!" she jabbered furiously. "If you get me in trouble again, I will kill you myself this time." Unconsciously she motioned with her free hand, signing.

Lucas got her point. He moved away with her reluctantly, shooting one last, hungry gaze back at the hunt.

They reached the new camp well ahead of the others, and Loses Something came not long afterward to drop a huge pile of bloody hides at their feet. Storm Whoever groaned, and he understand that they had been appointed to do something with them.

She pegged the first one out and gave him a long piece of bone that was razor sharp on one side. She had one, too. She began to drag it across the hide, and he followed her example. By the time the sun went down again, Lucas's back ached, and his wrist cramped where he was tied to the runt.

No wonder his buckskins smelled so bad, Storm Trail thought. He kept leaving tiny pieces of meat and fat so they had to go back over all his strokes a second time. Her throat closed in anger. There would be a buffalo tongue ceremony tonight, and she would probably miss it. By the time she and this stupid *tejano* finished here and washed up, the whole thing would probably be over.

"You are lazy, lazy, *lazy!"* She angled her feet around suddenly to kick him. "And stupid and slow! Why do you not just watch to see how it is done, then *do* it!"

Someone caught the rope that held her breechclout up and pulled her backward, away from him. She fought that, too, vexed beyond endurance.

"Stop this!" Star Line said sharply.

"Well, he will not do it right!"

Black Paint came out of their lodge. "Perhaps you should tell him why you are doing what you are doing instead of just showing him. Then he will understand and do it better."

"He understands nothing!"

"Have you tried?"

She hadn't, but she wasn't going to admit it or take any of the blame for this messy hide upon herself. "He just looks at me with those dumb, ugly eyes. He does not know what I say."

Loses Something stopped working on some meat she was cutting into thin strips. "It does not matter anyway," she called over to them. "That hide is not a good one. It is for him."

Storm Trail stiffened. For *him?* What would the crazy white-eyes need a hide for?

Loses Something came to them and squatted beside the place Loo-cus had missed. She took his flesher from him and gave one of the offending lumps a quick, deft swipe.

"Leaving anything makes the hide rot in that place," she told him, her hands moving gracefully as she demonstrated her point. "Then the piece will smell. It will not wear well, and the rain will ruin it as soon as it touches it."

Storm Trail stared at her mother. "For him?" she repeated.

"He cannot walk around in those smelly, torn ones forever. Besides, how is he ever to learn to ride with his buttocks and his thighs all covered up like that?"

"Ride?" she squeaked. She hadn't yet given up hope that they would kill him when her punishment was over!

She would rather die, she thought wildly, would rather go to Cannibal Owl and never come back, than have him stay with them much longer! And now they were going to give him leggings and teach him to ride!

As far as she was concerned, her life was ruined.

* * *

When they were allowed to leave the hides, the kid dragged Lucas to the water to wash up, then she pulled him right into the tipi with her again.

He'd harbored a mental image of a small, crowded rat hole, but the tipi was much bigger than it had appeared from the outside. Three beds lay around the perimeter, piles of hides with some soft fluffy pillows made of fur. Between the second and the third bed, a thinner hide was stretched upright, giving the appearance of two separate bedrooms.

Hanging along the walls were the big rawhide envelopes—parfleches, he remembered, *oyo'ts*. The liner that Loses Something pulled down every night when they slept went only halfway up to the top. More stuff was hung along its upper rim—a shield with long feathers streaming from it, a bow, and a quiver full of arrows. An empty pouchlike thing dangled halfway down one of the poles—it looked like the stomach of some animal. There was a cracked, chipped mirror and a couple of horns like the one the honey had been in.

He finally glanced back at the kid. Loses Something had combed her hair, and now she painted some red goop along her center part. It looked like blood and it gave Lucas a jolt.

They finally went back outside again. People were wandering over toward the arbor. The big guy who had tied them was there, along with another man who was even bigger than he was. In fact, Lucas thought, all those who were seated beneath the brush shelter were older men, a little ample around the waist.

"What's going on?" He motioned to the runt. He didn't actually think she would answer, but she was apparently too excited to remember to hate him.

"Lost Coyote will give the ceremony," she explained, signing. "He had more kills today than anybody, so he is supposed to share his meat with all of us. Not every man does, but he loses respect if he does not. A strong warrior is generous. Sometimes he will give away all his kills, or all his plunder after a raid, just to prove that he can always get more any time he wishes."

She moved down the crowded semicircle that was forming

around the chiefs. Some of the bucks were gathering beneath the arbor, joining the headmen.

"What are they doing?"

She answered him impatiently, signing as she watched the crowd. "They are getting ready for the dance. When the women are all finished cooking the tongues, the men will sit in a line. Then one of the girls will take the best piece to the warriors. The girl cannot be anyone who is wed. If any of the men have ever played with her, he shouts, 'No! No!' "

"*Played* with her? Oh, that way."

So *that* was what they called it around here. It was simplistically appropriate, he thought, but he felt an absurd discomfort at discussing such a thing with a girl. Then again, Storm Whatever was no girl. She was some kind of . . . hobgoblin.

The ceremony started. First one woman then another tried to take the meat to Lost Coyote. They were each turned away with a good deal of ribbing.

The crowd began hooting and laughing. A huge woman grabbed the tongue. She lumbered up to the line of men, thrusting her hips forward obscenely. All the men howled, throwing clumps of dirt at her. Lost Coyote leaned back so far, trying to avoid the meat, that he fell onto his back.

Lucas gave a bark of laughter. "Who is she?"

"Mountain." Storm Trail motioned again, talking as she did. "She is Paya-yuca's *pasaibo,* his first wife. She is just playing with them. She is not really part of it because she is wed."

He wasn't sure he got that right. He made her repeat it. When he was sure he understood, Lucas felt his jaw drop a little.

"How many wives do these guys have?"

"Paya-yuca has three, but that is because he is wealthy."

She pointed out Too Many Relatives and Sweet Water. Each woman diminished in size, and Lucas didn't think the youngest could be much older than he was. She was pretty to boot.

Suddenly the crowd quieted. Another girl approached the line. It was clear even to Lucas that she was going to be the one who didn't raise any objection from the warriors. There was something special about her. She had an elegant way of walking, her spine straight, her hips swaying ever so gently. Her dress was adorned with fur tails all along the hem.

"Who is she?"

Storm Trail motioned. "Winter Song. She loves my brother. She is Paya-yuca's daughter. They will marry some sun."

"Why does he wait?" Privately he thought the buck showed a lot more sense than that.

Storm Whoever was starting to look disgusted with all his questions. "Paya-yuca will not give her to a husband who still raids. Wolf Dream would have to stop riding to have her, but he is our very best war band leader. We need him. He asks Paya-yuca for her almost every moon, but Paya-yuca always laughs and says no."

Winter Song finally handed the tongue to Lost Coyote. The squaws hovering about began hooting their love chant. Lost Coyote took only a bite and immediately handed the meat to Wolf Dream, grinning.

The women loved that, Lucas thought. They hooted louder. All their wives aside, they were a pretty romantic bunch.

It was something else he would have to tell the folks in Texas when he got back. Then abruptly all thoughts of civilization fled from his mind. Loses Something came their way with a hide full of meat.

Lucas grabbed the biggest hunk before Storm Trail could reach for it. He pushed it into his mouth, closing his eyes, savoring the richness, the fullness of it. It was gamier than beef and fattier, and it was the most delicious thing he could ever remember consuming.

All this, he thought, and he still had his balls, too.

Six

By the time the grasses turned spare and brittle and golden, there was a red line on Storm Trail's wrist just beneath the braided sinew. She was marked *forever,* and her father showed absolutely no signs of relenting. Even her mother and her aunt seemed to be feeling a little sorry for her—at least Loses Something had finally let them leave camp to collect buffalo chips for the fires.

The wind whipped her hair into her eyes. She peeled strands of it away from her face and tossed her head. The crazy white-eyes smiled at her.

"What?" she asked suspiciously.

Lucas laughed aloud. He guessed he could have told her that for the briefest of seconds, he had caught a flash of the woman she would become. The truth of the matter was that he thought she would pretty much rival Winter Song someday. She had that same sort of breeding, he guessed, and the same grace, even if it was still raw.

But this wasn't someday, and he wouldn't let those words slip off his tongue if she had held a knife to his throat. He was, to his reckoning, roughly six weeks into his captivity here. If he had learned one thing during that time, it was that her nasty little ego didn't need any building up.

He gave her arm an extra tug to move her in the direction he wanted to go. "I see more over here."

Storm Trail followed him grudgingly. "Well, it is nothing to smile about. Why do you always smile?"

"Because it's a damned fine day, weasel. The sun's shining, it's not cool, it's not hot, our bellies are full." She Smiles had poked her nose out of her lodge as they were leaving camp to wave at him. "Not that I'd have necessarily chosen to run around collecting animal shit all day long," he went on, "but you've got to admit it beats doing laundry."

She dragged back and looked at him, scowling. He did this sometimes, started talking on and on, and she never understood him, even when he signed. The Nermenuh liked words. Stories made their winter nights seem warm. But with Loo-cus it was different. The Nermenuh liked to listen to others. Storm Trail thought this *tejano* just liked to listen to himself.

She gathered another pile of dung—it was old and dry and crumbly—and eased it into their gut bag. Then she straightened and looked up. Her heart leaped gladly, then dropped like a stone.

Yellow Fawn and She Smiles and Eyes Down were coming.

She Smiles was starting to be just another thing about the *tejano* that Storm Trail didn't like. She got all doe-eyed around the crazy white-eyes. And the white-eyes practically strutted when She Smiles was around.

"What do you want?" she called out to them crossly.

The *tejano* shot her a strange look at her tone.

"We brought food," Yellow Fawn called out.

Storm Trail decided that was all right. She dropped her gut bag and dragged Lucas with her to meet them. She reached eagerly for a cake. Loo-cus jerked back on their tied arms to stop her.

"Wash your paws first, brat."

Storm Trail scowled. "Paws?" she repeated carefully.

"Hey, I know where they've been all morning."

He grabbed her free wrist, turning her grimy palm up for the others to see. She Smiles giggled way too much. Storm Trail felt warmth slide up her neck.

He was making fun of her. There was nothing wrong with her hand. *Nothing!*

She planted both of her palms against his chest and shoved. But he only did what he always did when she got mad—he hefted her over his shoulder and took her wherever he wanted her to go. In this case it was the creek.

She gave him a good sharp blow between the shoulder blades. "You are vermin!" she spat. "Coyote dung! *Let me go!*"

He opened his arms and let her fall. She landed in the stream with a surprised cry and scrambled up to fight some more. But the white-eyes wasn't even looking at her now. He was flirting with She Smiles again.

The *tejano* was scrubbing his hands with sand and water while he grinned at her. She Smiles broke off a hunk of cake and gave it to him. She gazed at him through her lashes. The *tejano* sat down beside her, so close an ant couldn't crawl between them. This time when Storm Trail grabbed a piece of pemmican, Loo-cus didn't pay her any attention at all.

"You forget he is crazy!" she burst out suddenly, angrily, at She Smiles. She had told her again and again how he could be.

She Smiles's eyes flashed to her, startled. "Well, he only does crazy things to you."

Storm Trail opened her mouth to argue, then she snapped it shut again. It was true.

She dropped her cake back onto the hide in disgust. Loo-cus reached absently for his own piece, still making dopey eyes at She Smiles. When he realized he had picked up the piece Storm Trail had discarded, he scowled and pushed it away and found another.

Her face flamed.

Suddenly her head hurt and she backed away from the bank. What difference did it make? She didn't want Loo-cus to like her. She didn't want him to talk to her. She hated him, and half the time she didn't even understand what he was saying anyway.

But she knew that she didn't want him to like She Smiles either.

"It is your breasts," she told her friend knowledgeably four suns later. "He wants to touch them."

She Smiles blushed all the way down to her toes.

"How do you know?" demanded Eyes Down.

"I saw Wolf Dream and Winter Song in the pony herd once." At least it had looked like that was what her brother was doing.

She scrunched her fingers into the hide pegged out in front of her. A pernicious aroma wafted up from it, making her eyes tear. She was working Loses Something's special tanning compound into it, a mysterious concoction of liver and grease and brains.

She leaned back away from it, breathing deeply of the fresher air. Loo-cus was about as far away from her and the smell as he could get with the sinew holding them.

"That is not exactly what happens," She Smiles said very quietly, watching Loo-cus to see if he was listening. "At least, that is not all a warrior does. I asked my sister."

"Why would you do that?" Storm Trail demanded, but then suddenly she knew. Her mouth fell open. She Smiles would only ask her sister if she was going to sneak into Loo-cus's lodge the way girls did when they were sweet on someone.

But Loo-cus did not even have a lodge! Oh, spirit-protectors, would they do it right outside *hers?*

"He will have a lodge soon," She Smiles blurted as though reading her mind. "That is what you are doing."

Storm Trail scowled down at her hands. "I am?"

"Yes. That hide is for his lodge. That is what I hear."

Storm Trail snatched her hands away as though it had burned her. "Black Paint would give him a lodge?" she choked.

She Smiles shrugged. "It will be cold soon."

"But he is a slave."

"He belongs to your father, and that is lucky for him. Black Paint has always treated his captives well."

Storm Trail shoved the hide away in temper. "I will not do it!" She felt like crying. She felt like screaming. She had gone on that raid so long ago she could scarcely remember doing it! Would her father make her pay for it *forever?*

"I heard more," She Smiles whispered.

"What?" Eyes Down demanded, pressing close. Yellow Fawn sent an apologetic look at Storm Trail before she eased up to listen, too. Storm Trail clapped her hands over her ears. No! She would not hear this!

But then she couldn't stand it anymore because Yellow Fawn was gaping and Eyes Down was looking bemused. She dropped her hands. "What? *What?*"

"Black Paint likes him," She Smiles said. "He says he works hard and that he has decided he is not stupid. When it gets colder and the great buffalo herds break apart, he will see if he is any good at hunting. He will make him ride a mule so he cannot escape us, but he will let him ride after one of the small foraging herds."

"No!" Storm Trail leaped to her feet. She forgot about the *tejano.* Her arm jerked in its socket when he didn't move with her. She spun his way angrily.

His expression changed as soon as he saw her looking at him. But it didn't matter. Storm Trail knew suddenly and as clearly as she knew her own name that the white-eyes understood everything they had just said. He was *pretending* when he still made them motion everything out!

A lodge? Hunting? Oh, spirit-protectors, she *had* to think of a way to get rid of him!

"I need plums and some persimmons before the next hunt," Loses Something said the next sun. "Your father says it is all right for you to leave camp to get them. He does not think this *tejano* will hurt you, but he says please do not hurt him. He would like to keep him a while longer."

"I would like to—" Storm Trail began, then she broke off suddenly. *This was her chance!*

Lucas watched her eyes go wide, then narrow. She reminded him for all the world of a rattler sunning itself on a rock, peaceful and sluggish, smooth and warm—and God help the man who reached out to stroke those pretty little diamonds. She led him back to the river. By the time they reached the outskirts of the village, she was practically running.

"The best fruit is far from here, upstream," she gasped, out of breath.

Still she took a few persimmons and haws from the bushes as they passed them. Once she stooped suddenly to pick up a rock. He nearly tumbled over her, then she sprang up again and kept going.

"What the hell are you up to?"

"Go," she said suddenly, turning to him.

"Huh?"

"Go!"

She looked back wildly in the direction of the camp. She could not see it, she thought, so they could not see her either. She tried desperately to wrestle the sinew off her wrist. It had been there so long now, the knot on her end had strained and compacted tightly. She put it to her teeth, ripping at it furiously.

"I am letting you go, stupid! I will not tell!" She pulled her mouth from the sinew long enough to clap her free hand over it and shake her head hard. "I will not tell! Do you see? I have a plan!"

Black Paint would be furious that his slave had escaped. Maybe he would even hunt him down and kill him. She didn't care as long as she was not implicated in the turn of events. She would scrape her face with the rock, she decided, maybe even pound her arms and legs with it to make bruises. It would hurt, but it would be worth it. Even if Loo-cus didn't escape, even if her father didn't kill him, even if he just brought him back—at least Black Paint would hesitate to tie her to him again, because she would tell how he had beaten her to get away.

But Loo-cus would not go. He looked at her thoughtfully.

"I will wait until I cannot see you anymore before I go back," she vowed as the sinew finally came loose.

"There are holes in it, weasel."

Suddenly he snatched the twine from her hand. For one stunned moment Storm Trail only stared at it. He caught her elbow and pulled her close, lifting her up onto her toes.

"What are you doing?" she screeched. *"Let me go!"*

"So you can run back and tell everybody I hurt you? There's only one thing wrong with that. I've got the rope and if I take it back there, nobody's going to believe you. I'm damned well not going to get myself killed just so you can get rid of me. Even if nobody caught me, I'd starve out there, you silly brat."

Except he probably wouldn't, he realized with a start. He'd picked up some interesting information during the last couple of months, things the Rusts sure as hell never knew. Like which plants were edible and which could poison you in a hurry. Like how to make a fire out of animal dung. Like how to whittle down a snare so that the tread of the most feather-light rodent would spring it. So maybe he wouldn't starve—but his belly would be a hell of a lot fuller if he stayed right here. If he took this rope back to Black Paint, he'd earn the trust that would inspire the chief to finally let him hunt.

He let her go. Storm Trail's knees felt hollow, airy, and she almost fell.

"If you do not want to go, then give it back," she managed haughtily.

He stared at her a minute, then he laughed. "Not a chance."

Her eyes were burning. She tossed her hair. She would *not* cry. But if she didn't get that sinew back her father would send her to Cannibal Owl for sure!

"Give it back!" she tried again, jumping for it.

"Hell, no. This little baby is going to get me everything I want."

And he did not want to go back to Texas, he realized. Not yet. He had seen the buffalo. He had heard them, had felt them make the earth shake. He had breathed in their musky, magnificent scent. And he wasn't going anywhere until he had chased after one and killed one.

This sinew could give it all to him. Sooner or later the old man would probably let him hunt anyway, but if he took this back to him now, if he proved that he would stay without being physically bound into it—

"Please," Storm Trail whispered, her voice strangled. "Piamempits!"

"Pee-what?"

"Piamempits! The Owl! He has giant teeth . . . in the Wichitas . . . my father will send me this time for sure, and he will eat me!"

For a wild moment he thought she was actually going to cry. And in that moment she looked purely like a little girl.

He felt like a bully.

"Lucky for you I'm not sure what I want yet." Suddenly he felt so old. He felt a hundred, thousand years older than when he had slid out of that Philadelphia townhouse late one night over a year ago. After everything he had seen in these last many months, after everything he had done, waiting an extra week or two to hunt didn't seem like all that big a deal.

"Give me your arm, weasel," he said before he could change his mind.

She held it out to him. She was trembling. He pretended not to notice and tied the sinew back on. "There. Good as new."

Storm Trail couldn't swallow. "Why?" she croaked.

"Because I reckon the only thing that makes you so disagreeable is the fact that you're spoiled high-hell rotten. And it's just about choking you that you can't win with me. So I guess if I really want to torment you, maybe I ought to stay right here, attached to you."

He started back toward the camp and she stumbled dumbly after him. This white-eyes was the craziest, most contrary mongrel she'd ever laid eyes on. But he was wrong. She *could* win.

He should have had her sent to Cannibal Owl when he had the chance, she thought angrily. Because if she could not make him go, then she would just have to stop waiting for her father to get around to it and kill him herself.

Seven

Lucas wasn't sure that it was coincidence when Loses Something approached them in the pony herd two suns later.

Black Paint had suggested that he should consult with Medicine Eagle, the shaman-healer, about a tendon wound afflicting one of his favorite colts. Lucas got the distinct impression that he was supposed to administer whatever treatment the old one-eyed shaman suggested. The thing that made him leery, that made him raise a brow, was that he had never been allowed within spitting distance of the horses before.

When he got the necessary healing salve from Medicine Eagle, he only stood in front of the old man's tipi and looked around. The runt pulled at him impatiently.

"This pony will be dead before you do something."

So *she* thought they were supposed to work in the herd, too—but of course it was entirely possible that she was just setting him up. He looked at her closely. She was fidgeting, but she didn't have that overly innocent expression that had made his hair stand on end when she had tried to set him free.

Lucas finally went to the herd, but Loses Something came almost the moment he had finished smearing the foul-smelling goop on the colt's leg.

She reached for the sinew that tied them together. Lucas thought he saw one corner of her mouth move as she inspected it, for as certainly as the sky had stars she noticed that the frayed knot had been worked loose recently. But she made no

mention of it, just pulled her skirt up on one side and took
her knife from the sheath at her thigh.

As she sawed through the sinew, the Storm kid's jaw fell
open further and further.

"Loo-cus," Loses Something said, "you should go to the
council arbor. Daughter, you—*daughter.*"

Storm was staring at her wrist as though she had never seen
it before. She jumped, her eyes snapping up to her mother.
"What?"

"Star Line has work for you."

She nodded and hurried off, still looking at her free arm.

"You should hurry," Loses Something said to Lucas. "They
are waiting for you."

Lucas couldn't have hurried if he had wanted to. His pulse
was suddenly scrambling so erratically he felt dizzy. He
thought absurdly that he was going to miss the brat's company.
And what did Black Paint want him at the arbor for, of all
places?

Nothing he could think of was good.

He made his way slowly back into the camp. It felt sort
of like walking around buck-naked. Everything was different
without the runt attached to his arm. For the first time since
Star Line had given him his new leggings and a breechclout,
he felt acutely aware of his bare buttocks. He wanted to turn
around and face the squaws who remained behind him, to
cover himself somehow. It had taken him a while to get used
to the feeling of sun on skin he reckoned God had intended
to remain covered, but then he had pretty much forgotten
about it. Now that skin tingled again, feeling outrageously
exposed.

He kept walking. His steps didn't falter until he got close
enough to see the arbor.

Jesus Christ on a mule.

Practically every male in the whole damned camp had
turned out for this—whatever this might be. Suddenly Lucas's

bladder began to feel hot and heavy. Jesus, maybe they *were* going to kill him.

Then before his pulse could gallop out of control, he saw his own Kentucky rifle sitting in the center of the arbor. He didn't remember them bringing it along when they had captured him, but he had been understandably preoccupied.

"Loo-cus," Black Paint said as he approached cautiously.

"Yes, sir." Lucas winced. The only thing worse than dying was dying cowed and scared. He cleared his throat, made his voice strong and his grin just a little bit cocky.

"Thanks for taking the runt off." He showed his wrist to make his point.

Black Paint chuckled softly. "Sit, *haitsi.*"

Haitsi? Friend? Lucas looked at the ground. "Uh, no thanks." All things considered, if anyone made a move for that gun, he wanted to be able to start running fast.

Black Paint smiled slowly. "A wise choice."

Why? Lucas wanted to shout. Because you're going to shoot? The big man's smile was enigmatic but vaguely pleased, as though if Lucas had sat, he would have disappointed him in some small measure.

"We need your expertise," Black Paint went on. He motioned at the gun. Relief made Lucas let his breath out in a burst. All they wanted was to know how to shoot the damned thing.

He bent for it. The one called Wolf Dream barreled into him headfirst. The buck drove him backward. Lucas landed with a grunt that left him no air, but he managed to get away from Wolf Dream and roll to his knees, ready.

What he saw made no sense.

The old ones were watching him blandly, although many of the bucks had their knives drawn. Wolf Dream crouched a short distance away, clearly waiting for another move on his part, and Lost Coyote had picked up his Kentucky rifle.

Lucas dragged in air. "Do you want to learn how to shoot

it or not?" he demanded. Not, he realized suddenly. Oh, Christ on a mule, of course not.

They *had* firearms. Not many, granted, but he had seen one or two guns around the village. So what the holy hell did they want from him and his Kentucky rifle?

It came to him suddenly. The thing had taken most of Miss Myra's savings because a guy in Saint Louis had touted it as the newest, most effective thing to come down the pike. The new part had been true, at any rate, although insofar as fighting Injuns was concerned, it had turned out to be useless. They wanted to know about *this* gun, Lucas realized. They wanted to know how it was different from the ones they had already encountered.

Lucas felt something sour move in his gut.

All they were asking was that he aid and abet a few 'Manches in the slaughter of Texans. Unfortunately, aiding and abetting 'Manches in the slaughter of Texans would almost surely get him hung.

Black Paint knew that. Lucas looked at him carefully, and he could see it in the chief's smile. It was too mild, too patient. One brow was a little higher than the other.

Of course, Lucas thought, he could get hung only if he went back among his own kind. That idea shook him up, too, because more and more lately, he'd been wondering if he really *had* a kind. Certainly it wasn't the pompous, proper folks he had sprung from—The Banker and The Queen. Miss Myra? The Baptists? They had been a means to an end, and he didn't really think this 'Manche camp was the end, either. At least he hoped not. Just because he liked the way they lived didn't mean he was ready to settle here forever.

He decided abruptly that the only thing that mattered was his own skin. The question here wasn't one of getting hung, but of which course of action would benefit him the most.

"Tell you what." He motioned fast. "I'll tell you all about that gun if you show me how to shoot one of those bows."

Pandemonium erupted. The braves bellowed and the chiefs

hollered. One of the old guys looked damned near apoplectic. Lucas took an instinctive step backward.

"He dares too much!" shouted Wolf Dream.

"He forgets he is a slave!" someone else bellowed.

"Forgets?" Lost Coyote drawled. "Did he ever know it?"

"Kill him, kill him now!" This, Lucas realized, came from the buck he had beaten up on the trail—he had since learned his name was Kills In The Dark.

"Would you volunteer to do it?" Lost Coyote asked him dryly, and Kills In The Dark shouted in the affirmative without ever realizing that the buck was making sport of him.

"I never did think it was a good idea to keep one as old as him. Without that tether, he can kill us all in our sleep, or go back to Texas and get his brothers to come kill us," said Crooked Nose, who looked just like his name.

Black Paint's beady black eyes caught Lucas's and held on. "He will not go. He has already had the opportunity and he stayed."

Lucas felt surprise shoot all the way down to his toes. *How could he know?* He decided suddenly that it didn't seem like a good idea to toy with this man. Better just to tell them what they wanted to know.

He took a deep breath, motioned at the gun, and began signing as he spoke. "The day you took me was the first time I shot it under pressure. It's not a good fighting weapon, and truth to tell, I don't think you'll encounter all that many of them. They cost a bundle—upward of twenty dollars, and it's been my experience that the kind of men coming into Texas don't generally have that much money at their disposal. They're either running from something or trying to establish their own Garden of Eden, but either way they don't spend a lot on the way. Of course if a man is going to spend, I guess it would be on a firearm."

All around the circle, Injun faces scowled and nodded. "Anyway," he went on, "when I was target practicing with it, I thought it was accurate enough to take the pizzle off a bull at a hundred paces. It can't miss if you get the chance to brace it against something and aim it properly. But in the middle of an Injun fight, nobody's going to be likely to brace and aim anything. I sure as hell couldn't, and I was pretty safe in that cornfield. The only shot I got off took out his horse." He gestured at Wolf Dream.

Lost Coyote's brows went high. "I think he speaks true," he said. "The shot that hit your horse was powerful. It went all the way through his carcass and out the other side."

"I heard two shots," Wolf Dream snapped.

Lucas forgot that he wasn't supposed to understand Comanche. "The first one was your sister's doing. I think she was trying to shoot me."

Wolf Dream gave the look of pained exasperation that only his younger sibling seemed to be able to elicit from him.

"You are saying that we should not lose any men to these new guns if we take the *tejanos* by surprise?" Lost Coyote asked.

Something tightened briefly around Lucas's gut—something like guilt—then it was gone. "You can't hang around out on the hills this time. You need to burst out of concealment fast. Then they won't have time to brace their guns. Because I'm warning you, if they have time to aim, you're goners."

Wolf Dream nodded thoughtfully.

"Even if they do have time to situate their guns against a rest," Lucas went on, "they're helpless for a while after each shot. That's what got me mad—that I spent so damned much money on something that needs so much work to reload. It's the same as the old guns that way."

Wolf Dream straightened slowly. He did it like a predator, like an animal of the night. "So be it," he said. "We will ride tonight. If what you tell us is true, then we will come home with new captives."

The warrior's implication was clear enough. If the war party didn't come home with captives, then they would think it was because he had lied about the guns. If they didn't come home with captives, if they didn't fare well against the new Kentucky rifles, Lucas was probably as good as dead.

The war band was gone for three weeks. They came back on an overcast morning, and a cold heavy rain began to drench the camp just as Falls Into The Water, the youngest and most inexperienced of Wolf Dream's warriors, came in to announce the party's victorious return. The boy galloped down from a nearby hill, his lance held high. Two fresh scalps slapped wetly at its tip. Lucas was working in the herd again and he stood slowly to watch. His legs went hollow at the sight of the hair.

He had prayed for it of course. In the interest of his own scalp, he had prayed that the bucks would best those guns if they found them. And yet now, instead of relief, he felt only nausea.

She Smiles appeared beside him. *"Keemah!"* she cried excitedly.

Lucas forced his legs to move after her. She Smiles started singing as she jogged beside him, splashing gaily in the puddles gathering on the path. Mountain, Paya-yuca's first wife, took the scalp lance from Falls Into The Water. She Smiles stopped at the edge of the path to watch as the big woman moved about the camp, chanting, oblivious to the downpour. Others fell in behind her, and by the time she reached them, the parade was a city-block long.

The Penateka danced, their hair and buckskins streaming water. They were like children, Lucas thought. The bigger the puddle, the harder they stomped in it.

Lucas finally smiled.

The rest of the war band came roaring down from the hill. There were more scalps and four captives. Two of them— girls—were lashed to a pony the way he and the runt had been. A boy sat in front of Lost Coyote. And this time there was a woman. She rode a horse that moved wearily along behind

Kills In The Dark's, and she wore a tether around her neck as Lucas had.

The woman was naked, and blood dripped down over her small breasts, streaks and smears of it marking her midriff. Her neck was raw beneath the noose and her head lolled. Lucas noticed that the rest of the war band gave her and her captor a wide berth, as though there was something distasteful about the situation even by 'Manche standards.

The woman looked his way and her gaze slid past him. Something odd filled Lucas's belly as he realized that she did not even know he was white.

He looked down at his breechclout, at his leggings, at his skin. After so many months of exposure to the elements, it was weathered, scratched, bruised, and deeply tanned. The hair on his legs had bleached so white it was no longer easily visible.

His gaze moved on to the kids. They were clothed and terrified. He found himself walking toward them.

They saw that he was white. They began screeching and pleading as soon as they saw him.

He wanted to tell them that they would be all right. He had never seen such happy, beloved children anywhere as in this 'Manche camp. The Baptists worked the starch and the joy right out of their little ones, but here they went to get water and wood in the morning, then they laughed and played their way through the rest of day. It might be different for these kids because he guessed they'd probably be slaves, but even so, Lucas didn't think they would be treated cruelly. He certainly hadn't been.

He opened his mouth and for one blank, astounding moment, he couldn't for the life of him find the English words.

He realized with a start that he had begun to *think* in Comanche. A cold sensation filled his chest. He turned away and made his way blindly out of the camp.

Watching him, Wolf Dream stiffened. Black Paint put a hand on his son's arm.

"Leave him be."

"He will run."

"No. His heart is tearing. It is painful. There is nowhere else he wants to be right now, but a piece of him must die to allow him to stay."

Finally the chief turned back to the raucous crowd. "Tell me of this raid."

Storm Trail was poking at the meat in Loses Something's cooking paunch when she heard the scratching, thumping sounds outside the lodge that told her Loo-cus had returned.

"He is like a bear making a den out there," she grumbled.

Loses Something stopped what she was doing to cock her head and listen. "I hear nothing."

How could she not? There . . . there was the swishing sound of his bare feet as he kicked away the stones and debris that had gathered in the little indent his body made in the earth. And there . . . he grunted as he sat, and she could just picture the way he pulled that old robe they had given him up over his shoulders.

She reached a hand into the paunch to pluck out a piece of meat to throw to him. Her mother stopped her.

"No, daughter. Not this night."

Something thumped in the area of Storm Trail's heart as Black Paint ducked inside. "Why are we not feeding Loo-cus?" she demanded.

Black Paint sat at his place beside the fire. That was when she noticed that he held a bow and a small quiver with four arrows. The quiver was not of good quality—only a badger tail. The arrows were old ones, but Black Paint leaned everything against his bedding as though they were brand new and precious.

She didn't like the look of this at all.

"Daughter, bring Loo-cus inside," he said.

Inside? Storm Trail crossed her arms over her chest and lifted her chin mutinously. She would choke first!

Black Paint waited.

She gave a huffy sigh and went outside, giving the weighted door an extra hard shove as she passed through it. Loo-cus did indeed have his robe pulled up over his head and his arms were crossed beneath it, holding it closed. He looked cold and she was glad.

Oh, the words would kill her! "You should come in," she managed.

"Hakai, what?" She noticed that every once in a while now he let a Comanche word pepper his speech.

"Come in!" she screeched. "Are you deaf? My father would see you!" She was pleased to see that he looked a little worried. "Maybe he would finally kill you," she muttered.

He got to his feet and moved past her to the front of the lodge. He walked like a coyote, she thought, like he was up to no good and everybody knew it but nobody would stop him.

He went inside and she ducked in after him. Star Line had finally come, and she was seated beside the fire. Black Paint greeted him and waved at him to sit.

Storm Trail squatted on the other side of the fire. Their lodge was one of the biggest, second only to Paya-yuca's, but suddenly it felt cramped and small to her. She felt itchy, crowded.

Loo-cus took plenty of meat, she noticed grimly. She waited for him to do something to disgrace himself, but he had been with the People long enough to know not to eat until Black Paint held a piece toward the smoke hole and offered it to his spirit-protectors.

"You gave Wolf Dream good advice," her father said finally, belching and leaning back, indicating that it was time for conversation. He reached behind him, beneath his bedding, for his pipe and his smoking weed.

Loo-cus motioned that he did not understand.

"He lies!" Storm Trail cried. She jumped to her feet. "He understands me all the time and I never sign anymore!"

Black Paint only chuckled. He began motioning as he spoke, humoring the *tejano*.

"Everything you told us about the guns was true. The war band managed to get into the fort without mishap, and they killed all the men. They took the women and children. The woman was Kills In The Dark's coup and Wolf Dream will not take her from him. But he has claimed the children himself, and he will sell them, as he traded you to me.

"Do you know of that old warrior named Snow Dancing?" he asked suddenly.

Lucas scowled, pretty sure that the big chief was going somewhere with this rambling talk. He nodded.

"Snow Dancing lost his testicles when he was a young man," Black Paint went on. "The Tonkawas captured him. Have you heard of the Tonkawas? They have the land below that claimed by the Wichita. They are people-eaters."

He waited for this to sink in. Even Storm Trail could tell the moment Loo-cus understood. His face changed color, and he shifted his weight gingerly where he sat.

"Snow Dancing escaped his tormenters and came back to us. Luckily his marriage was one of love."

Lucas blinked at that, at the intimation that no matter how romantic these folks seemed, some marriages were not.

"His wife could have left him, and I do not think anyone would have blamed her for it. But she did not do that, and for many, many seasons now, she has pined for a child. Now of course she is too old for even another man to give her one. But because of what you told Wolf Dream, she will have one of those girls. Snow Dancing would buy her one. Wolf Dream will not ask for much in trade. It is enough to know that that woman is finally happy."

Storm Trail saw a strange look come to the *tejano*'s face, as though he had just found something beautiful and valuable in a pile of pony dung.

"So," Black Paint went on. "When I consider all that, I think you should have what you asked for."

Loo-cus's look became wary.

"You told us about your guns, and you wished to know about our bows. Perhaps you thought that because we did not smoke over it, the deal would not be upheld. But you gave honestly and should have something in return."

He reached a hand behind him for the bow. Storm Trail clapped a hand over her mouth to muffle a squeal of dismay.

Lucas looked at the bow and the quiver. Something both sick and triumphant filled him.

He thought of Kills In The Dark's woman.

He thought of Snow Dancing's wife.

It wasn't as simple as either one, he thought. He closed his eyes and saw scalps. He opened them and saw the bow and quiver again.

He could not undo what had already been done, he reasoned. He could only make the best of it.

Black Paint made a motion toward the door, saying he should go now. Storm Trail saw his *tejano* eyes gleam with triumph as he got up and ducked outside into the wind.

Suddenly Storm Trail's heart skipped a beat. An idea for killing him popped into her head. It was so glorious, so good, she could hardly stand it.

"Daughter?" Loses Something asked cautiously. "Why do you smile so?"

Storm Trail pursed her lips into a quick frown. "If the *tejano* hunts with that bow, I hope I am there to see it."

Black Paint looked at his wife. "Did I mention hunting?"

"No, husband, I did not hear you say anything about that."

Storm Trail flushed. "Well, that is a good thing, because he cannot even ride a pony."

At least that was what she was counting on.

Eight

"Buffalo!" a boy shouted, riding back into the camp.

Other boys ran to bring in the best of the hunting ponies. It did not matter that every squaw's parfleches were full to bursting with dried meat and pemmican. It was the last moon before the snows came. With each sun the sky seemed grayer and lower. And no matter how much the women had stored and saved, there was never, ever enough to see the band all the way through the winter.

"Daughter." Storm Trail spun about as her father came out of the lodge. "Go to my herd and get a suitable pony for Loo-cus." He handed her one of his bridles.

For a moment Storm Trail only stared at it. Oh, it was perfect! He was giving it right to her! Her new plan would come off flawlessly!

She tried desperately not to look too pleased. "He will be a danger to himself and to others," she grumbled.

"Do you think so?"

She nodded hard at her dusty toes. For an agonizing moment she felt a telltale blush creep up her neck. It was as though her father knew that she intended for the white-eyes to fall off and get trampled.

She finally looked up and managed a look of innocence. "Can I watch?"

"Come out with your mother and her pack ponies later. Then you can see how well your *tejano* has fared."

He moved away. Storm Trail hurried to the part of the herd

where his horses grazed. She stood there for a moment, looking around at all the ponies, then she grinned again. That old piebald would be the best one.

She slipped her knife from the sheath at her thigh and found the weakest part of one of the reins. She gouged it deeply. Finally she slipped the bridle over the old beast's head and led him away.

That *tejano* could not ride. She had told them that over and over.

Lucas looked up from the river where he was washing clothes. He saw the runt coming his way, leading a swaybacked old stallion. Out of the corner of his eye, he saw Black Paint approaching him from the other direction. He scrambled up the bank to meet them.

Black Paint nearly laughed when he saw the pony his daughter had brought. "Do you think this one will be safe enough for him?"

Storm Trail nodded solemnly. "It will not run very fast."

"It'll run," Lucas said. By Jesus, if he had to whip the mangy hide right off its old bones, it would run!

"Come then," Black Paint said to him. "Get your bow and meet me on the south edge of camp."

Lucas gathered his weapon. It was never very far from his side. He grabbed a handful of the stallion's mane and hauled himself astride.

The animal's jarring trot made his weight slide off to one side. He caught its mane and pulled himself upright again. The Injun bridle wasn't anything like those he was used to, he realized. It had no metal bit. He tugged on the reins and the horse kept going, plodding right past Black Paint.

The chief looked at him with a raised brow just as Lucas discovered the art of the reins—two hands and a tug downward, so a leather strip pinched into the pony's tender nose. "What do I do?" he asked, motioning at the distant herd.

"You watch. You observe. That is what this first time is for."

Lucas was sure he hadn't heard him right. "Watch?"

"Yes."

Fury burned in his head. *"Why?"*

"Because you are unprepared for anything else."

Black Paint watched the boy's jaw jut out. It was a look familiar to him. He had seen it a thousand times on his daughter's face.

"The hell I am!" Lucas shouted rudely. "Why did you tell me to bring my bow? Why did you give me a pony?"

"I did not."

"You—"

"I told my daughter to get you one," Black Paint corrected, "and she has provided you with a mount that will not hunt." In fact, Black Paint had counted on that.

He would kill her. This time the nasty little brat had gone too far.

"Did you look at your pony before you mounted him?" Black Paint asked.

"I—"

"If you had, you would have noticed that this one was not adequate. A warrior never mounts an animal he is unsure of. Too often his life depends upon the pony he is riding."

"I looked—"

"Then you must know that yours is blind."

Blind?

Lucas leaned forward cautiously to look down at the horse's face. It was, indeed, missing its left eye.

"If you had looked before you mounted, you would have known that," Black Paint pointed out. "If you had looked before you mounted, you might have exchanged this one for another. As it is, this is your first lesson, Loo-cus, the first thing I would teach you. There will always be buffalo, but you may not get so many chances to make the error you just made. Even once could kill you."

Lucas simmered. For weeks and weeks he had been scrubbing and washing, obeying and keeping his eyes down. He wanted one of those buffalo. He wanted it badly enough that he could taste it, wanted it so much it was a hum in his veins. He was damned if he was going to let that heathen runt take this opportunity from him.

The horse could see on its right side, he reasoned. He could just keep to the left of his prey.

He heard one of the warriors out on the plain give a thin pitched cry. Suddenly the throng of them lunged forward into the herd.

"It is important to kill as many buffalo as you can, as quickly as possible," Black Paint was instructing. "The meat will spoil quickly if the animal is slain when overheated from long running."

He would deal with the chief's anger later, Lucas decided. If he brought in meat, a hide, and all the other stuff they needed the buffalo for, then he didn't think Black Paint would castigate him for disobeying him, at least not severely.

He howled a cry like he had heard the first warrior give and plunged into the chaos.

First there was adrenaline, alive and powerful beneath his skin. Expectancy made his blood rush so loudly he could barely hear anything else. Ahead of him the mouths of the bucks moved as they shouted and whooped. Their muscles slid and bulged and strained beneath their skin. Then they were obliterated by rising clouds of dust.

Every moment seemed clear, perfect, honed in time, and he, Lucas Mazur, was a vital, integral part of it. He felt a howl leave his throat, a sound of primitive gladness.

He didn't have a quirt, so he used his bow on the old stallion's rump to goad him on. Then he spied a cow a little bit ahead of him and off to his right. Her gait was hitching and lame. She was the only one of the beasts slow enough for his old pony to catch, and that made her his.

Lucas brought an arrow ready. He had practiced avidly—his

ability with the bow was the only thing he had absolutely no doubt of now. His pony moved up on the beast's left side, and he let the missile go with a strong *twang*.

He could feel the arrow's release in his own muscles. It drove in perfectly, just between her hipbone and her last rib, just the way he had seen Wolf Dream shoot. But this cow did not drop.

She gave a roar of agony. She was so close to him that Lucas thought he could feel the air tremble with the fullness of the sound. Her head came around, and one big eye looked back at him balefully. Then she heaved her whole body about in midstride and came at him dead-on.

That was when Lucas felt the fear.

At first it was only a tickle of panic at the base of his throat. He caught one of his reins and pulled hard, trying to turn the old pony out of danger. But the horse was panicked, confused, and it only came to a standstill, trembling. Lucas pulled again. This time the whole rein came free in his hand.

He knew a moment of terror and disbelief. *This was her doing, too.* He knew it without doubt. But there was no time for him to dwell on it, because the cow roared again and charged into his pony's blind side.

The sturdy little animal went down with a scream of pain. Lucas went with it.

Storm Trail and her mother and aunt finally cleared the camp. When they got close enough to see the hunt, her eyes searched hungrily for Loo-cus and the old piebald. Then her belly plunged sickeningly down to her toes. She let out a little squeal and clapped a hand to her mouth.

Thinking of ways to make Loo-cus dead had kept her warm in her bedding night after night. The convoluted ideas she had come up with had made her smile through all the terrible chores Black Paint had assigned to her. But now it was real, now it was happening, and great waves of numbing horror rolled over her.

She had done it. She had really killed him.

All the best war and hunting ponies knew to swerve away from their prey as soon as they heard the *twang* of a bowstring, but the piebald she had chosen stayed close, and it was a lame cow, and a hurt buffalo was even more dangerous and unpredictable than a bull in rutting season. The *tejano* pulled at his rein to turn his pony away by hand, and the leather came free in his grip.

Storm Trail thumped her heels into her mare and galloped into the hunt. Maybe he wasn't dead yet. Maybe she could drag him free before he got trampled worse.

Lucas tried to notch an arrow in his bow as he scrambled back from his pony's carcass, but it all happened too fast. The cow came over him while the arrow was still fisted desperately in his hand.

Somehow, incredibly, the beast's front hooves missed him. One of her rear hooves loomed above his eyes for a split second, cloven and huge. Lucas bellowed in terror and thrust the arrow upward blindly.

The cow's back legs missed him, too. She went on a few feet, stumbling, and Lucas rolled onto his belly, coughing up the dust that burned his lungs. He felt the earth trembling again beneath him, not with the roar of the herd's retreat now, but with the impact of something much closer.

He looked around dazedly. The blow he'd struck had killed the cow. She lay dead not twenty paces from him.

Storm Trail sawed on her reins and gaped at the carcass. Lucas rolled in the dirt nearby. *He was alive.*

Her relief was dazzling. She slid to the ground, her legs shaking. Then her relief changed to disbelief, and her disbelief went to fury.

He was alive? And the *cow* was dead? This had been her best idea yet, and he had won, he had beaten her again!

The others began gathering around them silently. It was a

thick, throbbing, stunned kind of quiet. They looked from the *tejano* to the cow to the dead pony. Finally Lost Coyote let out a bark of laughter.

"This white-eyes is very hard on horses."

The voices of the others erupted. "He killed Wolf Dream's best war pony, too! Do you remember?"

"He reminds me of a raven," said Lost Coyote, still laughing. "Whenever you see an ailing horse, such a bird is always found nearby, waiting to feast on the carrion when it finally goes down."

"A white raven," Black Paint agreed, approaching on his big roan. Several curious squaws came along behind him. "It is a sure sign that a pony will die if he is about."

Laughter murmured through the crowd, then faded worriedly. Black Paint was staring down at his poor gutted piebald. "I liked that horse."

Lucas's eyes widened. Christ on a mule, did the chief value the damned thing that much?

Black Paint bent over the animal's bridle, studied it a moment, then grunted. "What happened, White Raven?"

Storm Trail was afraid to look at him.

"One of my arrows got caught in the rein and cut it," he said finally. "I have had only a few short weeks to practice shooting. I was not able to get it to the bow fast enough."

She whipped around to stare at him as he finished. He had lied for her. *Why?*

Her eyes darted warily to her father to see how he would take the explanation. He studied the rein a moment longer, then he shook his head and stood.

"If you had given me the chance," Black Paint chided, "I would have told you exactly how to aim. Shooting between the hipbone and that last rib is good, but you must hit the heart. It hangs low in her chest. You must not have understood that because you did not aim downward properly."

Lucas felt warmth flush his face.

"That is why your other blow killed her. You were able to

thrust upward into her heart from the other way, from beneath her. But we do not like to put ourselves in such a position for a kill. We like to eat what we have slaughtered, not be buried in its hides."

There was scattered laughter. Lucas colored even more.

He looked around and saw the runt trying to inch backward toward her pony. He grinned at her with evil intent. He didn't want her to think for a minute that he was going to let her get away with what she had done.

Storm Trail caught his look. Suddenly she wished Loo-cus had told her father the truth. She thought she might prefer any punishment that Black Paint could mete out.

The sky was bruised with purple clouds and mauve shadows when White Raven finally leaned away from his kill. He rocked painfully onto his heels, stretching his cramped muscles.

He had a strong suspicion they would be working out here, butchering the beasts all night. Usually the squaws were back in camp in time for the evening meal, but he did not see how they could possibly finish up with all these carcasses before full dark fell. He stood, grimacing at his stiffness, and turned around to look. He gaped and stared.

"We are the only ones left!"

She Smiles looked up. She was helping him with his cow. "Except for the dogs," she agreed.

Packs of mongrels fought over all that remained of the buffalo—long white ribbons of spine with only the heads attached. Raven knew that the brains had been scooped out of those skulls—for tanning, She Smiles had said as she had done the same thing to his cow. And all the sinews had been pulled off the spines for sewing. He had taken She Smiles's pony back to the camp three times, loaded with the meat that Loses Something was undoubtedly cutting into thin strips for drying even now. Each time he had come back, She Smiles had still another pile waiting for him—the bladder that would be a medicine pouch, bones that would make shovels and scrapers and awls, the stomach lining that would replace Loses Something's old cooking paunch. Now the plain was an eerie graveyard, looking as though meticulous vultures had stripped clean all that was usable.

"One last thing," She Smiles said, signing, and he looked down at her. "Then we are finished." She lay open the tail and fleshed it out. "Stew," she said, holding up the gristle.

"Stew? With that?"

"We dry it and use it to flavor the water when we have no meat."

White Raven scowled. Considering the rate at which these folks hunted, he couldn't imagine such a thing.

She Smiles tucked the piece neatly into a parfleche and handed the rawhide bag up to him. "This is yours," she said shyly. "I made it for you when I heard you would hunt."

His belly felt as though it had filled with warm velvet. "Thank you."

Then he thought about having to go back and face Black Paint, and his blood went cold again. Somehow he did not think that the chief's mild lecture earlier had been the end of it.

Loses Something sizzled his liver briefly in the coals that glowed like red-orange stars around the fire. The outside was charred, the inside just warm. Raven chewed blissfully.

The fire twisted and writhed and snapped, throwing heat back at his face, and the night was just cool enough for it to be a luxury. Someone lit a pipe nearby and the sweet scent of burning weed mingled in the air with the mouthwatering aroma of broiling meat.

"White Raven," Black Paint said.

He looked over at the chief warily.

"These autumn hides are best for sleeping robes," he began.

"Huh?" It was not what he expected to hear.

"You will notice that these have thick dark coats. In contrast, spring coats are mangy. In spring the buffalo shed, like all other beasts. Those are the hides to take the hair off of. At least ten spring or summer hides are required for a small lodge such as you would need. My wife has collected nine for you. You need one more."

Raven watched him bemusedly and nodded.

"Wolf Dream has several spring hides," Black Paint went on. "Perhaps he would be amenable to a trade for that thick hide you got this sun."

Raven nodded cautiously. "I will ask him."

"In the meantime you might not want to whoop and shout your way into the herd next time," the chief said finally, and Raven's chest tightened. "Your enthusiasm was refreshing—it has been a long time since I have seen anyone get so excited over a meager fall hunt. However, if you had scared the herd prematurely, you would have been severely chastised. There are distinct disadvantages to rushing in without observing first. That is your second lesson. If you had paid attention, you would also have realized that only one man, the hunt leader, gave any voice to the beginning of the hunt."

An oily feeling filled Raven's gut. Black Paint's point was clear. If he had somehow caused things to go wrong, he would probably be dead now instead of enjoying this feast beside the chief's fire.

He waited for more, but Black Paint only ate.

And ate.

More meat was brought to them and they gorged on that, too. Then they sat back, belching and smoking. They talked of the hunt and of gossip, then they started eating all over again.

Raven kept up with the chief until only a thin slice remained of the moon. Then Black Paint finally pushed to his feet with a laborious groan. Raven followed him back to his lodge and went to his dent in the earth beside it.

He reached beneath the heavy outer hide of the lodge wall and found his robe, then he gave an exploratory poke to Storm Trail's warm weight. He got no reaction. He pulled his robe up over his shoulder and rolled over.

A warm hand closed over his ankle where his bare feet poked out.

Raven jerked upright again, then his robe lifted and She Smiles slid in close to him. He ran his hands down her back and realized she was naked. Her body was firm and thin and smooth.

"Oh, God," he groaned.

Back in Texas he'd sure as hell get shot for this, he thought, but Texas was a long way away. He moved his fingers up to the little black tangle of hair between her legs and she cried out, loud enough to be heard all over the camp.

"Jesus! Shhh!"

"Je-sus," she repeated breathlessly.

"I—no, no! Don't do that. I mean, no, that's all right, what you're doing with your hand." It was better than all right, but he had to keep her quiet. "Shhh," he whispered again.

He was afraid to touch her now, afraid of what might come out of her mouth if he did, and unable to keep his hands still. She felt so good down there, hot and damp and exciting. But as he slid his fingers into her, she squealed again. Raven twitched, expecting to feel the cold blade of a knife at his throat.

Oh, God, he thought again, he was going to be shot, hung, gutted for this, and what a glorious way to go.

Storm Trail was not asleep.

When he had poked her, she had started to prod him right back except she thought that maybe he was trying to trap her. Maybe he would do something awful to her because she had tried to kill him earlier. She clenched her teeth instead and lay very still.

Now there were noises out there. She listened a moment, then she realized with a jolt what was happening, what he was doing *right on the other side of her lodge wall!*

Her throat closed hard and suddenly. She curled her hands into fists and tucked them down between her knees. It had to be She Smiles. Who else would do that with him, an ugly old *tejano?* White Raven sounded like a big, old, ugly boar, grunting and groaning! Then She Smiles cried out again, and she sounded like a bleating baby buffalo.

The lodge wall bulged inward.

Storm Trail sat up fast, horrified. She scrambled away from it, sick with the thought that they might bump into her, might *touch* her. Their voices got louder. She clapped her hands over her ears.

She would go outside and kick them both silly! That would stop them. She stumbled to her feet but then it got quiet out there. She let her breath out slowly, shakily.

She hated She Smiles, she decided suddenly. And, oh, how she hated White Raven!

She pressed a hand to the ache in her tummy. It was low and painful, but it wasn't so terrible that it could explain the sudden urge she had to cry.

Nine

The snows began four suns later. The first stinging, swirling flakes came down from the sky at dawn, and Bear Wound began moving along the pathways, chanting of their next move.

Storm Trail sat up in her sleeping robes, listening avidly. This move would be an important one. Wherever the band went now, they would stay all through the moons When The Babes Cried For Food. It would have to be a perfect place to sustain the four hundred Penateka for so long.

Bear Wound said they would travel up the *Ekakoma,* the Red River. He said they would send riders ahead to try to find that other band, so perhaps they could all camp together.

Storm Trail pushed her bedding off. "I will bring the ponies, *Pia.*"

She ducked outside. She needed desperately to pee, but she decided to bring the ponies in first. That way her mother could pack them while she ran down to the water to relieve herself.

She hurried into the herd. The ground was frozen, and ridges of sharp mud hurt her bare feet. She found *Pia's* best pack ponies, waving her arms at them, then she grabbed the mane of the last one to pull herself astride.

A sound behind her made her let go of it again. The pony trotted on without her and she turned about, scowling.

White Raven's big gun—the one that had made her faint when she had tried to pick it up on that long-ago raid—was visible just behind a knot of grazing geldings. What was it doing out here? She took a cautious step toward it, and the knot of ponies broke up. Raven held the gun.

He had caught her.

She squeezed her knees together fast before she could lose her tenuous control over her bladder. Her heart knocked once, so hard against her ribs that it hurt. Enough time had passed that she had stopped thinking he would get even with her for trying to kill him. She should have known he would never do that!

"No!" she cried out and turned to run. But before she could even spin fully about, his hand snagged her hair.

She went wild, fighting him, but he held her effortlessly away from him. "Do not irritate me, weasel. I have the gun, and I would love to shoot you."

"I am—" she began, but her voice sounded whiny so she clamped her jaw shut.

"You are what? Sorry for trying to kill me?"

Yes, oh, yes, she was sorry! Not for what she had done, but that he had not died! "No!"

"Then you give me no choice. I will just have to shoot you."

She almost lost her water. But if she lived to see a hundred thousand winters, she would never *ever* beg him for anything, not even her life.

He let her go. He had been holding her on her toes, and when he released her, her legs collapsed under her full weight. She fell into the grass, then she leaped up again, turned on her heel, and started running.

He got down on the ground with the gun, aiming it. "Say you are sorry," he called after her.

"No!"

He waited until she got far enough away that he could sight on her. Then he took careful aim at her scrawny little back and pulled the trigger.

It stung terribly, and it flung her down, or maybe she stumbled—Storm Trail couldn't be sure. Her knees got skinned on the hard ground, and she groped around behind her for the spot where the fireball had gone. Her hand came away bloody.

She shrieked, staring at it, and felt her bladder finally go. She stumbled to her feet and warm urine slid down her legs.

"No," she sobbed. He was coming toward her with the gun, and she staggered backward. *"You killed me!"*

"You are standing," he pointed out reasonably.

It didn't matter. Her hand was sticky and red, and there were small brown bits in the mess and she knew what they were. Her innards were spilling out of her!

She ran for the camp and dizziness swam up into her head. Loses Something's lodge was already down. Star Line was helping her fold the cover. Storm Trail reached them and collapsed at their feet.

"Daughter?" Loses Something looked at her curiously. "What is that mess all over you?"

"He killed me!" she wailed. "He sh-sh-shot his big g-g-gun—he was w-w-waiting for me and he *shot* me!"

"What?" Star Line gasped.

Storm Trail dragged in the last of her dying breath. She sat up gingerly, and the horizon and the sky tilted and spun around her. She groaned softly. She was definitely dying.

"He was waiting for me and he shot me," she groaned again.

Loses Something squatted beside her. "Let me see, daughter. Roll over."

She did, shuddering. Now Loses Something would see the truth. She closed her eyes, waiting for sounds of her mother's despair. At least Black Paint would kill him now, she thought, taking some comfort from that. And it would be good if Kills In The Dark saw this, too. He would remember the tragedy of her death forever.

"Be still, daughter. Let me clean you up. Raven," Loses Something said, "you did not pick a good time for this. We must hurry to move."

Move? Would they not even mourn her?

Black Paint approached. "What is happening here?" Then his deep chuckle joined Raven's laughter.

Suddenly it seemed highly suspicious to her that she was still breathing.

"You are not dying, daughter," said Loses Something.

"But you smell like the stream where we relieve ourselves," Black Paint said.

"What did you do to me?" Storm Trail gasped, sitting up.

"Spitball," Raven wheezed. "The white-eyes use paper." Then he remembered that they probably didn't know what paper was. "I used a little wad of doeskin."

"So that is what you wanted it for," mused Loses Something. "Yellow Fawn, please bring me water."

Storm Trail saw, aghast, that her friends had gathered. Her skin went hot even as something very cold filled her.

"I put rabbit dung inside," Raven went on, "to make it hard enough to feel like a bullet. And I got She Smiles to save me some blood from my kill. I soaked it in that and pushed it down into the rifle with just a little bit of powder. Lost Coyote gave me the powder."

Lost Coyote had betrayed her, too? Storm Trail stood, feeling fragile.

"Wait, daughter," said Loses Something. "Wait for Yellow Fawn to bring that water back. I would like to wash that mess away and make sure you really are not bruised too badly."

"No," she whispered.

"No wonder she smells so bad," Eyes Down put in. She wrinkled her nose. "Rabbit dung and old blood. Ugh."

"Worse," Raven said, "she was so scared she peed herself."

Storm Trail gasped. "Why?" she choked, humiliated. "Why did you have to tell them that?"

Raven put his face close to hers. "Because I have had the grandest coup over you of all, and I want everyone to know it."

Never in her life had she hated anyone more.

She shook with it. It was a great, racking trembling that

went as deep as her bones. She turned away from them and ran from the camp.

She heard Raven behind her. She spun about, running backward. "Go away! Leave me alone!"

He kept coming. He still had his gun. She turned around again and ran faster.

She reached the river and threw herself into the icy water. Beneath it, she would not have to look at him. The river felt soothing on her feverish face. When she finally came up, he was on the bank, and he was no longer smiling.

"Come out," he said. "You're going to catch cold in there." Standing there like that, with her hair slicked back, he thought she looked just like a boy. Her shoulders were skinny, her nipples flat and dark. Yes, she could have been a boy, except then he looked into her eyes. They were alive with fire. They were beautiful, and that jolted the hell out of him.

"Come out of there," he said again, his voice raw. He cleared his throat.

She turned away and dove back in, rubbing frantically at her back to clear the foul goop away.

"Goddamnit!" Raven dropped his gun and went after her. The water was so cold that the shock of it flew through his body. His heart seemed to freeze for a moment, his blood seemed to stop, then the feeling in his limbs went dead.

Contrary brat. He'd expected some screeching revenge, not this fragile horror and shame. It made her seem too old for such pranks.

He caught her elbow and hauled her up. "All right. We will finish this in the water. I can stand it if you can."

"We are finished." She bit off each of her words, then her gaze moved slyly to the bank. He'd left his gun up there.

He wondered if she'd guessed that it wasn't loaded. Lost Coyote and Wolf Dream had been willing accomplices, but neither of them had trusted him enough to actually give him lead.

"I am going to let go of you and turn my back," he said quietly. "Here is your chance, weasel—"

"Do not call me that!"

"All right. Storm, then."

"Storm *Trail*. My name is Storm *Trail!*"

"Huh? Oh." So that was the end part of it. It didn't matter. She would always be a weasel to him. "Well, Storm *Trail,* here is your chance. Just go up on the bank and get the gun. I will not stop you. Go up there and get it and shoot me. Either kill me now and be done with it, or shut up about it and leave me alone."

She moved away from him jerkily. *Kill him.* Of course he would try to stop her, but she had to attempt it. She reached the gun and pulled it up, grunting. This time she was neither dehydrated nor starved. It swayed a little, pulling her around, but it didn't drop her.

Her hands shook as she brought the gun to where she wanted it, and eased it down again the way she had seen him do. Her eyes burned and a hot wretched hand caught her throat.

Kill him. Yes! Suddenly she no longer believed even a little bit in Cannibal Owl. She would face her father's wrath, and she really didn't care what punishment he might give her, just as long as White Raven was finally dead.

Kill him. Yes. She lay down beside the gun as he had done and put her finger on the little curl of metal as she had seen warriors do.

And she found she could not pull it.

She made a little keening sound and closed her eyes. Maybe if she did not look at him . . . but that did not work either. She could not take his life when he was just *letting* her.

She launched herself to her feet again, trembling. "Every breath I will ever take is one in which I will loathe you."

He waded out of the water, coming toward her. Storm Trail turned on her heel and fled.

He wasn't done with her yet. He caught up with her halfway

back to the camp and lunged for her arm. He missed and ended up tackling her by the ankles.

She went down hard with a soft grunt, but just as he wondered if he had hurt her, she wriggled around to rake her nasty little claws down his face.

Nothing had changed. Yet somehow everything had.

"You are not a coward," he managed breathlessly. "Do you hear me? A coward would have shot me."

Her chest rose and fell with her short choppy breaths.

"It took more courage to turn away, knowing I can torment you for it every sun of your life."

Her eyes spat fire at him.

"But I will not, because we are just alike, really." He grew thoughtful, considering that. "Ruining you would be like crushing a part of myself: that part that dares anything, that wants to soar with the birds even if I crash and break my wings." He grinned. "The part that can't stand to be bested."

She sat up as well, easing backward, away from him.

"Truce?" he suggested, and chuckled at her appalled expression. "Do not worry, I do not think we will ever be friends. Things will never be that peaceful between us. But I am willing to let you go your way and never tell what happened down here—all you have to do is give me a wide berth as well. Do we have a deal?"

It took a while, but she finally nodded. He thought about it and knew her word was good. There was no sly hitching of her eyes this time.

She stood, and Raven watched her go. She moved away from him jauntily, her head up, her skinny hips swinging. No one watching her would ever suspect that she had just been shaken down to her nasty little toes.

Raven waited until she reached the first of the lodges, then in a white-eyes gesture not forgotten, he lifted a hand to salute her.

Part Two

Wildfire

Ten

In southeastern Texas, on the edge of Wichita country, a pair of wooden saloon doors swung open with an obnoxious screech. A brilliant shaft of sunlight speared into the dark, musty room.

"Mr. Thorn!" someone shouted drunkenly.

The man took off his hat, nodded, and went to the bar. It wasn't actually his name—that was Matthew Thornberg. But it was as close to accurate as anything else they said about him.

The bartender poured him a shot of whiskey—raw stuff, Thorn thought, but at least it warmed the gullet.

"Chasing Injuns?" the man asked. The Injun-chasing myth was another almost accurate thing they said about him. In actuality he was only after the rich reward the surviving Parker clan was offering to any man who could retrieve their lost loved ones.

Last May—May nineteenth to be exact—the Comanches had swept down off the Balcones Escarpment to kill most of the Parker men and carry off a handful of their women and children. Less than three weeks after that, they had come again to slaughter the Rusts. And then the *real* siege had begun. Since then some two hundred hardworking, God-fearing white men had died for their dream of settling the Texas frontier, and nobody had finished counting yet how many of their women and children were missing.

Thorn downed his whiskey in one swallow, then he held out his glass for another.

"They hit the Mueller place last week," the bartender offered.

Thorn drank again. "Yes, well, if you place a pot of honey in front of a bear, you can pretty much wager he's gonna snatch it up, and you've no business getting pissed off on moral grounds when he does."

"Hey, now! I thought you was an Injun *fighter!*" one man yelled angrily from the back of the bar.

Thorn glanced that way. It wasn't a popular opinion, but he remained convinced that the Texans had instigated this trouble. Thorn did not, however, care much about his popularity or lack of it. He did care about the money Isaac Parker would pay to anyone who found those kids. That money just might take him home to the States, back to his wife and his own kids again.

"We threw down the first gauntlet when our homesteaders went out there," he said flatly. "Now we're crying foul because our challenge has been met. All I'm saying is, don't get mad and cry into your whiskey. Do something about it."

"I'll fight 'em," someone shouted.

"With what?" Thorn drawled. "We have no warning of a Comanche strike, yet if we can't dig in fast enough with our rifles, our women and children are carted off. Those new rifles are useless. We need something we can shoot from horseback."

A slight, slim-hipped man approached from the darkest shadows in the back of the saloon. To Thorn's surprise, the stranger picked up where he had left off.

"And then there is the matter of our horseflesh," the man contributed. "Fine Kentucky breeding stock that is hopelessly inadequate to the job at hand. Our Eastern-bred mounts are too finicky and fine-boned to handle the great distances of these Texas plains. When the Injuns sweep away with our women, we have no means of pursuing the fight."

Thorn's brows lifted. "And who might you be, sir?"

The little man extended his hand. "Hays, Jack Hays."

Thorn had heard of him. At the age of twenty-three, he already commanded the San Antonio station of the newly formed Texas Rangers.

They shook hands. "I'd anticipated someone much . . . larger," Thorn admitted baldly.

Hays didn't take offense. He laughed as though he had heard it before.

"Buy you a whiskey?" Thorn offered, and Hays agreed.

Thorn followed the little man, twelve years his junior, back to his table. "So tell me about these Rangers everyone's talking about," he prompted.

"It's no secret that the Republic can't afford a regular army," Hays answered, "and more's the pity. But they've authorized a frontier battalion. They assigned six hundred mounted gunmen last fall. Next week they'll authorize six hundred more."

Thorn raised his brows. "That many?"

"Don't be impressed. My men have to provide their own horses, their own guns and ammunition, and God bless a one of us if we ever get paid in cash dollars. But the forts and the communities are supporting us as best they can—feeding us and what not. My only real complaint is the caliber of soldier we attract. We have no higher authority to govern us, so we tend to make our own rules and elect our own leaders as we go along. I suppose we're perfectly suited to the job at hand, but it's difficult channeling the energy of so many rough-and-ready men."

"The Injuns do it."

Hays raised his whiskey in a toast. "You, my friend, are a wise man. What they can do, we must do also, or we will never have Texas to ourselves."

Thorn's eyes narrowed. "It's going to be tough as long as they have that damned escarpment on their side."

Hays nodded. "The best my Rangers can do is patrol the land between that plateau and the westernmost settlements. Once they reach that jutting rocky barrier, they're gone. And we're bucking our president as well. Rest assured my Rangers were not Sam Houston's idea."

"They call him a bleeding heart."

"He is."

"He was married to an Injun."

"A Cherokee girl."

"That's a far cry from our 'Manches. They're civilized."

"So are rattlesnakes compared to our Comanche. But Houston refuses to build forts on the frontier as the Americans have done up north, because he says it will disrupt their hunting lands. He feels that altering their food supply will only increase their raiding. He won't send troops up onto the scarp to try to wrest the white women and children away again because he says the Comanche will kill their captives rather than let them be retaken."

Thorn sipped his whiskey thoughtfully. "So what's left? What can we do?"

"We need to defeat them on their own terms so that they come into San Antonio with their hands up, dragging their captives behind them. In the meantime Houston is sending emissaries up there to try to ransom the people."

Thorn's eyes sharpened. "When?"

"This very month."

He needed to be among the emissaries that Houston sent up there, Thorn thought. He could think of no better way to search for blond heads among the black. He could think of no other way in which he might get in and out of Comancheria alive—and even these circumstances were dubious.

But he was a Texan now, and as such, he was the kind of man to give it a try.

Morning broke over the escarpment with dazzling brilliance. Storm Trail poked her nose out her lodge door to find the last patches of snow sparkling in the pure light of the new sun. She went out and gathered the wood she needed for her mother, then she headed back toward her tipi, detouring past Kills In The Dark's lodge. She saw his *tejano* woman through the pegged-open door, struggling to build his fire.

"I could help you with that," Storm Trail volunteered.

The *tejano* woman's eyes snapped up. In spite of herself, Storm Trail gasped. Her face was so battered and bruised it was almost impossible to tell that she was a white-eyes.

Storm Trail recovered. "I will not hurt you. I come to help." She got no response. She put her wood down and slipped inside, signing more slowly and meticulously.

Still nothing.

"You must learn!" Storm Trail burst out, exasperated. "If you do your work right, he will not hit you!"

That was only part of it, of course. She also thought it was a perfect opportunity to impress Kills In The Dark with her more womanly skills. She figured she had perfected them pretty well through all the times she had been punished.

But it did not seem as though this captive was going to give her the chance to show anyone how good she would be at anything. The woman made a funny strangled sound and scrambled away, into the deepest shadows of the tipi.

Kills In The Dark's voice lashed out from behind them. "Leave her be!"

Storm Trail spun around. *"Hei, haitsi,"* she said cautiously. "Hello, friend."

"What are you doing here?"

"I came to help her get your meal." She eased backward. He looked angry.

She bumped into the white-eyes. The captive screamed as soon as she touched her, and this time Storm Trail's heart leaped into her throat. Kills In The Dark was upon the *tejano* in a second, grabbing her ragged, dirty hair. The woman went limp, falling to the ground.

"These white-eyes are too stupid to make food," he snarled. "Go. Mind your own business. Leave us."

Storm Trail opened her mouth, then she shut it again. He was wrong.

She hated to admit it, even to herself, but he was definitely wrong. All white-eyes were not stupid. *Raven* certainly wasn't. He had finally given up his pretense of not speaking their tongue, and now he was virtually fluent. But Kills In The Dark's white-eyes woman hadn't understood even the few simple words she'd signed just now, despite the fact that she'd had plenty of time to learn.

Suddenly the woman began screeching. She startled Storm Trail again so badly that she jumped. Kills In The Dark backhanded the captive, and the woman fell onto his bedding.

He started to go after her and Storm Trail gasped. Kills In The Dark turned, raising a hand to her now.

He would hit *her?*

The warrior caught himself in time and went still, his face mottling. The moment gave his *tejano* captive enough time to do what it was she wanted to do. She dug beneath his robes for his old, worn parfleches, then she hurled them at his feet, jabbering.

Storm Trail stared at them. They were empty.

She backed away, confused. Was the *tejano* saying that there was nothing for her to cook? Storm Trail turned on her heel and ran out the door.

Halfway to her own lodge, she finally slowed down to look for Turtle, the girl Snow Dancing and his wife had adopted. She wanted to ask her what Kills In The Dark's woman had been trying to say. Then she sighed. Even though Turtle had come here with Kills In The Dark's woman, it was as though she didn't remember her anymore. Turtle had become Nerm now.

That left Raven. He was the only other white-eyes she knew well enough to ask about this.

She ran out to the herd and regretted it as soon as she found him. He straightened away from the colt he was working on and gave her that crooked, knowing grin— like maybe he was thinking about the time he had made her pee herself. That episode still stuck in her head like a droning horsefly. She could shake it away, but sooner or later it always came back.

"Hei," he said. He peered behind her. "No guns? No knives?"

Storm Trail sniffed. "We had a deal."

"So we did, but you never went out of your way to look for me before." In spite of himself, he was oddly pleased.

Storm Trail planted her hands on her hips. "I have a question."

"Shoot. Or maybe I should not say that to you."

She ignored that. "It is about Kills In The Dark's *tejano,"* she blurted. "I do not understand her."

"And I hope to God you never do."

"What?" She scowled.

"Never mind." Sooner or later, he thought, she would grow up, and she would figure out the woman's defeat and debasement for herself. Then he looked at her again and realized it was probably going to be sooner. Once she got an idea into her head, it was hard to shake it loose.

"What do you want to know?" he asked resignedly.

"Why does she not want to please Kills In The Dark so he takes that tether from her ankles? That way she could run with the wind."

"She does not want to run with the wind."

Storm Trail shook her head. "She only seems to try to make him madder. This very sun she threw all his empty parfleches at him."

Raven raised a brow. Good for her. "So?"

Storm Trail swallowed carefully. "They were empty."

"He does not hunt very well. That is what I have noticed."

Storm Trail felt her temper stir. She had not come here to ask him about Kills In The Dark. Raven might tell her about white-eyes, but what could he possibly know about one of the Penateka's finest warriors? Except . . . she had heard Wolf Dream and Lost Coyote talking about him one night, and Wolf

Dream had said he was a little disappointed in Kills In The Dark's skills.

"Maybe the problem is not with the woman, but with the warrior," Raven went on as though reading her mind.

This time her temper exploded. "I was stupid to ask you!"

"Then go away."

"I think some of your people are just crazier than others."

Raven shrugged. "That is true, as far as it goes. It is also true that Kills In The Dark finds fault with everything his white-eyes does because he finds so much fault within himself. He is not nearly as strong as he wants to be."

She hated it when he talked like this! "I hate you!"

"I know."

He was watching her with that arrogant way he had, with one brow up a little higher than the other. Why had she ever come out here? But now that she had, she could not leave without winning. It was a matter of principle.

"Kills In The Dark is plenty accomplished to get the ponies he needs to buy me."

"To *buy* you?"

"For his wife! And when he does, you will never be able to talk to me like this again! He will *kill* you if you do!"

Raven laughed. It took all her willpower not to kick him.

"It will be seasons yet before you are of marriageable age," he said. "Look at you. You are skinny, a little girl."

That did it. She hurled herself at him.

Raven stepped quickly aside. "It is a good thing, too," he went on, dodging around to the other side of the colt to avoid her punches. "It will take Kills In The Dark that long to accumulate everything he will need to get you. Unless, of course, Black Paint just gives you away because you are so disagreeable and hard to get along with."

Suddenly he sobered. Suddenly he looked sad.

"What?" she demanded suspiciously. "What is it?"

"You would be better off with my teasing, weasel. At least

what I do to you is never mean-spirited, it is just to teach you a lesson."

Her head hurt. He was so . . . so superior, and he was only a white-eyes—only a *slave!*

Storm Trail whipped around to leave him again, and once again she stopped dead. She tried to cry out, but she was so surprised that no voice would leave her throat.

"Now what is it?" Raven demanded. He looked, following her gaze. She sensed more than saw that he went very still also.

There were more white-eyes coming over the snow-dappled prairie toward them. These were not women and they were not babes, and they were not being brought in by a war band. They were *men,* and they rode foaming, tired ponies.

Now these crazy *tejanos* were coming right into Comancheria on their own.

Eleven

Storm Trail ran. She reached the first lodges on the outskirts of the camp and skidded to a stop, breathing hard, looking around for someone to tell what she had seen. Then she thought of Raven again.

Her eyes went wide as moons. She had promised not to try to harm him, she remembered. She had said she wouldn't kill him. But she had never said anything at all about . . . well, about giving him back to his own kind.

She whipped around to look at the herd again. He was already gone, like a ghost.

There was no time to look for him now. She ran on into the camp. By the time she reached her mother's lodge, the people already knew what was happening. The strangers approached from the east, and word of their progress filtered back from that side of camp. Bear Wound, the crier, had been summoned, and he walked along beside them with an odd expression, as though he had caught a whiff of a very bad smell.

Suddenly Storm Trail became aware of the suffocating silence that had fallen over the camp. Sometimes, when old ones or babes died, it was almost as quiet as this. The people would be subdued for a while out of respect for the bereaved family. But even then, she thought, there were occasional howls of mourning. There were rustles and thumps as the others went about their work. *This* quiet made her skin pull into gooseflesh.

She looked about slowly. There was no laughter, no angry shouts as the old men gambled and argued. The dogs did not bark and the children did not shriek. Everyone just . . . waited.

She was not going to miss this, she decided, and dashed to the arbor. She was going to see every one of their faces, smell all their white-eye smells and hear their talk. She would learn all there was to learn about them, and then she wouldn't have to ask Raven or anybody ever again!

Bear Wound held out his hands for the strangers' weapons. They stared back at him dumbly.

"Keep looking," Paya-yuca snapped, clearly irritated. "They must at least have knives."

Bear Wound moved reluctantly to touch the white-eyes. He pulled open their big coats and moved his hands inside. As he worked his way farther down the line of them, his face grew more and more distressed.

The *tejano* on the end was big and fearsome looking, though not as big as Paya-yuca or her father. He was tall rather than broad, and he had blue eyes, like Raven's, only paler. There was black hair on his face, right underneath his nose. That was *very* strange.

Paya-yuca went to stand close to the strangers. "What is this? You come unarmed?"

"Yes, they come in peace," said their Kickapoo guide.

"The Nermenuh have no peace with you." Paya-yuca looked at Crooked Nose and at Black Paint. "Did we ever smoke with these people?" he demanded, though he knew as well as anyone that they never had. "No," he said, looking back at them. "We have never smoked with you. But come, sit. We will eat. We will talk about maybe making a peace, if that is why you have ridden so far without even a gun to kill a bear."

That struck him as funny. Storm Trail watched him laugh, great vibrations of sound that made his belly shake. "Wife!" he broke off to bellow. "Bring our guests food!"

Mountain already had the pemmican ready. She lumbered

out of her lodge, carrying a hide full of the cakes. Paya-yuca waved at the white-eyes impatiently and they sat.

"They thank you for your hospitality," the Kickapoo said, "but they are not hungry."

Storm Trail scowled, then with a sick, plunging sensation she understood. They were turning down Mountain's food!

She looked appalled at the chief's *pasaibo.* Mountain's big ruddy face went even redder with shame and anger.

"Kill them!" she cried. "Do you hear what they say? Kill them!"

Paya-yuca waved a hand at her. "They are only ignorant and rude, not even worth killing, and they come in peace."

"I would have some of that pemmican," the Kickapoo said helpfully.

The white-eyes seemed to know that they had lost ground. One of them began to paw through a sack he had taken off his pony. "He brings you presents," the Kickapoo offered, chewing.

"Why?" Black Paint asked warily.

The white man pulled a flat, black, square thing from his big bulbous parfleche. He gave it to Paya-yuca, and Paya-yuca passed it immediately and dismissively on to Black Paint. The white-eyes visitors had insulted his wife. As far as he was concerned, they were no longer there.

But Black Paint turned the thing upside down. There were gasps from the women as it opened. Thousands upon thousands of little white sheets fluttered inside.

"What does it do?" Black Paint asked.

"It will give you guidance and faith," the Kickapoo translated. The white man dug in his sack again. This time he brought out *toopah,* coffee. Mountain sighed mightily. Storm Trail thought that maybe she was rethinking being angry with these people.

There was sugar, too, and some cries went up from the other women. Such luxuries could be had only by riding far north into Pawnee country to trade. They came from the *tosi-tivo,* those Americans up there. Sweet Water moved into the circle and immediately snatched up all that these men had brought. Storm Trail decided that she would be visiting Sweet Water's lodge as soon as possible.

The white-eyes began talking in short twangy words like Raven had used at first. Then their Kickapoo guide told what they said, repeating it in Comanche and sign language.

"Pres-ee-dent Hoo-ston wants your warriors to stop raiding the white men."

Paya-yuca gave a great, rolling grunt and forgot he was supposed to be angry. He acknowledged the man by staring at him.

"Stop raiding?" Black Paint repeated.

"Yes."

"Who is Hoo-ston?"

"He is their biggest chief, over all the white men who live in Tex-us. He wants you to be nice to his children. He would also like to ransom any captives you have. Hoo-ston will pay you well in coffee and sugar and cattle for each of them you give up."

His Horses' eyes narrowed suspiciously. "Are cat-tul valuable?"

"No," Lost Coyote said. "We killed and ate one once. It tasted terrible."

"The mothers of the *tejano* little ones grieve for their children," the Kickapoo went on. "The men want their wives back, no matter what you have done to them. So if you will agree to this, Hoo-ston will have treaty papers made and sent to you by another messenger."

Black Paint felt something tighten around his chest. He had not been truly alarmed by any of this until they mentioned captives. He looked around and realized with a great rush of breath that Raven was nowhere around.

"I do not want to be part of this talk," Black Paint decided abruptly.

His Horses looked at him and at Paya-yuca. He smiled slowly. It was not often that he got to speak for the council.

"Captives are valuable commodities," he began. "I am not saying that this band has any. Look around you. You will see that we do not. But if we did, we certainly would not trade them for mere *toopah*. I have heard that your girls become strong healthy women who bear strong healthy children. The boys learn to be warriors and they hunt for us.

"I have heard sometimes of other bands selling their captives. We have none, but camped just behind us here are the Quohadi. Maybe Iron Shirt would talk to you. But I have always heard that when he trades back his Mex-ee-cans, they give him gold coins, not *toopah*. Maybe if your Hoo-ston gave us gold coins, we could talk to some of the other bands for you, the ones that maybe have white-eyes.

"As for our warriors molesting your people," he went on, "we have no control over that. Those of us who are gathered here are but humble old men. It is our warriors who ride and fight, and we would not dare try to tell them not to."

"He's lying," snapped one of the white-eyes men, and Storm Trail frowned because this time the Kickapoo did not translate. Oh, she wished Raven were here to tell her what was happening!

"Actually I think he's being remarkably forthcoming," Thorn said, stroking his mustache. "These bucks raid for the glory of it, and he's as much as telling us so. They're going to sweep down upon the closest, easiest, most lucrative prey, and I'm afraid, gentlemen, that as long as we keep settling along the Brazos and near the scarp, we are that prey."

This the Kickapoo felt safe in translating. His Horses listened and nodded eagerly.

"Ponies and plunder and coups are the mark of a man," he explained urgently. "We are all old, and we made our prestige long ago. But young men must buy wives. They must earn the right to someday sit on this council as we do. *Suvate,* it is finished. That is all I can tell you."

"So what do we do now?" one of the men asked Thorn.

"Well, they're not going to give up their way of life for a cup of coffee," he countered. "Would you?"

"You can hardly compare us to these . . . these savages," the man sputtered.

Thorn raised a brow. "That pony herd we passed on the way in is essentially identical to any fortune that any of us have amassed for ourselves." He shrugged. "I really don't know what to tell you."

He dwelled for a moment on the strange circumstances that had brought him to this place, that led him to more or less understand the old chief's position. He had left the States to avoid being hung for killing a scoundrel. Unfortunately that scoundrel had been the governor. He had made a pass at Thorn's wife. Thorn understood that killing was often necessary and unavoidable, and if a man was prone to do it, the censure of some old geezer was not going to stop him.

He got up and left the council. Houston's other emissaries caught up with him as he reached his horse. "How did you end it?" he asked them.

"I promised we would send a subsequent messenger with a treaty talk," Reverend Croll said. "Houston will probably want to try again."

They began to ride away when shouting erupted behind them. Thorn looked back. The first chief to have spoken to them—the big man who had then withdrawn from the council—was bellowing at them.

"What does he say?" he asked their Kickapoo guide sharply.

"That if you want to bring a paper talk, you should put in it that your white-eyes will go back to the big water and stay there. The only way to stop the raiding is to keep your *tejanos* away from Comancheria. Otherwise they will be killed simply because they are there."

* * *

Raven watched the white men depart. He lay on his belly atop a grassy cliff that rose over the spreading camps, the warm metallic smell of blood in his nostrils. Beside him was the freshly killed carcass of an antelope.

Go to them. Catch them. Go home. But he had no home, still had nothing to go back to or for.

You don't belong here, not really. He stuck a blade of winter-dry grass between his teeth. The hell of it was, he had forgotten what it was to be white.

There may never be another chance.

For what?

The white men—God save Black Paint, he thought, but that looked like a Baptist minister among them—headed for their poor, worn-out horses. They mounted and rode out. The squaws and the children followed them, knotting together near the last lodges to stare after them.

Raven could see She Smiles down there, running to the edge of the camp to watch with the others. Eyes Down and Yellow Fawn and Storm Trail were with her. She Smiles ran like the doe he had just killed. Storm leaped about like a startled cricket and made him grin. Leave them? Where in Baptist Texas was he going to find a warm sweet girl like She Smiles to crawl into his bed at night? For that matter, what kid had ever amused him quite the way Storm Trail did?

He could barely remember English. Soon the big buffalo herds would gather again. He would hunt them this year. What would he do if he went back to Texas? Slaughter the rare cow that made it south from Saint Louis as promised?

Hoe corn?

Shoe horses?

Work sunup to sundown and pray each evening . . . wear scratchy shirts and God-awful buckskins . . . watch pious Baptist elders fight the need to smile. Worry about another 'Manche attack, and next time maybe he wouldn't be so lucky? Maybe next time they would kill him for being a man, or someone like Kills In The Dark would claim him.

Raven finally knew then that he'd never really had a decision to make at all. He had made it some time ago.

Black Paint bit into the first juicy fresh meat he'd had in nearly a moon, not particularly surprised that it was Raven who had provided it. Wolf Dream had come to share it, and of course Star Line came inside the lodge as well. Only Storm Trail was missing. She had weaseled an invitation to Mountain's lodge to share Sweet Water's *toopah*.

The door flap rattled and Raven came inside. He gave Loses Something the liver from his kill.

"I do not know what you do to make this so good," he admitted.

"Do?" Star Line glanced at Loses Something, confused. Black Paint laughed. Wolf Dream scowled deeper.

Loses Something sizzled the liver for him. Raven sat and ate, too hungry to wonder what that had been about.

"Raven," Black Paint said. "I would ask you about those white men who came this sun. Do you know what this is that they gave us?" He produced the book from beneath his robe.

"They gave you *that?*" Raven choked on his food. "Why?"

"In exchange for a cessation of our raiding. If we stop killing them, I think they will bring us more of these. Also *toopah*, coffee, and sugar. But I cannot imagine what to do with this."

Raven couldn't help himself. He laughed.

He hooted until his throat felt raw. His eyes burned. "They . . ." he began, then he had to pause to catch his breath. "They gave you their bible."

Wolf Dream scowled. "Bi-bul?"

"What is it good for?"

"If you ask Reverend Rust right about now, I guess he'd

tell you nothing at all." Raven almost laughed again, but he sensed that Wolf Dream was getting angry. "The white-eyes have written signs for their words," he explained. "That book is full of them. See those marks there? They are all words. And in this book they have given you, all the words are about their god."

"Why would they think such a gift so valuable to us that we would want to stop raiding to acquire it?"

"We have no use for white *puha,*" Wolf Dream snapped. "So far what I have seen of it is not very powerful."

Raven shook his head. "I can think of one other use for it. You can use them to cook and warm your lodges."

He reached a hand out for the bible. Black Paint hesitated, then gave it to him. Raven tore a page out neatly and laid it against the coals at the edges of the hearth. The paper flared and ignited. Wolf Dream made a quiet, strangled sound and reared back.

Somewhere deep inside himself, Raven felt something squirm. It was more than just kicking aside a religion he had never fully embraced. As the page went to ashes, he knew he was committing the ultimate act of turning his back on his past.

Suddenly he realized he had never felt so alone in his life.

It was a sensation like the air in the lodge being abruptly siphoned off so he could not breathe. If he did not believe in the white man's god, and if he could not worship the one they had here, then he had nothing. He did not even know if they *had* one here. The 'Manches were not a very ceremonial bunch—everything he had seen so far was for fun or celebration. They seemed only to pay homage to their spirit-protectors, and then only with a passing reference now and again. He knew that the bucks wore small medicine bundles tied inside their breechclouts, but he did not actually know their purpose. He had always meant to ask Storm Trail about them, but he had never gotten around to it.

He held another page out into the fire, watching pensively as it burned. Wolf Dream watched it as well.

Was it power in the *tejano* words that had made those pages flare so brightly? Wolf Dream wondered. What kind of *puha* could cause such a thing? Wolf Dream knew, suddenly and with a sick feeling, that the white-eyes had to be strong in some respect in order to make such a bi-bul that could make fire explode.

Twelve

Raven's mood plunged after the white men came. He was here now of his own free will. He could easily have escaped with those *tejanos,* and the 'Manches had to know it. But he was still here, and now he wanted something to show for it.

He wanted his full freedom. His patience had run out with being owned.

They had finally given him his lodge when the snows got bad. He had a small hearth for warmth, but he had no reason to cook there since he was still largely dependent on what meat Loses Something sent his way. It was rare that he was permitted to leave the camp to hunt, as he had done the day the white men had been here.

By the time the buffalo came back, his dissatisfaction was a constant tight feeling in his gut. When he woke to feel the earth rumbling beneath him, he had a strong idea that it was about to get worse.

He rushed outside, clutching his bow. Black Paint lumbered out of his lodge nearby. Raven watched him expectantly as bucks buzzed out from their tipis like bees from a hive.

"It will be dangerous," the chief said.

"Yes."

"You think you know, but you do not know." Black Paint cocked his head, listening to the tale the trembling earth told. "This herd is over a million strong, I would say. They have just gathered together after the cold. That means the bulls are randy. The cows have borne their young and will fight violently to protect them."

Raven nodded, his pulse slamming. *Get on with it and let's go.*

"Come with me to the pony herd." Black Paint moved sedately and ponderously. "I will give you a good pony." But to Raven's dismay, he chose a weary-looking black.

He bit back a curse of frustration. By the time they mounted and headed out, all the other bucks were gone from camp.

They were already out on the open plain. Nearly a thousand Penateka and Quohadi men were gathered and ready. Behind him, Raven could hear the clatter and commotion of the lodges coming down. He realized the bands would go their separate ways now. This was all they had been waiting for to break the winter camp.

From somewhere in the tense shifting mass of hunters, the leader screamed. The hunting ponies plunged forward. Once again the air was filled with the thunder of hoofbeats, with the roar of his own blood, and Raven grinned through his teeth. This time he had a quirt, and he lashed it mercilessly against the old pony's flanks as the mustang strained to catch up with the buffalo.

Raven remembered what he had learned. These spring cowhides were best for lodges; calves had the sweetest meat. He took one of each, then he aimed for the prize he coveted. He wanted a bull. Black Paint had given him another old jaded pony. He would have to bring down the best prize just to prove to them that he could surmount even that obstacle.

He found one—an immense animal with huge bloodshot eyes and a tangled matted coat. Raven felt his own muscles bunch and tighten and burn as he came up alongside him and raised his bow. *Angle down, toward the heart.* It would be deeper than ever because this animal was so large. It disappeared all the way into the beast. The vibration of its release went up Raven's arm. The bull roared around, staggering, shaking its great mangy head. Raven shot again.

The beast fell.

He let out a whoop of exhilaration. Three of them! He had killed *three* of them—and he had gotten a bull. He reined in and sat staring down at it, grinning foolishly, breathing hard.

Then reality sank in on him again. He had three kills, and he still was not allowed a knife of his own with which to butcher them.

It was full dark this time before the People finished with the hunt and set up a new camp. The squaws put their lodges where the buffalo had fallen, and cook fires burned all around.

Raven started to take one of his livers to Loses Something, then he froze. His glance fell by happenstance on Lost Coyote's hearth as he passed it. Lost Coyote eased his own liver into his mouth, closing his eyes in pure happiness as he savored it—raw.

Blood rushed into Raven's face. Now he understood the looks he had received when he had brought Loses Something the piece from that antelope. She had been treating him like a child with delicate sensibilities—and she had been doing it because he was a white-eyes, because he was different, *owned,* not truly one of them at all.

He backed away from Loses Something's fire quickly. He sat down and bit into his raw piece deliberately and defiantly.

"What is wrong with you?"

He twisted around to see Storm standing behind him, her chin thrust forward in that way it did when she was ready to pick a fight.

"Go away."

She rested on her haunches beside him. "You are grumpy."

"What are you doing here? Do you not have something better to do? Is Kills In The Dark not sharing his bounty with you?"

She shot to her feet again. Her face reddened.

"He did not get a kill, did he?" Raven realized.

"He did! It just . . . his arrow hit the cow at the same time Lost Coyote's did."

For a moment curiosity overcame his mood. "So what happens then?"

"If both arrows truly went in together, then the hunters share."

"Who is to say what happened?"

She scowled. "Our men are honorable. They would not lie."

Kills In The Dark would, he thought.

Black Paint waved him over to join his fire. Raven got up, looking back, unable to restrain himself from a parting shot.

"Is your Kills In The Dark sharing a chief's company this night?" He looked around and found the warrior's lodge, sitting back in the shadows by itself. "No. There he is, all alone."

"I *hate* you!"

"Then why did you come over to talk to me?"

Raven realized he was feeling marginally better. He even laughed at her mutinous expression, then he sat beside Black Paint.

They ate for a while, then his glance went absently back to Kills In The Dark. What in the hell did she see in him?

The warrior's white-eyes captive woman was crouched by his fire, hugging her arms about her knees in the gathering cold. She stared at the spare pieces of meat roasting over Kills In The Dark's flames. Suddenly Raven understood something else. Lost Coyote had shared that kill out of charity. He had done it without fanfare or accolades because he was a great hunter. He had so many kills that it was not worth a fight over whose arrow had gone in first.

A long string of drool hung from one corner of the captive woman's mouth. There was only enough meat cooking for one person, and Raven knew that that person would be Kills In The Dark.

He tore a piece off his own rib steak and tossed it her way. Kills In The Dark's reaction was fast and violent. He snatched the meat from the woman's hand as she tried to push it into her mouth. The captive woman groaned helplessly and fought for it. She was so near starvation, she no longer cared what he might do to her.

Something snapped inside Raven's head.

"Raven." It was Black Paint's voice, a warning as he came to his feet, but he was angry with him, too. He was angry at all of them.

"Leave her be!" he roared at Kills In The Dark. "Let her eat! I did not throw that scrap for you, or do you need a *tejano* to hunt for you because your own skills are so inferior?"

Kills In The Dark seemed to ignore him, but the more Raven spoke, the harder he hit the white-eyes woman. He hauled her up by her hair and struck her again.

Raven felt each blow in his own head. He reached out and snagged the man's arm before he could strike the *tejano* woman again. Kills In The Dark made a strangled sound of rage. The sound choked off as Raven wrapped an arm around his throat.

He pulled him backward, spilling him violently into the grass. The buck leaped to his feet again, wrenching his knife free of his breechclout. Raven circled him warily. He'd kill him with his bare hands in spite of the knife if he had to. He'd always made do with the little bit they gave him.

He bellowed and plunged his head into Kills In The Dark's gut. The warrior went down beneath him and managed a shot to his belly before Raven rolled off him, onto his feet again. He assumed a fighter's stance.

"Come on, *come on,*" he muttered. Like most of the other 'Manches, Kills In The Dark was short legged and heavy boned. Raven figured that even back at Miss Myra's, he'd been at least six feet tall. No doubt he was even taller than that now. He knew his muscles were honed and hard, and he figured that he was just thin enough to be wiry. It would be an even fight.

He lashed out again, catching the buck with a sharp jab to the jaw. Distantly he became aware of the others' hooting.

Again he thought how things really hadn't proved to be so different here at all.

His next blow caught Kills In The Dark on the other cheek, and he kicked out with his foot. He tripped him, and Kills In The Dark fell hard onto his buttocks. Raven snatched the knife from his hand before the 'Manche could even think of using it. He leveled the man again, dropping on top of him, and this time he pressed Kills In The Dark's own knife to his throat.

Then he froze, his blood going cold.

He looked into the other man's eyes and saw a hatred there that made Storm Trail's venom look like honey. This man *would* shoot him in the back without a qualm. This man would see him die for what he had just done.

He started to ease off him. He knew he should probably kill him, if only to protect himself. But he couldn't murder a man lying defenseless beneath him. He didn't have it in him.

He threw Kills In The Dark's knife away, aiming it carefully over the People's heads. Kills In The Dark rolled onto his knees, spitting blood. Then suddenly he roared again and lunged for Raven's back.

Wolf Dream caught him, wrapping both arms around his chest to hold him. "Stop! Your choice is between shame or death. I fear that white-eyes will kill you this time."

That was the final insult. "He is a *tejano* mongrel!" Kills In The Dark snarled. "He cannot fight!"

"Maybe," Wolf Dream said diplomatically. "But the repercussions of this are for the council to decide, not you."

Kills In The Dark struggled; Wolf Dream tightened his hold. Raven turned slowly to watch them.

"I will cut his tongue out!" Kills In The Dark howled.

"It is a matter for the council," Wolf Dream repeated. "He is Black Paint's property. You cannot deface a chief's property."

Kills In The Dark wrenched free, and this time Wolf Dream let him go. The other warrior stalked to his lodge.

Black Paint felt the cold grip of shock finally begin to lift from his chest. He thought of Raven's deadly quick reflexes—unschooled, untutored, just raw speed and strength.

In all his winters he had never seen a man move like that.

"That was foolish of him," Paya-yuca said a short time later in council. Everyone knew that he did not mean Kills In The Dark.

"Does anyone have a smoke?" asked Medicine Eagle. "I always think better when I smoke."

"You always fall asleep when you smoke," snapped Bear Wound. "One of these nights you will set your tipi afire."

"Yes, but I will have very wise dreams while it burns."

His Horses and Crooked Nose chuckled, but Black Paint stayed grimly quiet.

When the pipe had been passed around and the fragrant smoke eddied up from the bowl to fill the tipi, Paya-yuca finally spoke again. "He interfered between a man and his property. Even if he were an independent warrior, that would be grossly rude."

"He is no more than property himself."

"Kills In The Dark has every right to kill him."

Bear Wound snorted unkindly. "That White Raven is too fast for him. I am still not sure how he got that warrior's knife."

They all began talking. "I want to know what kind of slave has a name," His Horses interrupted. "What kind of captive has his own lodge? You have encouraged this behavior in him. You treat him as one of us."

Black Paint sighed. "White Raven has courage. He does not often consider failure, and when he does, he does not fear it. I have sought to develop that in him. Perhaps I have given him too much. It seemed appropriate."

"Kills In The Dark cannot kill White Raven," Crooked Nose pointed out. "It would be a horrible affront to his owner."

"I think Black Paint should kill his slave himself," snapped His Horses.

Black Paint's face did not change.

"You are soft on that *tejano*," His Horses accused again.

"Because he has earned my respect," Black Paint said sharply. "Kills In The Dark has not."

Voices raised again at that. Black Paint was tired, tense, and as usual this council was threatening to go about in circles.

"I have a solution to this problem," he said abruptly. "I will simply release Raven. If I disclaim this white-eyes and remove myself from the issue, then Kills In The Dark can feel free to kill him without affronting me."

Bear Wound harrumphed. "I still think that white boy would kill *him.*"

Medicine Eagle began to snore.

"The stronger most capable man will prevail," His Horses mused, somewhat mollified. Despite what he had seen, it was clear that he did not think it would be Raven. "I guess that is an acceptable solution."

One by one, all the old men nodded their approval. Only Medicine Eagle did not vote. He was fast asleep, the burned-out pipe cupped loosely in his hand.

Storm Trail scrunched down in the shadows beside Paya-yuca's lodge. When the men began coming outside again, she reared back to avoid being seen.

She had not been able to hear anything this time.

Black Paint began moving toward Raven's lodge. When he had reached a safe distance, she fell in behind him, walking along nonchalantly, swinging her arms at her sides. But her pulse was thrumming, and her head hurt with too many thoughts.

They would probably kill him for this. They would finally kill him.

She stumbled briefly when Kills In The Dark's voice rose in outrage behind her. She whipped around to look back, her heartbeat picking up even more. What could that mean?

They were *not* going to kill Raven! she realized. That was the only thing that would make Kills In The Dark so angry.

Then, from the other direction, she heard Raven's shout of jubilation. She realized that that could only mean her father was setting him free.

She stopped at her own tipi and sank slowly down to her haunches.

He was not going to die. They were not going to kill him.

She began shivering so hard in relief that her teeth knocked together. She could not believe he had come out of this one so perfectly. Did the coyote never fail?

Thirteen

Storm Trail passed through the lodges on her way to the river, her arms full of clothing. She was being punished again. Eyes Down had dared her to put pony manure in Medicine Eagle's favorite pipe. She had gotten caught of course, and now she had to do laundry, but she knew that that would not last very long, maybe five or seven suns. But Eyes Down had lost the dare, so she would have to get *Pia's* wood every dawn for a whole moon. And Medicine Eagle had looked so funny, she thought, running about and flapping his arms like a turkey!

She reached the last lodges and Kills In The Dark's tipi, and her smile vanished. Suddenly her good mood fell like a bird shot from the sky.

The people were closing ranks against him. They would not leave any place for his lodge near the prestigious center of camp. And Wolf Dream had ridden out yesterday, and for the first time in Storm Trail's memory, he had not taken Kills In The Dark with him. If he did not fight Raven soon, she thought helplessly, his reputation would never recover.

She reached the river and dropped the clothing. Yellow Fawn was already there, looking for her.

"What is it, friend?" Yellow Fawn asked cautiously. "You look angry."

Storm Trail blurted her biggest worry. "Black Paint will never sell me to such a man!"

Yellow Fawn looked bewildered. "What man?"

What other one could possibly matter? "Kills In The Dark!"

"Oh." Yellow Fawn's eyes widened. "Did he ask for you?"

"No!" Storm Trail cried, exasperated. "Not yet." Having to admit that only made her madder. She *almost* had breasts now.

"How could he?" she demanded. "He knows Black Paint will say no because of what happened with Raven."

Yellow Fawn looked doubtful. "Well, you have not bled yet. There is time for this to be straightened out."

"Their fight happened with that first spring hunt! Any sun now, we will move to a winter camp! How much more time does he need?"

Yellow Fawn frowned. She, too, had thought Kills In The Dark would have done something by now.

"Even if Black Paint was willing to give me to him," Storm Trail went on miserably, "how will Kills In The Dark ever get a hundred ponies if he does not raid with my brother? That is what my father wants for me, you know."

Yellow Fawn nodded sympathetically. That was a *lot* of horses.

"He could ride with someone else," she ventured. "There are other war bands." Of course Wolf Dream's was the best, and if Kills In The Dark went with anyone else, it was as good as admitting that Wolf Dream had cut him permanently.

"I must think of some way to fix this," Storm Trail muttered.

"Oh, friend, your plans always get you into trouble."

"Well, this one will work."

She hoped.

The Penateka were on the trail, heading south to a winter place, before Storm Trail thought of a way to fix things. They stopped at dusk to camp, and she watched Kills In The Dark carefully as she dismounted.

She would do it tomorrow, she decided, with the first light, then she shuddered. Even she could not believe she was really going to try to arrange for her own husband.

* * *

Raven came out of his lodge carefully when dawn came. He glanced left, looked right, wondering if this would finally be the sun when Kills In The Dark attacked him. Nothing happened. Even as he waited, he knew that Kills In The Dark was not trying to lull him into a false sense of complacency, as he had first thought. Kills In The Dark was afraid of him.

It made his chest fill with a hot swell of power. He passed the warrior's lodge on the way to the river to relieve himself and spared it a disdainful glance. Then he paused, scowling.

A small shivering form was pressed back into the shadows near the lodge door. Raven looked closer. *Storm Trail?*

She did not notice him. His first absurd thought was that the weasel was sneaking into the warrior's lodge the way She Smiles was always creeping into his. Something odd and angry kicked reflexively inside him. But that couldn't be what she was doing. She was a *kid.*

A moment later Kills In The Dark came out of his tipi. Storm Trail fell into step behind him. Instinctively Raven pressed back into the shadows on the side of the pathway to watch them without being seen.

She was a weasel, a brat, but . . . well, she was *his* brat. He did not trust Kills In The Dark not to hurt her.

"Hei, haitsi," he heard her call out softly to the warrior.

Kills In The Dark had reached the creek. He jerked about to find her. The look on his face made Storm Trail pull her robe closer.

Maybe this was not such a good idea after all. She had the absurd thought that he could hurt her, maybe even kill her, and no one would even know it had been him who had done it. But that was silly. Why would he do such a thing? She was about to offer him a way out of this horrible mess!

"I know a way to help you," she blurted—and, oh, that was not how she had meant to say it at all! But now that she was here, she forgot all the perfect words she had planned.

"You do?" Kills In The Dark gave a sound of bitter laughter. "Your entire family has destroyed me."

She was dumbfounded. "Raven is not my family!"

"Whether he is Black Paint's slave or a free man matters little. Black Paint should have killed him for what he did to me."

"My father fixed it so you could kill him yourself, but you do nothing!" Storm Trail cried indignantly. Then she gasped and backed up as his face mottled.

Oh, this wasn't going right at all! "Probably you are right," she tried again. "Black Paint should have killed him. But he did not, and now I have thought of another way for you to come out of this."

Kills In The Dark looked at her without answering. Something in his eyes seemed dead and flat to Raven, but then a light shone there in the early light of dawn, a cunning sort of brightness.

"If you are not going to fight Raven, then you should try to buy a good wife right away," Storm Trail rushed on. "You have some ponies. You should try to grab a wife of good blood right now."

"Before too much more time passes and I lose *all* my honor?" he supplied too smoothly, and she flinched.

"I did not say that." But she had meant it, and she flushed. "Listen to me! If your woman's family is good enough, everyone will eventually forget what has happened."

"And who should I buy?" he taunted. "I guess you have thought of that, too."

Raven saw the pleasure, the hope on her face and something hurt inside him. *Oh, weasel, no, do not do it.*

But of course she did. She was Storm Trail.

"Someone young. Someone whose father does not want to take a chance that no warrior will want her later, if she grows up disagreeable or . . . or ugly."

"Go on," Kills In The Dark said tightly.

"I would not be able to come live with you until I bled of course, but I think if—"

"You?" he demanded.

Storm Trail realized what she had said. She colored to the roots of her hair, then she recovered and pushed her chin up. "Yes."

"Do you not think you can get a better husband? Are you disagreeable?"

Storm Trail floundered for a moment. "I am just trying to help you! If you go to Black Paint right away, he would probably agree because he feels guilty about what happened to you."

Kills In The Dark said nothing. Hope moved in her heart. *He liked the idea.*

"If he does not agree, I will beg him," she promised. "When I do that, he almost always gives in. It is perfect!" she cried. "If you buy me, it will not matter that you did not fight Raven! You would be part of Black Paint's hearth!"

Kills In The Dark smiled.

It was the very briefest of reflexes, and she would have wondered if she had really seen it, except then he nodded. Her pulse fluttered so rapidly, Storm Trail thought she might faint.

"Yes?" she breathed.

"It is a good idea," he allowed.

"Yes!" She nodded hard.

"A wife," he mused. "I am getting tired of that captive woman anyway. She does not even fight me anymore."

Storm Trail wasn't sure what he meant by that, but she shrugged knowledgeably. "I do not need her. I know all about women's work. I will take good care of you myself."

He gave a dark chuckle. "So eager. Go on. Go back to your lodge. I will think about this."

Storm Trail took a little stumbling step backward, then she grinned at him and turned to run back to her mother's lodge. She meant to run, but her feet floated. She felt as light as the air.

Raven watched her go, then he looked back at Kills In The Dark. He saw the warrior's expression, and his own heart fell like a stone plunging into the river.

"What?" Eyes Down demanded. It was driving her crazy that Storm Trail was up to something, and none of them could figure out what it was.

In fact, Storm Trail could scarcely contain the news any longer. She motioned her friends closer.

"Something glorious is about to happen. Something I have wanted forever, and now I will have it. It has to do with Kills In The Dark."

Eyes Down snorted. "Then it is only another lie."

Storm Trail shrugged, unperturbed. "If you do not believe me, then do not listen. I will tell the others all about it."

Yellow Fawn and She Smiles pressed closer avidly, and after a moment, so did Eyes Down. Storm Trail grinned wider.

"He is going to ask for me."

"You always say that," Yellow Fawn sighed, disappointed.

"He is going to do it soon. Maybe this very sun. He told me so himself."

"Oh, friend," She Smiles blurted. "What are you going to do?"

"Do?" Storm Trail looked at her blankly.

She Smiles floundered. "Well . . . no one respects him now."

"She is right," Yellow Fawn fretted. "You could do better."

"There is no one better!" Storm Trail said hotly. How could they do this to her? "He just lost honor because of that stupid white-eyes *you* play with!" She looked accusingly at She Smiles. "He will get all his old pride back when he marries me. *You* should think about doing better!"

Storm Trail forgot she was being punished. She left her mother's laundry and scrambled up the bank, back toward the camp. Kills In The Dark was *wonderful*. He *was!*

* * *

Raven watched Kills In The Dark for some sign as to what he was up to, but even so, when it happened, it blindsided him.

He was in the herd working with Black Paint's ponies when the warrior came to collect the ones he needed. Raven stood watching him, his elbows braced on the spine of one of Black Paint's broodmares.

Kills In The Dark didn't see him. His face was twisted with the beginnings of anger as he drove the ponies back toward the camp.

Raven understood what was going on. But who was he going to buy?

When he'd watched that dawn by the river, he'd been convinced that the warrior had no intention of asking for Storm Trail. He'd wholly believed that her rapture was going to be short-lived. Had Kills In The Dark changed his mind? Had someone changed it for him?

Raven was unprepared for the regret that suctioned the air suddenly from his chest. That buck would beat the fire right out of her, he thought. He swore softly beneath his breath. Then a new thought occurred to him, and anger filled him. How could Black Paint do this to her?

He raked a hand through his long shaggy hair and began moving after Kills In The Dark, back toward the camp. When he reached his own tipi, he saw Storm Trail come out of her mother's lodge nearby. For once she was alone. Her friends seemed to stick to her like burrs, but this time she carried a parfleche and all her concentration was upon it.

Kills In The Dark's face was livid as he came along behind his ponies. The animals pranced and snorted and their hooves threw up dust. For once the man was the center of amazed, titillated attention, and it did not please him at all—until he saw Raven.

He grinned slowly. Storm Trail looked up just in time to catch the look, and she stopped dead in her tracks.

Something scrambled in her chest—something like a small, wild animal, then it settled. Kills In The Dark was gaining a place at Black Paint's hearth, something Raven would never truly have. Of course that was why he smiled at him like that.

Her blood began roaring until she could hear nothing else. He was doing it—Kills In The Dark was doing it! He was going to buy her!

She pressed her hands together, knotting her fingers, and held them to her chest. Even if people did talk about him now, and sometimes he frightened her when he got angry, he was still so very handsome. He trudged along behind his ponies on his short sturdy legs, his head held high, his black braids glistening in the sun. From the other side of the chief's circle, she saw her friends running to her, and she grinned. Then the little animal in her chest began scurrying about again.

Why was he bringing Black Paint the horses *now?*

She had not even bled yet. She had thought that Kills In The Dark and her father would just smoke over it now and wait until she got a little older before Black Paint actually gave her away.

"Where does he go?" demanded Eyes Down.

"What?"

"He has passed your lodge."

"My father is not there. He is at the council arbor with Paya-yuca." But then she saw Kills In The Dark go past there, too. "He is going to make a grand procession of it, all around the camp," she declared hoarsely.

Yellow Fawn gnawed on her lip. "Oh, friend, I count only twenty ponies. I thought your father wanted one hundred."

"Kills In The Dark does not have a hundred yet!" she snapped. "He has made a deal with Black Paint of course. He will just give my father the rest of the ponies later."

"Yes," She Smiles agreed quietly, but there was something strange in her voice. And then her friend began gasping with an odd high-pitched sound. Then Storm Trail heard Yellow Fawn gasp, too, and Eyes Down made a sound that was almost like a snicker.

This could not go wrong!

She wanted it too badly. She had never wanted anything so much in her life! Then she saw where Kills In The Dark had stopped. He was standing in front of His Horses' lodge.

Her heart felt like ice crystals, shattering, shimmering down to her toes in a million tiny pieces. She Smiles? He would buy *She Smiles?*

"No," she whispered.

His Horses came out of his lodge, nodding. Then he handed Kills In The Dark a pipe and the warrior smoked. It was done.

It was done.

"He took my idea!" she wailed. "He stole it and he . . . he twisted it!" How could he do that?

But then she knew. He had done it to hurt Raven, to steal She Smiles from Raven. She looked at the *tejano.* There was disbelief on his face, and his white skin seemed to get even paler, but then—incredibly—he looked her way and he smiled.

She could not get her breath. His slow, wicked, arrogant grin flashed wider. He had shamed her, and he had ruined her life just when she had been starting to like him just a tiny little bit. This was all his fault. *Everything* was always his fault.

She made a single stumbling move away from the camp. Then she raced for the river, unable to bear it.

Fourteen

By the time the snows came, no one talked of Kills In The Dark anymore. It was a harsh winter. Though the Penateka had wisely gone south, drawing their lodges in close to each other to ward off the worst of the shrieking winds, there was little they could do about the dearth of game.

Raven went out every dawn, and he usually came back empty-handed. He finally saw the Penateka use their buffalo tails to flavor their stews without meat. In his estimation it made for a pretty awful meal, but he supposed it was better than starvation.

On a morning when he finally managed to snare a jackrabbit, he took it directly to Black Paint's tipi. He held it up by the ears just as the family was rising. He got sighs of appreciation, then he dropped the carcass at the hearth.

Out of the corner of his eye, he looked for Storm Trail. She jumped to her feet and left her bedding. She took her robe with her and ducked out of the lodge without a word.

Black Paint settled himself at the fire as Loses Something built it up. Wolf Dream came in, and Raven hunkered down to begin skinning the jackrabbit. Finally the door flap snapped back again and Storm Trail returned.

Now the games would start, Raven thought narrowly.

He wanted to be angry with her and couldn't quite manage it. She brought a dull deep ache to the pit of his belly these suns, a phenomenon he did not care to examine too closely.

But he knew that he vastly preferred the time when she had so diligently tried to kill him to this silence and withdrawal.

She blamed him for what had happened with Kills In The Dark, he thought. And she wasn't entirely wrong. That warrior *had* taken She Smiles because of him. And Kills In The Dark would not have married at all, not this season, if it were not for their fight.

Raven sighed. "Storm."

She did not look at him.

"You can have this." He tossed the rabbit pelt toward her as she settled down on the opposite side of the fire.

Storm Trail lifted her left knee disdainfully so that it would not touch her. "I have no use for it."

"The white-eyes say that the feet bring luck."

"I am not a white-eyes, bless the spirits."

His temper twitched. He didn't want to look at her too closely because that would be like admitting that she was getting to him, but his gaze was drawn to her against his will. She watched the rabbit cooking and her tongue slipped out to lick her lips. Then—*there*—her eyes danced up, met his, narrowed and darted away.

That was the new game, what she'd been doing to him ever since Kills In The Dark had bought She Smiles.

Usually she did it when she thought he wasn't looking, but even when he wasn't, it seemed like he always felt it happen. This was her twelfth winter, he thought, irritated. It was time for her to grow up and stop carrying on like this, time for her to stop driving him crazy.

"We need more wood," she said suddenly. Once again she grabbed her robe and was gone, as though she could not bear to sit still and be subjected to his presence.

Raven remembered a white-eyes phrase. It was amazing, he thought, the ones that popped back to him when he felt particularly aggravated about something.

"Damn her."

Loses Something looked at him, startled. "What is that?"

"It means I am going to go settle this once and for all."

Raven went outside. He remembered the last time he had truly locked horns with the runt, when he had given her his gun and had told her to shoot him. This time, he thought, if he gave her the opportunity, she might really do it.

He caught up with her far upstream. The sun was strong now, glinting off the snow so brightly that he had to shield his eyes against it. Her black hair shined where it poked up from above her thick bulky robe. The camp was quiet. The People stayed inside as much as possible these moons, close to their hearths.

He watched her pile the branches in the crook of her left arm, snapping them off the trees with quick irate sounds. A more muted crackling sound came from the river as the sun warmed the ice there, and her footsteps crunched.

"Hei," he said. She jumped and spun about to face him.

"What do you want here?" she demanded.

He started pushing toward her through the drifts. Storm Trail backed up.

"Damn it!" he snapped again, and then in Comanche he grated, "Stay still!"

"What is day-um-it?" she demanded, still moving backward.

"It means that I want to talk to you and I will be day-umed if I am going to chase you to do it!"

"I do not want to talk to you!"

"Well, you are going to. We are going to settle this business about Kills In The Dark."

"Why?"

That brought him up short.

Why indeed? Why could he not just let it go? So what if she avoided him? So what if she hated him? She had always professed to.

But this time, if he did not fix this, he thought maybe she really would.

He finally reached her, half-winded. That was when he realized that she was shaking. Not from the cold. From fury.

"How do you *dare* talk to me about that?"

"You blame me."

Her eyes went wide. "Who else should I blame? You were the one grunting with She Smiles every night outside my lodge! *Ugh, ugh, ugh!*" she mimicked the sounds he had made; she hated to remember them! "You were the one Kills In The Dark tried to hurt! If not for you, he would have wed *me!*"

"No."

"Yes!"

"Well, he might have, but—" He broke off. "I am sorry that you got caught in the cross fire."

She was too quiet for too long. He looked at her more closely. She dropped her wood suddenly and raked her nails down his cheek.

Raven remembered another white-eyes variation on the word. *"God*damnit!"

She broke into a strange lunging run through the snow. He took off after her, shoving his way through the drifts. Finally he caught her . . . or trapped her. He got her with the water at her back and planted himself in front of her, dodging left, then right, when she tried to step around him.

"You say you are sorry," she gasped, "but that means nothing. Nothing! You cannot take it back."

"Do you think I *wanted* it to turn out this way?" he asked incredulously. "I lost She Smiles!"

"You did not care!"

He looked at her dumbly. "Of course I cared."

"You *smiled!* You thought it was funny that he tricked me, that I lost what I wanted most in the whole world!"

In truth, she thought, as that sun slipped further and further into the past, it was not Kills In The Dark's betrayal that she remembered most. Sometimes she actually forgot what he had done to her. But she never forgot Raven's arrogant, knowing grin that sun, or the way he had looked at her before she fled.

And in that moment Raven remembered it as well.

His breath left him in a harsh burst. It was not his nature

to explain himself to anyone, and he felt a thump of surprise as he heard himself doing it anyway.

"Pride," he said tersely. "I could not let him know that he had hurt me."

"But you looked at *me* when you did it!"

"You were there! You were a convenient place to put my eyes. It was not because I was glad he had tricked you."

Her heart thumped. "How do you know he tricked me?"

He crossed his arms over his chest. He could have told her that she had just said so, but that would have been no fun.

"I was at the river that dawn when you practically threw yourself at his feet and begged him to marry you."

Her skin paled. "I *never*—"

"Sure you did, weasel. I *heard* it. Why would he want to marry you, anyway, you skinny little—"

Suddenly he choked. Actually she wasn't so little anymore.

He realized that her head came all the way up to his chin these suns. She tossed her hair angrily, and that gesture had stopped being at all weasel-like. The realization hit him like a blast of cold wind. She was growing up fast. And he found that he could not bear the thought that he had hurt her, that he had given her her first broken heart, even inadvertently.

"Ah, shit." He was just full of white-eyes words this sun, he thought bitterly.

"What is that?" she asked suspiciously.

"It means that if it is my fault that he did not choose you, then maybe you ought to thank me."

She went very still. For a moment she could not get her air. *"Thank* you?"

Raven raked a hand through his shaggy hair. "He did not want you, Storm. He never wanted you. He just wanted prestige the easy way, without working for it or risking too much to get it. Otherwise he would have fought me in the first place."

Oh, it was true—she knew it was true, but to hear him say it was horrible!

"You ought to be glad that he did not use you to do it," Raven went on relentlessly. "Sometimes getting what you want is not so glorious if you do not understand what you are getting." What was the white-eyes expression? *Rose-colored glasses.* He decided not to try to explain the concept to her.

Instead of looking grateful, she recoiled as though he had slapped her. She was going to cry.

Storm Trail?

"Oh, God." Guilt pummeled him all over again, just when he had been about to get rid of it. "You are doing this on purpose!" he snapped. He tore his eyes away from her and heard a ragged, rough sniff. He refused to look at her again. He simply would not do it.

He did it.

She was hugging herself, looking as horrified as he felt. She looked past his head at the tops of the trees, her small chin somehow hard even as it trembled. Raven choked and reached out a hand to pat her shoulder clumsily. She wasn't crying on purpose.

"Nothing ever hurt so bad in my whole life." She sniffed. "I wanted him *all my life.*"

"I know." He needed a handkerchief. His mind reeled, back to another life, and he even groped for his pockets before he remembered that he did not have those any longer.

Storm Trail looked up just in time to see a look of befuddled amazement touch his face. It was so out of character that it broke through the last of her control. She sank where she stood, going down into the billowing snow. She gulped against the urge to laugh and dragged a hand under her nose.

"The worst part," she gasped, "the absolute worst part is that he used my idea!"

Raven thought his throat would explode. If he laughed now, she probably would finally kill him.

He hunkered down in front of her instead, watching her carefully. She wasn't laughing, not entirely. She was still crying, doing a little of both.

"Oh, hell," he said again. He dropped down beside her and put an arm around her. "It will be better this way. Really."

"No," she sniffed.

"I do not think your father would ever have given you to him anyway. You are special. Kills In The Dark is . . . lacking."

He thought he felt her stiffen, but then she gave a soggy sigh.

Silence fell. It seemed that the ice stopped cracking for a moment. A distant bird cawed, then flew off. In that silence he felt contentment. Raven scowled, pondering it.

For one bizarre unforeseeable moment, he realized that he had no pressing thoughts. He felt a slow pervasive peace from the anxiety and from the hunger. He thought, for just a minute, that maybe he could sit here with her forever and never care about what he might be missing.

It really was a beautiful morning.

"Do not touch me!" she shrieked suddenly. Raven's breath burst from him hard as her elbow dug in just beneath his ribs. He rolled sharp and fast to get away from her.

"What is wrong with you?" he demanded angrily.

He had never touched her before, she thought, except maybe in the very beginning, when he had slid up against her on her pony, or when he had tackled her that day with the gun. But that had been different, though she could not truly put her finger on why.

She scrambled to her feet and stood staring at him, her skin feeling strangely itchy where she had leaned against him. She turned and fled back to the camp without answering him. She couldn't answer him.

She truly did not know what was wrong with her.

"Look for a deep chest," Black Paint instructed. "When the chest is deep, the horse will have good endurance. And the legs should be straight or the pony will break down young."

Raven nodded.

"Warriors like to fight on stallions, because of their *puha* and power," Black Paint continued, "but geldings make the best hunting ponies. There is no stronger drive than sex. Once that is removed, you have a far more useful animal. It is like a young man who is made crazy by a woman. He can think of nothing but her, so his thoughts are not where they should be."

"Do you speak of me?" Raven asked warily. He got the distinct feeling that that was the case.

Black Paint answered vaguely. "I think you will accomplish much now that Kills In The Dark took that girl from you."

Raven flushed. "Is she all right?" he asked finally. "You would know. You would have heard."

The chief began walking into the herd. Raven followed him. "Perhaps not," he answered. "It is not my business. But if I had heard something, and I told you that she fared badly, what would you do about it?" He paused. "There are women," he said, "and then there are those who are *sem-ah taikay.* I would not recommend doing anything about this situation unless She Smiles is the latter."

"What is that?" Raven asked suspiciously. *"Sem-ah taikay?"*

"It means 'one to cry for.' " Black Paint looked out at his herd thoughtfully. A haunting smile slid across his face then was gone. "It is true that the Nermenuh are the best warriors on the plains, but we are not without our romantic side."

He had believed that once. "You give girls against their will!" Raven snapped.

"No."

"Are you saying that She Smiles was *glad* to leave me?"

"His Horses did not give that girl a chance to make her choice. He was greedy to get her wed before you could make a babe in her—you are not even a warrior yet. If that had happened, he would not have gotten anything for her."

Hatred swelled in Raven's throat for His Horses. "So she was given against her will," he insisted.

Black Paint began to look almost angry. "The Nermenuh do not always marry for love, White Raven. In fact, most often we do not. But sometimes . . . sometimes the spirits will smile upon a man. Sometimes he learns to love the woman he buys, or it is like lightning strikes him, and he is able to get that one who makes him hot. And that is *sem-ah taikay*.

"But most often a marriage is arranged for economical reasons," Black Paint went on, "and those unions work well enough, too. Either way, you must establish yourself first. That is the Nermenuh way."

Raven nodded. He could see the sense in that, at least.

"All right then," said Black Paint. He resumed his instruction. "You will not find your horse wandering across the plains, carrying a sign that he is yours. The best horses are almost always owned by someone else. If that man is Nermenuh, there is nothing you can do about it. *Tejano* ponies tend to be of poor quality. Nonetheless, that is where you should look first. Theirs are at least good for starting a herd.

"A man must have ponies to survive here," the chief went on, "or he is a eunuch, worse even than the slave you burned so fiercely to rise above. And the best way to get ponies is to steal them from the stupid and the innocent."

And stealing, Raven thought, meant killing.

Something recoiled hard inside him, shrinking back and away from the prospect of taking another man's life for the purpose of acquiring a handful of four-legged creatures. He did not think he could do it. He did not know how he could not.

The wind caught his long thick hair, lifting it about his shoulders. He pushed it back and closed his eyes briefly. He was reasonably sure that he could take a man's life in self-defense. But for *sport?* For monetary gain? How could he raid into Texas, slaying men whose only crime was an unreasonable faith in their god?

He looked at Black Paint and saw that the chief sensed his revulsion, his uncertainty.

"I was stupid and innocent myself once," Raven said hoarsely. "I raced westward onto unprotected land, just as those *tejanos* who are in Texas now. By the grace of someone's god, I was spared."

"No," Black Paint said. "I do not think it was anyone's god. I think it was your spirit-protectors. You have strong ones."

Raven thought of the white men's angels. "Do they sit on my shoulder?" he asked roughly.

"Yes, perhaps."

"They have never leaned forward to look into my eye and say hello." Raven found that he did not want to accept it. He had been on his own a long time, without a god or any higher wisdom for guidance. Something within him rebelled against trusting anyone—anything—more than himself.

But Black Paint's mouth curled into a slight smile. "You need to start thinking of your vision quest," he answered. "It is time for you to meet your spirit-protectors, to introduce yourself to them. Then you will be ready to raid, to collect ponies and coups, to be a man."

Raven swallowed against something hard and round that lodged in throat. "This season? Will I raid this season?"

"No."

He honestly didn't know if he was relieved or angry.

"That would be impossible," Black Paint explained. "It is spring now. Some war bands have already gone out. It will take time to prepare you."

Raven finally let his breath out carefully. "So be it."

If Black Paint thought such patience was odd coming from him, he said nothing.

Fifteen

Just before sunrise on the day they sent him out on his vision quest, it began to rain. The first drops were only a delicate patter against the taut lodge cover, but then they grew into a deluge, drumming down.

"What does it mean?" Bear Wound worried.

The weather changed. Raven bit his tongue against speaking such irreverence aloud. They had been solemnly schooling him for suns now.

"His protectors would make it difficult for him," Medicine Eagle observed.

I have been wet before.

"They would make him strive harder, work for it."

You've made me do chores more difficult than slogging through mud.

Black Paint pressed upon him the things he would be permitted to take with him. Raven took it all and stepped outside.

The others did not come with him. They don't want to get wet, he thought sourly. He swung his old robe over his shoulders and set off.

The rain sheeted down. He had barely left the camp before he saw the necessity of holding the robe over his head rather than wearing it—otherwise he could barely see. But it quickly became sodden, and the muscles in his arms began to ache from holding it.

He thought of stopping, of waiting for the weather to clear before going on, but he would be just as wet and miserable sitting still. He abandoned the robe instead and went on without it. He wanted to get this over with.

The water sluiced down his chest, over his skin, chilling him. His arms felt better, but by midday the soles of his feet began to sting abominably. Each pebble seemed to have grown to impossible proportions and jagged sharpness. They dug into his flesh with each step, seeming to twist and gouge right through his moccasins.

Raven finally stopped. With a heartfelt sigh, he eased down to sit and rest. He closed his eyes for a brief moment, then finally he looked around. His breath seemed to stall in his chest.

How many times, feeling angry and frustrated, had he thought he could simply leave the 'Manches and strike out on his own? Now for the first time, the enormity of such an action struck him. The country around him was huge, and suddenly he felt small, insignificant . . . alone. Without the camp surrounding him, without hundreds of people buffering him, the vastness of Comancheria engulfed him.

The wind soughed. He thought he could hear each blade of grass drip and wave, could hear his own breath. He took out the pipe Black Paint had given him and tamped some weed into it, shielding it from the rain with his hand. He was beginning to feel vaguely hungry but knew he had to ignore the sensation. He was not supposed to eat for four more suns. He smoked and rested as he had been told to do, then got up and went on.

When he stopped the next time, he found he was having a hard time harnessing his thoughts. They wandered bizarrely and stubbornly to the Methodist god of his childhood. He was supposed to be praying while he smoked, but to whom? The image he'd always held in his mind of that old savior was foggy now, and how could he pray to spirit-protectors when he had no idea how they might appear at all?

A feeling of hopelessness began to take him over. He had gone into this thinking that he would camp for a few suns and go back, telling them whatever it was they wanted to hear. But now he found he wanted to succeed, and he did not think he was going to. He was neither white nor red and had no gods at all.

He went on, and when the sun set again, he simply stopped where he was. Medicine Eagle had told him how to look for a suitable place to camp, but as near as he could tell, one was the same as any other. There was grass to the east. To the south the land undulated beneath more grass. There was grass to the west and grass to the north, and not a sign of water.

Without a robe to lie down upon, he simply sat and drew his knees up. He rested his arms, then his head upon them. He would remain here for the requisite four suns, he decided, then he would go back and tell them . . . something. And that was still another problem. He had no idea what a vision was supposed to look like.

He sat through that night and another until he was so hungry it was a gnawing pain, and his buttocks hurt from his contact with the damp hard ground. He smoked until his tobacco was gone. He did not bother to relight his fire once he had no more use for its embers. He wasn't that cold. Too many other sensations occupied him.

By the fourth night, without food or drink, his head began to throb with a dull resonating pain. His tongue felt thick, swollen, as though it filled his entire mouth. He could barely swallow and persisted in trying because he craved the little bit of moisture his own body provided.

When night came again, he lay down once more and closed his eyes. He did not expect to dream. He was never convinced that he did.

He had been expecting something to happen to him while he was awake, and he wasn't sure he was asleep. He'd expected some sort of twitching trance, but there was only a pervasive hurt in his muscles that wouldn't allow him to move easily. He lay still and watched as the prairie around him caught on fire.

It started with a single leap of orange-red flame not far from his eyes. Raven jerked in surprise and stared. The flame caught the grass, and there was a *whoofing* sound as it ignited. And suddenly it was hard to breathe, as though the fire was consuming all the air.

It leaped across the prairie. Raven slowly stood to watch it, and he did not hurt anymore. The light grew strange and hazy behind the orange-red glow. It no longer seemed to be either day or night.

The heat beat at him. It fluttered his breechclout, flattening it back against his hips and his thighs. Its torrid breath singed his eyelashes and his hair. The flames teased him, banking, easing back, rushing at him again . . . stopping always just short of his toes.

For some reason it could not seem to touch him.

The next time the fire retreated, he saw carcasses. Antelope and buffalo and birds lay in the fire's wake. And he could smell them now—the crusty, roasting odor of a hundred kinds of burnt meat. His eyes began to tear from the acrid smoke.

There was something terrible about it all even as it was a stunning spectacle. The urge to flee finally clamored inside him, but stronger still was the need to see what would happen next.

Suddenly a huge white bird swooped up from the flames and he flinched back, his heart jerking in surprise. Up, up . . . Raven's eyes followed it, and somehow he knew it was his namesake. It rose higher and higher until it hung against the sun and the moon and the stars.

Terror exploded inside him. The bird spread its wings, and they hid the heavens. It opened its beak in a silent scream. Raven saw its throat strain until his own hurt, but he heard only the crackling, snapping anger of the fire.

Silence did not fall suddenly; rather it spread inexorably until it seemed as though it had always been there. Snow began to drift down from the white bird's wings. And then there was sound again, a hissing agony like a million snakes dying as the flames were doused by the cold wetness.

The bird spoke over it in a voice like thunder, Comanche and English intertwined. Raven understood perfectly.

"There is a nest in the copse of trees. Find the egg inside. It is your medicine, your power."

The bird gave a gigantic echoing caw. It rose even higher, spun about like it was caught in a whirlwind, then it was gone.

Raven dropped to his knees in the brittle burnt grasses. He breathed in deeply of the lingering smoke, then he slept.

He woke feeling disoriented and shaken. The images of his dream were still vivid. He half expected to find the massive bird still hovering above him somewhere in the sky.

He sat up and his head spun. His gut twisted hollowly, and now he was cold. Even his bones felt the crunch of ice, though the air itself was only tepid.

He'd build a fire now, he decided. One way or another, four days had passed and his vigil was over.

He couldn't find his fire starter.

He had placed it and Black Paint's pipe beside his head. He got to his hands and knees painfully, feeling around in the grass, but it was nowhere to be found. He shot to his feet, swaying.

And then he saw the copse of trees.

But that couldn't be. He had stopped, he had slept, in a place where there was only grass everywhere he looked. *There had been no trees*. He had not even been able to find water.

He began staggering in the direction of the thicket. His skin crawled. It had been a dream. Just a dream. But how had he gotten here from the place where he had slept?

He jerked around, looking out at the prairie, half expecting to see it charred and burned. But it was normal, its green and golden grasses untouched and twitching gently as the Co-

manche wind blew. Raven looked back at the trees again, and
he remembered.

A nest. An egg.

He made a grunting sound of disbelief. He reached the
woods and found a thin stream slurping along just behind the
trees. He dropped down to his knees beside it and plunged his
hands into its icy water.

It was real.

He drank deeply and got hold of himself. He knew beyond
a doubt that this place had not been here when he had arrived.
He had not missed it, had not overlooked it. It had not been
here. His fire starter was gone, too, so . . . so he had sleepwalked, he decided.

It had been a powerful dream, and he had sleepwalked.

He stood again and looked around. He spied a nest on a
low branch. It was small, normal, just the size one might expect a raven or a robin to build. He moved closer to it.

He had dreamed about a nest because he had seen the trees
in his sleep, of course, and it had put the idea into his mind.
He reached inside . . . and his fingers closed around a hard
solitary oval.

He took it and shook it gently. It was petrified. He slid it
into the medicine pouch that Medicine Eagle had given him
to tie into his breechclout. He started back toward the east.
Once, as the sun began to climb into a new day, he glanced
back.

There were no longer any trees behind him.

Storm Trail was the first to see Raven when he returned.

She was in the herd, watching a new foal to make sure it
nursed. Then her eyes shifted, sliding out to the horizon with
almost a life and a will of their own.

She definitely did not want him to come back this sun, so
of course he would. And of course when she looked again,
her gaze sweeping over the dipping dancing grasses, there was

something out there. She stood quickly, squinting. It was just a smudge of darkness. It could have been anything—a rogue bull, a pony that had wandered off from the herd the last time they had moved. But Storm Trail knew it was none of those things. It was White Raven.

She started to run back to the camp, then she came up short, hitching her weight onto one hip, her fingers plucking for the narrow string around her waist where only yesterday her breechclout rope had been. She found the string and tugged on it. Though she wouldn't have admitted it to anyone for anything, she was very uncertain about this padding between her legs. When she had bled this morning for the first time, Loses Something and Star Line had showed her how to put it there, assuring her that it would not slip or fall when she ran. They had given her this dress, too, a plain but soft doeskin. She felt confined in it, awkward.

She minced her way back into the camp. She paused at the council arbor where her father and the elders were gathered. "Raven comes," she told them.

She went on to Loses Something's lodge. Her mother was working outside with Star Line, stuffing meat and nuts into round little patches of antelope paunch for the feasting tonight. They would be placed on the coals and the paunch would burn away, leaving only the delicious, crumbly meat mixture inside.

"Raven comes," she said again.

Star Line raised a brow and looked at Loses Something.

"He probably failed," Storm Trail said helpfully. "He probably waited the four suns and failed."

The women began to gather up their work. Storm felt something inside her lurch in alarm.

"Will we not feast tonight?" she demanded.

Star Line looked at her with half a smile. "Of course. We must." The People did not have any great ritual for celebrating a girl's puberty, but neither did they let it pass unnoticed.

"But Raven—" Storm Trail broke off. Her throat began to

tighten angrily. "It will be to celebrate his vision. If he had one."

"It will be for both of you," Loses Something said.

"I do not want to share!"

No matter that she was worried silly about this stupid pad between her legs. No matter that her new dress was uncomfortable. She had finally done it. She had bled! Any sun now she would wake up to find she had great big breasts. She already had little ones, but of course they would keep growing now. She had waited for this sun *forever,* but just like when he had ruined everything with Kills In The Dark, Raven would spoil this for her also.

She did not care about the pad anymore. She did not care if it fell out and just lay right there on the path behind her. She turned away from her mother and her aunt and she ran.

Raven reached the council arbor and stood in front of the men. They seemed to measure him with their eyes, and he knew suddenly that if he had come back here and lied as he had planned to, his time here would have been over.

But he did not have to lie. The egg was in the pouch tied inside his breechclout. He still did not know if he could kill a man without damned good cause, but at least he had a spirit-protector.

"Toquet," he said simply, looking at Black Paint. "Can I eat now?"

Black Paint smiled slowly. "Yes, there is food."

Raven devoutly hoped that this would be one of those occasions when they ate through the sunset and the moonrise and the dawn. They ducked inside Loses Something's tipi, and Star Line came in after them. She gave him some pemmican, and he pushed it greedily into his mouth. It hit his belly painfully.

He looked around. Where was the weasel?

Anger twitched inside him. She had probably been praying

ceaselessly to her nasty little gods that he would fail at this. So where had she gone now that he had succeeded? Then again, he thought, she had never been a graceful loser.

The old men sat around him. "What will your name be?" Medicine Eagle asked.

Raven blinked at the *puhaket,* the shaman. He had said nothing about his name changing.

"It will stay the same," Raven guessed.

The council erupted.

"He is lying!" His Horses charged bitterly, his voice rising clear above the commotion. "This has never happened before, not in my memory, and I have seen sixty-seven winters!"

Suddenly Raven had had enough of him. "I cannot help that. I am sorry that you are so old and of such limited experience."

Breaths were sucked in. Raven heard a choking sound from behind the ring of men. His eyes flashed up. Storm Trail had finally come in.

She was wearing a *dress*. He could not believe that she had dragged out all the stops to help him celebrate.

Storm Trail knew in that moment that he really had had a vision. It was the only thing that could possibly make him even more arrogant and insufferable than before.

"You insult me," His Horses blustered.

"And you insult me," Raven said evenly. "I dreamed of a large white bird. That tells me my name will remain the same." He was sure of it now that he had thought it through.

"Did you find something of significance?" Medicine Eagle asked.

"I did." Raven touched his medicine pouch and the egg inside there. He could not bring it out to show it to them—the shaman had warned him that that was taboo. He was not inclined to prove himself anyway.

Black Paint nodded. "Tell us more of your dream."

Raven did, leaving out the part where the bird had spoken

to him and told him what to find. He saw their faces crease in concern.

"I do not know what this means," admitted Medicine Eagle. "Wildfire? A conflagration? As though Comancheria would explode and all its wealth and beasts would burn?"

"A white bird doused the fire," Wolf Dream pointed out. He had come inside to stand near his sister.

"But it happened too late," mused Crooked Nose. "The animals were already gone."

"What happens now?" Raven asked, looking around at all of them.

Storm Trail made another sound, a convulsive choking gasp.

"What is wrong with you?" he demanded.

"You steal her thunder," Black Paint said mildly. "This was to be her night."

"Her night?" That probably explained the dress. "Why? What did you do, weasel?"

"The little one bled this sun," Star Line said softly.

"Bled? Oh. Oh!" Perhaps he had had a vision, and maybe his heart really *had* become more Nerm than white, but some old ways died hard, he realized. He could not imagine his mother talking so openly and matter-of-factly about such a thing.

Storm Trail was watching him angrily.

"Well, congratulations," he managed. "I guess."

She nodded. "I thank you."

"Gave you a shot of manners, did it?" He needed to get back on an even keel, he thought. He lifted one brow slowly and gave her a half smile.

It was that same arrogant quirking of his mouth, a little bit cautious, a little bit above them all, that always made her so mad. And Storm Trail wanted very much to stay angry. Instead she felt laughter bubble up in her throat.

She choked back on it but not quickly enough. Her father looked at her oddly, and her brother's eyes narrowed on her. She reached down for a clump of dirt and threw it at Raven halfheartedly. She turned on her heel, started to run, and thought again of the padding between her legs. She slowed to a decorous walk and tossed her hair haughtily.

He had bested her again, stealing from her one of the most important occasions in her life. Still it was hard not to admire a master stroke when she saw one.

The celebration that night reminded Raven of Christmas.

When the People started gathering in Loses Something's tipi, he saw that they brought presents. They laid them in a clear area near the hearth, and the bundles were wrapped in doeskin and fur, tied with leather strips and strands of braided ribbon. In Philadelphia, The Queen and The Banker would have been solemn and dour, one at each end of the table, but here there were bursts of laughter over the hum of conversation.

It didn't take him long to figure out why Storm Trail had been disgruntled. The festivities might have been shared between them, but as he listened to the mingled conversations he realized that his vision took precedence over anything a girl could do. Something squeezed at Raven's belly as he watched her.

He counted the presents surreptitiously, those still by the fire pit and the few already in Storm's lap. He came up two short for the number of people present. That meant that someone other than himself had not brought a gift, so maybe it was not mandatory. He let out a breath, but his relief was short-lived.

There was a pause in the eating and Black Paint brought out his pipe. He tamped smoke weed into the bowl, then he leaned back and looked at his daughter.

"I, too, would give you a gift to mark this occasion," he said finally.

"I do not see it."

There was laughter, and Raven understood. If there was another gift absent besides his own, then it was because her father's could not be brought to the fire—and she knew it.

"A foal was born to one of my mares last night," Black Paint went on. "You know this of course because you have worked with her. I think that since she was born on the sun you became a woman, she should be yours."

Storm flushed with pleasure, and everyone began speaking at once.

Raven's pulse picked up in panic. As a slave it wouldn't have occurred to him to give her anything. But her father had bought him and then freed him. For that matter, he wouldn't even be here if it weren't for her. It was a special, once-in-a-lifetime occasion for her, whether or not it paled in comparison to his dream about the white bird.

He stood abruptly and went outside. He went to his own lodge and gave a heartfelt groan as he looked around. As far as possessions went, he was destitute.

He upended his one small parfleche, the one She Smiles had given him, and glanced down at the pile of odds and ends that had spilled out. And then he saw the bracelet.

He had forgotten about the bracelet.

He picked it up and examined it in the bare light from his fire. He had never seen a squaw wear such a thing, but he thought it would do. He had made it purely out of boredom. During those long nights on the hard ground outside her lodge wall, he had done it virtually one-handed because he had still been tied to her. That made it sort of fitting, he decided.

He had pulled tiny pieces of their sinew rope away, and he had braided the tiny, broken pieces together into a strand of their own. Later one of the warriors' wives had discarded some copper as useless plunder. He had scavenged that, feeding it in, too. The grapevines had grown especially wild at one of their summer camps, so he had put in a few of those silvery leaves as well. The end result was a woven strand that gleamed and shimmered.

More than once he had considered giving it to She Smiles,

but he had been unsure of any hidden significance there might
be in giving such a gift to one's lover. For all he knew, it might
have meant that he was marrying her.

He bundled it into a rabbit skin, then he hurried back to the
other lodge. He slipped inside just as Storm finished oohing
and aahing over Lost Coyote's presentation.

"Here." He thrust the furry parcel at her.

Storm's face changed. It occurred to him that maybe he had
made a horrible mistake after all. Then he wondered if he had
just asked *her* to marry him. His heart stopped.

"You would give me something?" she asked uncertainly.
"Why?"

"I . . . it is . . ." His temper sharpened. Trust her not to
just take the thing graciously.

"Open it!" Yellow Fawn urged.

Storm Trail looked down at the bundle. She was horrified
and confused to see that her hands were shaking. She pulled
the fur apart.

A tie. A thong.

She gasped, dropping it, and her skin flamed. *How could
he?*

She looked up at him again. Every time she thought she
started to like him, he did something horrible!

"It is nothing," he said, embarrassed. Why were the others
so damned quiet? "I made it some time ago. I am sorry if it
is not appropriate. I had nothing else."

He had *made* it? she thought, amazed. *Raven* had? It was
pretty, she realized suddenly.

He reached out to snatch it back. She held it out of his
reach. "No! You gave it!"

She brought it back cautiously to inspect it more closely.
At first she had thought he was taunting her with it, reminding
her of one of her most ignominious punishments, but now she
recognized the copper and the grape leaves, all delicately
woven together. Her throat closed. Suddenly, for some reason,
she could not meet his eyes.

"Put it on your arm," he said, motioning to demonstrate. "It is a white-eyes custom." And that, he thought, should certainly have her hurling it into the fire.

But she only nodded and slipped it onto her wrist. She held her arm out toward the firelight in a gesture that was suddenly so feminine, it made his hunting shirt feel hot and tight and itchy against his skin.

In that one strange moment, with that singular gesture, she had paid him back tenfold for every single time he had teased her. She looked . . . just like a woman. A beautiful woman. A magnificent woman with hot and wary eyes, with spectacular cheekbones and slow sultry movements that could haunt a man's dreams. She looked like a woman who made another English word flare into his mind.

Jesus.

Sixteen

The women left to their own gossip, and the talk of the men began to murmur and wander. It was late, and Raven was bone tired.

That was the only reason that that image of Storm Trail had . . . well, caught him by the throat. These vision quests were debilitating things, he realized. His senses were raw, his body battered and worn, and he had simply thought he'd seen something that wasn't there at all.

He pictured her again and had to swallow carefully.

He forced his mind back to the talk. They were discussing the white men now, that good Reverend and his party who had visited. No matter that seasons had passed since those *tejanos* had come here; on occasions when everyone gathered, they were still the favorite topic of conversation.

"Why have there been no more of them?"

Raven shifted his weight stiffly. He had done nothing to earn the right to speak among these men, but he certainly knew a thing or two about white-eyes. *"Tejanos* change a lot," he volunteered. "They are never satisfied."

"Like you," Black Paint pointed out thoughtfully.

Raven bristled, then he realized that it was true. He did not think he had ever been satisfied or content in his life. He always wanted more.

"I think probably this Houston is no longer their president," he explained. "They have elected someone new by now."

Black Paint scowled deeply. "Hoo-ston is dead?"

"Gone."

"Was he an old man, or did he die fighting?"

Raven shrugged helplessly. "I do not know if he is alive or not. I have been here. How could I know? I just do not think he is president anymore."

"Did he do something shameful and lose his people's respect?"

Raven realized suddenly that the only ways a Nermenuh chief might be replaced were if he died or did something so heinous his people no longer wanted him. "These white-eyes chiefs are different than you are," he explained. "The *tejanos* change their leaders every few circles of seasons just so that no single one of them can gain too much power."

"Power is good. A chief's power brings strength and continuity to his people."

"The white-eyes do not want continuity. They want change," he insisted.

"Nothing must ever get accomplished that way," Lost Coyote mused. "One pres-ee-dent says go. The next pres-ee-dent says stay. Those white-eyes must bump into each other, not knowing where to go."

And that, Raven thought, was pretty much on target, too.

"I think we should go to Tex-us and find out if this Hoo-ston is still there," Wolf Dream said. "If there is a new chief, I would know who he is and what sort of man he might be. We should raid and capture another white-eyes who can tell us what has been happening with them this past winter."

Raven felt something quicken inside him. He knew, suddenly, that this was the moment he had both dreaded and burned for. Wolf Dream would ask him to ride on this mission.

He still had not decided how he would deal with the killing part. A pain came sharply to his gut.

"Can you still speak your old tongue?" Wolf Dream asked him.

Raven nodded. With conscious effort, he knew he could recall the words.

Wolf Dream took the pipe from Blue Roan. "Then will you ride with us, brother?"

Raven closed his eyes briefly, in prayer to a raven image he did not yet fully trust. Then he accepted the bowl and smoked.

They left the next sun, and as the war band rode east, Raven thought about his ride into Comancheria over two years ago. He did not remember there being this kind of laughter.

Of course that war band had been retreating after a strike. Storm had been with them, and she had been in considerable trouble with her brother. This time they were twelve men alone in a sweeping, open land with no possibility of pursuit. They were riding to kill or be killed, and surely they would steal and shatter lives, yet they joked and told stories on each other.

After a while Raven began to feel an odd disjointed sensation. *This* was what he had dreaded?

When the sky was like ink, Wolf Dream finally stopped and ordered them to make camp. The moon rose and Raven wondered if he would die when the fighting happened. Perhaps his faith in his new power was misguided and foolish, but he just didn't feel as though his life was about to close. Surely if his death were imminent, he would sense it somehow. The stars would seem brighter, the moon whiter. He thought everything would be clearer, sharper, more precious.

He finally slept, and when he stirred in the morning, the others were already moving about. Lost Coyote stood above him, staring down at him with half a smile.

"We were about to drop you in the river, to see if that would rouse you."

Raven sat, stretching. "No need."

"Hurry. Wolf Dream would leave now."

By the time Raven came back from the stream, the war band was riding out. There was no time to paint his face the way the others had done. They rode harder now, and at midday they reached the edge of the escarpment.

They came upon it suddenly, the land diving off abruptly. A distinct trail led downward, the earth beaten into red-brown dust. Raven wondered how many thousands upon thousands of 'Manche men had ridden this path since the Parkers and the Rusts had died.

They started onto it, and the Comanche wind chased them a while as though reluctant to let them go. It tunneled over the edge of the scarp, tugging at their breechclouts and their hair, trying to hold them. Halfway down, Wolf Dream reined in. Raven sawed on his reins as well, surprised.

A solitary wagon lurched along far below them, transversing the Texas lowlands on a trail every bit as well beaten as the one the war bands had laid down. A fort would have lent testimony to a handful of white men easing surreptitiously and carefully westward, he thought. A trail was somehow worse. It told of the passage of too many *tejanos* to count.

They started down again. The little party of white-eyes did not see the Indians until the war band had positioned themselves directly behind them. The warriors hit the scrub grass in the valley and moved up behind the lurching wagon like snakes sliding silently through it.

Something alive and excited began to thrum and surge just beneath Raven's skin. Then they drew close enough to the wagon to see the people inside.

Children.

His throat closed hard, and suddenly he grunted in pain. Lost Coyote looked at him.

"We will take them with us."

Of course they would not kill the children. Even had Lost Coyote not spoken, Raven had lived with these people long enough to know that they did not kill babes, not as a rule, not as a breed. They needed them. As among the white men, there were wild hairs, odd men out, cruel and insecure men like Kills In The Dark who would hurt anyone for the sheer pleasure of it, but no such man was among Wolf Dream's elite party.

There were two men and a woman with the little boy and girl, and Raven knew that the men would die. He understood by now that they were considered too dangerous to take back to Comancheria. The woman would probably be the one to give them the information Wolf Dream sought.

One of the kids saw them and cried out. In the next second Wolf Dream began whooping. His voice had not finished echoing before his warriors caught up with the wagon and struck.

The white woman took the seat as the men got in the back to fire at them. She began beating the team, punctuating each crack of her whip with shrieks of her own. A pin came loose from her hair and soft brown curls danced down her neck. The children tried to clamber up beside her and were thrown this way and that. The boy finally managed to hold on to her, his bleating cries stitching the other noise.

Raven felt the vibrating readiness beneath his skin finally erupt into something jagged and violent. Wolf Dream rode close to him.

"Get the woman," he shouted. "Hold her for us. We will take care of the rest."

So that was to be his role—as simple and as bloodless as that.

In the crunching moment Raven felt no relief. He wanted to feel it, *needed* to feel it, because everything he knew about himself hinged upon him being glad that he would not have to kill anyone. But even if he felt no true bloodlust, the war whoops still made his blood sing. Though he felt no urge to actually kill, the screams of the woman sharpened some predatory instinct inside him. He spilled off Black Paint's pony, onto the seat of the wagon beside her.

The woman went off the other side of the wagon with Raven on top of her. They landed in the dirt, and the battle spilled on down the trail without them. Raven pinned the woman, straddling her, using a length of twine tied to his breechclout to rope her hands. He sat up, looking after the skirmish, breathing hard.

He wanted to leave her, to rejoin the fight—and he was horrified at himself.

It was the instinct of man, he realized, the nature of the beast. All of them, white or red, were born truculent at heart. All men could be incited to murder. It was why supposedly civilized men joined armies, why educated men belligerently provoked war and were so quick to grab up arms. It was their nature to be aggressive, to kill, given any righteous excuse.

Wolf Dream and the other warriors finally galloped back toward him, and he stood slowly to meet them. They drove the white-eyes team of horses ahead of them, as well as the one Raven had been riding. The little girl clung behind Too Much, and a warrior named Snow Sign had the boy lashed in front of him. The boy struggled fiercely and bravely. Snow Sign laughed at him, pleased.

"Bring the woman," Wolf Dream said to Raven. "We will camp back by the scarp."

They stopped just before sundown in a glade near a low hill. Raven pulled on the rope that held the woman to his pony. She went wild. He caught her arms just below the shoulders and shook her a little. She gasped, staring at him.

"She just now sees that you are like her," Wolf Dream observed quietly.

Raven realized that it was true. He alone wore no war paint. The woman's eyes flew over him, and she reached a trembling hand out to his face.

"Sweet savior," she whispered.

Raven understood her well enough, but he couldn't find the English words to answer her, couldn't reach them in the back of his mind. She began to grope at him, jabbering like a magpie. Suddenly the word Raven wanted blasted into his head.

"Stop!"

She went still again. Her breathing was labored, raw.

"Ask her about Hoo-ston," Wolf Dream ordered.

Raven cleared his throat. He dredged for more words—and the ones that came to him were not the ones Wolf Dream wanted him to speak.

"You think—I am hope," he managed angrily. "You think—at least I am white. You think not kill you because I am. Because white." It was Lucas's language, a white man's words, but the truth of them enraged the Indian in his soul. The English words came clearer. "Fool!" he spat. "Your men kill, too! You think them heroes, yet you call us savages!"

"Us?" she breathed, blanching.

He was so furious his head throbbed with it. "I want something from you."

The *tejano* woman nodded frenziedly, desperately eager to please him no matter what he had just said. Raven felt nauseous.

He leaned close, putting his face to hers. "I want words."

"Words?" she repeated, confused.

"Talk." He motioned. "Slow."

He posed his questions carefully. Rusty memory continued to squeak and loosen in his head. He kept remembering the syntax and the language that had been his through most of his life. After a while, it amazed him that he had forgotten so much of it in the first place.

Darkness had fallen hard before he gathered from her everything that Wolf Dream wanted to know. He left her and went back to the war band's fire, rubbing his temples.

"Well?" Wolf Dream demanded.

"It is not good," he said quietly. "She says that Houston is gone. I was right. During his . . . term—"

"Ter-um?"

"The time he was chief. We took hundreds of women and children from his settlements. The *tejanos* got angry and . . . and they voted him down. They picked a new chief in their last election. His name is Lamar."

Wolf Dream stiffened. "Why did we not hear from this man?"

"Because, given time and good leadership, he thinks the Republic of Texas will reach all the way to the western sea, 'Manches or no 'Manches." Raven realized from their faces that they did not even know there was an ocean out there, at least to the west. It didn't matter.

"What is important is that this Lamar has declared war on all red men standing in his way. He proposes to solve the 'Manche problem by force."

Wolf Dream made a growling sound deep in his throat. It raised the hairs on Raven's nape.

"Wait," he said sharply, holding up a hand. "There is more. Lamar does not want peace, so he sends no men with bibles. He has mustered an additional one thousand men into something this woman calls the Rangers. Do you know what these are? I was not able to get a clear answer from her, and they were not here when I was."

"They are the white-eyes war bands," said Lost Coyote. "We outrun them easily. Their ponies break down after even one good hard sprint."

"A thousand?" Wolf Dream repeated, scowling. Raven looked at him and saw that his eyes had gone very dark. It was easily three times as many warriors as the Penateka had in all their war bands.

"She said that this thousand is in addition to whatever they already had," Raven pointed out. He could scarcely imagine that there were that many men moving west onto the Texas plains in the first place.

"Douse the fire," Wolf Dream ordered suddenly. Falls Into The Water immediately began to shovel handfuls of dirt upon it.

Lost Coyote didn't argue with Wolf Dream, but he looked up at the sky and made a salient point. "The weather changes, brother."

"We have been cold and wet before." Wolf Dream got up and went to the *tejano* woman. He stared down at her thoughtfully, but he spoke back to his men.

"We have always passed through here easily, but perhaps now is a time for caution. It is late so we will rest here for a while, but at first light we will take these white-eyes and go home. We will talk to the council, then we can make adjustments to our tactics and come back later for plunder and ponies."

He began to cut the white woman's clothing from her. She screamed, trying to scramble away. Raven went to help him.

The woman breathed hard, groaning, her eyes squeezed shut as she tried to cover herself by rolling half onto her stomach. Finally Wolf Dream began to cut away her ropes.

That startled Raven past caution and respect. "What are you doing that for?"

The warrior flashed him a glance and decided to answer. "These white-eyes squaws are benumbed when they are undressed. I do not think this one will try to escape if she is naked. If one of those Rain-jer parties should appear, then she can be dragged along more easily with us if she is not bound."

He finished with her ties and straightened again. Raven glanced at the woman and felt an uncertain feeling swell in the pit of his stomach.

He was not sure he agreed with Wolf Dream. As far as he was concerned, a human being was liable to do anything when faced with a fate that he or she could not bear. Of course such humiliation did seem to take the starch right out of white women. And he did not think this one would leave the children.

The wind began to blow up almost before Raven got back to the cold fire pit, pushing rain and hail ahead of it. He found his robe still tied to Black Paint's pony, and he folded it around himself. He lay down in the cold oozing mud and closed his eyes.

Raven would never have believed that he'd be able to sleep, but he knew he had because his next conscious feeling was one of tripping surprise. One of the men began shouting and he sat up, disoriented.

It was dawn. Chunks of hail still littered the ground in the frigid cold the northeaster had left behind. Wolf Dream was spitting out directives and epithets. Raven looked where the white-eyes woman had been lying.

She was gone.

Too Much moved quickly, belying his size. "I will track her," he said. "She cannot have gone far."

But, Raven thought, there were many places to hide this close to the escarpment. And suddenly his neck prickled, as though all those places had eyes.

"No, let her go," Wolf Dream snapped. "The news we received here was all bad. I think her preposterous escape is an ill omen. My *puha* is not working here."

Raven noticed that several of the warriors froze. Actual fear flicked across several faces. Something was happening here that he could scarcely believe.

Yesterday this war band had been murderous. Now they were quivering in their moccasins—*because a white-eyes woman had escaped their clutches?* It was a perfectly understandable development, yet they seemed to see it in terms of their magic.

The People's belief in their medicine was so damned powerful, he thought. He knew warriors would ride into a hail of enemy fire when they believed their *puha* was strong, and more often than not, they would come out unscathed. But now he saw that it worked both ways. If they thought that their medicine was gone, then they would retreat at all costs.

Raven turned about and reached for one of the children. The girl shrank from him, crabbing away in the dirt and the ice. He caught her and dragged her to his pony. She screamed.

His heart ricocheted in his chest. The sound was not one of terror, he realized, not this time. He whipped around. Rangers came across the creekbed from the concealment of the plum and haw bushes there.

He started to swing up behind the girl, then the *tejano* boy dashed by in front of him. Lost Coyote had not finished tying him before the Rangers appeared. Raven lunged for him instinctively. He caught him by one ankle and dropped him, scrambling up on top of him to hold him as Lost Coyote swept by on his pony. The warrior leaned down, and Raven passed the boy up to him.

Raven turned back to Black Paint's horse and the girl. He did not think that these Rangers would split hairs over the color of his skin. He did not think they should. A fight was a fight, and he was among the enemy.

He *was* the enemy.

He grabbed his pony's mane and finally pulled himself astride. He drove his heels into the animal's ribs and smacked its rump. Bullets spat through the air around him. He glanced ahead to gauge how far the others had gone without him.

He saw Snow Sign go down.

The war band was well ahead of the fallen man, most of them racing pell-mell up the escarpment to safety at the top. He would have to get Snow Sign himself, but he didn't know how he could possibly do it without dismounting.

Then he thought of what Lost Coyote had done to grab the boy. He galloped up close beside the fallen warrior, preparing to dive for him. He looked down at the bloody pulp of the warrior's chest and felt his gorge rise. Snow Sign was not alive. He could not save him. Still . . .

He lunged off the side of his pony. Too late he knew how foolish his attempt was. Lost Coyote had probably learned to ride at an age when Raven had been sitting in The Queen's buggy. *Too late.* He felt the rain-slick hair of his pony sliding under his thigh. *Too late.* His upper leg dragged across its back and he squeezed helplessly, his hands flailing. Then he was flung forward, pain and heat ripping through him as a bullet punched into his shoulder.

He felt a strong hand close around his ankle at the same time. He caught one of Snow Sign's braids and wrapped it around his fist.

Fire seared down his arm, into his chest. He dragged the warrior with him, groping back with his other hand until he found the girl's leg. She wailed, but she was tied and he was able to use her to pull himself up.

The hand that had held him belonged to Lost Coyote. That warrior galloped around to his other side and took the dead warrior from him. In spite of everything, to Raven's amazement, he seemed to be laughing.

"What?" Raven demanded, feeling dazed.

"Wolf Dream's sister was right. White-eyes truly cannot ride."

Seventeen

The warriors painted their faces black—two streaks downward across each cheek and vertical lines on their chins. The stuff was thick and noxious, and as it dried it pulled Raven's face into a painful rictus.

They shaved their ponies' tails. Out of the corner of his eye, Raven saw Wolf Dream take Snow Sign's body from Lost Coyote. Someone else came and took the girl from his own horse.

"When you go in, do not look at anyone," Lost Coyote instructed, somber now. "Go straight to your lodge and go inside. I will send someone to tend to your wound."

Raven rolled his shoulder. It was stiff, a knot of hard pain.

Once he was alone inside his tipi, that pain seemed to wake up and come alive. He lay down carefully beside his cold hearth and closed his eyes, breathing shallowly. Almost immediately his door flap clattered. He angled his gaze to see Medicine Eagle come inside.

"So," the *puhaket* said, kneeling beside him. "Your new power saves you already."

"Saves me?" Raven choked. "They *shot* me."

"In your shoulder. By contrast, Snow Sign is cold. Roll over."

Raven eased onto his belly. He thought he had known pain before, but it shrieked through him, blinding and white, when the healer began to dig for the bullet. He finally passed out.

When he woke again, it was to a dull throbbing kind of

hurt that pulsed into his body with each beat of his heart. The *puhaket* was still working on him.

"What happens now?" he asked hoarsely. "Will Wolf Dream's reputation suffer?"

"Some."

"And what of mine?" He wondered if he would be somehow tainted by association.

Ah, yes, Medicine Eagle thought, this white boy had the spirit of a Nerm warrior. "They say you were courageous," the healer allowed finally. "Even after Wolf Dream's medicine broke, you stayed to keep the boy."

Raven craned his neck around to look at the old man. "Lost Coyote took him from me."

"You kept the girl as well."

"She was already tied."

"You retrieved Snow Sign's body."

"I thought he might still live."

Medicine Eagle chuckled. "Do not argue with them, White Raven. A time will come when you will do much and no one will notice."

The stones of the bottom of the door hide rattled again. Loses Something came in. "My husband sent us to finish for you," she said to the *puhaket*. "They need you at the arbor."

Raven pushed up a little to look around. Storm Trail was with her mother.

She had watched him come into camp. From the moment the first wails of grief had gone up, she'd had to know if the dead warrior was him, but he had ridden in seventh. She had not seen that he was hurt right away. She'd thought he slouched because he was tired. He was only a *tejano,* after all.

But then he'd reached his lodge, and he'd slid bonelessly from his pony, and she had seen the blood, and her heart had nearly stopped. She did not want to be here, in his lodge. She didn't want to care if he was hurt or not.

Suddenly she grabbed a prickly pear pad from Loses Something and jammed it down hard on his wound. Raven came inches off the ground.

"Daughter!" Loses Something cried, shocked.

She leaped to her feet again. *"You* fix him," she muttered, turning for the door.

Star Line poked her nose inside just as she ducked to go through it. Storm Trail straightened fast, backing up.

"I need you," Star Line said to Loses Something. "Lost Coyote has taken a small nick in his thigh."

They could not leave her alone with him! "No, wait!" But Loses Something hurried out with her sister.

Storm Trail looked warily at Raven and got her breath.

"It is interesting that the first time you go out is the first time something bad happens to us at the hands of these white-eyes," she managed. "What kind of medicine did you get on that quest anyway? I would not be surprised if it killed us all!"

"Go listen to the talk, weasel," he managed. "That is not what they say about me."

She knelt again carefully and began binding his flesh together with thin strips of doeskin. She did it absently, but her hands were cruel.

He sat up suddenly and grabbed her arm. She squealed out of reflex. She had forgotten how fast he could be. His fingers curled around her wrist.

"Stop it," she hissed. "Let me go!"

"You still have not learned how to lose with good grace, have you?"

"I have lost nothing!"

"I am a warrior now, and that just about kills you."

"You get ahead of yourself, *tejano!* I see no war pony tethered outside, just my father's bony old gelding! I see no scalps hanging about this lodge!"

He flinched and hoped she didn't see it. "I will have them soon enough. I will gather them more quickly than any natural-born Nermenuh man." And he would, he thought—*now* he would. The bastards had shot him.

Her eyes glared at him. Suddenly he realized that they looked the way they had on that night before he'd left—hot, wary. The image of her holding her wrist out to the fire flashed at him again.

He dragged her closer if only to defy the strange, sudden fear that came to him.

"I wonder," he said quietly, "just why you cannot be glad of my success for the sake of your people. Why is it so personal for you?"

She twisted her arm in his grip, trying to get away. "It is not personal! Why should I care what you do?"

"You care."

He pulled on her wrist so that she was forced to lean into him. She could feel his breath on her face and her heart started thudding.

"No," she whispered, though she did not think she could have told anyone exactly what she was denying.

"It is personal because you do not truly hate me."

"I do!"

"It is personal because I make some kind of fire burn inside you." He was not at all sure he was right, but he had always enjoyed provoking her, and this was definitely getting a rise out of her.

"No!" she cried again, twisting against his hold frantically.

He laughed and the sound was like a growl. She was horrified to realize that it stroked her skin into gooseflesh.

This time when she jerked against his grip, he let her go. She fell backward, but she sprang up again in the same motion, all long fluid limbs, still skinny, too tall . . . but filling out nicely, he realized, and, oh, those eyes. Like black flames, and they threw sparks at him.

"You are crazy," she whispered, backing away from him.

"We are just alike, Storm," he went on. "I told you that

before. I think our spirits match." The more he talked about
it, the more he decided it was true.

"Crazy!" she repeated.

"When you brought me here, you tied my life to yours."
He paused, as though to consider it. "Now there's an interesting thought."

"Get out!"

He laughed. "This is my lodge." Oh, yes, she was definitely
provoked.

She realized it at the same time he said it, and she flushed
to the roots of her hair. She bolted for the door herself, stumbled blindly against the wall, reeled away from it, and was
gone.

Raven put a hand to his shoulder. She hadn't finished ban-
daging his wound.

He smiled slowly to himself, not particularly caring. *Well,
now, what have we here?*

After she left, Raven dozed out of sheer exhaustion. The
sound of drums woke him again. He sat up slowly, his head
feeling muddy and hazy.

Darkness had fallen, and the inside of his lodge was pitch.
The drums were a rhythmic, urgent *Thump-thump-thump* coming from the camp center. He had never heard them sound like
that, and he knew somehow that they were war drums. They
stirred something inside him, something hostile and hungry.

He rubbed the back of his stiff neck with his good arm and
got to his feet. There was just enough thin moonlight outside
to make the path snaking by at his feet glow white. He began
moving along it toward the arbor.

The council fire leaped there, sparks and smoke spiraling
up from it to disappear into the night. The chiefs gathered
around it. Raven hesitated as Too Much danced into the circle
they formed.

"Sun, Father, you saw me do it!" he sang. "Earth, Mother,

you heard me do it! Do not permit me to live another season if I speak a lie!"

Too Much left the circle and a warrior Raven did not know went in. Alarm began to fill his chest. Whatever was happening here was bigger than anything he had ever seen before.

Where had Storm gotten to?

He looked around and found her hunkered down behind the circle. Her knees were drawn up, her arms wrapped around them. She reached up absently and tucked a shiny hank of hair behind her ear. Then she felt his eyes on her, and she came half to her feet before she froze, holding herself in a crouch, one slender arm bracing her weight. A doe ready for flight.

"What?" she demanded. "What do you want now?"

"What happens here?" He motioned toward the dancing.

"They will avenge Snow Sign's death."

He moved closer to her so he could hear her over the warrior who was shouting and singing. She shot the rest of the way to her feet and took two quick, stumbling steps away from him.

"Stay away from me," she hissed. "Just stay . . . over there."

"Why?"

"Because you ask stupid questions, and I want you to leave me alone."

He wondered if she referred to his curiosity about the dancing or their discussion in his lodge earlier. He smiled slowly.

"When will they go?"

"Who? Oh." She flushed again. "As soon as this dancing is done. They tell of their best coups so that their spirit-protectors will remember them and know how fierce they are. Then they will go."

"No one has spoken to me about it."

Her mouth curled into the old nasty grin. "You cannot go. You have no coups."

"No coups?" He remembered what Medicine Eagle had said about taking credit when it was due. "I nabbed the boy when

he would have run back to those Rangers. I carried the girl home. I collected Snow Sign's body."

"Those are not coups," she said triumphantly. "You did not kill anyone. You did not touch an enemy who was alive."

"Those kids are alive!"

"They are not enemies. They are ours now."

She smiled too sweetly. He realized that he couldn't deal with her looking like that right now, on top of everything else.

"Stop it, damn it."

"What?"

"Grinning like that."

She turned on her heel and moved off obligingly, her arms swinging jauntily at her sides.

"Come back here!" he shouted.

She started running.

He took a step after her, then he hesitated. He wanted to drag her back with such heat and intensity that he decided it was better to let her go.

He had other matters to attend to anyway. Coups or not, he was going on this ride. He had a score to settle with these *tejanos*.

In spite of herself Storm Trail paused and looked back at him when he didn't chase her. She found him staring at the pony herd. Her heart thumped.

No, he would not do such a thing, not even Raven.

Would he? Would he sneak out after the war band?

He began walking, and she looked about wildly for someone to stop him. The warriors were just beginning to ride out. People were straggling back to their lodges. She did not want to go near him after what he had said to her in his lodge!

Let him go. But if she did, it was not just his death that would happen. She groaned in anger and frustration and ran after him as he started for the herd.

He was already astride when she got there. He had taken the gelding that Black Paint had given him for the last ride into Tex-us, but her father had not loaned it this time, and that alone would probably get him whipped. He was just so stupid sometimes!

"Raven!" she shouted. He did not even look around at her.

She gathered her breath again. "Raven, you stupid, scab-ridden, maggot-infested, foul-smelling *fool!*" she shrieked. "Stop right now!"

He began trotting.

She swore and ran again. She dodged and shoved her way through the horses, and when she got close enough she leaped and hurled herself at his pony. She landed belly down over the animal's rump.

Raven cursed as the surprised pony began bucking beneath her weight. She caught a handful of Raven's shaggy hair as she began to slide down the animal's other side.

"What the—" He broke off. Her weight alone was enough to topple him with her. She landed with a little grunt of pain, and he came down hard on top of her.

"What . . . crazy . . . thing . . . are you up to . . . now?" he gasped.

Her hip rolled into his groin and pain exploded in him, and her head shot up, smacking into his unbandaged shoulder. Agony burned through him, leaving him no strength. He groaned and slumped on her weakly.

Storm Trail couldn't speak. For one horrible fascinating moment, she could not even breathe.

Get off me, please, please get off me. She felt him hitch his weight, trying to. *No, don't!* She found herself grabbing him, holding on to him to make him stay, then she snatched her hands away as though he had burned her.

His left leg was tangled with her right one, but his chest was flush against hers. She could feel his heart beating, and she knew, she just knew that he could feel hers, too. He was warm and heavy, and something happened inside her. She had a sense of dark secrets beckoning. It made her shiver with a hot skittering excitement.

It left her terrified, and she was never scared.

It appalled her.

This was *Raven,* the stupid *tejano.*

She twisted away from him. She dragged for air until some finally filled her chest, then she wiped a shaky hand across her mouth.

He got to his feet unsteadily, then he gave that slow grin. "Felt it too, did you?"

"No!" But then she realized that the single word was an admission in itself because he hadn't said *what* he thought she was feeling. She colored fiercely.

"Sure you did."

"What . . . why are you looking at me like that?" she demanded breathlessly. He was definitely looking at her . . . differently.

Because you are magnificent in the moonlight, he thought. *Because you look beautiful with that fire in your eyes, and I do not know exactly when you got that way.*

"Because you have grass hanging from your left nostril."

She made a choking sound and swiped at it. "I should have let you die."

"Die?" He jerked with the single word. "Who would kill me this time?"

"All of them! My father, the council, the women, everybody!"

Raven blew his air out. "For going after the war band? You did it once, and you are still with us."

She shook her head hard. "That was not a vengeance ride."

"So?"

"So Medicine Eagle made *puha* for every man in this war band! He made powerful, antienemy *puha.* That is why he was called to the arbor when he was fixing your wound."

Raven's eyes narrowed. "Go on."

"He made none for you! It is taboo for anyone without such protection to join them. Do you not see? If you went, you would break it!"

"Break what?"

"Their power!"

There it was again, he thought—that fine mystical shield of magic.

"I saw it happen once," she went on, taking an unconscious, urgent step toward him. "I *saw* it. I was very small but I remember. A boy sneaked out after them—a chief's son. And the whole war band was killed. It was in a fight with the Pawnee. Star Line's husband died."

"What happened to the kid?"

"The People killed him."

Raven swallowed carefully. "They did this to a *chief's* son?"

She nodded fervently.

Raven felt something ghostly touch his spine. He knew how reverently the warriors believed in their medicine, and if they believed that some sacred taboo had been broken, they probably would all ride to their deaths.

He took a shaky step away from Black Paint's pony.

"What are you doing?" she demanded. "Where do you go now?"

"To punch something that won't kick me back."

She scowled. He was so *crazy.*

Understanding in no way lessened his need to ride, Raven thought. It only fed the fire. And there was absolutely nothing for him to do under the circumstances but wait for the war band to return, to wait for next time.

Eighteen

Raven eased his right calf against the pony's ribs, but it was Black Paint's gelding, trained to Black Paint's touch, and the animal would not turn.

Raven swore. He could not truly practice his riding without a pony of his own, and he could not get a pony of his own until he rode well enough to raid. He had convinced himself that that was why Wolf Dream had not included him on the vengeance ride. So he thumped his heels hard into the horse's ribs, making it burst forward into a run. They went at a gallop toward the buffalo robe he had laid on the distant prairie. He raced closer and closer to it, shifting his weight onto his thighs, easing forward.

He crooked an arm in readiness around the gelding's neck, and then he went down with his weight, easing lower and lower as he came upon the robe's bulky form. He had asked Loses Something to sew rocks into it so that it would more closely approximate a man's weight. He skimmed his hand along the ground, got the hide in a good grip, heaved it up—

—and crashed into the grass at a full gallop.

Raven came to a painful stop flat on his belly. He pushed up on his hands, looking at the robe disbelievingly.

He got up and went to it, lifting it. It was much heavier than it had been just a short time ago.

The brat—not a brat, a *vixen*—had switched it on him. Somehow, when he had not been looking, Storm Trail had crept over here in the grass and she had replaced his robe with this heavier one.

Once he would have laughed.

He bolted around angrily, looking for her, and saw her running back to the camp. His first instinct was to go after her, to shake her until she apologized, but of course she would never do that. She ran like a doe. Her short black hair danced, and the golden-green tips of the grass teased her hips. She leaped over something, then paused to look back at him.

"Go ahead," he said tightly under his breath. "Just . . . go."

As though she had heard him, she turned again and loped away.

He wanted to throttle her. And he was afraid of what might happen if he got his hands on her. She was like his *sister,* he thought. No matter that he had taunted her about not really hating him—the reality of what had happened in the pony herd was something else again.

The more he thought about it, the more it scared him.

Storm Trail was out of breath when she reached Mountain's lodge. "Where is Winter Song?" she demanded.

Loses Something was working with Paya-yuca's wives. She looked up at her daughter curiously. "What do you want with her?"

I want to know what is wrong with Raven. I want to know about touching. The truth was that she had hardly thought of anything else since the night she had stopped Raven from running after the war band. The whole thing had taken on the dark urgency of the deepest kind of secret.

"I want to visit," she said finally.

"She is out looking for roots and turnips," Mountain supplied, but Storm Trail had already wandered off again.

There was another way to find out what she wanted to know, she realized. It was so simple, so obvious, she couldn't think why it hadn't occurred to her before. She didn't need Winter Song's expertise. She would just touch somebody else.

She'd find someone more suitable. When the warriors came home, she would pick someone accomplished, someone with many coups and a *huge* herd of ponies. She'd just sneak right into his lodge. She couldn't imagine why she hadn't done that in the first place. Except, of course, that she had never wanted to until Raven had landed on top of her.

Three moons passed before the war band returned. When Falls Into The Water gave his first ear-numbing whoop and galloped triumphantly into the camp, Raven's blood rushed with his own private relief. The waiting was finally over. He was determined that the next time they went out, he would be among them.

Storm Trail stood on tiptoe outside her mother's lodge so she could see the camp center. The scalp pole was planted there, hair streaming from it. When the warriors began dancing and acting out their new coups, she would watch very carefully and pick the very best one for herself.

Something oily moved in her belly.

She clapped her hands to her flushed cheeks and bent to go back inside to dress. When Black Paint came in, he gave her a smile that reminded her a little bit of Raven—like maybe he was going to laugh about something behind his hand.

"What?" she asked warily.

"You are beautiful, daughter."

Storm Trail scowled. She certainly did not *feel* beautiful. She felt nervous. And that made absolutely no sense at all. She had *liked* the way it had felt when Raven had fallen on top of her. She could not imagine why she should feel all squirmy inside at the prospect of it happening again with someone better.

Well, for one thing, her breasts had not kept growing the way she'd been certain they would. What if she picked a war-

rior only to have him laugh at her? Her heart galloped horribly
at such a prospect.

No, no, of course that would not happen. Even if he was
horribly disappointed with her breasts, even if she was too tall,
she was still Black Paint's only daughter. She put her chin up.
All things considered, she was a very good catch.

Rich smells filled the air as the women poured honey and
tallow over antelope as it roasted. Tripe had been laid over the
hot coals to sizzle. Turtles and terrapins had been thrown live
into the big fire near the arbor. The chiefs broke open a few
of the shells and great wafts of pungent steam puffed out. They
ate the tender juicy morsels inside.

Raven sat behind the people gathering around the scalp pole.
Nearly every male in the village strode about like a hero, gnawing meat off bones, shouting in deep strong voices and laughing. Only the very young and the very old did not have new
coups to tell of after this trip—the very young, the very old,
and him.

But it was hard to hold on to his irritation because the mood
was, as always, infectious. He swallowed steaming hunks of
the antelope, so hot it hurt his throat. Finally squaws began
spilling into the circle to join the warriors. They formed a long
line, swaying with the drumbeats, lifting up on their toes, coming down on their heels. Raven figured it was probably all
right if he went in there as well. This was the social part of
the evening.

He glanced at the girls who were not yet in the circle. His
eyes slid over one who stood shyly beside her mother, but then
something about her drew his gaze back. In a way she reminded him of She Smiles. When he caught her eye she gave
a sweet delicate blush that was just discernible in the firelight.

Something inside Raven stirred, willing and randy. He realized with a start that it had been a very long time since he

had had a woman. He couldn't imagine why he had let it go on so long.

Storm Trail watched the dancing, gnawing her lip. Falls Into The Water was too young, she decided. He had only gathered his first coup on the ride that Raven had gone on. Scout was too skinny. He was not even a very good warrior—he just tracked well. Too Much was fat and soft. His body would not feel the way Raven's had.

Where *was* Raven?

She saw him dancing into the circle with the daughter of one of Wolf Dream's older warriors. Her stomach twisted strangely. She looked away again fast.

She had to find someone. She had to do it right away. Maybe Too Much was the right warrior after all.

Raven left the girl at the end of the line of women, then he went to join the men who danced across from them. He imitated their rhythm, and she smiled at him timidly.

The dancers moved closer together. He put his hands on her hips and thought he felt her shiver. Something hot flashed through him again, then his breath stalled.

What was the weasel doing?

In an instant he forgot the girl he danced with. He looked past her shoulder to where Storm Trail was leading Too Much into the circle. *Too Much?*

The big warrior's paint was smeared with perspiration. His immense naked belly jiggled over the string of his breechclout. Raven shook his head, his eyes darting to the scalp pole. Too Much had had a very successful ride, he realized. He'd brought home more scalps than anyone else. And Storm was sure enough the type to suck up where the bounty was.

He raked a hand through his hair and pushed her out of his mind. He let his hands slide up the girl's hips, to her waist, to skim over the sides of her breasts. He grinned to himself as she sucked in her breath in delicious surprise. Then the line of dancers veered, turning around the scalp pole again, and Storm came back into his line of vision.

Something else was at play here, he thought suddenly. She wasn't just dancing.

It was the *way* she danced. She was all loose-hipped and graceful. Where the hell had she learned to move like that? He had been with her the whole summer, and he hadn't ever noticed her tilt her head back like that when she laughed. And there was something in her eyes. They were too bright, too speculative . . .

Raven's heart slammed into his ribs. She was going to sneak into Too Much's lodge tonight, he realized.

He clenched his hands into fists, and the girl cried out and pulled away from him. He thought about the way Storm always walked, her arms swinging at her sides with jaunty purpose. He found himself thinking of her sly sideways grin when she thought she had won a point. And the way she tossed her hair. He shook his head and the images shattered, leaving only one—her strong slender body overcome beneath the mounds of Too Much's own.

Let it go.

She had grown up. So let her have her share of the fun.

She was leaving the circle with the big warrior.

Raven left the girl he was dancing with. "Storm!"

She did not answer.

He dragged the back of his hand over his mouth. She was heading back to her lodge . . . alone. Too Much had peeled off to go to his own tipi, and she was waving goodbye. Black Paint and Loses Something were right ahead of her. Raven breathed again, but then she paused and looked in the direction of Too Much's lodge with a strange thoughtful scowl.

She wouldn't just waltz over there beneath her parents' noses, he realized. It wasn't done that way. She would wait until they slept.

Raven sat down stiffly outside his lodge door to wait for her.

And then what? Stop her? How? And *why?*

The thought of turning her aside when she had set her mind on something made him laugh aloud. It was a strangled sound.

Nineteen

Storm Trail waited until her father began snoring, then tucked her robe securely around her and rolled outside.

And screamed.

Raven clapped his hand down hard over her mouth. "Hush! You will wake up the entire camp! Do you want everyone to know what you are doing?"

He held her so tightly she couldn't fight back.

"They probably already know, the way you were acting," he went on. He pitched his voice and imitated her laugh. " 'Ha, ha, ha!' Jesus!"

She didn't know what he was so upset about, but she knew he was because he was using *tejano* words again.

"Gftns—fff—mm!"

"What?" he demanded, lifting his hand a little bit.

"Get your hands off me!" she shrieked.

Someone shouted irritably from a nearby lodge that they should shut up. Raven smacked his palm back down over her mouth and held her tighter.

He was touching her again.

He had one arm wrapped around her right below her breasts, and that was agonizingly delicious because if he moved ever so slightly he would touch her there as Wolf Dream had done to Winter Song, and she didn't know why that occurred to her—she didn't want him to do that—but something started tingling in anticipation anyway. It was the strangest tightening ache.

She finally twisted her neck just enough to be able to sink her teeth into the web of skin between his finger and his thumb. She bit and Raven howled.

"What man would have you, you little beast?" he demanded, pushing her away, sucking on the wound.

"What are you doing out here?" she gasped.

"Waiting."

She inched away from him, then she stopped when she realized that she was heading away from her own tipi and toward his own.

"For what? If you are still expecting someone to creep into *your* bedding, then I think you should get some sleep. All the best squaws are already with the war band."

He shot a brow up in that arrogant way. "That does not say much for you."

"Too Much is waiting for me! I told him I would come."

He knew that of course. But for some reason he'd needed to hear her say it. He'd wanted to know for sure.

So now he could go into his lodge and sleep.

"Why?" he heard himself demand instead. "Why would you want to go and do that?"

He realized immediately that it was one of the most inane things that had ever come out of his mouth, but she had him flummoxed, he thought, all off balance. He had dreaded seeing her come out from beneath that dew cloth as much as he had wanted her to.

"It must be a long time since you have done it yourself if you do not know." She tossed her hair back with that sly slow smile.

His heart squeezed. Maybe this *wasn't* the first time she had done this. He had just assumed it was, because he had never noticed her slinking around like this before.

A cold bony hand closed around his throat.

He went on doggedly, "I want to know why *you* are doing it."

"Because."

"Because why?"

"Because it feels good!"

"How do you know?"

Because suddenly she remembered that night in the pony herd so clearly she could almost feel the weight of him all over again. "I know," she breathed, her throat closing. "It will be wonderful."

He didn't know whether to laugh or to cry. She was a virgin, and damned if she wasn't going to serve herself up to the highest bidder.

Raven choked. Would Too Much even know what he was getting? He was so slow, so complacent and quiet. He could never match her touch for touch!

"I bled four whole moons ago!" she wailed, startling him. "I have seen fourteen winters! And the closest I have come to playing with anybody in all that time was *you!*"

"Do not go," he said hoarsely.

"What?"

"If you are that eager, then you do not have to go any further." He heard his own voice and he was shocked, amazed, terrified. *What the hell was he doing?*

She went very still. Why didn't she say something?

"You are not going to find what you are looking for in Too Much's lodge," he went on roughly. "That . . . that hunger, that excitement—you want what happened between us that night in the pony herd. Well, it will not happen with him."

"It will," she breathed.

"No."

He took another step closer to her, and she jumped away like a rabbit. "You do not know that!"

"I do. I have done it and you have not. That . . . that feeling is different. If it was not, people would be rutting all over the place, all the time, like animals."

"They do!"

"Well, yes, but . . ." He raked a hand through his hair. Why did she have to be so stubborn? "They are looking for it, searching."

"Searching?"

"To feel the way we felt that night."

She started shaking. He could see it in the rising dawn, the way the little tremors went through her body, making her teeth snick together. She was trembling, and he was sounding like some cow-eyed, softhearted romantic and he knew he didn't have a romantic bone in his body.

What was happening here?

"I was with a whore in Saint Louis—"

"Who-are?"

"She *sold* it, Goddamnit!"

"Stop saying *tejano* words so I can understand you!"

"You could understand me if you would listen! This is important!"

Somehow they had both taken a step closer to each other. Their faces were inches apart now, and he could see that her eyes were snapping and her breasts were rising and falling with her harsh breaths. And Christ, he was getting hard just talking about this.

She was like his sister. But she wasn't, not really . . .

"I was with the whore, and then I was with She Smiles, and it wasn't like that with them," he said, strangled. "It was not . . . sudden, not . . . sharp." *Like a knife edge.* "It did not leap." *From you to me and back again.* "Do not go to him," he ground out. *I'll show you.*

"No," she whispered.

"Prove it was not a fluke," he challenged her, and knew, as always, she would rise to it. "Maybe it was just the War Dance that made us feel that way that night. Maybe it was all the shouting and . . . and the violence. The only way we will know is to touch again."

He took the plunge first. He caught her elbow and dragged her back to him. She was too startled to fight him, and she stumbled, tilting her head back at the last moment to look at him incredulously. He swore in English words again, then he kissed her hard.

Something liquid and hot shot through her, pooling between her legs.

Something amazing and explosive crashed through his blood, gathering violently, readily, at his groin.

At first she was astounded. Then she was horrified. Then she was scared.

Storm Trail planted her free hand against his chest, shoving at him as hard as she could while she struggled to hold her robe closed with the other. "What are you doing to me?"

He felt dazed. He could still feel her mouth on his. "Uh, that is a white-eyes custom."

"Well, I do not like it."

"You did not give it a chance!"

"You would bite me?"

"No!"

"Hurt me? You would have hurt me!"

"When have I ever done that?" he demanded, suddenly angry. "Just tell me one time when I ever hurt you! God knows I have had cause to, but I never did!"

She ran a trembling hand over her mouth. "Do it again," she whispered.

"No." He looked at her warily. If he tried, she would probably bite him again. He knew he was out of his mind, but he did it anyway.

The first time she had stood as rigid as stone. This time she relaxed for a treacherous moment, her mouth softening beneath his own. And it happened again.

Sudden need came back inside him, tightening and howling. He caught both her shoulders, dragging her closer.

A strange indefinable urge rushed through her like a great wind. It raged, becoming more and more painful as the pressure of his mouth increased on hers.

His teeth hurt her lips. She didn't care. Then he did something even crazier. His *tongue* slid along her teeth and she started to jerk away again, but she had been startled when he had first touched her mouth, too, and that had ended up being good, so she stayed where she was. She wanted more. She wanted it desperately . . . and he was giving it to her. *White Raven.*

"No. *Not you.* Not with you." She pulled away from him and staggered backward.

He couldn't think. His blood pounded. She whipped past him, running back toward her lodge. But then when she reached it, she went still. Instead of crawling back beneath the dew flap, she only stood there, hugging herself, her back to him.

Where would she go? Storm Trail wondered wildly. If she went back to her bedding, she knew somehow that she would lie there with this jagged unfulfilled need inside her. She could go to Too Much, but what if Raven was right? What if touching him was not the same?

Too Much would not know about that mouth thing, she reasoned. That was a *tejano* custom.

A reckless laugh worked up in her throat. Raven had something she wanted, and it was only two steps out of her grasp if she would only turn around and go back to him. She did not have it in her nature to leave this unexplored, not while he was standing right here, offering it to her.

Raven?

She made a little keening sound in her throat and looked back at him.

When she made up her mind, she came up against him with such force that they stumbled together to his lodge. Raven finally managed to bring his arms up and hold her, and it seemed like even through her bulky robe he could feel the heat coming off her. He pressed his mouth down on hers again, and this time there was no hesitation in her, but then she went very still. He realized that she was waiting to see what he would do next, so that she could do it as well.

He pushed his tongue past her teeth again. This time she

slid hers into his mouth. He bit her lower lip and she slid her tongue over his upper lip. He held her head still, his hands in her sleek short hair. She reached out a hand to touch the ends of his own where it curled against his chest, but still one hand struggled to keep her robe closed.

"Come on," he said hoarsely, "inside."

Rather than walk around him, she pushed into him again. He fumbled his way backward and together they spilled through his pegged-back door. He pulled at her robe as he kept kissing her, but she clutched it even tighter.

They went down hard on his bedding. He lowered himself on top of her, somehow managing to accomplish it all without breaking the contact of their mouths.

"Wait!" she gasped.

His blood was on fire. If she played games with him now, he thought he might kill her. "What?"

She started to get up, and he realized that he had forgotten about his door. "I will get it. Just stay put. Don't . . . move."

He got up and pulled the flap back into place, then he hurried back to her again, shrugging out of his hunting shirt. She had moved. She had scrambled up onto her knees to kneel, facing him. Her eyes were huge and she held her robe together more tightly than ever.

Finally he thought he understood. "Are you shy?"

Her eyes flashed. "No."

He eased down onto his own knees in front of her. "Scared?"

"No!" She hesitated and her eyes slid away. "What do we do next?"

Was he going to have to keep up a running commentary, discussing this every step of the way? Why was nothing ever simple with her?

"We were doing all right before you stopped me," he grumbled.

She shrugged. When she moved liked that, the front of her robe finally opened. *Now* he knew why she had been clutching it.

She was naked under there.

He had seen her that way a thousand times, and if he closed his eyes he could visualize her still . . . her flat brown nipples and her narrow chest, her long, skinny legs and tight little bottom. But she wasn't ten winters old anymore, and he realized that his hand trembled as he reached out to push the robe the last of the way off her shoulders.

Her nipples weren't flat anymore. They were tightened in anticipation, hard. Her breasts were soft and round and just big enough for his hand to cover. Her knees were pressed together as she kneeled, but there was soft black hair at the juncture of her thighs, and his head spun.

She kept looking doggedly away from him. "You, too!" she gasped.

"I . . . what?" he asked dazedly.

"Take your clothes off."

"Oh. Right." With She Smiles he had simply flipped his breechclout aside, but that seemed somehow wrong with her. He sat back to struggle out of his leggings and he untied the string of his breechclout. "There. Okay?"

She was watching him, her eyes hard on his face now. "Are you embarrassed?"

He thought about it. Impatient, yes. Embarrassed? "Not even a little."

"I . . . no, me neither." Her throat was suddenly dry hot sand. She couldn't swallow.

"Do you want to talk about this or do it?" *Do it, please say do it.*

She hesitated, then she gave her head a little shake. No, he thought. No *what?* What was she saying no to?

She put her palms flush against his chest. He was afraid to move.

She could feel his heart beating. It slammed there, and that ache started inside her again, full and throbbing, and she *wasn't* embarrassed. It felt as though all her blood was gathering at crucial places in her body, in the pit of her stomach, at the base of her throat, between her legs. She splayed her fingers and ran her hands down his ribs and felt rigid muscle.

Her eyes fell lower, to his hardness, and she followed with her hands. She breathed in fast because she hadn't expected him to feel so smooth and hot there. She closed her hand around him and jumped a little when he groaned more *tejano* words.

He moved fast then, surprising her with it the way he always did. But this time he only caught her around the waist, taking her down onto her back, covering her body with his. One of his big hands came up and covered her breast and she stiffened, waiting for some taunt from him. But he was not arrogant now, and he did not tease her. The ache inside her seemed to catch fire, flames licking at her from the inside out.

He covered her mouth again, moving his head this way and that so he could thrust his tongue deeper, and he was wild, she thought, wanting her, and that was the most magnificent, amazing thing of all. All the while his hand stroked her breast. He opened his fingers and then he squeezed ever so gently, and she thought it was like nothing she had ever felt before.

"Oh!" she gasped. "Yes!" His hand slid down to her hip. "No!"

He moaned. "No what?"

"Go back."

He did not do it quickly enough. She caught his hand and yanked it back to her breast. This time his thumb moved over her nipple and she cried out, because that felt even better.

She shifted her weight underneath him, greedy, trying to feel all of him at once. She wanted to match their naked bodies together, but he was so much bigger than she was, and in the end their legs twined together like they had when she had pulled him off the pony, and that was good, too. His hardness pressed into her belly. He had a mat of fine, scratchy hair on his chest, on his forearms—that was so different from the other warriors, too, but she liked it. It tickled her breasts even as his weight flattened them.

When his hand moved this time, she was too delirious to stop him. It slid up to her neck, pushing her hair out of the way, and he put his mouth to the skin under her ear. She started shaking again, more and more violently as his hand went back down to slide between her legs.

She was slick and hot and all her skin had taken on a rosy flush. No matter where he touched her, she writhed and wriggled to gain all the pleasure from it she could. She was as greedy and hungry as he had ever been, as avid to experience, as desperate to learn. She was not gentle and melting. She demanded and she took what she wanted, giving back with careless random innocence that left him dazed.

Some part of him realized that he was not in control of this. Part of him thought he should probably feel emasculated by the way she saw to her own needs. But his body thrived on her gifts, clenching and trembling under her urgent touch, and nothing had ever felt more right.

His fingers probed, easing inside her. Then he slid them out again and she gave a wordless sound of protest.

"Wait," he managed. "This will be better."

Her eyes opened, and they were smoky.

"There is more," he promised. "I will show you."

He positioned himself over her and knew a stabbing moment of regret that he would hurt her. Then she lifted her hips and caught him. Her tight heat wrapped around him.

Storm Trail felt a moment of searing fire, almost pain. Then a sensation of fullness swelled inside her. She wrapped her legs around him instinctively. He slid out of her. She caught her breath in anger. No! But he did not leave her, only stroked in and out, out and in, making it better, making it more.

Her hands flew over him, over the long tight muscles of his back, his buttocks, his thighs. He wanted to give her everything, every sensation he could think of. He needed to prove that he had been right, that what he could give her she'd find with no other man. They *did* belong together, as odd as it seemed. But she made it so difficult to remember all the things he wanted to do to her and show her. She melted over him, her breath hot and gasping at his throat.

He tried to slow it down, but she would not let him. He groaned and kept pumping into her sweet tight heat while her fingers raked at his skin and her teeth closed over a ridge of straining flesh near his neck. Beneath her hands his muscles flexed, gave, tightened.

Yes, she thought, this was everything. This was harder, faster, better. It was glorious, and she was terrified.

She felt the fire raining through her like a million igniting sparks, even as his muscles clenched beneath her touch. He made an inarticulate sound that melted into her name, and this time he did not call her a weasel.

Twenty

When it was over, she left him haughtily. She gathered up her robe again like a cat that had just lapped up a bowl of cream it fully considered its due. Raven felt amazed and dazed at what had just happened, euphoric and oddly frightened.

He did not see her again for days.

He finally went to Lost Coyote's lodge, because it had one of the best vantage points in the camp. He sat just outside the door in the weak autumn sun, keeping an eye out for her. Was she embarrassed, hiding from him? The warriors talked of the latest party to have gone down the scarp—there were few now, because there was snow in the lowlands—and she finally came out of Loses Something's lodge directly across from him.

If she even glanced their way, she did it so quickly Raven could not catch it. She began walking toward the pony herd, and she did it in the way that had started haunting his sleep. Her hips swayed beneath her dress and her arms swung. Her black hair slid and shifted above her shoulders. That was all it took to make need spear through him again, hot and immediate, making him hard.

What was she doing to him?

Suddenly he was nearly wild with panic. It had not been this way with She Smiles. It had never been this way with anyone. It was as though she had some sort of spell over him, some power . . . and she did, he thought helplessly. He realized that he could barely think for wanting to taste her, to touch her all over again.

He waited for the tension in his body to ease, then he stood up stiffly and headed back for his own lodge. He bent and scooped up his rifle from where he had left it in front of his lodge door. Black Paint had finally given it back to him for good. He was working on a plan to saw the barrel down so that it might be more manageable on horseback. He had left it notched open and now he slammed it shut again—and caught his finger in the barrel.

He yowled in pain and stuck his finger in his mouth.

Curse her.

Storm Trail watched him from the river, from behind the herd. She sat down and pulled her knees up to her chest, hugging her arms around them.

Her heart was still thrumming just from walking past him, just from trying to ignore him. He really had something on her now, she thought desperately. She had loved touching him—she had not stopped thinking about it since it had happened. Oh, if he knew that he would tease her mercilessly . . . and she thought that his grown-up way of teasing might be more than she could bear.

She wanted to do it with him again. And that was exactly why she knew she could not.

She did not dare want anything as much as she wanted him. It gave him some . . . some power over her.

As long as she stayed away from him, she thought, then what had happened between them would not change anything. But, oh, it was going to be a long winter before he rode out with a war band again and gave her some peace from this ache inside.

It was the coldest October anyone in Texas could remember. By Halloween there was a foot of snow on the eastern Texas frontier. Even as Jack Hays stood with his back to the blazing fire in the saloon, the gunmetal gray skies promised more.

Thorn leaned back in his chair and downed his whiskey in a neat shot. "The weather's slowed the 'Manches down early this year," he muttered.

"No, they won't be back down off the scarp now," Hays agreed. "Snow season truces are universal among the plains tribes. The Sioux and the Cheyenne, the Apache and the Pawnee, they all lay down their bows with the first good frost. They'll grab them up again with gusto come the thaw, but the deepest part of the winter is a time of peace and planning."

"You agree, Johnny?" Thorn asked.

"I defer to Mr. Hays," said the other man at the table. John Moore was a Ranger as well, though he was neither as shrewd nor as gutsy as Hays, at least not in Thorn's opinion. Still Moore was a decorated soldier from the East, and as far as President Lamar was concerned, that made all the difference in the world.

"Truth to tell," Moore went on, "I wouldn't know a 'Manche if one walked in here right now and tipped his hat to me."

"More likely he'd take your hat *and* your hair with it!" a drunken voice shouted from the bar.

Thorn straightened, planting his boots back on the floor. "So let's go up the scarp and get 'em."

Hays's eyes popped, then went narrow and thoughtful. "Are you serious?"

"Very. We're going to have to pursue them into their home camps sooner or later if we're going to stretch Lamar's Republic to the sea. Why not when they least expect it?"

"They've certainly been harassing us worse than ever lately," Hays grumbled.

"It was an atrociously bad summer," Moore agreed. "Do you suppose that killing that buck was the start of it?"

Hays thought of the poor naked Blanchard woman who had come crawling into their camp last spring. She had led them back to that war party camped near the slope, to the bucks who had taken her and had stripped her of her dignity. But the experience had bent her mind—she'd tried to tell them that the savage who'd done it to her had been white.

"They surely got fired up after that," Moore ventured.

"Colonel, our president seems to hold a great deal of respect for you," Hays said suddenly. "Do you suppose you could get an audience with him?"

"Almost certainly."

"Then why don't you meet with him. Convince him to take the war to the Comanche this winter."

Thorn nodded his support of the idea, eager to go back up there. Stories of a white buck interested him greatly.

The night was bitter cold, and an icy draft snaked inside even past the dew flap and the hide wall and the pegged-down door. The fire burned fiercely, trying to battle it, but it wasn't enough.

Loses Something and Storm Trail had both retired to their bedding despite the presence of the men, if only because it was warmer there. *Do not look at her,* Raven told himself. But he knew without looking that she had dozed off. She made a little sound in her sleep, and it scratched right through his skin to tweak at his nerves. He wanted to slide underneath that bulky robe with her, wanted to push his fingers into her warmth, and he knew just how she would awake, startled at first, then her eyes would spit fire. Sensation would catch up with her. She would get that smoky look again, and without preamble this time he would roll on top of her and drive into her hard and—

"What?" He jerked as Wolf Dream snapped his name a second time.

"I want no man with me who cannot concentrate."

"I concentrate."

"But on what?" Bear Wound speculated dryly.

After a moment they went on instructing him on the ways of the warpath. "And when do I get to utilize all this knowledge?" Raven asked finally.

Wolf Dream leaned back, relaxing infinitesimally. "It is not a time for riding. We cannot get through the snow right now."

Raven swore silently and got to his feet. He was young, he was strong, he was hungry, and it did not seem that he could have anything he hungered for. He cast a dark look at Storm Trail's sleeping form. She was burrowed so deeply under her robe that he could barely see her. He ducked outside and went back to his empty lodge alone.

But he couldn't sleep. He tried, rolling in his robe, but the ground felt unconscionably hard beneath him. What was wrong with her? She had *liked* it. He knew she had. So why wouldn't she come back to him?

When dawn touched the eastern side of his lodge, he was still half awake and he still had no answer. Then a smile spread across his face. He heard movement outside.

The sound was furtive. She'd display a bit of decorum this time then, he thought. Then his smile faded. *Decorum?* Storm Trail?

A moment later his skin prickled. There was more than one set of footsteps outside. It sounded as if every squaw in the camp had suddenly decided to get up and sneak about.

He eased to the door of his tipi and peered out. His heart whaled into his throat, choking him. *Ah, Jesus. Oh, Christ.*

English words tumbled through his head again, brought on this time by stark fierce panic. There were Rangers practically right outside his lodge door.

He moved back inside in a crablike crouch, then took his sawed-off rifle from the liner rim and went to the side of the tipi closest to Wolf Dream's. He pulled up his dew flap, then the outer wall, and looked out warily.

There was no sign of boots, no Ranger left or right. He lay down and rolled out, then he ran the few steps between their lodges.

Wolf Dream came awake with a grunt and half a smile before he opened his eyes fully and saw who had come. The look of shock on his face would have been comical under other circumstances.

"What are you doing here?" he asked harshly.

"Tejanos," Raven hissed. "In the camp."

From outside came the first cracking sounds of gunfire. Wolf Dream roared a sound that Raven thought he would hear in his nightmares for an eternity. Then the warrior charged out the tipi door like a wounded bear and Raven followed him.

The Rangers were back among the outermost ring of lodges. A few must have crept in to get the lay of the land, then gone back to form their ranks with the others. Falls Into The Water came out of his own tipi to gape at them, and in the next moment the young warrior staggered back, his chest exploding in a spray of crimson.

A squaw screamed, then another and another as lodge doors popped open and they came stumbling outside, holding their babes and clutching their children against their legs. Out of the corner of his eye, Raven saw Storm Trail and Loses Something and Star Line racing out of the camp, then Raven lost sight of them as fresh gunfire exploded from behind him.

He reeled about, bringing up his sawed-off rifle, jamming a load into it. The Rangers were coming back now, forming a line on foot. *They could not shoot their rifles from horseback.*

He remembered that even as Lost Coyote sank hard fingers into his upper arm, jerking him about. "Scatter!" he shouted. "Run! All in different directions. Then we will regroup and circle the camp. You will have your fight now, white warrior."

Lost Coyote began running out of the camp. The squaws continued to bolt for a ledge of high ground beyond the camp.

A bullet spat past him, spraying snow entirely too close for comfort. Every instinct Raven possessed screamed up in him to fire back. He forced himself to run instead, going opposite the way Lost Coyote had gone.

He reached the pony herd and caught a gelding. He swung

up on it with a single hard scissoring of his legs, then he gouged his heels into the animal and began galloping back toward the tipis. The warriors were already circling them and the white men were trapped inside. The *tejano* horses were still milling on the east side of the camp, behind the advancing line of Rangers. Raven's pulse stuttered with the magnitude of such a coup as claiming them.

The Rangers' long rifles would be deadly to anyone trying to press in on them. The warriors still raced around them, screaming, their lips pulled back from their teeth in feral snarls. The white-eyes began to get down to brace their rifles.

Raven's pulse boomed once, hard, and he screamed a war cry.

He gouged his heels into his horse again and galloped through the warriors' circle. He raced into the white men, howling. Suddenly the Rangers were no longer thinking of digging in with their long rifles to pick off the circling warriors. Shouting, confused, they tried to shoot after Raven, but their guns were inaccurate at close range, just as he had counted on.

He galloped through them to reach their mounts and drove the horses out beyond the warriors' ring. *His.* He heard voices shout in disbelief, and at least half of them were Nermenuh. Every last one of the ponies was *his.*

The Rangers were beginning to break rank. Some of them tried to flee, and a few miraculously got through. The women streamed back from the ridge and hurled mauls and fleshers and anything else within reach at those who remained.

The confusion allowed even more white men to get past the warriors, back to the open prairie. They ran on foot, just barely holding the warriors off by dropping down one after the other to fire their long guns.

One of the Rangers still in the camp got down on one knee, ignoring the buzzing horde of Indians, to level his gun on a single squaw standing alone in the middle of the lodges. Raven looked that way and his heart twisted in his chest and threatened to stop.

Storm Trail. He brought up his sawed-off rifle. He did not have to get down to brace this one, and it was still loaded with the bullet he had shoved in when the fight had started. He squeezed the trigger as he raced back into the camp, urging out a single perfect shot.

The Ranger jerked and fell. His hand spasmed on his own trigger, and his long rifle belched and went off.

Raven felt the pony beneath him stagger gracelessly. A dull wet redness began to spread at its glossy neck. He had killed another one.

He leaped from the animal at the last moment and saw Storm Trail ahead of him again, back at the lodges, oblivious to the white man who had nearly shot her. She bent over the crumpled body of a squaw, and a horrible relentless wail ripped from her throat again and again and again.

Raven ran to her, knowing somehow what he would find even before he got there. The dead woman was Loses Something.

Twenty-one

Raven had no chance to give vent to his own grief. Storm Trail managed to get to her knife and she began stabbing the blade into her arms and hands.

Bile collected in Raven's throat. It hadn't shocked him when he'd seen Snow Sign's kin grieve like this, but he couldn't bear it when she did it.

"Stop," he croaked, trying to catch her hands. *"No! Stop!"*

He finally had to hit her, flinching as he did, his blow catching her above her ear. She reeled backward, shaking her head like a little dog, but her wailing finally stopped, and in her shock the knife dropped from her hand.

Her eyes swam to him. She shrieked again, but this time it was a sound of venom, not pain, a sound of wrath, not grief. Her anguish ebbed for a moment and her fury focused on him.

She lunged for him. He held her, pinning her arms to her sides.

"If you are going to cut something, then do it in a way that can make a difference! Do not hurt yourself! Hurt the men who have done this to you!"

"You are not Nermenuh! You do not know—"

"Mourning is always a crutch for the weak," he went on, and if it was cold, if it was cruel, then she could hate him for it later. "The strong brush themselves off and get revenge."

He finally let her go. She wiped the back of her hand over her mouth and stared at him, then she looked around, jumping skittishly at the last sounds of gunfire.

"Where . . . where did they go?"

"There. Out there." Far in the distance the last of the Rangers hurried along on foot, still just barely holding off the warriors.

"We should have had guards out," he went on hoarsely. But who in the name of the spirit-protectors would ever have thought that white men would come *here,* in the dead of winter?

The grieving began in earnest all around them. Raven watched a woman fall to her knees beside the body of her child, and his belly turned sourly.

The Nermenuh stole children. Perhaps it was wrong, but they loved and raised them as their own. *What justification do you have for slaughtering them in cold blood?* he railed silently.

But even as he thought it, he knew. He had been one of them long enough to know their thinking. This child had been red and therefore less than human.

He knew, in that moment, that he would never consider himself a white man again.

"I must . . . I have to take care of her," Storm Trail whispered.

"Let me help."

Her eyes slid to him and she gave him an odd look, partly her old disgust, partly something so soft that it nearly buckled his knees.

"You cannot. Only a woman can tend to the body of another woman."

She moved away from him, stumbling once, catching her balance, going on. She went to her aunt, sitting on a pile of ransacked parfleches. Star Line was huddled, weeping.

Raven turned away, unable to watch any more.

Storm Trail could not do this alone, but Star Line made no response to her pleas.

"Help me!" She could not take care of her mother herself! She knew the rituals, all the tender ministrations that needed to be performed, but she did not know how to hurt like this, had never bled inside like this before.

Still Star Line did not answer her. Storm Trail stood again, swaying. *Make it small.* Yes, that was what she had to do. She swallowed hard, pushing down all the grief and horror until it felt like a cold, hard rock inside her.

She went back to Loses Something's body. She struggled with her mother's knees, pushing them up against her chest, then she bent her head down upon them.

"Can I help?"

Storm Trail looked up vacantly. This time it was Yellow Fawn who was offering.

"Thank you." She could barely get the words past the hurt in her throat. "Your kin?"

"They live."

"Ah. That is good."

They carried Loses Something to the river to bathe her, then they painted her face with vermilion. Yellow Fawn had brought red clay. They sealed Loses Something's eyes with it.

They dressed her in her finest clothing and wrapped her favorite robe around her body. Yellow Fawn went out onto the prairie to find Loses Something's mare from the ponies that had scattered in panic. Again horror and denial tried to scream up in Storm Trail.

Push them down. Make them small.

Raven stayed back, feeling helpless. He watched Storm Trail leave the camp. Star Line had roused herself somewhat, and she stumbled along with her.

They crested the ridge where the squaws had gone during the fight. Raven saw that Wolf Dream and Lost Coyote and Black Paint waited for them there. They put Loses Something in a crevice at the top of the slope wall. They sat her up, facing east, without pomp or circumstance, and piled rocks over her.

I do not belong here, Raven thought. He took a step backward. But Loses Something had been good to him. *She had cooked his liver.* He remembered his first glimpse, from the ground up, of her neat beaded moccasins. Pain slammed in on him.

Storm Trail slashed the pony's throat and it screamed. Black Paint's bullish body was hump-shouldered and shaking. The big chief wept unabashedly. Loses Something had been his *sem-ah taikay,* Raven realized wildly. May the spirits help him.

His gaze skipped to Storm Trail. The pony's gurgling scream finally undid her, and he saw her sway.

He moved fast, catching her as she fainted. He hefted her into his arms and turned blindly for the lodges again. She roused again almost immediately. When she began struggling against him, he put her down and she planted a hand against his chest.

"Kill them all!" she wept. "Do it not for the coups, not for the ponies, but because they are *animals.*"

She did not give him a chance to promise. She rushed into her lodge.

Raven made the vow in his heart.

The snow took on a blue tint in the gathering dusk. Ice sparkled at the narrow frozen creek and glittered like diamonds over the drifts.

Raven hesitated outside his lodge for a moment. He heard a babe cry, a single thin wail. On top of everything else, he thought, there was precious little food this snow season. The cold had come too quickly, and then the *tejanos* had struck and there had been no time to slaughter the last straggling herds of autumn buffalo.

Raven turned and went inside. A thin rapier of smoke eddied

up from his fire, disappearing into the smoke hole. He sat down and poked at the hearth, agitating the embers back into flame. He fed some new wood into the fire and pulled his robe more tightly around himself.

Then he heard quick footsteps outside, crunching in the snow.

Instinct stiffened inside him. He rolled fast and silently to his haunches, reaching for his sawed-off rifle. *Not again.* He had a bullet rammed down into it before his door frame rattled. Storm Trail rushed inside.

Her short hair was tousled from the wind. Her black eyes seemed too big. Disbelief made his air leave him. She had not come back to his lodge since the first time, and he had finally stopped expecting her.

Her own voice was a gasp. "You are still awake."

He nodded dumbly. What was she doing here? To assume the obvious would make him a fool. There was nothing obvious or uncomplicated about her. Even if she had slid in under his lodge wall in the usual way of squaws, he would not have assumed that she had come to burrow under his robe with him again.

Storm Trail wailed silently. What was she doing here? For so long now, for so many moons, she had held herself in control. She would not, could not, let wanting him get the best of her. But those Rain-jers had changed everything.

"Make . . ." she whispered, then she paused to clear her throat. "I want you to make me feel alive again."

Raven wondered if she could see his heart slamming up against his chest.

She wondered if he knew how hard this was for her.

"I worked so hard on that sun not to . . . to feel," she explained. "I pushed all that hurt, all that heartache down so deep inside me. Now it feels like there is nothing left in there at all. I think I buried all the good with the bad." She finally looked at him directly. "I need to feel warm again."

"I suppose I can accommodate you."

Her eyes widened. Something like temper shifted behind them.

He wanted to go to her. He wanted to gather her up and make love to her again with all the sweet fumbling simplicity of the last time, and nothing at all was simple anymore. He knew, somehow, that if he did that, he would be cheating her. The coldness inside her would not go away.

Loving was not all she needed. If it were, she could have gone to any man in camp, and, he thought, she probably would have.

She had come to him because she needed to feel temper as well as warmth. She needed all the rushing emotions of life, and for whatever reason, they were things he alone could make her feel.

"Do you want me or do you not?" he asked quietly. "Take your dress off."

This time her temper flared clearly in her eyes. "Is that how the other women do it when they crawl to you now? Now that you have forty-two ponies and a scalp?"

Raven shrugged. "They are friendly enough now that I have proved myself."

Her breath hitched. "You are glad for what happened to us that sun!"

That brought him angrily to his feet. "No," he said, his voice suddenly dangerous. "I would have gotten ponies anyway, as soon as spring came."

"And girls," she sneered.

"Many of them." *Not a one. Curse you, if you had only once looked at me in all these moons, you would have seen that!*

"They practically beg for your attention! It is disgusting!" *And I hate it that they should have what I am so afraid of!*

"You beg as well. You are here," he pointed out. *But not begging, never you.*

How could she have even considered for a moment that he was worth coming to? Storm Trail spun for the door again.

He was upon her before she could take a step, his hard hands catching her arms, holding her, his breath hot on her nape.

"Is the cold melting now?" he asked quietly.

Storm Trail jolted all the way down to her toes.

She made a sound that was almost a growl and turned on him. Before he could react her mouth was pressed to his ferociously. She stayed with him, her mouth clinging as he dragged her down onto his bedding.

He rolled her beneath him, struggling with her, needing to keep control this time. He captured her wrists in one hand and held them over her head. He moved his other to the hem of her doeskin, sliding it along the long cool length of her thigh.

She shuddered and made a move as though to twist away from him, but then she groaned and licked her lips, staring at him, breathing hard.

"Please," she whispered wretchedly.

"Are you begging?" He laughed hoarsely, but he did not make her answer. He leaned down to kiss her again. When she opened her mouth to him he pulled back.

"Touch me," she gasped. "Touch me again, Raven, please, like before."

He finally kissed her fully, plunging his tongue past her teeth, sweeping it around all the deep dark spaces of her mouth. She groaned and bucked, needing her hands free to touch him, but he would not let her go. He lowered himself so that his weight kept her pinned down, and sensation tingled and tightened at her nipples.

He kept a grip on her wrists but his other hand began moving. It slid over her skin until her muscles contracted, tensing deliciously. When he pushed impatiently at her dress, wadding it at her waist, when his palm slid beneath it again, over her tummy to her breasts, she arched her back, pressing herself into his hand.

"Get inside me!"

But he wouldn't, not yet. He pushed her dress up even further, above her breasts, baring them until the heat of his gaze and the chill in the lodge made them burn and tingle and tighten again. The place between her legs began to ache. Then finally he let her wrists go and he covered her breasts with both hands, kneading them until she cried out, a thin, greedy sound. Oh, yes, this was what she loved, what she had craved. He swallowed her voice from her mouth, kissing her again and again, then eased back to watch her face.

She felt as though her very soul was naked, and that was so much more vulnerable than her body.

"Please, get inside me," she said again. "Put yourself inside me like you did before."

He chuckled, a hoarse, rough sound that prickled her skin into gooseflesh. "Oh, no, Fire Eyes. You made *me* wait. You made me wait moons and moons to have this again. Now *you* will wait until you cannot stand it."

Her pulse pounded. Already she could not stand it.

He finally moved his hands from her breasts, only to do another *tejano* thing and put his mouth there. He took the pebble of her nipple between his lips and suckled it. He wanted all of her, wanted to taste her, wanted to leave no inch of her skin unexplored and unexposed. He wanted to torment her and set her on fire again so that the flames never went out. He wanted to make her burn for him so completely, so endlessly, that she would not be able to stay away from him again.

But his own body betrayed him. He was so hard it was agony, so desperate to sink into her again that it was unbearable. He finally straightened away from her, braced his weight on his hands, and drove himself into her hard.

Storm Trail yelped in surprise, then moaned in pleasure.

She tightened around him again like wax melting. And it was as it was before, tremendous sensation spiraling and curling, building and screaming through him toward release. He moved in and out of her, faster, harder, deeper until his blood exploded and he thought he could weep with it.

She hated him for making it so good even as everything shattered inside her, and she finally laughed again even as she cried.

Twenty-two

Wolf Dream's war band rode out with the first hint of a thaw. This time he left one of his best warriors, Too Much, behind. Never again would a Nermenuh man assume that his women, his children, were safe simply because they were home in their own country.

Raven went in Too Much's place.

Storm Trail stood beside her father's tipi, watching the warriors depart. *Kill them, Raven, kill them all.* He had given her warmth back again—now she wanted vengeance. She wanted blood for her mother's blood, white-eyes tears for her own grief.

Her eyes clung to him until he was gone. She felt filled with a strange hollow feeling. Finally she turned away and ducked back into her lodge.

She shivered because it was still cold, she thought, because winter still had teeth. It had nothing at all to do with knowing that she had been right. By the sheer gift he had given her in a time of treacherous need, his power over her had grown to an unbreakable web.

She was helpless.

The warriors did not come back before the spring moon waned, but more and more game returned and the prairie came alive. The squaws spread over it with their digging sticks, unearthing roots and wild vegetables. The men still in camp went out to follow the buffalo, the small trailing herds that moved about Comancheria, looking for others, trying to join together again into the immense herds of summer.

The People ate again, and they healed.

Storm Trail was working an antelope hide into doeskin, kneeling outside her father's lodge, when she heard her name spoken. She looked up to find Too Much standing beside her.

"Hei, haitsi," she answered absently, bending back to her work. But he didn't move on and finally she looked up again.

"There is some buffalo sign half a sun's ride from here," he said suddenly, urgently. "We are going out to hunt. I, ah, your brother asked me to watch over you, so would you come with me then? I will share my kills with you if you help me butcher."

Why was he so nervous? He was making her jittery. Then Storm Trail's heart skipped a beat. He was flirting with her. Suddenly she knew she could prove that she was just as happy without Raven as with him. She loved the things he did to her body, but he was gone now.

She could live without him just fine.

She would not miss him. She did not need him.

She would not.

"Yes!" she agreed a little breathlessly. And she hated herself for thinking that Raven would never have asked her to hunt. He would simply have gone, and if she had wanted to follow him, then she would have had to hurry to catch up.

"Thank you." Too Much's big moon face smiled back at her. She wondered if the whole huge bulk of him would actually swoon.

"For what?" she demanded, feeling very, very irritated with him all of a sudden. "You are sharing meat. Of course I will do it. I do you no favor."

She got up and went inside. He watched her in an agony of wanting. Her flashing smiles and swinging hair bedazzled him hopelessly. He did not know why she had changed her mind about coming to him that night of the Scalp Dance, and he had lived each sun in a maelstrom of hope and despair since then.

He finally turned away, his normally heavy footsteps light.

Yellow Fawn watched from behind the reeds at the river. She pressed her hands to her mouth as her timid heart broke.

Lamar's penchant for American military officers was truly regrettable, Thorn thought.

Because of his credentials, the president had enlisted Johnny Moore, rather than Jack Hays, to lead Rangers up the scarp when they had taken their plan to him to attack in winter. Johnny had barely gotten out of that Penateka camp alive. He had lost all his horses and his men had walked home, and Johnny wasn't too proud to admit that he didn't have the frontier experience to have attempted such a strike in the first place. He had been adamantly opposed to doing so, and had refused to come back up here onto the scarp a second time.

But he had managed to kill a few 'Manches, and Lamar was thrilled with that. Lamar was more convinced than ever that all that glittered was eastern brass, and now he had unearthed another United States soldier for this latest mission.

This time Thorn had managed to horn in on it.

Several of Moore's men had come back from that debacle insisting that the brave who had ridden suicide-fashion right into their ranks had had wild golden hair. Thorn did not doubt the stories of those survivors at all, and not only because poor Mrs. Blanchard had talked of the same man. Anyone familiar with the long Kentucky rifles would know that such a move was not suicide at all. *So who was this son of a bitch?*

If all reports were accurate, then he was too old to be a Parker. The Rusts had claimed that all the bodies of their kin were accounted for. Maybe the buck wasn't even from Texas at all—it could be that he had joined the savages from up north somewhere. But Thorn's instincts told him otherwise.

And he hoped to have more clues soon. Fifty Rangers, led

by Captain John Bird, had crested the Balcones at dawn. Bird
was not a particularly energetic man. He was much more concerned with details than with progress, with precision rather
than due haste, but Thorn figured even he could find some
'Manches with a little luck. The heathens crawled all over this
part of the plateau like maggots.

In fact, they'd barely finished lunch when an old Injun, one
of their Lipan Apache guides, came racing back from a rise
of land just to the northwest of them. "Cap'n!" he shouted.
"Got us some sign after all. Good sign!"

Bird bolted down the last of his food. "The hell you say!
'Manches?"

He nodded hard. "Hunting, maybe. Big dust far west, near
Little River."

"Pack up, gentlemen," Bird announced. "I do believe we
have a fight to go to."

The wind was glorious, cold enough to be bracing, wild
enough to be exhilarating. As she rode, Storm Trail threw her
head back just to laugh. It was so good to be away from the
camp, away from all her pressing chores. Since her mother
had died, and Star Line was so vacant, nearly all the work of
keeping her father's lodge had fallen to her.

She looked over at Too Much. "I will race you!"

He scowled doubtfully. "You are a girl."

She could not imagine what that had to do with anything.
"I will beat you anyway."

"But I do not wish to tire my pony before we get to the
buffalo," he said seriously.

It made sense, she supposed, but she was disappointed. She
set her heels to her pony and began galloping by herself.

They found the buffalo moving through a snug valley a short
time later. Her pony tried to get away from her as Too Much
gave the signaling cry to charge, and the hundred warriors
who had ridden with them lunged past her. Storm Trail kept

her mare to an easy gallop. She reached the first carcasses and almost hoped *not* to find any of Too Much's arrows. She was not ready to dismount yet and work.

But as the hunters and the herd thundered away, she found one of the warrior's green and white shafts. She sighed and got off her mare. She had to use both hands and brace her foot on the cow's ribs to get the arrow free. It came lose with a sudden, burping sound and she stumbled backward a few steps. She lay it neatly in the grass beside the kill.

She was pulling at the hide, trying to peel it back, when Too Much finally returned.

"How many did you get?" she asked warily.

"Four. It was a very good hunt."

Four carcasses to strip down. Suddenly this ride did not seem to be such a good idea after all.

A popping sound came from behind her, interrupting her thoughts. It wasn't the sound of a hide coming off, but it was eerily familiar all the same. Storm Trail scowled and looked about, then she screamed.

It was happening again.

White men galloped across the plains toward them. Suddenly her blood began boiling with rage. She heard Too Much shout at her as she started toward them, brandishing her knife. His big hand wrapped painfully around her arm, but she fought him off, screaming at the white men.

"Leave us! This is ours, *ours!*"

One of them shot at her and she reeled backward, absurdly stunned. Her knife finally slipped from her hand. She shrieked again and stumbled blindly into a gutted calf. Then another bullet came, thudding wetly into the carcass, and she mewled a sound of terror and began to run.

"Go back!" Too Much shouted at her. "Go back to the camp!" He caught her again and dragged her bodily toward her mare as the Rain-jers came closer. He caught her around the waist and lifted her onto the back of her pony.

"We will keep the Rain-jers busy while you go! Run!" He

hit her pony's rump, and the animal bolted directly toward the Rain-jers.

Storm Trail screamed again, but the same thing happened that had occurred on that other sun when Raven had rushed at the *tejanos* to get their ponies. When they saw her, they jumped down off their horses. They were startled and they couldn't manage their big cumbersome guns fast enough to do anything with them. She was past them before they could even brace them to take aim.

Paya-yuca went very still as the wind carried the distant popping sounds of gunfire to him. Black Paint heard it, too.

"*Tejano* rifles."

Paya-yuca lumbered to his feet, bellowing a call to the warriors who remained in camp. But they did not need to be told what to do. They began to spew from their lodges and leap up from their own fires to mount the war ponies that were never far from their sides.

"They've gotten the hunting band," Bear Wound groaned disbelievingly. "What is happening?"

Crooked Nose spoke the impossible. "Perhaps we should move the women, the babes. Perhaps those Rain-jers will make it back here."

"No," Paya-yuca said harshly. "They could never get past all our warriors."

Still they waited, watching the horizon, just to be sure, and it occurred to Black Paint that that was unprecedented in itself.

Suddenly his bones felt cold.

The men fought like jack-in-the-boxes, Thorn thought in helpless disgust. They leaped off their ponies, took aim, fired, then lunged back up to mount again. But Bird would not make the same mistake that Johnny had and leave the horses unattended.

The trouble with his strategy was that by the time the Rangers saw the opportunity for a good shot and dismounted, the moment—and the shot—were often gone. So far not a single red body had fallen.

The bucks were running, and that bothered Thorn, too. He thought Johnny had said something about this happening in that other fight as well. The 'Manches had taken off, then they had come back in a circle surrounding Moore's pathetic bunch of horseless Rangers. These 'Manches would not easily be able to encircle them. It was a running fight, and yet . . .

"Captain!" Thorn roared suddenly.

When they had attacked nearly an hour ago, they had closed in on no more than a hundred bucks. Now Thorn realized that the Injuns were racing the same way the escaping squaws had gone, presumably back to a camp somewhere. And that camp had to be emptying of its fighting men as quickly as Thorn's heart could beat, because they were no longer chasing a hundred Injuns. It looked to Thorn like they were on the tail of closer to two hundred.

Bird finally realized it as well. The captain sawed on his reins in panic.

"Retreat!" he shouted. "Turn about!"

That was a mistake, too, and Thorn knew it with a rushing, sick sensation. The bucks had drawn them off from all means of suitable cover. As Thorn watched, they, too, wheeled around in a furious turnabout pursuit.

Thorn went after Bird and the beleaguered Rangers, but when they scrambled into a creekbed to take a stand, he kept going. There was no doubt in his mind that the Rangers were all going to die in there, and he was right.

It was nearly dawn before the men began returning to camp. They brought Ranger scalps, and they had retrieved the new hides and meat. Life went on, and the buffalo still had to be reaped at all costs.

Women stood outside their lodges in the darkness to watch them, wide-eyed and dazed. Paya-yuca and the chiefs gathered at the arbor. Storm Trail looked around and noticed with a rush of relief that Yellow Fawn had come out of her mother's tipi.

They would laugh and gossip, she thought hungrily. They would make this strange new fear go away and everything would be like it once had been before the white-eyes craziness had touched them.

"Friend!" she called out. *"Hei!* Come visit with me!"

But Yellow Fawn shook her head. "I have things to do for my mother."

She rushed off to the river. Storm Trail scowled and went after her. Yellow Fawn would not even look at her. Her eyes kept going skittishly back to the camp.

Storm Trail followed her gaze. "Oh!" she gasped, surprised. Yellow Fawn was watching Too Much, and when she heard Storm Trail's cry, she flushed.

"Why did you not tell me?" Storm Trail demanded.

Yellow Fawn's expression twisted. She started back up the bank without answering.

Storm Trail caught her arm. "If you want him, then go after him! You should sneak into his lodge!"

For the first time in Storm Trail's whole memory, temper showed in Yellow Fawn's eyes. "How can I?" she cried.

Storm Trail was dumbfounded. "Well, you just wait until everyone goes to sleep and—"

"No!"

"No?"

"I know what to do, but I do not dare do it! How can I go to him when he wants you? Why would Too Much settle for me when you are fluttering all around him?"

Fluttering? "I do not flutter!" she answered indignantly. "Besides, you are pretty, and—"

"I am *not* pretty. I am fat."

Storm Trail scrambled for a response. "So is he!"

Yellow Fawn's face crumpled. "You are horrible!"

"Why?" What had she done now?

"You do not want him! You just tease him! The only warrior you want is Raven, and everybody knows it. You are just too stubborn to admit it that you really do not hate him!"

She had admitted it, Storm Trail thought wildly . . . oh, she had definitely admitted it. She remembered the way he had loved her the last time, before he had left on this ride, and her heart started thrumming. She had gone to him, hadn't she? She had stopped fighting it. She had gone back to his lodge time and time again lately.

"This has nothing to do with Raven!" she managed. "Too Much asked me to go out on that hunt! He gave me meat, hides, while my brother and cousin are away! That was all it was!"

"You did not do it because of meat!"

"Of course I did!"

"No! You went because Raven is not here, and you are bored . . . or . . . or you just want to prove he has no hold on you! But everyone can see it like the grass on the prairie. You love that *tejano!*"

Yellow Fawn turned and fled. Storm Trail felt as though the blood was draining out the bottom of her feet.

"You are *crazy!*" she screamed after her friend, then she sank down slowly to sit beside the creek.

"She is crazy," she muttered again.

But all the same, she was very scared. Because somehow she thought that maybe she hadn't admitted anything. She went to him, and she accepted that he had some strange *puha* over her and her body craved his.

But Yellow Fawn was just a little bit right. She could not admit—did not dare admit—that her heart was lost and lonely while he was gone.

Twenty-three

When the youngest apprentice warrior went down into the camp to announce Wolf Dream's war band's arrival, there were none of the usual howls of jubilation from the women. The men rode into the lush narrow wrinkle in the earth where the Penateka were camped this time, and their families looked up at them dully. The chiefs stood at the arbor. Children stopped playing and ran to the camp center, but there was more a weariness to it than an urgency.

"What has happened?" Wolf Dream demanded, riding to Paya-yuca.

Where is she? Raven looked about for Storm Trail. Something had gone wrong.

"They came back after you were gone," Paya-yuca said.

Wolf Dream gave a crazed sound of disbelief.

Where was Storm Trail?

Raven finally saw her at the river. His pulse staggered, then steadied. Finally he realized that there were no wails of mourning. If anyone had died, the people would be keening still. They were just . . . stunned by the latest turn of events.

Paya-yuca looked at the bounty they brought. Everyone seemed to be holding their breath, waiting for him to speak.

"It is good," he said finally. "We struck back even as they hit us. We will have a Scalp Dance."

"And then," Wolf Dream said tightly, "we will turn right around and go back there again."

* * *

Raven was torn between anger, bemusement, and laughter. He had harbored a sweet mental image all through the ride of coming in with his scalps, his ponies, and handing everything over to her triumphantly. He had promised her. But as he pulled a clean hunting shirt over his head in his tipi, Storm Trail had still not approached him.

He finally saw her when he stepped outside. She was headed in his direction. She reached her own lodge near his and shot him a scathing look before she bent and went inside.

Raven's brows went up. Even from her, that look was severe.

He briefly considered going into the tipi after her. He thought of tumbling her onto her bedding while she was still pliant with surprise. It had been so long. He ached for her, for more of what she could do to his body, and that alone astounded him. But who knew when Black Paint might return to his lodge? Fast enough, he thought wryly, if she started caterwauling.

He scrubbed a hand over his unshaven jaw and went to the big central fire instead. Tonight he would have a coup to contribute. He would dance. And if she didn't come to watch it, he thought he might choke her.

A crowd was beginning to gather. As soon as the People saw Wolf Dream enter the circle, even those still at their tipis stopped what they were doing to watch. For a while they would not be afraid. The fear itself was an unprecedented thing, and they seemed eager to escape it.

Storm Trail was not among the others. Raven's temper surged from irritation into anger. When a warm body slid up against him from behind, he almost relaxed, but the breasts were too full, the hips too voluptuous.

He kept his arms crossed over his chest and looked back over his shoulder. It was Eyes Down.

"When will you dance?" she asked breathlessly.

Raven lifted a shoulder in a shrug. He would prefer going

toward the end, he decided, and it had nothing to do with Storm being there to see. It was just that he wanted to find out what the other men had done first, he told himself.

"Where is she?" he asked suddenly. "Have you seen Storm Trail?"

The look that came over Eyes Down's face was one he was growing accustomed to—bitter and irritated. "Maybe she went to the herd."

"The herd? Why would she go there in the middle of a dance?"

"Maybe she was sneaking out there to meet someone."

"To meet someone?"

"You know," Eyes Down said slyly.

To *play* with someone? Something hot began to swell inside him, then he scowled. That did not make sense. If she was going to do that, she would go to the warrior's lodge, not to the pony herd.

Eyes Down was trying to stir up trouble. For the first time he realized that she was inordinately jealous of the others, of Yellow Fawn and She Smiles, but especially Storm.

"I will go look." He would not find her there, he was sure of it, but at the moment he just wanted to get rid of this girl.

"Maybe you will not like what you find," Eyes Down taunted.

"Maybe I will find nothing."

"Maybe you will find her with Too Much."

Raven stopped dead in his tracks. *Too Much?* Were they back to that again? "I do not think so," he said slowly.

Eyes Down smiled, very pleased with herself. "She has been playing with him."

She was lying. She had to be lying. Raven left her and went to find Twice As Good, Lost Coyote's second wife.

Four hundred people could not live in such close proximity to each other in what amounted to tents without gossip living a good and healthy life. If anything was going on with Storm and Too Much, then Twice As Good would definitely know about it.

The woman was on the other side of the circle. Lost Coyote was dancing now. She tapped one small moccasin in time with the drums and grinned widely. Raven stopped beside her.

"Has Storm been playing with Too Much?" he blurted.

Twice As Good raised a pretty brow at him, then looked back at her husband. "That is what I hear."

It was like a blow to his chest. The cold inside him fragmented into sharp jagged pieces.

She was his now, he thought. How could she— But she was not. She wasn't his. Not in any way that mattered. Confusion seeped in to tangle with his anger. He moved away again, his limbs feeling as heavy as stone. He had no claim on her, he realized, shaken. She came to his lodge when *she* wanted to. That was the Nermenuh way. They had in no way promised themselves to each other. He could only imagine her reaction if he ever had tried to claim her.

He could not stand it.

He wanted to choke her.

He finally found her at Star Line's lodge. When she saw him coming, she tried to duck inside. Shame? Guilt? But he could not imagine her ducking her head over anything she had done.

He closed the distance between them at a run, just barely catching her elbow and hauling her out again.

"What is wrong with you?" he demanded.

"Why should I want to watch you dance?" she muttered.

"How do you know I have not yet?"

She colored and tried to struggle away from him.

"Why are you mad at me?" he went on. *I am the one who has been wronged.*

"I am not."

He snorted, then changed tactics. He knew that Too Much could never make her feel the way he had.

"I have thought of nothing but you for suns now," he said

quietly. "All on the ride back here, I thought of touching you again. I stayed hard the whole time I was gone, wanting you."

Her black eyes went a little wider and her breath caught.

"I intend to have you," he went on. "I will not wait any longer, not past this night. If you do not come to me before dawn, I will come to your lodge and get you."

She almost choked. "You would not dare! My father—"

"Of course I would," he interrupted. "I am a crazy *tejano*, and given the mood I am in right now, I am liable to do anything at all."

She opened her mouth to retort, then she snapped it shut again. He turned about and left her, going back to the dancing.

She came to him.

It was late, and Raven had very nearly drowsed off. His belly was so full it hurt, and his head still pounded with the vibration of the drums.

It had been good to dance. Storm had given a snorting sound of indifference, but her eyes had remained on him, rapt. And now she was back, he thought, sitting up groggily at the scratchy rustling sound at his wall.

She wriggled inside beneath his dew flap, then she scrambled to her knees to look at him. She said nothing, only hugged her robe around herself, but he could tell by the soft gape of her mouth that she was breathing hard. He did not speak either. He had already said everything that needed to be said.

He reached out, caught the edge of her robe, and gave it a sharp sudden tug. Storm Trail tumbled toward him, onto his bedding.

He pushed the hide out of the way roughly. She was naked beneath it and the sight of her smooth rosy skin went through him like flame. He had thought perhaps she would put on layers upon layers just to thwart him.

But she was as desperate as he was. He felt it instantly when her hands moved hungrily over his own skin. Perhaps she was still angry about something, but she *did* want him. She had ached for him as he had ached for her, and he knew it all over again in the way she groaned softly and writhed beneath his hands.

Too Much had not satisfied her. But, oh, the thought of that man touching her this way!

Raven ground his mouth down on hers angrily. He plunged with his tongue, demanding a response from her. She gave it, her hands going to his tangled hair, pulling him back to her when he would have moved away again.

She kept her mouth pressed to his, her body molded against his own as she wrapped her legs around him. There was no time for teasing. He was already too hard. There was no time for exploration, to reacquaint himself with all the sweet warm places of her body. She would not allow it.

He covered her breasts with his hands, squeezing, feeling them heat beneath his palms, and even as he did he found himself on his back as she rolled over, taking control. She straddled him and fit herself over him, taking what she wanted. She gave a gasping sound as he filled her, and then she rode him.

Raven watched, mesmerized, as a fine sheen of perspiration seemed to make her lithe body shine red and golden in the last of his firelight. She braced her hands on his chest and her head fell back. Her throat was a narrow column, and her hair spilled down her neck. He caught her around the waist and tumbled her again without breaking the heated connection between them.

She made a little sound, half in frustration that she could not have her way, half in exhilaration that he alone could overpower her. He drove himself into her again and again until his anger was gone, until there were only her soft sweet murmurs. He spilled his seed into her and collapsed atop her.

It was a very long time before she began shoving at him.

"What?" he asked huskily.

"Get off me."

He raised up on his elbows to look down at her. "You are fickle, Fire Eyes. You are enough to make a man crazy."

"You were crazy from the first time I saw you, and now I am tired," she muttered. "I came only to spare you trouble with my father in case you really did come after me."

He laughed aloud at that. "Oh, I could tell."

A delightful blush touched her face. She went back to the dew flap. Raven scowled.

"Why are you doing that?" he asked sharply. "You never sneaked in and out of here before." Was it because she did not want Too Much to see her coming and leaving here?

She had never realized before that everyone was talking about them. She would die before she did anything else that would make them believe that what Yellow Fawn had said was true.

She did not love him. She did *not*.

She scrambled out beneath the dew flap again and was gone.

A Quohadi war band arrived three suns later, and Wolf Dream decided to join with them in riding east again. Once again, Too Much offered to stay behind.

Raven felt something entirely too much like panic. Wolf Dream had asked him to ride again, but he could not risk going out and leaving that warrior behind. What would he come home to find *this* time? The possibilities made his head hurt. Too Much had a huge herd and many coups. He knew it was not out of the question that he could come home and find Storm Trail wed to Too Much. She would be snatched away from him just as She Smiles had been. He didn't want to examine too closely why such an outcome seemed so much worse this time.

He had to prevent it. And then suddenly he knew what he needed to do. It was crazy. It was delicious. It would work.

Raven planted himself outside his door to wait for Black Paint to come back from the Smoke Lodge. The moon rose, and still there was no movement over there. He scrubbed his hands over his face and wondered if it would be considered inappropriate for him to interrupt the elders. Then the door rattled, and Bear Wound and Medicine Eagle came out.

Medicine Eagle looked bleary-eyed, as though he had been sleeping. Black Paint emerged. Raven cleared his throat as the chief passed by him.

"*Hei.*"

Black Paint stopped, looking around until he found him in the shadows. "Do you think you are so strong that you need no rest this night, White Raven? Wolf Dream would leave to-morrow, and I heard you are going again."

"I am. I will be able to rest only after I speak to you." And that was certainly true enough.

Black Paint nodded. "So be it. We will talk in your lodge. Do you have smoke?"

Raven nodded. It was a *tejano* pipe with white-eyes tobacco that he had taken on the last ride, but it would have to do.

He hurried back inside. Black Paint came in behind him and settled himself by his fire. Raven passed the pipe and found that he could not speak.

The words got tangled in his throat. This was a *good* thing to do, a smart thing, he thought desperately. Not only would it prevent Too Much from usurping something he wanted, but it would add tremendously to his reputation besides. And it would be a coup over her to end all coups. He could not imagine why he felt panicked.

"I want to buy your daughter," he croaked.

Black Paint raised one brow mildly. Raven thought he did not seem surprised.

"That could be good," Black Paint said finally. "It gives me a feeling of comfort to think that you would provide for her once I am gone." With Raven providing for her, Black Paint thought, he could finally die. Storm Trail was his last responsibility in a long life full of them. A misty image of his wife's face hung before his eyes for a moment.

The chief was going to say yes, Raven realized. His heart whaled so hard against his chest it hurt.

"No other warrior has asked for her," Black Paint went on, "and I am beginning to worry about that. She has seen fifteen winters. She should be wed soon. I think it is partly because the Penateka men all know she would be hard to handle. But many Quohadi warriors are here now, and none of them have brought me a pipe, so maybe even they have heard of her antics." He paused. "But I worry about your motives."

"My motives?" Raven repeated. For one terrifying moment, he was sure Black Paint was going to ask him if she was *sem-ah taikay,* if she was the one he would cry for.

His throat closed tight and hard. She was the perfect wife for him. And it was time he had a wife. Lost Coyote's wives and sometimes Star Line took care of him now, but that wasn't fair. Storm was interesting. She was beautiful to look at. He thought of having sons with her fire, her courage.

But *sem-ah taikay?* That was like . . . loving her, and no, no, he could never be that . . . bound. She just suited him.

He took a deep, steadying breath. "You said . . . you said a man should marry for disposition and family ties, for respect and economy."

"Yes. And I am the first to admit that my daughter does not have much of a disposition."

In spite of himself, Raven gave a caw of laughter. Oh, she did, she did, he thought. He never had any idea what to expect from her at any given time.

"I greatly respect her family," he offered finally.

Black Paint smiled and nodded. "But those are not the kind of motives I was speaking of."

He was going to do it. Sweet spirit-raven, the chief was going to ask him if he loved her.

"I worry that if I comply with your wish, then I am somehow abetting you," Black Paint said instead.

"Abetting me?" Raven was not sure he had heard him right; he had been expecting something so entirely different.

"Helping you establish a coup over her."

"No." *Yes.* "Well, that is not all it is." He took a deep breath, compelled to be honest. "It is an extreme measure to take just for a coup over her."

"I am relieved that you realize that."

"I would relish the expression on her face all the same when she finds out."

"I thought so."

"But I want her."

"Ah."

"I like the way she laughs, the way she walks. And I hate the idea of Too Much claiming her. I want her for myself." That was as baldly honest as he could be.

Black Paint's brows went up. He finally nodded, and Raven's breath came back to him. Black Paint did not seem to care if she was *sem-ah taikay.*

"I will allow you this coup over her because it will be a very expensive one indeed," the chief said finally. "I put her price at one hundred ponies long ago."

A *hundred?* That staggered him, but it pleased him, as well. Having an expensive wife would add greatly to his prestige.

"You do not have that many," Black Paint reminded him, and Raven's air left him in a rush.

"I could ask for a deal such as Kills In The Dark made with His Horses," he ventured. "Did he not promise more horses later as he acquired them?"

Black Paint chuckled. "His Horses is greedy. I am not. I have all the ponies I could ever need. My daughter's price is for her sake, for her pride, more than my own needs.

"I would not ask you for all your ponies now, and I would not ask you to raid for horses that you already owe. I would not give you my daughter now. I am not ready to let her go. Star Line is not herself. If I sell my daughter now, I would have no one to take care of me."

"What do you propose?" Raven asked warily.

"It will take you a while to collect enough ponies so you

can give me one hundred without depleting your herd. We will not yet smoke to seal this pact, but you have my word that I will not renege. Do you trust my word, White Raven?"

Raven nodded. He realized that he trusted this man implicitly, more than he ever could have trusted his own father.

"That is good. I will not accept any other offer for my daughter for one circle of seasons. Until then you can change your mind without blemishing your honor. I want you to be very sure that you want her and of what you are doing. She will not be easy to live with. I want you to be sure that you think she is worth one hundred ponies."

Raven rubbed his temples. He imagined that there would be many times when he wondered about that.

Then he thought of the way they touched. He thought maybe she was worth twice that much.

"At the end of that circle of seasons, if you do not bring me her bridal price, then she will be open to any other warrior's offer," Black Paint went on. "And we will not speak to her of this to anyone until then. You cannot have your coup until you pay me. That is fair."

"So be it," Raven said. He wanted to see her face when he told her, he wanted to see it *now* . . . but he felt a certain relief, too. He could, theoretically, change his mind. He was not trapped.

But she was.

He smiled slowly. This time when he rode out, he had some sort of claim on her, even if she did not know it.

Twenty-four

He did not see her again before the war band left at dawn, but images of her flashed into his mind constantly while he was away. Sometimes they made his throat close in panic. There were times when he was sure that claiming her sealed some kind of fate, ensnaring him far more than the lenient Nermenuh vows of matrimony or that silly sinew thong. His instincts were to buck it, to fight it, to change his mind.

Those thoughts almost always came near dawn, when the fire was low and the ground seemed too hard. When the sun came again, he would think of what her face would look like when he told her, assuming he could ever collect an extra hundred horses.

When, after only ten suns out, Wolf Dream decided abruptly to go home again, Raven panicked.

"Why?" he demanded, and winced when he heard his own voice. One of the first things they had taught him was never to question his leader.

Wolf Dream gave him a hawkish glare. Raven felt his belly fill with ice. *He knows something*, he thought. *He feels something . . . some danger, some trouble.* Frustration pounded against his temples because he wanted to question him, wanted to know.

But he could not, and the thought of one hundred horses made him sensible again. "Can I go with you?" Raven asked Nokoni.

He saw Nokoni's eyes move to Lost Coyote. Raven realized

that he was not at all sure about including a white man in his ride, though it was said that he had bought a stolen white-eyes girl for his wife.

Lost Coyote nodded his support.

"So be it," said Nokoni.

They split up at dawn. Wolf Dream headed west again, and Nokoni rode east. A handful of Penateka followed Raven's choice and determined to keep riding with the Quohadi.

The sun was high in the sky when one of Nokoni's scouts came galloping back. "Rain-jers!" the warrior reported. "Traveling northwest along the Pedernales River."

"How many?" Nokoni asked tersely.

"I counted fourteen."

"We will take them," Nokoni decided. "The Rain-jers tend to have better mounts than the average *tejano.*"

He shrilled a sound that ended in a whoop and gouged his heels hard into his mount. His men followed him. Fourteen ponies, Raven thought dismally. This war band was big, even without most of Wolf Dream's men. Fourteen was not enough to go around, not even barely.

Still maybe he would get lucky enough to claim one of them. He beat his horse into a gallop, but when he caught up with the others, some sharp presentiment twisted deep in his bowels.

The white-eyes did not race for cover this time. They always did that with their long rifles so they could brace them, but this time Raven did not see any guns among them at all. The others noticed that as well. Their screams grew louder, more frenzied, as they smelled easy blood.

But the Rangers would not be riding without weapons, Raven thought.

"No!" he roared. He sawed on his reins. This was what Wolf Dream had known. This fight was wrong.

The Ranger leader howled a cry of his own and turned his men directly into the warriors. The momentum of the Indian ponies took them into the *tejanos* in a blizzard of arrows and bullets. Their war cries turned to screams of pain.

Raven howled a cry of his own and charged into the melee. His arrows would be useless. He knew it before he got there. The fighting was knee-to-knee, and there was so much blood. He realized wildly that he did not even know if that on his hands was red or white. *Red. It has to be red, because no white-eyes are falling.* A *tejano* leaned into him, reaching toward him. Raven caught a flash of silver and black in his hand.

He brought his shield up reflexively. There was a stunning report, and feathers and hide and wood spat into the air as the shield came apart.

A gun—he had a little gun. It was small enough to shoot from astride, something like his own sawed-off weapon. But the *tejano* would have to reload, Raven thought, while his own adapted rifle was packed and ready. He brought it up and felt his air leave him in a stunned gasp. The white man did not have to reload. Another bullet spat from his little gun, creasing Raven's right thigh. The pain was bright, searing.

All around him warriors were hurling down their useless shields with crazed sounds. Those shields had always stopped bullets before, but they had never been shot at this closely before. Their medicine was breaking. Warrior after warrior fell from his mount, and others fled.

The white-eyes bullets kept coming, cracking out of neat little guns that fit virtually into the palms of their hands. Even Nokoni broke rank and rode away, his eyes almost demented as he hunched low over his pony's neck, howling. This was white *puha* at its greatest and most inexplicable.

But Raven knew that these guns were not magic. Amazing, yes. Deadly, certainly. But there was nothing mystical about them—some *tejano* had just finally invented something better than the old breech- and muzzleloaders.

He came up behind another Ranger and thrust his knife upward into the *tejano's* kidneys. The Ranger's grip began to loosen in death, but Raven leaned across him and caught his little gun before he dropped it.

He thrust it beneath the string of the breechclout, then he whipped his mount around, praying that he could escape this swirling, bloody scene alive. He was horribly outnumbered now. Only Ranger horses remained, spinning and rearing, some riderless, some not, and far too many red men were on the ground.

Raven swerved after the few ponies the war band had stolen earlier in the ride—the warriors had left them behind in their terror. He set them to galloping and jerked his own mount around to ride behind their cover.

He knew without being told that this was the worst defeat the Nermenuh had suffered in generations.

It was near dawn when Raven arrived back in the Penateka camp with the few warriors who had survived. A ground mist swirled around the ponies' legs.

At once, it seemed, the People spilled from their lodges and raced toward them. Their eyes were disbelieving, darting, as though if they looked hard enough they would find the missing warriors. Raven moved his pony through the gathering crowd, feeling an illogical shame. Though it had not been his war band, though he knew—*hoped*—there was nothing he could have done to have kept it all from going wrong, his sense of disgrace was bone-deep.

But you knew, a cruel voice inside him chided. *Wolf Dream knew, and you would not listen and go back with him. Your greed insisted that you go on.*

Raven stopped his pony in front of his tipi and slipped clumsily to the ground. Pain flared up his thigh. He limped toward the arbor.

He looked around at all the faces: Storm Trail's seemed inordinately white. He watched her for a moment, and it seemed to him that she was searching him for wounds. That pleased him and bolstered him somewhat.

Kills In The Dark nosed his way into the council. He smells blood, Raven realized, and he wondered again if his own reputation would somehow suffer for this.

"You chose to stay with Nokoni. That is what I heard," Kills In The Dark charged before Raven could even sit. "If you had not, those other men would not have stayed either."

Raven carefully lowered himself the rest of the way to the ground. "I made my own choice. I did not ask others to join me."

"You prompted them to do it by doing it yourself! Now we have eight men dead!"

"They were young men, hungry for coups," Paya-yuca said harshly. *"That* is why they went on."

But Kills In The Dark did not desist. This was as close as he had ever come to being able to discredit Raven since that horrible night when he had interfered with his slave woman. The warrior was not about to back off.

Scout cleared his throat. He was one of the four men who, with Raven, had survived.

"That man speaks when he was not there," Scout said, looking distastefully at Kills In The Dark. "It is true that White Raven asked to ride with Nokoni first. Then several of us decided to go as well. When we encountered those Rain-jers, I heard this man yell out a warning that something was not right. He tried to stop the fight. But those Quohadi were already galloping. Our blood was hot and ready, and we all ignored him. Raven saved the ponies we had already stolen. And he took one of their magic repeating guns. I, for one, turn my own raided horses over to him now. Nokoni did that as well.

We stole them first, but then this *tejano* reclaimed them from the white-eyes in the next fight."

A hush fell over the council—not because of the ponies, Raven realized, though he felt vaguely stunned at the odd acquisition of more horses. It was the gun.

"Where is it?" someone demanded.

"I would see it."

"How is it magic?"

Raven held up his hand. "I will show it to you, and then I will tell you what I know." He pulled it from beneath his breechclout string and laid it carefully on the ground in front of him. Bear Wound leaped to his feet to take a wary step backward.

"It must possess amazing white *puha*," Medicine Eagle said quietly, "to kill so many Nermenuh."

"It is just new, different."

Lost Coyote reached forward to touch it with a single finger, but several other warriors backed off with Bear Wound to watch from a safer distance. *Oh, their magic, their reverent sense of magic.*

Raven picked up the gun again and opened it. "There are places for six bullets inside. That is why they were able to keep shooting at us without reloading."

They did not believe him. One of the younger warriors shook his head angrily.

"I saw what it can do. I will not fight against them again."

Wolf Dream made an abortive sound of disgust. "Are we cowards to hide from them?"

Another man jumped to his feet. "I would live long enough to dance my coups!"

"Then we must get these guns ourselves," Lost Coyote snapped.

"I do not see the purpose," His Horses said darkly.

"So that we might live through fights against them," Lost Coyote argued with far more heat than was usual for him.

Paya-yuca waved his hand to draw their attention back to

himself. "I agree with His Horses. I do not think we should try to get these guns. They possess white-eyes magic. Maybe they would even turn on us if we tried to shoot them.

"We must continue to fight these *tejanos* as we have always fought our enemies, with our bows and arrows," he went on. "That is where our strength lies. Shall we give up our horses and start walking into battle because that is what that white-eyes did who first came here to attack us? Of course not. And neither should we try to shoot them with their own guns, guns that possess their *puha,* not ours.

"Suvate," he finished. "That is all I have to say."

He got up and left the council. Raven looked at Black Paint.

"We cannot fight these guns with bows and arrows," he warned carefully, not wanting to disparage Paya-yuca. "With these guns, the Rain-jers can come right up into our faces and shoot us."

"What does that one know?" His Horses sputtered angrily. "What does he know about fighting? How many rides has he been on so far? When he goes out, there is almost always disaster!"

"He knows white-eyes," Lost Coyote said angrily. Raven looked at him, amazed. Rarely had he seen him so emotional.

It was the guns, he realized, the wonderful, amazing, new magic guns.

As he stared at him, Lost Coyote finished. "We need to get them at any cost."

Raven nodded, not sure why he felt suddenly wary, as though that cost might prove to be devastating.

Twenty-five

Storm Trail was cutting meat, biting her lip as she drew her knife through a flank steak to make it just the right thickness.

"I heard they are hidden in caves somewhere," Eyes Down said from beside her, still talking about the magic guns, as everyone was.

"No." Storm Trail bent over her work. Things were dismal indeed when the only company she had was Eyes Down, she thought, but She Smiles seemed so depressed lately, and Yellow Fawn was still mad at her.

"You do not know that," Eyes Down protested.

"I know." She said it without venom, and wished she could feel the old fierce pride at having information that no one else did. "Raven told me."

"You should make up your mind who you want to play with, him or Too Much. Then someone else could have the one you don't want."

"Who says I am playing with either of them?" she snapped, irritated. But thinking of Raven made her wonder where he was. She looked around, then she made a choking sound.

Tejanos, more *tejanos.*

Voices rose suddenly from the east side of camp. Eyes Down began running that way, children streaming past her. When the little ones reached the white men coming in, they began pelting them with pony dung and rocks. Women shrieked and cried out, trying to drag them back out of harm's way.

The white-eyes came on stoically. Storm Trail stumbled backward as they approached her. They went past her toward the council arbor, and she jerked into motion as though someone had struck her.

Women were already gathered there, knotted closely together as though they would shield each other from harm. None of Paya-yuca's wives offered the strangers food this time. Storm Trail's head spun. She had so often accused Raven of being arrogant, but this . . . this was mind-numbing, that these white-eyes would take advantage of their traditional hospitality when they were such enemies now.

Raven was nowhere in sight. Storm Trail thought he would probably hide again, and she felt no chagrin this time, nothing but a knee-weakening relief. She realized that she did not want him to go back among them, not at all.

You *love* that *tejano.*

No, she thought, no. It was just that if he went away, she would have no one to play with. No, that wasn't quite right, either, she thought wildly. But no one else's gaze made her pulse stutter the way Raven's did when he looked at her as though he was thinking what he would like to do to her body if they were alone.

She took a deep breath and closed her eyes, and when she opened them again, she saw him approaching. *What was he doing?*

He strode up to the council arbor from the direction of the herd. It seemed to her that everyone stiffened at the sight of him—the Nermenuh and the white-eyes. Her heart started banging. The sight of his golden hair, of his pale eyes, would surely make this council escalate past any semblance of civility.

"No," she whispered as he passed her. "Raven, go back." One look at his face told her that he was very angry. A feeling of hard hot power came off him in waves. A fierce thrill, a feeling of pride, scooted through her blood.

She did love him—yes, oh, yes, she did, she realized helplessly. And she did not want anything to happen to him.

"Leave us," she whispered fiercely. "It is too dangerous!"

He barely looked at her. "You have nothing to fear."

"I do! They will want you back!" Too late, she flinched, wondering what he would do with the knowledge that she cared. But he was not even thinking of such things now.

"What would they do? Ransom me?" he sneered. "I am my own man, Fire Eyes, and who would pay to get my scarred old carcass anyway?"

She shook her head frantically.

"I was white once," he said more quietly, his gaze finally settling on her and seeing her distress. "I alone know enough about these *tejanos* to judge their motives."

The white-eyes were watching him cautiously. They were as aware as she was of the restrained violence in his stance. There were six of them this time. They put their heads together to talk.

"Whoever he is, he has gone savage," one man said, and Thorn tried to keep all expression from his face as he nodded his agreement. But excitement was alive inside him. *He had found the bastard.* He was finally face to face with the legendary white savage so many had spoken of.

"It doesn't matter," he said levelly. "A fight with him would still incite the other warriors, and that doesn't serve our purposes. Lamar wants them in San Antonio no matter what it takes. Fighting with them is not going to achieve that, and they'll only end up taking our hair with them if they go."

He cleared his throat and took a step closer to Raven. "Do you speak English?"

And there it was again, Raven thought, that tantalizing thread of recognition dangling just out of his grasp. If it had been difficult to talk to that woman they had captured two years ago, now the white-eyes words were like a twangy buzzing in his ear, bringing memory frustratingly close but just out of reach.

Raven pointed at Thorn's chest and tried. "Talk. Want?"

Interesting, Thorn mused. His limited command of his own tongue indicated that the buck had been here for a while. It had been four years now since the Parker children had been stolen and the Rusts had been killed.

"I bear a message from President Lamar," Thorn began, speaking carefully and signing. He saw the white buck's eyes flare. *He knows who Lamar is.* And Lamar had been president for only a little over two years. "Our president desires peace." He mimed a laying down of arms.

Raven watched and his eyes narrowed. "Your price?" he asked.

"Well, you'd have to come to a council. Bring your captives into San Antonio. We'll buy them back from you. We'll smoke and reach a peace."

No, Raven thought, we would be without bargaining power.

"Peace," Thorn repeated. "No more Rangers will come up here, up the scarp. But you must not come down into Texas anymore, either."

Raven nearly laughed at that. "When council?"

"In one month."

Thorn drew a map in the dirt to illustrate where San Antonio was, but Raven barely glanced at it. He knows the place, Thorn thought.

"Will you come? Will you bring your captives?"

"Talk. See." He motioned at the headmen.

Thorn nodded.

He did not, in all honesty, care if they came to San Antonio or not. He had learned what he had come to find out. He knew with which band this man could be found.

He had one last question for him. "Do you know where the Parkers are?"

Raven had begun to turn away. He went still, then looked

back over his shoulder at the man. Something pulled hard at his memory.

Par-kerz. The people who had died just before the Rusts had, he remembered. He nodded cautiously.

"Are they here?" the man asked excitedly.

Raven drew a line across his throat. He thought the man got a little paler.

"Dead? All of them?" Thorn asked. "Even the children?"

Raven shook his head and his eyes flicked over the crowd of red faces. "Dangerous for you to ask."

Thorn understood. He took a step closer and spoke in an undertone so the rest of his party would not hear him. "I don't give a tinker's damn if you've got white kids here. I just want the *Parker* kids."

"No children here."

"Where then?" Thorn demanded. "Goddamnit, just tell me where they've gone!"

The white buck stared back at him impassively.

"I'll follow your ass all over the plateau," Thorn warned, too angry to talk carefully now. "You're damned easy to spot— people are talking about you all over Texas. I'll hound you, and I'll dog every move you make until you lead me to them. Sooner or later you'll lead me to them."

Raven turned away.

In spite of himself, he knew a brief rare flutter of nerves. It would have been a simple matter to admit that he had never had any idea what had become of the Parkers, but the battle lines had been drawn when Loses Something had died, when the bastards had shot little kids.

Never again would he give a white man anything.

Storm Trail lay beneath him, still breathing hard, her eyes still a little bit wild. Raven started to leave her, but she tightened her legs around him.

"Again," she gasped.

Raven would not have thought that he'd be able to oblige her, but her mouth found the hard ridge of his collarbone and her teeth nipped and her tongue laved, and his body responded. It was only a low faint stirring at first, deep in his groin, but then he caught a fistful of her hair, pulled her head back, and kissed her again, and the rest of him ignited. She was in one of her frantic moods. He had thought to spend some leisurely moments exploring the dark wet recesses of her mouth and catching his breath, but her tongue plunged to meet his.

"Again," he agreed. He moved inside her and her legs tightened around his hips even more, melding him to her, and she moved in perfect counterpoint to his own rhythm.

Storm Trail felt excitement tunneling inside her, and it was all she wanted to feel. She did not want to think beyond the heat of his mouth and the hard readiness of his body. She did not want to think about her feelings for him. She just wanted to feel what he did to her as his fingers moved to find the hidden nub of her pleasure while he slid his hardness in and out of her.

She panted and writhed and refused to think at all, because Raven did not have anywhere near a hundred ponies, and she was not sure she wanted to be given to him even if he did. He would own her, and she did not know if she could bear that, not him, not a man who would take such glee in it, but of course her father would send her to someone else soon, and how would she bear going to another?

Her hands moved feverishly over his back and his buttocks. But she could not make it last forever. The excitement inside her built fast, as it always did, and exploded into shards and pieces.

He followed her a moment later, and this time his groan was a depleted sound. He pushed up on his elbows. "You would kill me, Fire Eyes."

He waited for some retort about his manliness and virility,

but she watched him almost warily. This time when he sat up, she let him go.

She was so beautiful. Her fast breath made her breasts rise and fall, and that rosy blush still touched her chest and her cheeks. *His weasel.* Sometimes when the light was just right, he could still see the child he remembered in her finely arched brows and in the flashing black fire of her eyes, and that could make him feel strange and amazed inside. But then she would seem like a stranger again, a mysterious woman of untold thoughts and passions who had seemed to have come into his life straight out of his fantasies.

She took a deep breath and sat up. "Will you go?" she asked idly, and he *did* know that much about her, that whenever her voice was like that there was nothing idle about her words at all.

"It is not decided that anyone will go yet," he said carefully.

"We will." She looked at him defiantly. *"I* will."

And that, Raven thought, was another issue entirely.

He got up and went to peer out his lodge door. The council fire near the arbor was still burning. The chiefs had been there since the white-eyes had gone, and it was nearly dawn. They were talking about going to San Antonio. The very thought of that place brought such a feeling of cold pressure to Raven's chest that he could scarcely breathe.

He did not trust this Lamar.

Maybe it was because he had been the one to talk to that *tejano* woman, because he had heard of Lamar's ambitions almost straight from the horse's mouth. Perhaps they had lost something in the translation, because Wolf Dream did not seem afraid of the man. He and Lost Coyote wanted to go to San Antonio. They thought they could get the magic guns by trading with the white-eyes.

Raven turned back to Storm Trail. "I am going over there. I have to try to talk sense into them one more time."

She stood impatiently. "They will not listen to you. You are only a warrior."

He grinned fleetingly. Once it would have been *only* a *te-jano*. "You are mellowing, Fire Eyes."

"Why do you call me that?" she asked suspiciously.

Because it is what I love most about you. The unspoken thought, caught back from his tongue just in time, drained the moisture from his mouth.

Oh, what she would do with that knowledge . . . if it was true . . .

He shook himself. "It is just a name, a special one that suits you." He fumbled around in the near-darkness for his breech-clout and changed the subject before she could make more of it. "You hope they do not listen to me because you want to see a white-eyes village. And I am very much afraid that it will be the last thing you see."

"That is stupid!" she sat hotly.

"I hope so." He thought of telling her that he didn't want her to go because he didn't want to lose her. He realized with a thump in the area of his chest that it did not matter if he loved her or not. He did not want to live without her.

She snorted, and he put his attention back to her.

"It is just a council," she said. "They invited us to talk and to trade captives. And I am going no matter what you say."

He watched as she went down on her knees to work her way beneath the dew flap on the side of the lodge that was closest to her own. He caught her elbow suddenly and pulled her back to her feet.

She tilted her head back to look warily into his eyes. Oh, to be able to tell her that she was *his*. If only a year had already passed and he could forbid her to go. Then Raven gave a short scraping laugh. As if that would stop her. As if claiming her for his wife would make any difference whatsoever in her stubborn determination. This was one woman who would never be owned, no matter what custom decried.

He covered her mouth impulsively instead, kissing her deeply and fast. How he loved doing that. Her eyes widened in the murky light of the new dawn, and he was pleased to see that it left her a little unsteady on her feet.

"Come back tonight," he said hoarsely, and he grimaced as soon as the words were out. He never asked her to come to him. He had always been sure that if he did, she would stay away out of sheer contrariness . . . or maybe, maybe, it would just let her know how much he needed her in his bedding. Neither possibility was tolerable.

He wasn't sure if he was shaken or pleased when she just smiled fleetingly this time and nearly nodded.

Mirabeau Lamar arrived in San Antonio with no less fanfare than Thorn expected. He and his entourage set up camp at the old Alamo, next door to the small limestone building where the council would be held—assuming any Comanches ever materialized.

"I see Anglo faces and Spanish faces and Pueblo faces," Lamar muttered, looking out on the main plaza, "but there is nothing out there that even vaguely suggests braids and feathers."

Thorn was playing cards with one of the president's officers. "Full house," he said to his opponent, collecting the kitty. Hays and Moore grinned at each other.

Lamar paced away from the window. "Let's go over this one more time."

The brass who had been appointed to run the council crowded obligingly around him. They were the most venerable of the Republic's upper crust. Colonel Cooke was the secretary of war. Hugh McLeod, a colonel himself, was the Texas adjutant general. And Lieutenant Colonel Bill Fisher of the newly organized First Texas Regiment would lead the proceedings.

We surely are getting civilized out here, Thorn thought dryly.

"We expect full surrender of all the prisoners," Fisher began.

"Two hundred fifty of them," Lamar muttered. "By all

counts, they have at least two hundred and fifty of our women and children up there by now, and I want all of them."

"If they don't bring them in, the chiefs will be seized and held hostage," Fisher went on. "Of course we'll give them every opportunity to surrender their captives peacefully first."

"In addition, the peace we offer comes on three conditions," McLeod contributed. "They must remain west of a line drawn through central Texas—"

"West of the scarp," interrupted Lamar. "I want at least a hundred miles of land between them and that goddamned ridge."

"They must never again approach any white settlement or community east of that line," Fisher went on, nodding, "and they must not interfere with any of our efforts to settle any lands *west* of it, assuming those lands are vacant."

Thorn had finally put his cards down. He watched them as though one of them had just proposed to make the endless prairie wind stop blowing simply by telling it to.

"Just out of curiosity," he asked, "what are you offering them in exchange for all this?"

"Nothing," Lamar said flatly.

Thorn's brows went up. "You had me promise them that we would ransom our women back—"

Lamar waved a hand dismissively and impatiently. "That was to get them here. This custom of giving presents to Indians is ludicrous. Unless their captives are offered up willingly, there will be no peace and they themselves will be taken hostage. The only way to deal with these savages is by force."

Thorn caught Hays's eye. Jack cleared his throat.

"I'm not entirely sure that resorting to high-handed trickery will work with these particular savages."

"It's civilized all the northern and eastern tribes," Johnny Moore pointed out.

"Unfortunately," Hays said, "I don't think the Comanche have much in common with those other tribes."

Lamar's face turned to stone. This conversation would be like spitting into the wind, Thorn realized. No matter that Jack Hays had led the only truly successful fight against the 'Manches with those new guns he had found back East. He wasn't a decorated soldier, and, as such, Lamar had little respect for him.

Still Hays tried. "You can only twist the arms of subjugated desperate people," he pointed out. "The Comanche are neither. If their backs are up against the wall, I daresay they don't know it. We have nothing they need, nothing with which to coerce them into this agreement."

Thorn attempted to back him up, although he doubted if Lamar was much more impressed with him. "We can promise them peace, but those bucks will want it on their own terms." During all his trips up onto the scarp, he had met a breed of people every bit as arrogant, as domineering, and as self-assured as these Texans. He wondered if there was any way to avoid temper and bloodshed when two such similar factions clashed.

He would find out shortly enough. Over at the window, Johnny Moore gave a shout.

"The first of your Indians are arriving, sir."

Lamar pushed up behind him. "How many captives have they brought?"

Thorn went to look for himself. He didn't see a single white face astride any of the procession of Comanche horses.

The Penateka council had decided to go to San Antonio. Word had reached them that the Kotseteka were already there.

As the party rode out, Raven tried frantically to count them all. His best guess put the Penateka at sixty, maybe sixty-five. Storm and Star Line and all Lost Coyote's wives would go. Eyes Down and Yellow Fawn and She Smiles were among the crowd as well. Of the chiefs, only Paya-yuca steadfastly refused to have anything to do with these white-eyes, and Medicine Eagle complained that he was too old for such a long journey.

Raven watched Storm Trail swing a long slender leg over the back of her mare, and his throat tightened. He had not intended to leave his lodge, had not meant to intercept her. He knew it would do no good. He found himself jogging to catch up with her anyway.

She looked up at the sound of his footsteps and he almost stumbled. For one breath-robbing moment, he thought he saw pure delight on her face . . . for *him*. It was the kind of look she usually reserved for times when he was touching her.

"Will you come?" she asked quickly. "Have you changed your mind?"

He wanted to. He needed to be there to protect her . . . and he could think of no way that he could manage it. There was no way he could blend in with all these dark burnished faces. His skin was white, even if his heart had become red, and Lamar wanted his *tejanos* back.

They would have to kill him to take him, Raven thought, and too many others could die as well if they tried. He did not worry so much for the warriors, but there were so many women and children among the party.

"I cannot," he croaked, his throat hurting. He had already told her why.

Storm Trail's jaw hardened and she looked away. He realized, astounded, that he was hurting her, that she really *wanted* him to be able to come, wanted him to share this with her. That opened so many glorious uncharted possibilities between them that it made his pulse speed.

"It is your turn to ride, and my turn to wait," he went on quietly, trying to smile. "I will be here when you come home."

She did not say goodbye, although she glanced back at him quickly as the long line began moving. Suddenly he had the horrible feeling that this was the last time he would see her, that fate was laughing at him and he did not even know it. Now—when things were finally so uncomplicated and good between them—she would slip through his fingers like sand.

Raven shocked himself by groaning aloud.

Part Three

Season of Yellow Leaf

Twenty-six

It was going to be a wonderful adventure, Storm Trail thought, with or without Raven.

For the first time in many seasons, She Smiles began to look like her name as they rode toward San Antonio. Her friend's silent despair had been one of those things that you did not see clearly until it was gone, Storm Trail realized.

"You must truly hate your husband," she ventured. "Is that why you have been so different lately?"

She Smiles did not even look at her. "He hurts me."

"Hurts you?" Then she remembered the time he had raised his hand to *her*, and she thought of the sneaky thing he had done to her and Raven. And now, suddenly, she was glad he had, because perhaps otherwise Raven would still be with She Smiles.

She sighed in confusion.

"You are lucky he did not choose you," She Smiles said finally, as though reading her mind. "Anyway, for a short time at least, he is there and I am here."

"How did you manage it?"

"I lied to him."

Storm Trail felt her jaw drop. "You did?" She Smiles had always seemed as sweet and guileless as Yellow Fawn. That was more like something she would do.

"I told him that my father wanted him to sit on council in his stead while we were gone. He let me come because I told him that His Horses thought I should have some small bit of pleasure, and of course he would not want to displease my father in case he changed his mind."

Storm Trail laughed out loud, delighted. "Your father will be wild when he finds out."

A hint of a smile touched She Smiles's mouth. "It will be worth it. And he cannot punish me." Her smile vanished again. "He has already sold me."

A shout sounded from up ahead, distracting them. San Antone-yo. It was a spot of darkness on the horizon, but already she could tell that it was bigger than any Nermenuh village she had ever seen. As they drew closer to it, she saw that the buildings were made of stone, not hides or wood. They gave off a feeling of defiant permanence.

They went into the town past a very large building where many *tejanos* stood outside. Despite the bravado she had displayed to Raven, Storm Trail felt herself shiver. One of the men came to stand in front of them, holding up a hand to stop them.

"Welcome!" he called out.

His Horses and Black Paint, Bear Wound and Crooked Nose all looked down at him impassively from their ponies' backs. Then Bear Wound offered a happy smile.

"Hei, haitsi, we are glad to be here on this fine sun."

Storm Trail laughed. The old man looked as though he was already counting the trade goods.

The white man's eyes seemed to dart around, looking for something. A Kickapoo man ran up to change the white-eyes talk into words and signs that the Nermenuh could understand.

"You should camp back there, back behind that building," he said. "And come straight to the council. They want to get to it right away. It will be in that building over there. Where are your captives?"

His Horses looked over his shoulder at the people behind him. "Bring my son-in-law's woman."

Kills In The Dark's *tejano* was cut from her pony. Storm Trail did not know how His Horses had succeeded in talking the warrior into giving her up, but the woman was the only one the Penateka had brought. Her father said they would give up just one captive now, to see how the trading went. Later, perhaps, they could sell back some others who were not working out.

Kills In The Dark's slave woman slid from her pony. When her feet touched the ground, she seemed to collapse into a human puddle.

One of the white-eyes yelled. The people riding closest to Kills In The Dark's woman sawed on their reins and backed quickly away as a bunch of *tejanos* ran for her. They pulled her back to her feet, but when they eased their hold on her, she threatened to crumple again. She looked vacantly at the faces of her own kind without even seeming to recognize them.

The *tejanos* carried her off. Some of them were shouting. The Kickapoo no longer tried to translate.

Another white man rushed from the building to wave Black Paint on to where they were supposed to camp. Storm Trail realized with a jolt that she recognized him. He was one of those who had come to them long ago with those bi-buls, and he had come again with the invitation to this white-eyes village. He was the one who had yelled at Raven.

Her good mood vanished and Storm Trail gave a small cry of alarm.

Her father looked at her mildly. "They will be happier with the captive that Spirit Talker brought from his Kotsoteka band. That one is a boy. He has not been beaten so badly."

The tipis want up on the outskirts of the town, the sturdy pale hides catching in the wind, rippling, then snapping taut as the women struggled with their lodge poles to pull everything into place. When Black Paint's tipi was up and finished, Storm Trail threw her parfleches inside.

"That is good enough," she decided. "I will straighten everything out when I come back."

She Smiles agreed eagerly. Storm Trail was startled again by how brave her old friend had become. Marriage to Kills In The Dark had truly changed her.

She looked around briefly for Yellow Fawn and Eyes Down, wishing suddenly, fiercely, that they could all share this together. But Yellow Fawn was still angry with her, and she did not see Eyes Down.

They hurried onto the first path they came to, a rutted stretch of dirt. It was packed hard beneath their moccasins. Storm Trail looked about at more stone buildings that sat pressed close to the trail, then she walked backward to look at everything again as they passed it.

"Smell," She Smiles urged.

Storm Trail drew in a deep breath. The air was amazing—ripe with pungent spices like she had never before encountered and fetid with too much unwashed humanity. "These *tejanos* are dirty," she muttered.

The sun glinted off the white stone of the buildings. She had to shield her eyes and squint to see the people—not just *tejanos,* she realized, but Mex-ee-cans and other Indians, too.

"Watch out!" She Smiles cried.

Storm Trail spun about. A white-eyes child rushed up to her and tugged on her short sleek hair.

"Why did he do that?" she gasped, batting his hand away.

"I do not know," She Smiles admitted. "Do you want to go back to our camp?"

Storm Trail pushed her chin up. "I am not afraid."

"No," She Smiles agreed. "But the council will be starting soon. I want to see that."

They hurried back the way they had come. As they reached the outskirts of the town again, more white-eyes men came from one of the stone buildings. Her father and all the other chiefs stood waiting for them in a big area where grass still grew—only it was not wild and lush like in Comancheria. It was short and looked matted. Storm Trail pulled up short.

The chiefs began walking to one of the buildings. Storm

Trail felt another thrill of fear run down her spine as her father bent and went in through a yawning black door.

"We should sit right here," she decided. She sank down in the grass. "We can see everything."

Even as she said it, other people began to join them. Her skin crawled as *tejanos* bumped into her, and she fought the urge to scrub her hands over herself where they touched her.

She could wash their dirt off later. For now, she glued her eyes on the shadowy door through which her father had gone.

After a while she grew bored. She wondered if there was a way she could actually see inside.

She Smiles noticed her expression. "Uh, oh." But then she shook her head with that strange new bravery. "Unless . . ."

Storm Trail nodded. "Yes. Look. There is a hole in the wall. See it halfway up there on the other side?" She motioned at the window, then she got to her feet. As she moved toward it, gunfire suddenly exploded.

In the space of a moment, the air filled with the stench of gun powder and the reeking metallic smell of blood. Screams echoed from the building as bullets pinged and ricocheted off the stone inside.

Storm Trail stumbled in horror, her feet suddenly getting tangled with those of hundreds of others. Everyone, white and red and Mex-ee-can, began rushing toward the council house.

She screamed as someone crashed into her, driving her down to her hands and knees. She looked up and saw her father stagger out of the door. He put his hand to his bloody forehead.

She had to get to him. There were bullets in that place. They had taken her mother! They could not take him, too!

What had happened?

She clawed her way up someone's leg—a warrior—and stood again just as white men burst from the building behind her father. They gunned him down.

Someone tried to hold her back—She Smiles, she realized. She beat at her with her fists and finally broke away. She shoved through the people, and got to where Black Paint had fallen.

"No," she choked. *"No, no, no!"* She fell to her knees beside him, sobbing, then looked up wildly. *"What have you done?"* she screamed at the milling white people.

Dazedly she registered that everyone was running away from the council house now. Squaws and children grabbed up weapons as they fled. She saw a Nermenuh boy shoot a *tejano* in the thigh with his little toy bow.

Get up. Help them. You are Nermenuh. She rocked back on her heels again and pushed to her feet, her hands wet with her father's blood.

Find a weapon, take Black Paint's knife. She bent over him, fumbling at his waist to find it. She sensed more than felt that still more white men were coming out of the building behind her. She shrieked again and spun on them, raising the blade.

She drove it into the chest of the very next white man who came through the door. He collapsed into her and even as she started to fall beneath him, the *tejano* behind him clubbed her with the butt end of his rifle, again and again. Pain cracked through her head like a million explosions.

The *tejano* kicked her, catching her in the belly as she went down. She felt her whole body jerk backward. Pain reverberated behind her eyes, but now it was as though she was floating above it all, as though she was watching someone else suffer. The white man kicked her again, grinning in satisfaction when he felt one of her ribs give way. Storm Trail tried to scream, but she had no voice.

The white man finally turned back to the plaza and opened fire.

Thorn nearly fell over the squaw when he finally made his way out the council house door. *Oh, Jesus, oh, God,* he swore, and then he said a prayer of thanks that the Injuns had not brought any more captives into the city because he had the terrifying feeling that everyone, white and red, was going to die here.

Most of the 'Manches were fleeing now, though some still tried to fight. But they were too outnumbered this time, Thorn thought, and their ranks were chaotic and disorganized. Squaws raced for the river. Even as he watched, one threw up her hands in a grotesque dance, her body twitching as bullets riddled her.

Bucks seized any available horse and raced for the outskirts. And the populace of San Antonio spilled into the streets, hating them for four years' worth of torment, for their arrogant superiority over white men, and for the women they had stolen and forced themselves upon. Thorn started to follow the swirling, shouting, shooting mob, then his feet stumbled to a stop and he only stared.

He saw the exact moment when the mood of the mob changed and became insane. At one point they were simply angry, and in the next moment they no longer cared about past insults. Plain simple bloodlust ran through them. Many of them had no idea why they were fighting any longer—they simply streamed through the streets, chasing down Comanches because the others were doing it. They killed without thought or provocation, and Thorn knew that later many would honestly wonder how they had come to have blood on their hands.

The wild throng surged along, firing after the fleeing Indians, killing many of their own people in the fusillade.

"Enough," Thorn whispered hoarsely. "Sweet Jesus, we're supposed to be *men*."

He looked around for Hays, for Johnny Moore, for any man he might count on to have some scruples and common sense. He turned back to the council house, and that was when he noticed the young squaw at the door, the one he had stepped over to get out here.

He had thought she was dead, but now she moaned and stirred. This time he noticed another young woman bending over her, sobbing.

Thorn made his way to them clumsily. "Come on."

The conscious girl saw him and shrieked in terror. He caught her arm and pulled her to her feet.

"Come on," he said again, forgetting that she couldn't understand him. "I'm not going to kill you. Let's go."

She fought him, then he realized that she was scrambling to get her friend.

"I'll bring her! Go on, get over there into the jail where you'll be safe. They won't look for you there. Go on!"

He bent and scooped the other squaw up in his arms. Only then did he see what was beneath her. The other girl wailed again. The one he held must have been with child. One delicate slender arm fell away from his hold, dropping downward—her hand was stained crimson as though at some point she had roused, had known what was happening, and had tried to hold the babe inside her.

"Jesus," he muttered again. He doubted if he would find a medic willing to care for her, not for a squaw. She was probably going to die anyway. But he carried her into the jail, laying her in a cell, and went to find a blanket to cover her with.

When he returned with it, the other girl was working frantically to warm her. Thorn watched them for a while, then went back out onto the streets to see if he could gather up any other survivors.

Maybe if he did, God would forgive him for being even marginally a part of this.

Twenty-seven

The hot, closed white-eyes building reeked of bodies and blood and excrement. Storm Trail opened her eyes and realized that the blood she smelled was her own.

Though there were at least twenty people squeezed into a space half the size of her lodge, no one touched her. She Smiles ferociously stood guard over her, pushing anyone away who would lean on her. An ache swelled in her belly.

The babe.

Her babe was gone. She felt a unique hollowness, as though she had been emptied of everything good and precious. She had not wanted a child. She hadn't been ready yet, still had winds to chase and games to play, and she could not imagine the shame it would bring, not because she had played with Raven—everyone played with someone—but because Raven would not be able to give her father all she was worth.

Until now, until this very moment, she had not even truly accepted that it had lived inside her. She had played with Raven so much, had stopped bleeding several moons ago, but she had not known what to do about it, so she had ignored it.

Now she grappled with the impossible pain of accepting that it had died. It had died unloved and unwanted . . . and now, when it was too late, she wanted it back. Unshed tears burned at her eyes. *Her babe.* She finally found her voice and gave a little keening sound.

She Smiles hunkered down beside her. "Friend? Are you awake?"

Storm Trail nodded and She Smiles began to cry.

"They killed us."

Yes, she remembered that part. She remembered being sure that she, too, would die when that *tejano* had bludgeoned her.

"Where are we?" she asked hoarsely.

She Smiles dragged a hand under her nose. "It is a long stone building. It looked safe so I brought us here. Then they brought others. But I do not know what this place is."

Storm Trail struggled to sit up. She Smiles helped her. They were in a long building with a path down the center. The People were crowded into cubicles up and down each wall. She did not see a single man among them.

She began to shake.

"Is this . . . all who live?"

She Smiles shook her head. "I do not know. I have not been outside to see. They will not let us out."

The men were probably all dead then.

A scream swelled in Storm Trail's throat, but she did not dare let it out because it would never end. Her father and His Horses, Crooked Nose and Bear Wound—all of them. Her brother? Her cousin? Had they killed them, too?

There was a commotion at one end of the strange building. Dazzling light speared into the rank-smelling gloom. A door opened. Some *tejanos* came in, and when the Nermenuh women saw them, they began screaming and howling.

A white-eyes threw meat into the cubicles. Long before they reached her, Storm Trail could smell that it was rotten. She did not care about food. She pushed at She Smiles. "Go to the front!"

Her friend looked at her dumbly.

"Go to those bars!" Her voice cracked. "Tell them you are a chief's daughter!"

She Smiles looked doubtful. "It will not do any good."

"Tell them!"

She could not do it herself, Storm Trail thought. Though she had managed to sit, she did not think her legs would hold her to stand. She Smiles was their only chance. If they did not get out of here, they would all die.

Raven, oh, Raven. Suddenly, crushing terror filled her chest. She could not breathe.

He had been right. He had been right about coming here, and if someone did not get back to the Penateka camp to warn him, he would die for it. She clawed for She Smiles's arm.

"Think what they will do to Raven! Our women will kill him. They will kill all our white-eyes when they learn of this!" She remembered again what had happened to that chief's son after the Pawnee fight. "You must get back there and tell him to go!"

She Smiles finally understood. Her expression changed, going from confusion to a gape of horror.

She shoved and pushed and elbowed her way through the others in their cubicle. She hurled herself at the metal bars. "Our fathers will kill you if you do not release us! They will come back here and burn your village!"

Storm Trail shuddered. *Oh, friend, our fathers are dead.* But the white-eyes did not know that, could not know that there were not hundreds more men in the Penateka camp, plotting vengeance.

Storm Trail managed to add her voice to She Smiles's. "My father is one of the most important men in council! They will avenge my death! You think you have won but you will die for this! You will *die!*"

The little bunch of white-eyes stopped in front of their cell. Storm Trail's heart hurtled. There was a Kickapoo with them.

"Tell them!" she shrieked at him. "Tell them who I am and what they have done!"

The Kickapoo responded uncertainly, in words and in sign. "They have come to release one of you. One of you must go back to your people and tell them that you will all be held hostage until they get all their white-eyes back. They will trade—the chief's families for their own."

"I will go!" She Smiles gasped. "I will tell them."

Storm Trail felt something wild pound at her temples. *She* needed to go. She had an instinct that it was imperative that she go, that she see Raven, touch him, one last time . . . her very own crazy *tejano*.

That numbed her. She would not know how to say goodbye to him. She thought maybe it was better that she could not travel.

Spirits, to have to watch him go!

"Tell Raven first," she croaked. "Then tell the others what has happened. He must have a chance to get away."

There was a horrible clanking noise. The bars opened. Those in their cubicle surged forward as one, trying to get out. Someone clawed at Storm Trail's hair to get leverage to climb over her. Feet punched into her thighs, and knees gouged her belly. She screamed aloud. Something was broken inside her. The pain was excruciating.

One of the white men reached inside for She Smiles, wrenching her out before the others got too close. Storm Trail closed her eyes, slumping against the concrete wall, and she prayed to her spirit-protectors that this time Raven would listen, he would go, he would know it was not a trick but a gift from her heart.

Though the night was deep and the camp slept, Raven heard the faint scratching sound at his door flap as soon as it came. He had been waiting for it.

Too much time had passed. Too many suns had gone by without word from San Antonio. The feeling of doom that had dogged him as Storm Trail had ridden out had grown with each passing day until it was a black gnarly thing inside him.

She lives. Surely she lives.

He kneeled and reached for the door flap, pushing it out. He found She Smiles there. The grief that assailed him made him rock back on his heels, almost dizzy.

"Where is she? Where is Storm?" he asked hoarsely.

She Smiles pushed past him and scurried inside. A new flash of horror crossed her face at his question. Then she shuddered, feeling the ache of losing him all over again.

"Storm Trail is in a building with many others," she managed. "They are prisoners. All the chiefs are dead. They shot them at the council."

Though he had been expecting such an atrocity, the truth of it pushed bile up into Raven's throat. "Black Paint?"

"Gone," She Smiles whispered. "You must go."

He looked at her dazedly. "Yes. Yes, I will gather the warriors who remain here and—"

"No!" she cried. "Not to San An-tone-yo! Some of the warriors live. Wolf Dream and Lost Coyote . . . they encircle that village now, hiding, waiting for some way to get in and get our women and children back. I saw them when the white-eyes let me go. The *tejanos* sent me to tell Paya-yuca that until we return their people to them, they will keep our women."

"We will trade nothing," Raven snarled. "Wolf Dream needs help."

"No!" She Smiles shook her head frantically. "You cannot help him! You must go back to your own kind now."

His face blanched, then fierce color came to his cheeks. "This is my home."

"Soon I will have to go tell Paya-yuca what has happened!" She Smiles rushed on. "When the women learn of it, they will kill you. They will kill all the white-eyes we have here."

"They adopted us, took us in as their own!" he yelled. "I am a warrior! I have coups, a herd—"

"It will not matter now!" she shrieked, then she, too, went pale, wondering if any of the others had heard them.

Raven wrenched his sawed-off rifle from the lodge liner.

"No!" she wept. "You must listen." And then she knew the only way he would. "She will not live, Raven." She flinched with the lie. She thought Storm Trail would probably survive. If anyone did, it would be her, so stubborn, so strong. But perhaps she would not . . . how long could she live in that place without a healer to tend to her?

"She was . . . barely alive when I left, barely breathing." It was the only way to make Raven go, to make sure that he, at least, lived. That was what she told herself.

She watched the fury drain from Raven's face until there was no expression left at all.

"They beat her," she whispered. "I was with her. I saw it. She killed one of them when the fighting started, but then the next one hit her, over and over again, with his gun. He kicked her. Her babe is gone."

He jerked visibly. "Her babe?"

"You did not know?"

"I . . . no." On top of everything else, betrayal clawed at him, ripping at his throat. Raven began gathering parfleches.

"Please," She Smiles whispered. "Take me with you. I do not want to stay with my husband!"

He looked at her incredulously. "Why do you speak of that now? Your friend is dying—" the word was vile in his throat, on his tongue "—and you worry about Kills In The Dark?"

His words made her recoil, but she was desperate. "You need my help. I will go tell Paya-yuca what has happened, then I will go to the herd. I will get two of your ponies and meet you on the east side of camp. You cannot make it to the herd on your own. It is on the other side of the camp from here. If you try, they could see you. . . ." She trailed off uncertainly. She could no longer read his expression.

Raven knew she was right. She was right in so many ways, and he felt his stomach heave. He dragged a hand over his mouth and tilted his head back to control the reflex, staring at the smoke hole.

Yes, he would have a hard time getting to the herd on his own, and, yes, the women would probably try to kill him. He remembered Storm Trail speaking of something like that the night she had thrown herself at him in the pony herd. She said they had killed a chief's son who had inadvertently been responsible for mass slaughter.

A chief's son. Someone born Nermenuh. He was only a mongrel captive whose blood kind had destroyed them, and now his mentor was gone.

"I do not care," he said, his voice strangled. He looked down at the parfleche he held, the one this same girl had made for him so very long ago. Everything was gone, he thought, everything was torn, ruined. "Come if you like."

She Smiles gave a sound of breathless relief. It was not the response she had hoped for, but once they were away . . .

"Leave the camp now, before I go to Paya-yuca," she urged, and left the lodge.

Raven gathered the last few possessions he could easily take with him. He should have told her to bring more than two ponies. *His herd.* He would lose his whole herd, everything he had worked for. He had nearly had enough to buy her. Rage boiled up in his throat again, urging him to fight back somehow, to do *something* to save it all, but there was nothing.

Then he had a new thought, one for all the white children in the camp. He would not be able to save them either. He should have told She Smiles to try to get some of them, but of course she would not have been able to do so without waking and alerting their parents.

He left the lodge quietly, making his way to the outskirts of the camp. He looked back once. The tipis glowed a ghostly white in the moonlight, and his throat ached with intolerable loss.

Twenty-eight

Kills In The Dark bit down on his tongue as he looked around the camp from his seat beneath the arbor. It was the only way he could make sure he did not smile.

The Penateka were numb, shattered, their numbers decimated between those who had been killed in San An-tone-yo and those who remained captive there. But he would help them collect the ashes of their defeat, he thought, and they would be grateful. They would revere him now, finally.

He had plans. He bit until pain throbbed.

It bothered him not in the least that his wife was gone. He had never liked her much to begin with. With or without her, His Horses had requested that he sit in his stead on this council. Now that greedy nagging chief was dead, and Kills In The Dark intended that his seat here should last for a very long time.

Best of all, Raven was gone.

The People still spoke of him, but they were mostly words of speculation, and soon that would die down, too. Fate had truly smiled upon him, Kills In The Dark thought. His spirit-protectors had finally returned to him. They had been gone for a long time, as though they, too, were ashamed of him for what had happened with Raven. But now they were back, sheltering him with their power.

Kills In The Dark could no longer restrain himself. He grinned.

"I wonder what you find amusing under the circumstances," Paya-yuca snapped.

Kills In The Dark sobered. "I have a plan." *And if it is successful, you will never get me off this council.* He knew that Paya-yuca, and especially Medicine Eagle, disliked him. He had even wondered briefly if there was a way to kill them as well. He had tasted a little bit of power now, and he liked it. He intended to get more.

"I think I will give these white-eyes what they want," he went on. "I would ransom back our women."

Medicine Eagle made a sound of disgust. "That is your plan? What would you ransom them with? Your twelve ponies?"

Kills In The Dark colored. For a moment his temper blazed. He clamped down on it. "With *tejano* captives, of course."

Paya-yuca waved a dismissing hand. "Do you see any? I do not."

"Not all of them were killed," Kills In The Dark pointed out. "Some of them ran."

Medicine Eagle nodded, reluctant to agree with this man about anything. But it was true. Raven had escaped, and Snow Dancing had taken his wife and their adopted daughter, Turtle, away from the camp at the first sign of trouble as well.

"And not all of the other bands killed their white-eyes," Kills In The Dark went on.

"Why would they give them to you to get back Penateka women and children?" Paya-yuca demanded. It was mostly Penateka who were being held captive.

"Because some of those Penateka women are kin to them. They probably will not give their white-eyes to us, but perhaps they would be amenable to a token trade."

Kills In The Dark shot to his feet. "I will ride out and talk to some of these bands now. I will leave this sun. I need only one or two children. I can tell the *tejanos* that it is a show of good faith. If they release our women, I will bring back more of our captives."

They would respect him then, curse their mangy old hides.

* * *

Storm Trail could not believe her eyes when she saw who walked down the center path of the building. *Kills In The Dark?*

Memory and emotion assailed her so swiftly she felt dizzy. There was sweeping relief, then a curious, almost detached wonder. How could she ever have thought she loved this man?

He walked with the same bandy-legged strut that had once made her shiver. But now she could plainly see the avarice and the bitterness that etched his face and made it ugly.

"Hei, haitsi." She tried to say it softly, seductively, but her voice cracked and it was nasal. The *tejanos* so rarely brought them water. Someone had died in the next cell this sun, and no white-eyes had come yet to remove the body. The stench was sickening, and she had to try to talk without breathing too much of it in.

It did not matter. Kills in The Dark heard her anyway.

His eyes snapped around to her. Selfish satisfaction flared over his face.

He was not glad to see her alive, she realized. He was only glad that someone of such good blood was still living, someone who could serve his purposes. She wondered what those purposes were this time, who he wanted to hurt. She thought he probably just wanted to take credit for bringing at least one of the prisoners back, something no other chief or warrior had yet been able to do.

Anger and revulsion made her head hurt. She wanted to refuse to go with him. But if she did not go, he would just take someone else. She had to live. She had to get out of here. He would know if Raven had gotten away safely.

"Please, *haitsi*," she breathed, smiling at him.

"This one," Kills In The Dark said shortly, and she let out a weak breath of relief. "I want this woman."

She fought the urge to cry out in joy as one of the *tejanos* slid open the bars. Kills In The Dark caught her arm and twisted it painfully as he dragged her from the cell. Her blood moved wildly with this first pitiful taste of freedom. She stumbled into the pathway, then gasped and shrank back.

Behind Kills In The Dark was the white man who had come to their camp twice, with the bi-buls and the invitation here. She had dreamed of him so many times while she had been trapped here—horrible, terrifying dreams of blood and screams and bullets, dreams of this man carrying her. And she knew in that moment that they were not dreams. They were memories. But She Smiles had said *she* brought them here. A strange unsettled feeling began to make Storm Trail's pulse skip.

He spoke in his twangy white-eyes tongue. "Tell them that for each white child they bring back, we will release a prisoner of their choosing. Can you understand me at all? If you do not cooperate, they will begin killing the prisoners in another month."

Storm Trail shook her head mutely. A Mexican with them translated halfheartedly.

"The buck, this one here, brought a woman. He gets you," he said shortly. "If you bring back more girls and boys, then more of you can go home."

Kills In The Dark took her arm again and tried to pull her down the center path to the door. Storm Trail nearly fell.

"Come," Kills In The Dark snapped, "before they change their minds. They gave me one—*one*—woman and I do not intend to lose you."

Storm Trail struggled to walk. She had not done it in so long. Then strong hands caught her and steadied her from behind.

It was the white man.

Revulsion and loathing did the impossible. Heat burst through her and with it came strength, allowing her to walk again, if only out of sheer determination.

She made her way outside unsteadily behind Kills In The Dark. The sunlight was blinding. Tears sprang painfully to her eyes after so long in her dark dank hell. He reached back for her, but she wrenched away, blinking.

She was free now.

"Do you think I am grateful?" she sneered. "I know what you did to my friend, I remember how you betrayed me! Now I thank my spirit-protectors that you did *not* buy me. You will never be half the warrior Raven—"

"Raven is gone. He took my wife. He thinks he got the best of me again, but now I am rid of both of them. And you will be mine after all. When we get back, I will claim you." He laughed, an ugly sound. "It seems I need a wife again. Did you not offer your father's hearth once before? He may be dead, but Wolf Dream is not, and you will still bring me prestige."

Storm Trail's vision finally cleared. She stared at him. "You lie," she breathed.

"You will see for yourself when we get back and the white warrior is gone with her." He shrugged, unperturbed. Somehow in that moment, she knew he was telling the truth.

Raven had left with She Smiles.

She shrieked again wordlessly, flailing at Kills In The Dark when he would have held her. It did not even matter that Wolf Dream was alive after all. She wanted to go back inside where it was dark and nothing mattered, where maybe this time she would die.

The ride home was a nightmare. Storm Trail had thought nothing could be worse than that white-eyes cell, but perhaps she was wrong.

She rode behind Kills In The Dark, holding herself stiffly away from him. She could not bear touching him. Once when they stopped to camp, he grabbed her breast, laughing again when she jerked away. Both She Smiles and his old captive woman had given up wrenching away from him a long time ago.

Then he left her alone because he said soon he would own her and he could do with her what he liked. He could wait. Storm Trail shrugged. She was dead inside, almost beyond caring. She could barely deal with this pain. She could not cope with the future.

It took them five suns to get back to the camp. The Penateka closed their love and care around her. Lost Coyote carried her to Paya-yuca's lodge, and she thought she saw her brother's eyes shine with something more than disbelief that she was alive. Mountain took her in and cut the tattered doeskin from her body. Medicine Eagle came to tend to her bruises. Then Mountain wrapped her in a warm robe and left her beside the fire. But Storm Trail did not sleep.

For a while she only stroked the buffalo hide, whole and untattered, smelling neither of death nor dying. Then her thoughts slid back to Raven.

He had told her that touching had not felt the same way with She Smiles. The night when she had nearly gone to Too Much, when he had stopped her, he had said that. So why would he prefer that other woman?

How could he do this? None of this made sense!

They had just been playing, as everyone played, but . . . it had felt like more than that because she had been with him so long, in such a different, special way. She had been playing with her best friend, she realized with a jolting pain, the only person she had ever known who could best her. Their bodies had matched, melded, created new life, and she could not bear the ache of losing him to another.

It was more than pride. It was the utmost betrayal.

She hugged herself, groaning silently. She had known she would hurt if he went, but he had taken her gift of life and he had shared it with another. If she could just touch him now, she would claw his eyes out, she thought, then she sobbed softly.

If she could just touch him now.

* * *

In the morning she roused herself enough to find Wolf Dream. She went to his lodge and scratched softly on the door.

"*Tahmah,*" she whispered. "Brother."

Wolf Dream came, though it was forbidden that he should. She was grown now, and should not be alone with him. She was afraid he would be angry, but Wolf Dream only looked steadily over her right shoulder, and his strong, handsome face was haggard.

Suddenly she was afraid. He would do it, she thought wildly. Kills In The Dark had saved her. Wolf Dream might feel he owed that warrior something and give her to him even though he did not have the bridal price.

"Please, do not let him claim me!" she gasped. "I could live with anything but that! Do not do it out of gratitude!"

Something ticked at Wolf Dream's jaw. "What are you talking about?" he asked impatiently.

"Kills In The Dark."

He scowled. "He has not spoken to me."

"He will."

Wolf Dream shrugged. "It will do him no good, not yet."

Relief was the first good thing she had felt in over a moon. Her knees almost bent with it, then something about her brother's choice of words alerted her.

"What do you mean? Not *yet?*" She thought fast. "He is not worthy of me! She Smiles lied. Her father never asked Kills In The Dark to sit on that council! It was something she made up so that she could go to San An-tone-yo!"

Wolf Dream's face hardened enough to scare her. "How dare you girls meddle with the council?"

Storm Trail's spine went straight. "She was desperate, as I will be if you give me to him." Why was she defending She Smiles after what she had done? Because the whole world felt shattered, she thought, and nothing made any sense anyway.

"He would only try to claim me to make sure he stays on that council," she managed more calmly.

"He cannot claim you," he said impatiently. "Not until the first spring moon."

"The spring moon?" She looked at him dumbly. "Why then?"

"Our father already made a bargain for you," he said flatly. "I cannot give you until then. He gave his word, and I must stand by it. I would not disgrace his memory."

It felt as though her heart shrank. It went very, very small and still, and then it exploded, making her blood rush. "Who?" she managed. But she knew. Of course she knew.

"Black Paint told me of the pact before we went to that place, that town. Perhaps he knew something would go wrong. He wanted me to know of the deal he had made so it could be upheld."

"Who?" she cried again.

"It stands only until the first spring moon. If he does not return by then, then I can give you to another. You have no one now, and this is your sixteenth winter. You need a man."

If he does not return by then. "Raven bought me?" *Then* he had gone back to She Smiles?

She reeled away from her brother in confusion. Raven had bought her. Then she laughed wildly, hysterically. He was also her only hope.

If he did not come back and make good on his pact, Wolf Dream would almost certainly give her to Kills In The Dark.

Twenty-nine

She Smiles wept quietly, rolled in her bedding on the other side of the lodge. The endless broken sound clawed at Raven's nerves.

She had wanted this. She had wanted to come with him. And now, night after night, she wept for her choice.

She wanted to go home. It was not possible, even if he wanted to oblige her. Winter had come to this north country with bone-crunching cruelty. The snow was too deep for their ponies to get through.

When the thaw came, he would be ready to go himself. He would do it in triumph, he thought, not ruined by the Penateka's betrayal. He only prayed that the thaw came to this high country before it was too late. *The spring moon.*

He reached over to his own bedding from his seat beside the hearth. He rummaged around beneath it until he found his magic repeating gun. He laid it thoughtfully in front of the fire. She Smiles quieted and sat up to look at it as well. "What are you thinking?"

So many things. "Nothing. Go to sleep."

"You hate me."

If he said yes, she would start crying again. He wanted to do it if only to prevent further discussion. But in fact, he did not hate her. It was not her fault that she was a constant reminder of everything he had lost.

Neither one of them could have anticipated his longing.

When he looked at She Smiles, he saw her and Yellow Fawn

and Storm running through the high grasses, laughing. He did not think of their brief time together as lovers. He saw her as the friend of the woman he had bargained for, then had been forced to leave behind.

He was absolutely sure that Storm Trail was alive. He had taken She Smiles that night and had left impulsively, without thinking it out, because she had said there was no time. And she had probably been right. Before they had ridden very far from the Penateka camp, he had heard the first screams of the children. Those screams still echoed in his dreams. He hated the Penateka fiercely for what they had done, and he hated the white men for causing them such grief and anguish as to bring it about.

But as the moons had passed, he had become more and more convinced that if Storm Trail had died, he would have *felt* it somehow. He thought something inside him would have died as well. Instead, it ached. It reached back to that Penateka country.

Finally he had to ask the question that had been tormenting him for moons now. "Why? Why did you do it? *Why did you tell me she was dying?*"

She Smiles began trembling. She pulled her robe more closely about her. "She was." They all had been, she thought desperately. None of those people in San An-tone-yo could have survived unless they got out of there. And those white men had not been about to let them go.

But rumor was starting to come back to them, even in this high country, that some of those people had escaped anyway. The rumors said that many of the Penateka in that horrible building had gotten out of that place and had come home. And after that, She Smiles thought, Raven barely spoke to her at all.

She began weeping again.

"Stop it!"

"You think I betrayed you," she sobbed, "but I did not. You are alive, and you would not be if I had not made you go."

Some of the rigid tension went out of his shoulders. In truth, he felt sorry for her.

Had she thought that by coming with him, they would be lovers again? Had she thought he would want her as he once had? Color crept up Raven's neck as he remembered that first moon after they had left, before he had understood that if Storm had died, he would have felt it. He had tried to make love with She Smiles, had tried to heal himself with the warmth she offered. But even then, perhaps, his body had known what his heart had not realized yet.

Storm Trail was alive. She was waiting for him. Maybe she would try to kill him again for this when she saw him, but she waited.

His body had not cooperated, had not allowed him to make love with She Smiles instead. And that had been the first time she had bleated that he hated her. Then she had come to realize that he was not going to try again, that she had exchanged her home, her remaining kin, for nothing. And that was when she had started crying.

He picked up the gun and examined it. "I have over forty ponies now, from those rides into Mexico." He had gone with Nokoni again. He had a goal again, and he would work toward it wherever, in any way he could. "If I trade this gun for one hundred more, that will be enough to go back and get her."

If time did not run out on him, he thought. If the spring moon got near and the snows still had not melted, he decided he would find a way to travel through them on his own.

This was the only magic gun among the Nermenuh. If there was another, surely he would have heard of it. The weapon was precious beyond compare, but if he could ever talk another war band into going east, he was reasonably sure that he could get another one.

Across the lodge She Smiles finally lay down again with a noisy wet sniff. Raven closed his eyes, gritted his teeth, and got up to find Nokoni, taking the gun with him.

Thirty

Jack Hays was drunk for one of the rare times since Thorn had known him. He was also very angry.

"Never in all my years have I encountered such a bumbling, half-assed, ineffectual group of . . . of nincompoops!"

Johnny Moore choked on his whiskey. *"Nincompoops?"*

"It's not funny," Hays said darkly. "This imbecilic legislature has thwarted my good efforts at every turn. Lamar took a misguided stand, and now . . ." He finally trailed off morosely, as though someone had let his air out.

Thorn thought he did have a gripe. Of the sixty-plus hostages they had helped retain in the San Antonio jail, only twelve remained. Of those twelve, two were toothless old men. Three were toothless old women. And one was a child barely old enough to toddle. Almost the entire remainder of the seized Comanches had escaped.

"Well," Moore said, drinking again, "welcome to politics, gentlemen. Our grand ol' Republic covers a good many square miles. I daresay Lamar is concerned with the God-fearing men back east in Galveston and all those towns along the Gulf. No one's raped *their* women. No one's stolen *their* children. And they're not likely to re-elect a president who orders the cold-blooded murder of a bunch of elderly folks and swaddling babes, no matter what color they are."

"There's no way Lamar could have put those hostages in front of a firing squad," Thorn agreed bitterly. "Jesus, the hue and cry that would have resulted!"

"Then he should not have promised such retribution," Hays snapped. "My God, we look like fools!"

"Assuming either of those squaws took the message back," Thorn said. "We can't be sure they told their chiefs we were going to kill the hostages."

"It doesn't matter. We *are* fools," Hays muttered. And he was one of the biggest ones of all.

The captive who had been traded for the second woman had turned out to be young Rachel Plummer—not so young now, Thorn thought. She had been among those taken from the Parker Fort, and she was presumably back among the bosom of her family now, with no ransom having been paid for her. That sly-looking buck had brought her in of his own volition.

It had been rumored that her husband had divorced her in her absence. Still Lamar was looking like a hero in the Parkers' eyes. And Lamar had never risked one greasy hair on his precious scalp going up on that damned scarp.

Thorn turned his attention back to Hays and Moore.

"There was nothing Lamar could do but let them escape," Johnny was expounding. "To release them outright would mean eating far too much crow from the locals."

"So the guards turned their backs and whistled 'Dixie' while the vermin slipped away," Hays grated.

"Ah, but there's hope yet, my friends," Moore promised. "They say Houston is going to try to wrest the presidency back from Lamar come this next election."

Hays groaned. "Our resident bleeding heart."

"At the very least, that bleeding heart never stirred up a hornet's nest with false bravado that he couldn't possibly back up," Thorn snapped. "Now we've got a bunch of pissed-off savages on our hands with nothing to show for it." He stood up irritably, slamming his glass back onto the table. "We have no hostages," he muttered. "We have none of our own captives. We have *nothing*."

* * *

"We must strike back with our full fury. I say we should go all the way to the water," Kills In The Dark pronounced.

Satisfied, he sat back, a grin on his face that raised the hairs on Storm Trail's nape. The men were gathered beneath the arbor, and she was helping Mountain serve them from the antelope skewered over the nearby fire.

She could not believe he was still sitting on the council after she had told Wolf Dream the truth. But His Horses was dead and could not verify her story either way. She Smiles was not here to tell what she had done. It was Storm Trail's word versus Kills In The Dark's.

Still his seat was precarious. His Horses' supposed request would not be enough to keep him on the council indefinitely, and perhaps that was what Wolf Dream was counting on. Already She Smiles's family was looking elsewhere for advice and wisdom, bypassing her husband, and a man held his seat on council only through the respect of his extended family. Lost Coyote was sitting in Black Paint's seat for just that reason. Lately all her family went to him when they had a problem.

Storm Trail was thinking that when she finally registered what Kills In The Dark had said. The water? "What water?"

He ignored her. She could hardly blame him. She was a woman. She had no right to ask a question in council.

Raven would have answered her. *Do not think of him. Do not.*

"I say we can gather all the Nermenuh war bands together," Kills In The Dark went on, and his voice was more strident than forceful. "We can burn a path of death and destruction from the scarp all the way to their *tejano* towns by the big water. We will destroy everything we come across and leave no white man standing. They killed our chiefs! Our council!"

"Not enough of them," someone dared to murmur.

"Other tribes have attempted such rides and failed," said Paya-yuca. "I heard of the Shawnee doing something like that once. Now the white men live in their valleys."

"The Shawnee are not Nermenuh!" Kills In The Dark shouted.

Oh, he was getting good at this, Storm Trail thought, shuddering. Even her brother looked his way with narrow-eyed consideration. Everyone gathered around the arbor began talking heatedly and excitedly, in a way they hadn't done for a very long time.

Kills In The Dark looked her way in the commotion and grinned slyly. Her belly heaved. *A hundred horses.* And the spring moon was coming fast.

Kills In The Dark jumped to his feet with a flourish. "I will enlist the help of other bands, and I will lead them in ultimate vengeance against those coyote-scum white men!"

Storm Trail's mouth went dry. It was perhaps the only way he could gather the necessary ponies to buy her. If he did that, Wolf Dream would *definitely* give her to him.

She had promised herself that she would never forgive Raven. She could not bear the thought of being *his,* especially after what he had done. But now, she was beginning to want him to come back more fervently than she hated him.

Word of the Penateka's ambitious ride reached the Quohadi before the snows began to melt.

Raven was seated at the Quohadi arbor when it happened. There were seven chiefs, including Iron Shirt, Nokoni's father. Iron Shirt wanted to buy the magic gun. Nokoni had arranged the deal. Iron Shirt had been avid to smoke over it and close it for moons now, but something within Raven had kept holding back . . . waiting.

For what? For this, he realized instinctively, watching strangers approach the camp.

They were Nermenuh, but not Penateka. At least he did not recognize them. They traveled on foot, struggling through the drifts. Raven leaned back again just as he was about to place the magic gun on the ground in front of Iron Shirt.

"Give me that," the chief said harshly as Raven tucked the little revolver back into the string of his breechclout.

"Not yet. We have not smoked yet."

"You are a liar, a cheat, like all of your kind!" the chief charged. The others stiffened. "We had a deal!"

"My kind is Nermenuh now," Raven said absently as he watched the approaching warriors get closer. "And I know as well as you do that no deal is final until it is smoked upon. You are trying to take advantage of ignorance I no longer possess."

Someone dared to chuckle. Iron Shirt sighed. "What do these men want?" he wondered, looking up at the visitors now as well.

"They are Yamparika," someone murmured.

Raven's pulse picked up. Something alive and rushing replaced his blood, though he could not have said why.

"What could possess them to travel in this moon?" someone asked.

Something urgent, Raven thought. Something big.

It took an infernally long time for the two travelers to be welcomed and fed and warmed. Iron Shirt shared a smoke with them. Raven was careful not to indulge in the pipe when it came his way. He caught the sly old man looking at him, then Iron Shirt grinned and shook his head.

"You are a clever one. A smart one."

Raven nodded. Modesty had never been one of his problems, at least not to hear Storm Trail tell it.

His heart spasmed again with the memory of her.

"We bring word from the Penateka," one of the Yamparika said finally. "Their horses could not make it this far north in this season, so we carry their message for them. They would take the war back to the *tejanos* again, at the very first thaw."

One of the Quohadi chiefs nodded. "Of course they would want to do that. They suffered atrociously at the hands of those white-eyes."

"They want us to join them. All the Nermenuh."

"What for? We have no quarrel with the *tejanos,* at least not as those Penateka do."

Raven scowled. None of the Quohadi had gone to San Antonio. It had simply been too far for them to ride to meet with enemies they would just as soon kill anyway. The white-eyes had nothing the Quohadi wanted. They were still very leery of the magic guns, and with the exception of Iron Shirt, few of them coveted them enough to want to trade for them.

"The Penateka say they are only the first band to be decimated by these *tejanos,*" the Yamparika man explained. "They say that if the white-eyes are not destroyed now, if they are not swept from their Tex-us once and for all, our other bands will suffer next."

"If we do not go near them, we have nothing to fear," one of the old chiefs muttered.

Raven cleared his throat. "The Penateka did not invite contact with them. Those white-eyes just kept sending messengers into our camp."

"The Penateka would bring together all the war bands, from every faction of the Nermenuh," the Yamparika man went on. "Every man of fighting age. Any woman who wishes to go. The *tejanos* could not hope to best such strength. The Penateka talk of going all the way to the water, killing everyone and everything in our path."

The idea appealed to Iron Shirt's Nermenuh heart. So strong, so destructive and powerful—no enemy would be able to touch them. "Will your Yamparika war bands go?"

"Yes, we will send many men. If nothing else, the trip should provide many horses and scalps."

"And the Tanima? The Tenawa? What of the Kotsoteka?"

"All of those bands will send warriors as well."

"I will think about this," Iron Shirt decided.

"I will go. Any man here who wishes to be a part of this can ride with me," Raven said, standing abruptly.

"You think you are a war band leader now?" Iron Shirt demanded, amazed.

Raven looked at him levelly. "If any men choose to follow me, I suppose I will be."

"You would do it to claim that woman without parting with your gun," Nokoni said quietly. Of all the Quohadi, Raven had confided only in him. They had become strong friends over the moons. Nokoni knew what it was to crave a certain woman beyond all sense or reason, to be willing to try anything to have her.

"Other men going on this ride could claim a hundred ponies as well," Nokoni pointed out. "A ride like this holds much opportunity for warriors with even moderate skills."

"Yes," Raven agreed tersely.

"If your friend—" he used the Nermenuh word for father, and Raven flinched "—if he did not tell of your bargain before he died, then your woman could go to the first man who offers a hundred. Perhaps she already has. You should take my father's ponies and go back for her right away."

Raven smiled thinly. "No." Oh, he was tempted. But it was more than just going back. It was a matter of going back stronger, more powerful than before. He'd rather go back with the gun *and* with a hundred horses to spare.

He doubted if Storm Trail would expect him to do anything else.

"You are crazy, my friend," said Nokoni. "I think I will go with you just to see if you can do this."

Raven was surprised. "What of the magic guns?" Nokoni was more wary of them than anyone.

Nokoni shrugged. "Some day I will have to sit in that old man's place," he joked, motioning at his father. "Who will respect a coyote with his tail between his legs?"

Raven laughed, then sobered. "Thank you, *haitsi*, friend."

There was a low moaning sound from outside the council circle. They both looked around sharply. Nokoni's beautiful blond-haired wife stared at them, aghast, her throat working.

"Do not go back there." Naduah mouthed the words. "Please."

Nokoni reached for her hand, drawing her away from the council. "It will be fine," Raven heard him say. "I must do this."

Raven watched them go. He understood what Naduah was afraid of. He had talked to her a great deal when he had first gotten here—a white woman who had joined these magnificent proud people in much the same manner he had. Naduah was afraid that if her husband had anything at all to do with those *tejanos,* they would somehow find out where she was and steal her back.

Raven knew her terror was not entirely groundless. He knew of at least one white man who wanted very badly to find her, the man with the dark mustache and the rude, intrusive eyes who had invited them to that treacherous council in San Antonio. Raven remembered what that man had asked him. Then he had not known the answer.

Now he did. Now he knew that Naduah, wife of Nokoni, was Cynthia Ann Parker.

Thirty-one

"This will be glorious," Yellow Fawn said as Kills In The Dark's great war band left the Penateka camp.

Eyes Down came to ride with them. Nearly everyone had escaped from San An-tone-yo this past winter. Even Star Line was back. And now, every band except the distant Quohadi would exact vengeance for what had been done to them, and for the chiefs' deaths.

Perhaps even the Quohadi would join them eventually—Storm Trail had heard Wolf Dream and Lost Coyote talking about it, and they had both thought they would. It was just that those men had to ride so far to join them, and Kills In The Dark had been impatient to set off, unwilling to wait for them any longer.

Every other band was represented, and nearly all the Penateka women and children were riding as well. There were easily fifteen hundred Nermenuh, all told.

From somewhere in the immense moving throng, people began singing. Storm Trail kicked her mare and went after them. She hesitated, then warily lifted her voice to join the others.

This time would be different. Nothing bad would happen. This was a war band, not a council, and the Nermenuh were simply too strong.

Jack Hays was out patrolling somewhere with his Ranger battalion. Johnny Moore was upstairs in the room he had rented above the saloon. By now, Thorn thought, Moore would be dandified and spit-polished, every buckle and every bit of brass on his old American uniform gleaming. Moore had been invited to a gala event at the president's home to raise funds for the Republic. Thorn's company had not been requested.

He pushed his glass back at the bartender, putting a spin on it. "Another."

The bartender obliged. Thorn was about to put the glass to his lips when the saloon doors banged open. They swung wildly back and forth as a man came inside. Thorn recognized him as a Ranger, though not one of Jack's men.

"Where's Hays?" the Ranger demanded.

"Out and about somewhere, chasing 'Manches," the bartender supplied. The three men were his most regular customers. He estimated his take upon whether or not Hays, Moore, and Thorn were all in town, and when they would be back.

The stranger nodded at this information. "Pray God he doesn't find them."

"Why?" Thorn asked, startled.

"Because Ben McCulloch—Fifth Battalion—just picked up sign of a war party coming down off the scarp. Sent me back here to find Hays, to alert everybody. We got trouble."

"We've always got trouble," Thorn said dryly, but, in truth, he knew McCulloch to be a sensible pragmatic man. It wasn't like him to throw a fit over nothing. "Must be a hell of a lot of sign," he mused aloud.

"Yeah," the man said, dragging in breath. "Looks like they're thousands strong this time."

Thorn felt his heart stall. "A *thousand?*"

"No. No, sir. *Thousands.* More than one, Ben says. Maybe three or four."

Thorn pushed away from the bar. "Sweet Jesus."

The man headed for the door. "Grab a gun, mister. Ben says the way they're headed, they're on a beeline straight here to San Antonio."

* * *

The war band approached the town of the treacherous council four nights after they left the scarp. The darkness became sibilant with the terrified voices of the women. The warriors rode among them, motioning at them furiously to be quiet. Wolf Dream rode close to Storm Trail and her friends, forcing them to turn their ponies southward.

"Why?" she whispered. "What are we doing?"

Wolf Dream kept to propriety and did not answer her, but Too Much slowed his pony to explain.

"We will not strike that place," he said quietly. "It is a death place. There's too much bad medicine there. Our women will not go close to it, and it is probably still well guarded anyway."

"So what will we do?" asked Yellow Fawn.

"There is a small town not far from here," he explained, his gaze lingering on her. "They call it Vik-toor-ya. We will strike there."

It was dawn before any of the warriors talked to them again. They had gone many suns without sleep, but no one seemed to care. Storm Trail felt something hot and ready scoot through her blood.

As light began to spread over the sky, she saw that they were surrounded by low rolling hills. They had reached Vik-toor-ya. She saw the town out beyond the dip of a valley.

Someone shrieked from that direction. It was not a Nermenuh voice. One of the scouts came racing back to them.

"They had a guard out with their horses. We killed him, but the sound has alerted the town."

Kills In The Dark gave a curdling war cry. "Now!" he screamed. "Now!"

Raven and Nokoni closed in on Victoria just behind Kills In The Dark's war band, with seventy-two Quohadi warriors. They dismounted and melted into the hills to stare at the place. Some charred adobe walls still stood. Embers glowed red.

The wind carried the faint echo of women sobbing and the stench of burnt animal flesh.

Raven laughed softly. After a moment Nokoni's voice joined his, and then other men chuckled as well. One of the warriors howled like a wolf, a sound of triumph. From the town the weeping turned to screams again as the man's cry echoed down from the hills.

"There is only one problem with this, White Raven," said Nokoni. "I see no horses."

"No. The others have gotten them all already." Raven shrugged. "We are closing in on the war band quickly," he pointed out. "They are moving slowly with so many women. We will catch up with them before they reach the water. Then I will steal what I need."

He stood suddenly from his crouched position. Nokoni looked at him sharply.

"What are you doing?"

"There are no ponies, but there are still a few buildings standing," Raven pointed out. Below them a dark hunched figure moved furtively from the charred remains of one to the next. "There are still scalps to be taken."

Nokoni felt his skin crawl. "You want to go *in* there?"

Raven began walking toward the town.

"You are crazy!" Nokoni hissed from behind him. "Men died in paths like this in San An-tone-yo."

Raven glanced back at him. "Yes, I am crazy. And once I was a crazy *tejano*. I know these . . ." What was the white-eyes word? "These streets. I can use them. They are not my enemy. Will you follow me?"

Nokoni groaned. This was rapidly becoming Raven's war band rather than his own.

He looked around at his men. Some of them were already standing, preparing to follow the crazy white warrior, leaving their horses behind.

Nokoni moved fast, into the shadows cast by the next hill. Then he darted to the next, and the next, his men following him. They caught up with Raven again at the first smoldering buildings at the edge of the town.

"This is what we are going to do," Raven told them. He explained how to hide in the alleys, in garbage bins and watering troughs. "Strike, and then disappear before they can strike back. Be like snakes. Slide from shadow to shadow, darting out only fast enough to kill."

By full dark the screams echoing above Victoria were in earnest once more.

"Goddamnit," Ben McCulloch snarled.

He had never believed they had averted catastrophe. When the tracks of the immense 'Manche band had swerved, giving San Antonio a wide berth, the folks there had breathed a sigh of relief, but McCulloch had followed the trail, knowing the bastards would strike somewhere. They hadn't come all the way down here for a tea party.

Now he knew where they had gone.

He stood on one of the hills, looking down at the ravaged remains of Victoria. A Mexican, one of the survivors, had rushed out to meet him and his Rangers. The man babbled in Spanish, sobbing, waving his hands as he tried to tell what happened.

"They came in waves," a tracker translated for the Mexican. "They struck and moved on, then another bunch came and hit them again. He says they must be ten thousand strong."

Ben felt his stomach drop clear down into his groin. *"Ten* thousand?"

"They kept coming," the tracker repeated. "In waves."

McCulloch mounted his horse again and dragged its nose around violently. He looked east along the incredible swath the 'Manche passage had cut into the earth.

"What're those?" A Ranger pointed at a series of long narrow furrows.

"Travois," Ben snapped. "They've got women with them."

But how many? How many of the ten thousand were fighting men, and how many were just their squaws?

Then a light dawned in his head. For the first time since this whole nightmare had started, McCulloch smiled slowly.

"They're going east," he murmured aloud. To the Gulf. And once they got to the Gulf, they had no choice but to turn around again.

He gave a bark of laughter. "Hays should be behind us somewhere by now. You there—Buckley. Go back and tell him to stay put."

"Stay put?" The Ranger named Buckley gaped.

"That's right. There're too many of these bastards for us to attack outright. Good God, they'd waste us. But once they turn around to go home, we'll drive them right at Hays. We'll get on their heels just enough to send them headlong into Jack's troops, and then we'll hit them from behind at the same time."

"Ten thousand of 'em?" Buckley gasped. "You wanna hit ten thousand of 'em on the tail?"

But another man laughed. "Damned right!"

"In the meantime I need a few of you guys to peel off," McCulloch went on. "Go to every settlement, to every town between here and the scarp, and muster every man who can hold a gun. If there're ten thousand 'Manches, we need twenty thousand armed civilians."

"Don't reckon we *got* that many," Buckley muttered.

"Raise them!" McCulloch shouted. "Raise as many as you can. Tell them to find Jack Hays and join him and wait for us. We're going to have to let them get to the water, not a damned thing I can do about that. But when they turn around, we got the bastards."

Storm Trail looked to her left, then to her right, as they rode on. *Finally, once again, the Nermenuh were strong.*

After they had left Vik-toor-ya, the massive war band had poured over the Guadaloupe River. They had streamed down

Peach Creek, surrounding rickety little settlements and homesteads as they found them, killing the white-eyes, stealing their horses and their cat-tul, setting their places ablaze. Now as they neared the water, Kills In The Dark moved their haphazard ranks into a formidable crescent.

They came upon another place—five squat wooden buildings littering a creek. Her breath snagged and stayed just short of her chest until she was sure that Raven's shaggy blond hair was not among the heads bobbing and racing for cover. Then the war cries of the men started up again. There was no longer time to think about him.

Storm Trail raced toward the buildings with the others.

Twenty-six miles behind the war band, Ben McCulloch studied the incredible sign of the 'Manche passage one more time. Then he got back on his horse and fixed his looking glass on the horizon.

It was quite possible that he might have given his left arm to be able to actually see them, but he did not dare get that close. Behind him, two hundred men rode along impatiently. It wasn't nearly enough to risk the savages spotting them. Sure as hell they'd each be decorating somebody's lance by nightfall.

"Slowly, slowly," he cautioned as one his men trotted past him.

He wondered how many men had joined Hays by now. He prayed to God it was a hell of a lot more than two hundred.

All in all, he couldn't help being just a little bit impressed by the savages' answer to the San Antonio debacle. This, he thought, was an Injun raid such as no white man had ever experienced before.

At her first glimpse of the water, Storm Trail reined in, stunned. *So much of it.*

Silver and blue, its colors winking and shifting as the sun

peeked through a cover of clouds, it stretched horizon to horizon. She had not expected anything so big. Even the sound of it was huge, rushing at them like a giant ghost sighing in the sky.

White-eyes buildings were clustered together near the bank. A cry of alarm rose from somewhere among them. Kills In The Dark gave an answering howl, and the People swept down.

Storm Trail shook the daze from her senses and went after the others. As soon as the People reached the paths of the town, they fanned out and disappeared. There were so many shadows, she thought, her heart skipping. There were twists and turns and places between buildings that you could not see until you were practically on top of them. It reminded her of San An-tone-yo. She felt panicked and disoriented, but the warriors did not seem dismayed. They were strong now, unimpeachable. They had not encountered a single Rain-jer on this whole amazing ride.

She dismounted, feeling safer, smaller, more invisible on foot. But then something panicked her mare, and the horse wrenched away from her, galloping back up the street. "No!" she cried, but the mare kept going. She hugged herself and began to move down the path on foot.

Most of the People had gone toward the water. She went after them and nearly stumbled over a fallen white-eyes. His hair was gone, and an arrow protruded from his chest.

"Yes," she whispered fervently. She knew he was not actually the one who had beaten her, who had killed her babe. It was not his fault that Raven had gone. But none of that mattered.

She saw another *tejano* body and another, then she found something that made her stop and stare. A man was sprawled, dead, against one of the buildings, and he had skin that was a burnished black-brown. She inched around him warily, giving him a wide berth.

She looked for familiar faces as she reached another pathway. She stopped there because she could go no farther. This one ran along beside the water.

The warriors were destroying the big buildings. They were tearing open wooden boxes in one place, flinging out sheets like those that had been in that bi-bul the white-eyes had brought to the Penateka. But these sheets were not all bound together. They flew about like big strange snowflakes.

Four more warriors spilled out of a building in front of her. They dragged another screaming *tejano* woman with them. As Storm Trail watched, two of the men cut away her clothing. She had something all wrapped around her waist, underneath her long cumbersome dress. It pushed her breasts up, stopping just beneath them.

One of the warriors backed up in confusion, studying it warily. Another tried to cut it off her. His knife bounced off the thing.

Storm Trail felt her mouth go dry. So much strangeness . . .

From somewhere to her left there was an immense explosion. She spun that way and saw fire leaping into the sky. One of the buildings was suddenly ablaze and warriors ran from it, but even as it burned, others carted more flaming boxes outside. They swatted at the sparks that would have ignited their breechclouts and leggings, jumping about as the embers burned their skin. Storm Trail laughed nervously. Finally they ripped the boxes open and she saw that they were full of strange hats, and something else in big white-eyes gourds. The warriors put the tall hats on their heads and drank from the gourds, golden liquid spilling over their mouths and splashing down over their chests.

No, no, this was not good.

She wanted these *tejanos* to die, to pay for what they had done to her and her family. But the war bands were looting and burning everything in sight and not paying much attention to the white-eyes at all.

Storm Trail looked back at the water, then gaped all over again. The *tejanos* who had not fled from the town were escaping that way, going out into the water in small flat vessels. Some Penateka men galloped up to the waterway path and began shooting their arrows and guns at them.

Storm Trail heard one *tejano* voice rise louder than the rest. A man stood up in his floating wooden thing. Then to her astonishment, he leaped over the side, splashing into the water, coming back toward them.

The warriors all around her stopped what they were doing to stare at him. He had long, very white hair and he brandished a gun that looked old and tarnished.

"Damn you! Damn every one of you to Satan's hell!" he screamed. "You destructive sons of bitches!"

"Why does he not shoot?" one of the warriors asked worriedly.

"Perhaps the gun does not have bullets in it. Perhaps it has magic instead. Is it one of those repeating things?"

"No, those are small."

"This could possess a different kind of *puha."*

The white-haired man kept approaching them. Storm Trail backed up quickly. The man walked right among them, still yelling, then he blinked and looked around at all of them. He staggered away from them, and his large body swooned. He collapsed into the water with a splash and sank below it.

"Did he curse us with his magic?"

"Kill him!"

Storm Trail spun around, recognizing Kills In The Dark's voice. "No!" she cried. "Leave him. *Please!* We must all leave. Something is wrong here!" Suddenly she was sure of it. It was all like a distorted bad dream, a nightmare.

But the women and warriors began moving back into the paths again, and Kills In The Dark only sneered at her. After a moment only Yellow Fawn remained by Storm Trail's side.

"Come," Storm Trail whispered. "Come. We must get out of here." Maybe it was that the sky was already turning orange-red behind them with the sunset. The thought of being trapped in these paths after dark terrified her. She felt danger skittering along her skin now, pulling cold gooseflesh behind it. And suddenly, impossibly, she thought she could feel Raven, so close it almost brought tears to her eyes.

She knew—as certainly as she knew her name—that if she stayed in this place one more moment she would see him. She began running frantically back up the path she had taken to get to the water.

Raven spotted the town of Linnville when the Quohadi were still several miles away. It was an angry orange conflagration on the wrong horizon as the sun set behind them.

His spine turned to a rigid line of tension. *Tejano* phrases flew into his head—more images and thoughts than words, and he couldn't have spoken them aloud. *The eleventh hour. End of the road.* Perhaps, he thought, it was the product of being back in their world these past several suns, though never a part of it . . . never would he be a part of it again.

The Quohadi had rampaged through every ruined white-eyes settlement on the heels of the big war band, but there had not been any ponies left at any of those places. And, now, finally, he had to wonder if there would be any in Linnville, either.

He cast a sideways glance at Nokoni's wild-eyed stallion. The speed of the animal was legendary among the People.

"Last man there shares his woman," Raven taunted. *If I can find her.* Women were obviously traveling with the war band. He was sure Storm Trail was among them. She would never be left out of something such as this.

He pounded his heels into his horse and took an early lead on Nokoni if only because he caught the man by surprise. Then he heard his friend's shout of incredulous laughter behind him, and the thunder of his stallion's hoofbeats came after him.

When they reached the outskirts of the town, his own horse was stumbling and heaving. Raven was not displeased to lose by a nose—he was actually surprised that he had kept it that close. And he knew that Nokoni would never call him on the bet.

If I can find her.

The town was all burning rubble. Steam hissed up from the banks of the water as burning roof beams splashed in and were extinguished. But Linnville was not deserted. Comanche men reeled and swayed through the narrow pathways. Raven felt the tension in his spine spread suddenly around to his chest.

"They are drunk," he spat.

"Drunk?" Nokoni repeated. "No, Wolf Dream would not—"

"Wolf Dream is not leading this mission." Wolf Dream never lost control of his men. Who then? Raven wondered. Who?

He heard a distant whinny from behind one of the hills that sheltered the town. He turned his exhausted animal sharply and the Quohadi men followed him. When he topped the hill, Raven shouted. A herd milled in a corral, still untouched. There were at least two hundred horses.

"Either you have magnificent spirit-protectors," Nokoni said dryly, "or the man leading this ride is a fool."

Raven could not immediately find his voice. The pressure in his chest took his air. Though it seemed incomprehensible, he was beginning to think he knew which Penateka man led this ride.

A moment later he recovered himself. *"Ahe!"* He howled the coup cry, once again taking every other man off guard with the challenge.

He galloped to the fence. At the last moment, when his stallion balked and swerved at the obstacle, he leaped off its back and over the railing. He scrambled astride the closest animal in midfall and pulled it around by leaning over and grasping its nose.

At the same moment he kicked it and headed for the gate. He had to pause briefly to lash out at the bar with his foot, dislodging it. Then the gate swung slowly open and he plunged through, the remaining horses following him to freedom.

"He is crazy," one of the Quohadi men breathed to Nokoni.

"Yes, a crazy *tejano* red man," Nokoni agreed, then he laughed. "Will we let him keep all of them?"

He plunged into the herd the white warrior had stolen, managing to cut off twenty of the animals. Together they raced to the top of the hill. Another warrior managed to cut out a few of the mares, then another man claimed a few more. All in all, Raven thought, he lost perhaps fifty of them by the time it was all over.

It did not matter. The remainder were enough. He looked at those he had left, breathing hard, then he threw back his head and laughed.

Finally he looked at the town again and sobered. It did not seem as though anyone was making any move to leave the place. That worried Raven. Then a familiar voice came to him, carried on the breeze that was rushing up off the Gulf.

"Leave her or kill her! We have no time for women now. Claim your spoils and go!"

Kills In The Dark. Raven squinted in the gathering darkness. Where was the bastard?

Nokoni made a move to go down into the town. Raven's hand lashed out with lightning quickness, snagging his rein to stop him.

Nokoni growled a sound of surprise and anger, and Raven cut him off. "I have never asked a man for anything. I will never do so again."

Nokoni went still. "What is it then? What do you want?"

"Leave this place. Go home to your yellow-haired woman. Leave now. And take my ponies. Keep them for me. I will join you later and reclaim them."

Nokoni's men began arguing loudly. "We have ridden nine suns!"

"You say we should leave without scalps, without plunder?"

"Go!" Raven snarled. ".The man who leads this raid would not even fight me for his honor. There is going to be trouble."

"Yet you would go?" Nokoni asked.

"She is in there."

Nokoni hesitated, then nodded tersely. He swung his stallion around.

"My horses are yours, brother, if you do not see me again," Raven called after him. "Go south. Take the Mexico trace home. Do not pass through Texas."

Still astride the stolen mare, riding bareback, Raven put his heels to her and sent her walking cautiously down the hill into the burning town.

Storm Trail found some tall grass and tangled weeds growing behind the smoldering embers of the last building at the edge of the town. Most of the growth was blackened and brittle, but farther out it was still healthy. She pulled Yellow Fawn that way.

They reached it and hid themselves in it, then Storm Trail looked back at the town. Kills In The Dark was trying to get everyone to leave. But no one heeded him—they did not seem to care what he said. They were drinking from those gourds and laughing.

He had lost control.

Raven fought the *tejano* mare he had claimed, trying to turn her around a corner without benefit of a bridle. When he managed it, he nearly collided with Lost Coyote.

His first sentiment was rage. A clawing furious anger ripped through him, for this man and all his kin who had betrayed him. Then there was relief that the warrior was alive, that he had not died in San Antonio, because Lost Coyote had always been a man of intelligence and reason. Perhaps together they could save this from turning into a nightmare . . . perhaps they could save her.

Lost Coyote gaped at him a moment. Then as he took in Raven's weathered leggings, his breechclout, the bow and quiver over his shoulder, the warrior threw back his head and laughed.

"If I were not in such a hurry to get out of this place, I would ask you to stay right here until I found Wolf Dream." He leaned sideways to look behind Raven. "Are you trailing a hundred ponies, by any chance?"

Some of Raven's anger cracked under a thump of surprise. "You know of my bargain?"

"We all know of your bargain, my friend."

"It was supposed to be between Black Paint and me, no other."

"Be glad Black Paint shared it before he died." Lost Coyote sobered. "Kills In The Dark would try to claim her, and now it would seem he has the horses to do so. But Wolf Dream says he will stand by the word of his father, at least for the remainder of this moon."

Raven did not know whether to laugh or weep. There was relief—and terror—that he was actually going to do this. He would throw his freedom to the wind . . . willingly, to have her, to be with her, and he had never wanted anything more.

"I have one hundred ponies," he said shortly. "Where is she?"

"Here, somewhere. I was looking for those closest to my hearth to get them out of here when I found you."

It was the Nermenuh way to strike fast and vanish, Raven thought—it had been one of the first things they had taught him, and he had never forgotten it. But Kills In The Dark was not following that dictate. Raven did not think he could if he had wanted to. He heard that man's voice rise again, some-where distant, sounding petulant, and he knew that no one was paying him any mind any longer.

"Why?" he snarled. "Why Kills In The Dark? How could you follow him?"

Lost Coyote lifted one shoulder in half a shrug. "It was his idea, and that gave him the right to lead us. You know that."

Raven nodded. There was no sense in worrying about it

now. "You go to the north part of this place and the paths there," he told him. "I will ride to the south. Tell anyone you recognize to come back to this point. We will leave from here and go home by way of Mexico. I think it will be safer to avoid Texas."

Raven spun away. He would save the Penateka who had betrayed him. He would do it because they were *her* people. He could not live with them because he would never trust them again. But he would save them because he had made a spiritual vow to fight for all the Nermenuh. And if he put aside his own anger to do it, perhaps his spirit-protectors would allow him to find her as well.

Wherever she was, he thought desperately . . . in all these streets, wherever she had gone.

It was full dark when he returned to the place where he had first met Lost Coyote. His heart moved so fast it was painful as his eyes skimmed over those who waited.

Star Line, Eyes Down, Winter Song, and Sweet Water. There were warriors he recognized and some he did not know. He felt sick, feverish, with loss.

She was not here. Lost Coyote had not found her either.

Wolf Dream galloped up. When he saw him, his jaw dropped. Lost Coyote had not warned him.

"You?" Wolf Dream asked hoarsely.

"Where is she?" Raven asked.

"Perhaps she has already left," Lost Coyote suggested. "I did not see her."

"We must go," Too Much warned, looking out at the western plains as though expecting to see Rain-jers materialize.

Raven nodded. "You should go." But he made no move to leave himself.

"You are not coming?" Lost Coyote asked.

"I must find her."

"It is suicide to stay here," Wolf Dream said harshly. "Or have you come back just to get killed?"

Raven looked up at the hills and saw people—mostly squaws—streaming out of the camp, heading directly west. Lost Coyote was right. She had probably left already. But that was not all that comforting. Kills In The Dark appeared to be leading his people home directly westward, right across Texas.

"Fool," Raven snarled suddenly. "That man is a fool."

Wolf Dream's eyes narrowed as he looked west as well. "He has gotten an amazing number of horses and cat-tul. I think he wants to get them home as fast as possible. He is impatient to bask in the glory of his raid."

"Do you think those Rangers do not know we are here just because we have not seen them?" Raven snapped.

Wolf Dream gave a guttural curse. He dug his heels into his stallion and spun the animal about. Behind him, Winter Song cried out.

Raven turned his own pony toward the town. He would turn over every inch of this deadly place until he was absolutely sure she was not here. Then he would go after Kills In The Dark, just in case she was there.

"Now!" Storm Trail cried.

She darted from the grass with Yellow Fawn on her heels. The Penateka warriors were collecting the vast herd of stolen ponies from where they had left them when they struck the town. She raced that way and caught one of the mares, swinging herself astride.

They were safe now. It would be fine now. Thank the spirit-protectors, they were leaving.

There were no Nermenuh left in the town, and it was becoming a lethal place to be found.

Raven pulled his horse back into the shadows of a building

as white men began splashing in from the water. He had to leave this place. He did not know if they would see a red man or a white man when they looked at him, but it was not a chance he could take.

He had not found her.

Raven gave vent to a sound of frustration and pain. The white men near the banks froze when they heard him. They began shouting, running his way, brandishing their guns.

Raven fought his mare around and beat her into a gallop, leaving Linnville behind.

Thirty-two

Kills In The Dark was not entirely oblivious to the need for haste. He drove his people hard, refusing to stop until the sun set for the second time.

By then Storm Trail ached in every one of her bones. Her eyes kept drifting closed as they rode. Without the adrenaline of knowing they would make another attack at any moment, she dozed so deeply she nearly slid from her pony.

When they stopped to rest, she looked around blearily and did not see anyone she knew. Then Yellow Fawn came up beside her.

"They must be coming behind us," she offered. "I saw dust back that way earlier."

Storm Trail nodded and dropped to her knees. She curled her body inward, hugging herself, without even a robe to cover her. That was still with her own mare, the one that had taken off with the white-eyes in the town.

She felt Yellow Fawn snuggle down beside her, and then there was only blessed sleep—fractured by a shout.

She sat up again groggily, responding instinctively to the urgency in the voice. "What?" she croaked.

Someone else shouted, and then there was a scream.

How long had she slept? She looked around, struggling back to her feet. The eastern sky was paling, so it was nearly dawn.

A cracking sound exploded in the air, one she knew too well now. A gunshot?

People began running for their ponies. Then Storm Trail heard the single word that made her blood run cold.

"Rain-jers!"

No, not again, never again, she thought despairingly, remembering the horrible building they had put her in. Anything but that. She caught another of the stolen *tejano* horses as it trotted past her and pulled herself clumsily onto its back in front of the plunder that was tied to it.

They galloped. Whenever anyone slowed, a warrior appeared behind them, beating at their ponies to make them go faster. The white men did not seem to get any closer, and she could not understand that because the war band was traveling slowly, with so many weighted-down ponies. The air was filled with clanking and banging as the plunder lashed to the stolen horses was jarred and jostled.

Another bullet spit into them, then another, but not half as many as she remembered from San An-tone-yo.

There was a constant shooting pain through Storm Trail's hips with each ground-eating lope of her horse. When she tried to swing off onto a new pony to rest the one she had been riding, she could not scissor her legs fast enough. She landed on her belly as the pony strained. Someone caught the back of her doeskin and lifted her, helping her until she was astride.

She groaned and rubbed the dust from her eyes with her free hand so that she could see. The black and red shadows of the jutting scarp were just ahead. *Home.*

The warriors began falling back, riding behind the rest of them and the stolen herd. When they reached the trail, they could shoot down at anyone attempting to follow them. They would be between the Rain-jers and the women.

Storm Trail's horse staggered as it hit the creek that traced around a swell of land toward the scarp trail. They surged up out of the water again, and she was nearly at the front of the throng. Then she galloped around the swell of land, and her pony crashed into a writhing knot of animals.

She screamed again and again, not believing what she saw

even as she believed too well. There were more Rain-jers on the scarp trail. Rain-jers and white-eyes—there seemed to be millions of them, and they began shooting the women.

They poured down the trail toward the People. Their bullets rent the air—popping, cracking, and the *tejano's* shouts of jubilation rose over the chaos.

Women and horses exploded around the swell of land behind her. They slammed into those who were already there and could go no farther. They were hopelessly caught in the bend between the creek and the scarp, and the white-eyes were shooting into them.

She was going to die.

"No, no, no," she sobbed. She used her hands to brace her weight against her horse's withers. Her limbs trembling from exhaustion, she struggled to stand. The churning screaming ponies and cat-tul were packed in so tightly that she could step from one of their backs to the next. She could make it.

All the white-eyes were down off the trail, surrounding them, shooting into them. She flung her arms out for balance as one of the ponies tried to climb up onto the back of the one ahead of it. From the corner of her eye, she saw Yellow Fawn following her. Then there was another cracking burst of gunfire, and her friend went down.

Storm Trail dropped as well, reaching for her across the neck of another pony. "Please," she wept, "please, you are all right, just get up. Please . . ." But Yellow Fawn did not move. She grabbed her shoulders, shaking her, and her head lolled back. There was blood, crimson and gushing, at her breast.

Medicine Eagle could fix it, surely he could, if she could only get her back to the Penateka camp. Another bullet cracked and another. Blood spattered and flew from the head of the pony Storm Trail squatted upon.

"Help me," she groaned. "Please. Someone help me. I have to get her—" She broke off, screaming again as a babe was shot against its mother's back. The bullet passed through both of them and the cradleboard.

Sobbing, Storm Trail pressed her hands to her eyes so she would not have to see.

She finally managed to push up onto her knees again. Some instinct for survival drove her. She moved without conscious thought, crawling across the horses' backs this time. If she stood up, someone would shoot her.

When she got to the scarp trail, she reached up and wrapped her hand around a bared thrusting tree root above her head. She held on and dared to look back. Wolf Dream and his men were galloping around the edges of the jammed herd, shooting at the white-eyes, trying to hold them back. But more Rain-jers were coming in from behind them, and she finally understood they were trapped.

As she watched, her brother flung his arms up suddenly and slid from his stallion. "No!" she wailed. "Not him, too!"

She started back across the horses again, crazed. She would kill them. She would kill every one of them. They could not do this to her! Wolf Dream was all she had left!

Horseflesh shifted suddenly beneath her. The first of the ponies finally gained the now-clear scarp trail. She felt herself slipping down between two of them, and grabbed frantically at manes, tails, anything that would keep her on top. She dropped hard through them, landing in the mud. So many hooves, kicking and thrashing.

Storm Trail closed her eyes as one clipped the side of her head and another came down on her thigh. Pain exploded. Then finally, blessedly, she blacked out.

As Raven galloped through the white-eyes, some of them swung about to gape at him as though doubting their eyes. Then he saw Storm Trail. She was here, she was alive—but what was she doing?

She seemed to be climbing over the horses, coming back the wrong way. He shouted her name and never knew if she heard him. She disappeared abruptly, plunging down through the animals.

A bullet spit at him, coming in from his left. Every instinct he possessed told him to look that way, to find out who was shooting at him, to ascertain where the danger was coming from. But he could not take his eyes off that horse. A single bay pony marked the place where she had gone down.

He leaped from his own pony and began climbing over the horses, moving as she had done. *There, right there.* Then the herd moved.

The bay he had been trying to keep in sight ended up several paces farther ahead. Raven counted backward one horse, then two. He scrambled that way and flattened himself against the back of a pony, reaching down blindly.

Nothing.

He sat up and wrenched his magic repeating gun from his breechclout. It had six precious bullets in it. He had never dared to shoot it, not knowing where he could find more ammunition. Now he aimed it between the ears of the horse he crouched upon and pulled the trigger.

Blood flew and the beast sagged. The other horses jostled again, and the dead pony fell, opening a fleeting window in the writhing swell of hides.

Raven looked down and saw gold and silver.

For a precious moment, he only gaped, then he gave a howl of triumph. He scissored his legs off the animal as it fell and his feet sank into mud. The horses pressed in on him again from all sides. But he had seen her bracelet, the one he had given her so long ago. He plunged a hand down, caught her hair, and pulled with all his strength.

She was unconscious. Even the pain of his grip did not rouse her. He worked her up through the ponies, driving his elbows viciously into the animals' ribs when they would not, could not, allow him room.

He locked an arm around her chest. She groaned. *She was alive.*

He pushed through Kills In The Dark's wretched stolen ponies again. He beat them with his gun to get them to lunge into each other, giving him spare inches of precious room. Finally he reached the trail. The horses that had survived—those whose legs had not been broken and who the white-eyes had not shot—were breaking up into pairs and threes.

He could not catch one without releasing Storm Trail, so he dragged her up the scarp, to safety, on foot.

Thirty-three

Storm Trail opened her eyes slowly, believing in an after-world where the grass smelled sweet and green and there was peaceful silence. Then she saw Raven's face.

She gasped and her eyes flew open again. She screeched a sound of fury. Raven moved fast to pin her arms. He knew without a doubt that she would try to strike him.

"Easy." He grinned slowly, then he added, *"Wife."*

He was disappointed by her reaction. How many moons had he waited for this moment, to tell her? How long had he dreamed of finding her again, of seeing her relief and surprise that he was back, alive? He'd expected shock, something wild, but she only turned her head to the side, pressing her cheek into the grass.

Before she did, he saw tears well in her eyes.

What? She had to know he had not left her willingly. Something like anguish exploded in his heart as he wondered if she still wanted to go to Kills In The Dark after all.

"You have no deal," she managed. "Wolf Dream . . . my father . . . they are all gone."

And then he understood. The pain inside him did not ease; in fact, it bloomed. He had known about Black Paint, but Wolf Dream? He had been with that man only suns ago, before they had left Linnville.

"The Rain-jers." She spat the word. "Everything . . . gone."

"No." He found her shoulders and pulled her up, making her sit. She grimaced with pain but her eyes finally swam back to him. And then she was weeping hard, as he had never seen her cry.

She groped for him. Maybe later she would find her temper again. Maybe later she would spark, laugh, taunt him, but now she clung as she had never done. He held her as tightly as he dared.

"No," he said again, hoarsely. "You live, and I live. . . ." And they could make another babe, he thought—five of them, ten of them—until they filled all the gaping holes the white-eyes had shot into her life.

She placed a hand on his chest and pushed back from him hard. "What of She Smiles?" she spat. "Where is your woman?"

He flinched. Of course she would not be pleased with that turn of events. But *he* was. Her jealousy bemused him, almost made him smile.

"Here," he said cautiously. "My woman is here."

She looked around wildly as though actually expecting to find her old friend standing nearby.

"You," he managed. "You are my woman."

She turned back to him, her eyes narrowing, but he thought he saw tears there again. "It was not *me* you took from our camp."

"How could I? You were not there."

"Why? Why did you do it?" *She would not cry.*

"She asked me to."

Storm Trail gasped with an incredulous wild sound. That was it? That was what she had tormented herself over for moons now? She Smiles had asked and so he had simply done it? *"Without a thought for my heart?"*

"I thought endlessly of your heart and many other parts of you," he said, trying to make her smile, but she only continued to stare at him in disbelief.

He could have said that She Smiles told him she was dying, or that there had been no time to think. But he would not offer excuses, and he did not want her to hate She Smiles. He could withstand her wrath. Let her be angry with him.

It wouldn't last.

"I had to go," he said instead. "If I had not left, I would have died. You know that."

Storm Trail pushed unsteadily to her feet. He rose to stand in front of her. Beautiful, she was so beautiful . . . even with her eyes haunted and her face so chiseled and gaunt.

"So you think you can just come back and . . . and . . ." But she didn't know what he intended.

"And claim you?" he finished for her. "I had a pact with your father."

"I know that," she snapped. She needed to know if he was going to honor it . . . or go back to She Smiles, wherever she was. Until she knew, she could not seem to breathe.

"If your brother is gone, then I will find Lost Coyote and deal with him. Is that how it works? There must be a way. I will buy you. You will be mine."

She didn't answer. Her expression changed until she looked almost panicked.

"I . . . missed you all through me," he tried. "It was a loss that filled me. I want you. Kills In The Dark cannot have you."

Finally she realized that that was true. He *had* come back in time, and he would uphold his half of the pact. She struggled purely for pride's sake to keep her relief—the sweet, sweet relief—from her face. No matter where he had been, no matter what he had done, Raven had at least saved her from that man.

Suddenly it was all too much. The scent of him filled her senses. She had longed for him through so many suns, even as she told herself she hated him. She had ached for him through so many moons, even as she hated herself for doing it. Her throat tightened, and she knew it didn't matter how he had gotten here or why he had come. He was back.

She managed to toss her hair off her shoulder. Raven laughed.

"What?" she asked suspiciously.

How could he tell her that an image of her doing that had filled every one of his sleeps while he had been away from her? He could not, he realized, not without mewling. He would not get down on bended knee and snivel of his love for her. He laughed again. He could only imagine her reaction if he tried.

"Come," he said instead, turning her west again. "We must go back to the Penateka camp." With any luck Nokoni waited there for him, with his horses. Without luck, well, then he would have to give Lost Coyote his gun.

It did not matter. She was alive. She would be his.

Together again, they began walking.

It took them five more suns to find the Penateka camp. After three suns Storm Trail began to wonder if she could walk any farther.

It was not the pain. She could live with that, and already many of her aches and bruises were healing. But sometimes as she looked ahead, her vision swam with exhaustion. She was so enormously hungry that she had stopped feeling the pangs and only felt weakly nauseous.

Raven tried to carry her. Her pride would not allow it. She fought him off and nearly passed out from the effort, but he let her keep walking on her own after that, watching her occasionally with a raised brow. She glared back at him.

It was so good to be with him again. As though he had never betrayed her, as though they had never parted.

She watched him out of the corner of her eye. His tangled golden hair spilled down his back, past his shoulders. For the first time she realized how much he had aged since she had first met him. There was nothing of the boy in his face any longer. The relentless Comanche sun had roughened his skin, darkening it. His eyes were startlingly pale in his ruddy face, so blue, now gray as the sun slipped behind a cloud. His shoulders were broad, hard, his body so lean.

She wanted—*needed*—to touch him again. She needed it with something almost like agony.

"Can we rest?" she gasped.

He looked at her sharply. "Are you all right?"

"I . . . yes. No."

Something flared in his eyes. As always, he knew what she was thinking.

She took a fast step backward, putting distance between them.

"I will never forgive you for leaving me!" She would always want him, she admitted that. She loved him, and she had admitted that, too, at least to herself. He was a craving in her blood. But she would never forgive him. How dare he leave her to go with another woman!

"You would have sent me away yourself if you had been the first one back to camp," he pointed out mildly.

"I was *not* the first one back, and you betrayed me. You made a vow to buy *me.*"

"And I did not buy her." One corner of his mouth crept upward in that arrogant grin. She loved that grin. She hated it. She began trembling. She hated it when he was so cocky . . . so right.

"Come here," he said quietly, reaching for her.

He knew no remorse, she thought wildly. She scooted out of his reach.

"Did you touch her? Did you play with her?"

Hell—if he had, he would have committed no crime. He had not smoked with Black Paint before he had left, and even if he had, the Nermenuh were not notoriously long on chastity. He thought briefly of mentioning that she herself had played with Too Much. And in the end, he was just inordinately glad that he did not have to lie.

"No," he said quietly, then he thought he'd better qualify that. "I did not play with her," he said precisely.

Storm Trail's eyes sparked. "You took her with you, but you did not touch her? What was wrong with you?"

You. "My body wanted you." And that was true without qualification.

She hurled herself at him. For a moment he thought she would strike him, but she slid her hands up his chest and into his hair. She took fists of it on either side of his head, and her mouth was firm and greedy on his. He caught her reflexively, his hands on her hips, kissing her back. *Oh, spirits, it had been so long.*

He was glad she had not asked him if he had kissed She Smiles. He would have lied fiercely if she had, because it had not been like this—never, with anyone, had it ever been the way it was with her.

The recesses of her mouth were warm, her tongue desperate as she sought his. He found her own short hair and pulled her head back to make her open to him wider. She gasped and he drank the sound from her, covering her mouth again. For once, if never again, he was in no hurry. It had been a lifetime without her, without this—and it was true, he had missed her with a physical ache.

He stroked his tongue over her teeth, then bit gently on one corner of her lip. He covered her mouth fully again. And still she gripped his hair, holding him as though she were afraid he would stop or go away again.

He laughed hoarsely. Never—never again would he leave her.

She felt the strength in her legs give out and finally moved her hands, wrapping her arms around his neck as much for his warmth as for his support. His hands moved up her ribs to the sides of her breasts, and his touch was everything she had ever needed—brazen, unapologetic, strong. She never felt like herself anymore unless he was with her, beside her.

He stroked her nipple, hardening it, and she growled an inarticulate sound, reaching down to press his hand more firmly against her breast. He bent suddenly, catching her legs, scooping her up in his arms, and then he stopped as though in confusion.

"What?" she gasped. "What is it?"

He had been planning to take her to shelter, somewhere private, but there was nowhere . . . just the endless, rippling grasses of Comancheria. That was good, too, he decided. It felt . . . right. He lowered her again as suddenly as he had picked her up, easing down on top of her as they both sank into the concealing grasses.

The sun beat down on his back as he traced her jaw with his tongue, trying to savor, needing more. She arched her neck, tilting her head back to allow him access. Her eyes closed and she groaned. He pushed her hair back from her neck and nuzzled there, and her hands began clawing his back. Her fingers caught the string of his breechclout, and she dragged at it desperately.

"Yes," he murmured. "Yes."

He pulled the string away himself, and when his hand swept up again, he had the hem of her doeskin in it. He fought it with his own growling sound, pushing it up to her neck, finally getting it off her. She lay beneath him, breathing hard, watching him watch her. His eyes moved over her breasts, her dark nipples puckering in the wind that teased gently through the grass.

In spite of himself, he remembered the way they had looked just before he had lost her. He had known her body so well, and her breasts had been fuller then, with a trace of blue veins just beneath the skin. He had not wanted to see that, had not wanted to know. He had not been willing to claim her quite yet. A babe would have sealed his vow with Black Paint more fully than any pipe ever could . . . and he had not been ready.

How wise that man had been, making him wait, making him need first.

He closed his mouth over one of her nipples, suckling, forgiving her with his touch for not telling him about the child. Through it all, he thought, through every cruel thing they had done to each other, they had both been to blame.

She needed him to fill her. She needed it desperately. She

spread her legs and brought them up, wrapping them around him. He slid both hands up her ribs to cup her breasts and bent his head to slide his tongue over her skin. But his hardness, the hardness she had ached for, was pushing against her thigh and he made no move to enter her.

She worked her hand down between them, closing her palm over him and he went still, his muscles rigid. She could see his jaw tense, and she laughed wickedly.

She knew then that he had not lied. He had not been with anyone recently. He was too ready.

If she had not burned so much herself, she would have punished him, made him wait. She told herself that even as he moved, pushing his weight up onto his arms, and she guided him into her.

The first instant, the first moment, was almost more than she could bear.

She arched back against the grass, sensation carrying her too quickly, too far, right away. He moved inside her fast and furiously and she cried out, wanting it to last, knowing it could not. She felt him stiffen above her even as her own body tightened, and it felt as though her blood crashed in heated waves.

It was only then—only after it was over and he lowered his face to her neck—that she realized she was crying. She had been crying silently all along, but they were not tears of grief this time.

She was whole again.

They found a watering hole near dusk, a low place on the prairie that was muddy with rare ground water. Some antelope drank there, and Raven used another of his precious magic bullets to take one.

Storm Trail tried to stop him.

"And what do you propose to eat if I do not?" His bow and quiver were with his war horse, with Nokoni. He caught the back of her neck and made her look at him. "I will provide for you always. That is my vow to you. It has nothing to do with your father or your brother, with any other man."

In truth, Storm Trail was not at all sorry he had done what he had. She could not even wait for the meat to cook fully. She hacked a piece off and pushed it into her mouth.

"Slowly," he warned. "Your belly will be surprised by it." He tucked a strand of her hair behind her ear, then his face hardened. "Did he not feed you?"

She stopped chewing. "Who?"

"Kills In The Dark. Your beloved warrior."

Storm Trail grimaced at the way he snarled the words. She thought of telling him that he had been right about that sly coward all along, then changed her mind. Let him wonder, she thought.

"There was little time to hunt after we came down off the scarp," she explained. "There are . . . so many white-eyes there now." Her voice dropped. "So many times we saw settlements to strike, more than I think anyone anticipated. There was no time to rest, to eat, to do anything but press on toward the water and kill as we went. There was so much rage carrying us." She swallowed, then asked the question she had not wanted to ask. It was not that it hadn't occurred to her. It was that she had not wanted to know.

"Raven, why do we walk?"

He finally took a piece of meat for himself. "I have been with the Quohadi all this time," he said finally, without really answering. "We heard of Kills In The Dark's ride and wanted to join it. We were riding along behind your war band, toward the water, trying to catch up with you."

"Where are all the ponies?" she asked again. They had stolen so many horses, thousands of them, she thought. Had none of them made it up the scarp?

"My war stallion is still with Nokoni. I left him to capture a herd in Linnville, then I was riding one of those mares."

She nodded slowly. He *had* been there then. She wondered if she would always feel him like that, when he was near.

"I was riding behind the white-eyes after that, the ones who were behind you," he went on. "Then I got close enough to see you go down. I left my mare and climbed over the horses as you were doing. She got lost with the rest of them. I found you and carried you up the scarp. *Suvate,* that is all." He thought of that glimpse of silver and gold again and looked down at her arm. She had taken the bracelet off. He grinned anyway.

"But those ponies, all those ponies . . ." She trailed off.

"I do not know what has become of them. I left, took you far enough that it was safe to lay you down and let you wake up." He remembered the strangling fear, as the time wore on, that she would not.

"But we have not seen any horses pass us," she persisted. "None."

"No."

"Some of them were starting to move up the trail when . . . when . . ." *When Wolf Dream had died.* In her chest, pain twisted.

Raven did not make her say it. He nodded. "Most likely the Rain-jers slaughtered the rest, or maybe they took them back to the *tejanos.*"

She moaned softly.

"Some people passed us while you were still unconscious. Some survived and were heading home."

"How many?" she whispered. "How many died?"

"I do not know."

Storm Trail took a deep shuddering breath, then she groped for her knife and grimly began cutting at the meat.

"We will need this," she said tightly. "I think they will be hungry when we finally find the Penateka."

Thirty-four

The camp was worse than either of them had imagined. They heard it first—the wails of grief floating to them on the wind. Raven saw Storm Trail stumble briefly, but then she kept grimly on.

His first glimpse of the lodges left him stunned and speechless. When he had come to these people, there had been nearly four hundred Penateka tipis. He remembered with etched perfect clarity the first time she had led him from the camp to get her mother's ponies so the band could move. When he had turned to look back, the tipis had stretched along the water for miles.

Now his eyes flew, looking for more than what he saw here. Maybe they were behind a hill somewhere . . . but he knew they were not. There were less than a hundred Penateka lodges left. They had taken the brunt of both the San Antonio massacre and Kills In The Dark's ill-fated raid. With a bible and an invitation to council, the once-mighty Penateka had been destroyed.

There were two well-beaten trails snaking into Comancheria from Mexico, swaths worn into the earth after centuries of Spaniards and war bands traveling back and forth. Lost Coyote brought the women up the western one, as far from white-eyes interference as he could manage. But Nokoni was traveling with only fighting men, and he came up the quickest, eastern way.

Raven was asleep beneath the arbor when he arrived in the Penateka camp with his horses. He got to his feet and went to meet the war band. Nokoni studied his face briefly as he swung to the ground.

"I took a chance I would find you here. Did you find her?"

Raven nodded slowly. "There was trouble."

"You said there would be." He looked around, measuring the devastation of the Penateka with his eyes.

Raven allowed a quick grin. "I will take those horses now."

"And then?"

Raven sobered. "Are you in a hurry, friend?"

"I would like to see my woman."

"Can you give me another sun? Perhaps two?"

Nokoni finally allowed a brief twitching smile. "You always ask a great deal of me. When I finally ask a favor in return, it will stagger you."

"I will take the chance. I would like to go back with you, but I need some time."

He had his woman. He had his herd now. All that remained was to wait for Lost Coyote to surface so he could tie up loose ends, then he could ride on.

He hated waiting.

He finally caught Storm Trail alone when she went to the river to bathe. She stood by the bank, pulled her dress over her head, and his breath snagged as he watched her from behind a tangle of plums and yaws and vines that hid the creek from the camp.

She was too thin and too beautiful.

He crept down, coming up behind her, putting his mouth to her smooth bare shoulder. She squeaked reflexively, jumping around.

"Hush. It is only Raven."

His mouth found hers. His kiss was hungry. She pressed herself against him, but then he lifted his mouth.

"I swear to my spirit-protectors that I will get you away from this place," he murmured. "I will take you where you will never again fear that footsteps behind you are those of an enemy. Soon," he promised. "Soon now."

She wondered if he guessed that the enemy she feared most here was Kills In The Dark. She did not think that warrior would accept losing to Raven again without a fight. But then again, Kills In The Dark was a beaten man. He barely even left his lodge these suns.

Storm Trail nodded, then his words registered and she stiffened. "Get away?"

"I will give Lost Coyote the horses to buy you, then we will go back with the Quohadi."

She did not want to leave her father's band! And she realized suddenly that once he bought her, she would have no say in the matter at all.

"I will kill those ponies!" she burst out, surprising even herself. "I will see to it that you have nothing with which to claim me!" She pushed past him, leaving the bank, before he recovered. He snagged her elbow to stop her.

Anger punched at his temples. "After so many seasons you still do not know me?"

"You are a man!" The tears were hot and gathering behind her eyes. She had longed for him, had begged her spirit-protectors for him to return in time, because the alternative was terrible. But she would never forget She Smiles, and she had never relinquished her horror of being *his*.

She loved him—loved him wildly. And maybe because of that, maybe because he was the only man she *could* love, she did not want to give up her choices to him. It would change everything between them. Their heat had always been that of two equal souls colliding. If he owned her, controlled her, it would destroy the delicate precious balance between them.

She fought his grip, but he would not let her go.

"I am as much Nermenuh as any man in this camp. But—"

She turned her head so that she would not have to look at him.

"But—" he went on, shaking her, making her look at him, "—but even when I was white, I did not hold with the idea of women as chattel. If that was what I wanted, I would not love you!"

His words stunned both of them. Storm Trail felt her belly roll over. She stopped struggling.

"I love you," he said again, almost wonderingly. His own heart slammed hard.

She opened her mouth. Nothing came out.

"You are mine, but I would not bend you against your will. I will not force you to leave if you do not want to go, not even now, after they would have killed me merely for the color of my skin."

He loved her, she thought, dazed. But love could be cruel when it had to be, and he had not said he would fight fair.

"If you will not go, then we will stay," he went on, "but I will not hide my head in the sand with you."

"What?" she breathed, not understanding.

"If you choose to stay here, then you must know that you are destroying those last few of your people with any will to survive."

Her eyes blazed. "What are you saying?" she hissed. "I would never—"

"If you stay, you will," he interrupted harshly. "I give them an alternative to dying."

"No!"

"To dying slowly," he reiterated. "Their last hope, their only chance, is to go west, to get as far away from these bible-toting *tejanos* as possible. We are vulnerable in Penateka country, at their mercy. They come up the scarp now. It is not as it was when you were a child!"

She knew that. She trembled in his hands.

"We must go where they cannot find us, so that our children

can grow without fear. Away from here, we can be strong again, without always looking over our shoulders." He dropped his hands suddenly and turned his back on her. "Think about it," he finished stiffly. "I would like you to tell me what you decide before Nokoni goes."

She watched him walk away, but she could think of only one thing.

He loved her.

When Lost Coyote came back, there was a renewed frenzy of mourning. As long as that party was unaccounted for, there was hope that this woman or that child had survived and traveled with them. But when Lost Coyote returned, faces were still missing, and grief erupted anew.

The worst was Winter Song.

She looked about and did not see Wolf Dream at the arbor, where he had always stood tensely, hovering nearby. She dismounted and ran from lodge to lodge, looking for him, but she knew. She did not keen. She shrieked. Again and again her cries rent the air.

Mountain and Too Many Relatives finally caught her. By now the squaw had her knife out, and she cut savagely at her hair, at her arms and hands. Blood flew and spattered. Someone wailed at her to stop.

Raven's heart thumped in sick alarm. Winter Song's knife found her breast. But then, blessedly, Too Many Relatives caught her hand before she could plunge it in again.

They took her to Mountain's lodge, and she spat epithets at her father as she went. Raven looked at Paya-yuca. The big man's face was stony and unmoving, but his cheeks seemed to shine with wetness.

Foolish, pompous old man, Raven thought. You believed you would hold her until Wolf Dream retired from the trail, that it showed your power over him. You did not know that the ulti-

mate power lies with the white men and the death they dis-
pense.

In that moment Raven knew that if he and Storm stayed
here, Paya-yuca would somehow destroy them as well.

When everyone was accounted for—those who lived and
those who had died—the Penateka council finally gathered beneath the arbor. Raven drove his ponies into the camp for Lost
Coyote, and the whinnies and thunder of hundreds of hoofbeats
roused the Penateka somewhat. Squaws dropped their work
and spilled from their lodges to gape at the commotion.

He saw Storm Trail as he reached the camp center. She was
hugging herself, smiling bemusedly. He drew up with a flourish, his own stallion rearing. The herd milled, and he heard
Mountain shout as a few of them crashed into her meat rack.

Lost Coyote stood up and stepped out from beneath the arbor. His handsome face was haggard. Raven knew what he
was thinking. Wolf Dream should have been accepting this
bounty.

"So be it," Lost Coyote said quietly. "It would take a more
foolish man than I to try to stand in your way now." He looked
around almost absently. "I need a pipe."

Sweet Water ran off to get one of Paya-yuca's. And then
with no more fanfare than that, they smoked and it was done.

Raven looked around for Storm Trail again. This time he
could not find her. That was all right. He was not sure he
wanted her to hear what he had to say.

"I want to leave. I want to go with Nokoni with the next
sun." He had lied to her, he realized. He would not let this be
her decision. He would keep trying to convince her with every
breath he took until she finally relented.

"Join us," he said urgently, looking around to include the
warriors who stood behind the council.

A corner of Lost Coyote's mouth pulled up. "I think I would,
if I were not nearly the only one left." Raven understood. The

Penateka's best war band was shattered. They needed Lost Coyote to ride, and they needed his wisdom on council. They needed him to hunt. They needed him for far too much, and he was only one man.

Raven looked at the other warriors. "My offer still stands for the rest of you. I would take my woman to a place where she will be safe when I ride out to kill the *tejanos*. How many times have they crept in here while your backs were turned?"

There was a murmur of voices, and his own got stronger.

"The white-eyes have never found the Quohadi. They have never gone to their camps. The only time they even got close was when they came east to meet us and we all wintered together."

"Has your wife agreed?" asked Nokoni quietly. Raven looked at him sharply, but before he could answer, Storm Trail's voice came from behind him. He whipped around to find her.

Oh, yes, she was the perfect wife for him. After all this time she still managed to surprise him.

"I will go," Storm Trail said quietly, but then her chin came up. "Because *I* want to."

Thirty-five

In the end, twelve men brought their families with them. As war bands went, it was not a big one. And as a practical matter Raven knew there was no guarantee these men would stay with him. Once they reached Quohadi country, they were free to split off and ride with Nokoni, if he would have them, and there were at least seven other active Quohadi war bands as well. But Raven did not think they would.

He laughed aloud as they rode. Storm Trail looked over at him. "What?"

"Not bad for a white man," he chuckled.

She tried to scowl, but her mouth curled.

He thought it was quite possible that she grew more beautiful by the sun. The livid bruise on her cheek where the pony had kicked her was fading now to be replaced by a soft glow. With these last several suns of rest and food and plenty to drink, she seemed less gaunt.

Her hair was agonizingly short, just covering her ears. It had barely had time to grow in after the loss of her father before her brother had died. She kept it from flying into her eyes with a thin braided twine around her forehead. A feather was stuck in the back of it, pointing down.

She rode with her spine straight. In every respect she was still a chief's daughter, arrogant and confident, cunning and unpredictable and strong.

She was everything he had ever wanted, and she wore the bracelet.

Suddenly a chill slid down his spine as the sun eased behind a cloud. He felt almost too good. He wondered how long the spirit-protectors would allow him to keep this sense of satisfaction.

As they traveled westward, the land changed.

Storm Trail had never seen Quohadi country. When the bands had wintered together, they had met halfway. Now the curly tipped, yellow-green grass stretched as far as the eye could see, and that was the same, but there was something new on the horizon, another plateau like the scarp that protected the land she had once called home. The Balcones had stretched so far that one could not see the end of it. It was as though the whole of Mother Earth went up a step there. But this scarp was smaller even as it was somehow more imposing. It was yet another step up, flat-topped, much more narrow, dark and solid against the sky.

She knew that Raven had been right to bring them here. No white man could sneak up there if warriors were at the top, waiting for them.

They rode until the Quohadi scarp loomed above them and blotted out much of the sky. "I will race you to the top," Raven yelled impulsively to Nokoni.

The man looked at him incredulously. "You are one crazy coyote."

Raven did not hear him. He was already galloping. Nokoni cursed and took off after him.

Storm Trail watched in disbelief as their horses raced and scrambled up the sheer dangerous rock face. She thought it was possible that if she ever lost Raven, it would not be to a white-eyes or a rogue buffalo, or even to another woman. It would be to his own reckless abandon.

She picked her way up the scarp more carefully with the others. When they reached the top, she was startled all over again. The crest was arid in a way the Penateka land was not. There was little grass and no visible water.

The flat land was pockmarked with canyons. As they drew close to one, she looked down into a lush well. Here there was water and grass.

They went on, Nokoni and Raven finally coming back to join them again. They reached another canyon and found hundreds of smoke-yellowed lodges snaking along a creek at the bottom. Storm Trail's pulse stirred a little fearfully. The tipis were not set in a circle the way the Penateka's always were, but she was sure there was some sort of hierarchy here as well. Would they have to camp in the back, with the lowest warriors? They were newcomers, after all.

They were halfway down when she heard a short aborted scream. Her skin prickled. Nokoni picked up to a canter. As the rest of the party continued their descent, he rode to a white-eyes woman who was even fairer than Raven. Her hair was so blond as to be almost white, and Storm Trail tried hard not to stare at her.

As they got closer, she realized that the woman's eyes were the most beautiful cornflower blue she had ever seen. For some reason they immediately endeared her to her.

"She is Naduah," Raven explained quietly. "Nokoni's wife. His only one. I think he could afford many—he is their first chief's son and a very successful leader—but he keeps only her."

Storm Trail narrowed her eyes on him. "Would *you* have another?"

Raven laughed. Even if he could afford one in ponies, he could not do so in energy. She was all he could handle.

Storm Trail was satisfied with his wordless response and his wicked grin. A smile tickled her lips as well as she imagined what he was thinking.

"Why did she scream?" she asked finally.

"Because she noticed me before she saw her husband."

Storm Trail shook her head. She thought that if a thousand

men rode into her camp, her eyes would always be drawn to Raven first. Then she realized that it would not happen just because he had taken her heart from her, but because, with his wavy golden hair, he stood out.

"Naduah lives in fear, even here," Raven went on. "She worries that somehow her old people will find her and try to take her back. I have come to like her." He hesitated, wondering if he should tell her who Naduah was. He could think of no reason not to. That mustached man could not possibly find them here. "She was taken just before I was," he added finally.

"Before you?" Storm Trail scowled. The war bands had made only one raid on the *tejanos* before they had captured Raven. That meant that this woman was one of those captives she had heard of when she had eavesdropped on that council.

That made her feel yet another tug of warmth toward her. Because of rumors of her, she had gone out after that war band and had found Raven. It seemed to tie their fates together somehow.

Naduah finally left Nokoni and came their way. *"Hei, haitsi,"* she said with a combination of shyness and warmth. She reached up for Storm Trail's reins. "I have food in my lodge. You must be very hungry."

Storm Trail dismounted. She followed the young woman into the camp. Naduah kept up a soft flow of conversation.

"I will help you move Raven's lodge closer to mine. I have helped his . . . woman friend make a tipi of her own. She will not be with us."

She Smiles. Storm Trail stiffened. Of course she would still be here. In spite of herself Storm Trail looked around for her.

Naduah watched her assessingly. *"Suvate,* it is done with them. He is yours now."

Naduah gave her pony to a boy to care for, then led her to a lodge sitting close to an immense one that could only belong to a chief. "That is Iron Shirt's," Naduah said. "He is Nokoni's father. Here, beside mine, is where you will stay."

Storm Trail was filled with a rush of gratitude that she would not be relegated to the outskirts of this camp.

She looked at Naduah again and knew that they would be fast friends. She was not poor Yellow Fawn, so sweet and compliant. She was not She Smiles, pretending friendship only to slice her heart out. In fact, she thought Naduah was very much like herself. Storm Trail decided that she liked the mischievous twinkle in her eye.

Naduah seemed to read her mind. She tossed back a lock of white-blond hair and grinned. "We have a good deal in common, after all."

Thirty-six

It took Storm Trail less than a moon to realize that she had never been as happy as she was living upon this Quohadi plateau.

Her nights were full of Raven. Sometimes they were sweet and sometimes they were fierce. He would pull her from sleep with his hands on her body, knowing the places to touch to bring her instantly awake, sliding an exploratory finger between her legs. But there were times, too, when he could not wait for darkness, when he would pull her, laughing, into his lodge even as twilight gathered, stripping her bare almost as soon as they ducked inside. She loved him. She loved what he did to her. She loved being safe.

She told herself she was without fear.

They were almost inseparable from Naduah and Nokoni, their lodges ending up side by side no matter how many times the Quohadi moved camp. The only times the men parted were when Raven went into Texas. Nokoni would rarely go there.

Storm Trail's only clouds were her glimpses of She Smiles. Each time she spotted her old friend, it was like a claw raking through her chest to scratch at her heart. She still could not accept how either of them could have done that to her. She knew Raven sometimes hunted for her, and she told herself doggedly that he was only doing it out of some misguided responsibility for bringing her here. He never gave her hides or anything valuable, just some of the lesser cuts.

One sun, as Storm Trail worked with Naduah to make pemmican, Naduah followed her gaze to She Smiles. "Why do you still hate her so?" she asked.

Storm Trail flushed. It was the first time Naduah had mentioned She Smiles since they had arrived.

"Raven was never hers," she said. But that wasn't entirely true. He had been hers, before Storm Trail herself had even bled for the first time.

"He was not hers when they came here," she tried again. "He had already smoked for me." But that wasn't true either. He had had a pact with Black Paint, but he had not actually smoked over it yet.

Storm Trail sighed and rocked onto her heels. "I sent her from San An-tone-yo to save him," she whispered finally, wretchedly. "She took him from me."

Naduah sighed. "You should let it go. I see the way he looks at you. I see the way he is now, and I know the way he was then. He was sad and . . . driven."

"He is *always* driven," Storm Trail muttered. But she was mollified to know that Raven had not been happy without her.

"In the meantime," Naduah said mildly, *"you* have his child."

Storm Trail's eyes flew open again. Something cold and violent shook through her.

"No. That is crazy."

Naduah scowled and put a hand to her friend's tummy. "I think it is very real."

Storm Trail's heartbeat gathered into thunder. She launched herself to her feet. "No."

She was still afraid, she realized. When had it happened this time? It was possible that the babe had gotten into her as long ago as when they had been coming back from Kills In The Dark's horrible raid. She had not bled since before that ride. But she had not thought about it, had been unable to even consider it, because . . .

She looked at Naduah, her eyes pleading. "The *tejanos* took one from me."

Her friend's eyes widened. "Stole it?"

"Beat it out of me."

Sympathetic tears sprang to Naduah's eyes. "Oh, friend, no."

Storm Trail gripped her arm. "I cannot do it again! I cannot give them another! I do not want to have it!"

She darted into her lodge. Naduah hurried after her.

"You must not say such things!" Naduah breathed. "The spirit-protectors—"

"The spirit-protectors do not know what it is to wake and find the blood of your child all over your legs!" Storm Trail cried. "They do not know the pain! It was my child! And I did not want it until it was too late, and then the spirits punished me. I am so scared." It was something she had never said aloud before. She covered her face with her hands and sobbed.

"The white-eyes will not find us here," Naduah said soothingly, stroking her hair. "The white-eyes will not come here. Nokoni tells me that often."

"But you fear it anyway."

"Yes, but . . . wildly. Without really believing it will come to pass."

Storm Trail sniffed hard and looked up at her. For one precious moment she dared to believe that it would be all right, that her spirit-protectors had forgiven her, and the *tejanos* would stay away, and this child would live to be healthy and strong.

"You have not told Raven?" Naduah guessed.

Storm Trail laughed, a soggy sound. "I did not tell *myself*."

"He can probably tell. How long have you been together?"

Storm Trail blinked. She thought about it, then she began shaking.

She had caught him—he had caught her—when she was ten winters old. This would be her seventeenth winter.

She had been tied to him and had tried to kill him. He had pretended to kill her. She remembered stopping him when he would have done the craziest thing ever and ridden out after

Wolf Dream's vengeance ride. She remembered lying beside him, on the other side of the lodge wall, while he had played with She Smiles.

So many memories. The first time he had ever touched her in the pony herd, and then again when she would have gone to Too Much. He had killed for her on the sun that her mother had died, and he had gone away, only to come back and strike the biggest coup over her of all. He had claimed her without ever letting her feel that she had not been the winner in his victory.

They matched . . . her and her reckless, crazy White Raven, and, if only for a moment, she believed that they would love forever, that they would be young forever, defying death and the white-eyes, laughing at anyone who would try to hurt them. A heady exhilaration filled her. Look at all they had been through, and they had survived! They would always survive. It would be all right. Especially here, on the Quohadi scarp, they would be fine.

Naduah clapped her hands. "I think we should make a feast. We have enough meat that we do not have to put it all into pemmican and dry it. We will stuff sausages and get prairie turnips. And then later we can tell both of them."

Storm Trail scowled at her. "Both of them?"

Naduah smiled, blushing. "I have a babe in me, too."

"Ah!" Storm Trail gasped. And then they were hugging, laughing, and she wondered if these babes would be born together, in lodges side by side. She truly hoped so.

Raven had raided east again, and he rode into camp that afternoon with scalps and ponies. He found Storm Trail in Naduah's lodge.

"What is all this for?" He looked around at the food with a raised brow.

"It is to welcome you home," Naduah said mildly before Storm Trail could answer.

"There will be a Scalp Dance," he said uncertainly.

"But later. This is for now."

He finally nodded. "Where is Nokoni? I would speak with him."

Something about his tone made Storm Trail's pulse skip. If he had news to impart, she wanted to hear it.

"Wash up and do it here," she urged. "He will be back soon."

Nokoni returned from hunting, and for a long while the four of them ate heartily in Naduah's lodge. They talked of nothing of consequence until Raven leaned back against some bedding and wiped the grease from his fingers on a scrap of old hide.

"Houston is back," he said abruptly.

Nokoni looked up sharply. "How do you know this?"

Raven told him how, long ago, he had caught and questioned a *tejano* woman to help Wolf Dream's war band. "I thought it was time to do that again. I wanted to know Lamar's sentiments after Kills In The Dark's scarp fight. And I found out that Lamar is gone." He paused. "There is something worse."

Storm Trail's heart plunged. "What?" she breathed. She dared to interrupt the conversation of war band leaders, but here, in this lodge, no one looked at her askance.

"The Republic has . . . annexed . . . with America." Raven used the unfamiliar English word because he could not think of one in Comanche to equal its meaning.

Nokoni was quiet for a long time. "What is an-ecks?"

He struggled, illustrating with his hands in a way he had not done in a great many seasons. "Joined with. As if the Penateka and the Quohadi decided to become one."

"Are there so many of these Aye-mer-i-cans? Are they good fighters?"

Raven scowled. "There are . . ." How could he convey the thousands upon thousands of people in places like Philadelphia? He could barely remember the place, but the one thing that stayed in his mind was an image of congested streets, of horses and carriages spewing up mud, and people pushing past each other on crowded sidewalks. He thought of other cities, Baltimore, Richmond, New York, and he knew it would be the same there.

"There are many," he said finally, pensively. And he prayed to his spirit-protectors that none of them would care enough about some Indians in a far-off southwestern land to fight them.

And that of course was no doubt what the Texans were praying for, he realized—that in achieving annexation, the Republic would share American tax dollars and militia to help them hold their own in this endless war against the Comanches, against a rare tribe who just would not lie down and die.

He glanced at Naduah. She had said she'd seen only eight winters when the Comanche had claimed her, and he did not know how long she had been in Texas or where she had come from before then. Her expression was calm. Perhaps she did not know how many Americans there were, either. Perhaps she did not remember.

"It will not affect us," Nokoni said, "as long as we have nothing to do with them." He looked pointedly at Raven.

"I will stay away from them," Raven agreed. *For a while.*

"How long will Hoos-ton be their chief this time?"

Raven struggled to explain, as he had once tried to convey the concept of elections to Black Paint and the Penateka council. "But this time he is not a president," he finished. "He is just a governor. That could be different. I do not remember."

He did remember, but he was testing Naduah. He glanced at her again curiously. She remained silent.

It struck him that it would be the worst kind of cruelty to take her back into that world. She seemed to recall none of it—it would be as alien to her as it would be to any natural-born Comanche. The difference was that white-eyes would expect her to be grateful and elated. "We should get ready for the Scalp Dance," he said, helping Storm Trail to her feet. They made their way back to the opposite lodge.

When they were inside, Storm Trail looked at him levelly

for a long time. "You are worried," she said softly. "You worry about this an-ecks thing."

He shrugged. "I will always worry. After San Antonio, after Kills In The Dark's fiasco, I never trust anything I hear about those people. I always wonder what they are up to with any given move."

Storm Trail hesitated, then nodded. His answer did not frighten her. In truth, she would have been more alarmed if he had *not* kept one watchful eye on those white-eyes.

Now there were more important things to discuss. She took a deep breath and realized she was shaking again.

Abruptly she pulled her doeskin over her head. Raven looked at her with a bemused grin.

"Even with the moccasins, I like it," he said slowly.

"Look at me," she whispered. "Please."

"When you are naked, I find it difficult to look anywhere else."

She took a step closer to him. *"Look,"* she said again.

He reached a hand out to her and traced one finger along the delicate blue webbing beneath the skin stretched over her full breasts.

"I wondered if you were just going to tell me you found the babe under a . . . a . . ." What was the word? He had thought about white-eyes too much tonight, he realized suddenly. "A cabbage patch this time," he finished finally.

Storm Trail scowled. "Cab-ij? What is—" Then her heart whaled up into her throat. *This babe? This time?* "You knew!"

He looked sad as he gathered her to him. "I keep telling you that I am not a stupid *tejano*." He found her skin, smooth and warm, and ran his hands down her back, over her buttocks.

"Why did you not . . ." She paused and gasped at his touch.

"Say anything?" His strong hands cupped her bottom briefly, then moved down to knead her thighs. "What would have been the use? For every cruelty we have perpetuated upon each other, we have both been to blame," he explained quietly.

He found her mouth with his. His hands swept up again,

over her ribs, to her breasts. He cupped them now as well, and bent his head to them. "Mmmm . . . I like this. You are not so skinny anymore."

Her head was swimming, her body alive with his touch. It took her a moment to realize what he had said. *Skinny?*

She found the will to pull away and pop him in the shoulder. He laughed softly and pulled her down onto his robes.

"What . . . what about the Scalp Dance?" she managed.

"I am tired of looking at that hair. I would rather look at you. Open your legs," he said huskily.

"Why?"

"Because I want to see if you look different there as well."

He traced her most intimate flesh with his fingertips, as though discovering her there for the first time. And then he followed with his tongue and her mind spun away. She heard her own gasps as though they were coming from someone else.

"We are a pair," he said, his voice muffled.

No, we are three.

Thirty-seven

The robe season in the north country was harsh, and when the thaw arrived, it was deceptive. Storm Trail woke one morning to a vague feeling of warmth in the air.

Raven was gone. She poked her nose outside to look for him. The sun was up and it was brilliant, glaring off the snow. She shielded her eyes and saw Naduah instead, coming back from the stream, her hand pressed to the small of her back.

Naduah was nearly as swollen with her babe as Storm Trail was with her own. Storm Trail wondered if she, too, moved with that strange, rolling, side-to-side gait. She certainly hoped not.

Naduah saw her and called out. "Do you have wood?"

"Some."

"You should get more." Naduah licked her finger and held it up in the air. A delightfully balmy breeze came strongly out of the north.

"This weather will not last long," explained Naduah, "not when the wind comes from that way."

Storm Trail's jaw dropped. "It will snow again?"

Naduah nodded.

Storm Trail groaned. So much for spring.

She went down to the creek to wash and gather branches. She had to reach far up the trunks of the cottonwoods to get them. The Quohadi had been in this canyon long enough that most of the wood had been picked over. It was difficult in her condition, and when she heard a sound behind her she was glad for the break.

She glanced over her shoulder, expecting Naduah. But She Smiles stood there instead, her hands clutched together in front of her.

"I followed you. I—"

Suddenly a sharp grinding pain hit Storm Trail. "Oh!" She dropped her wood and reached for the tree to brace herself.

Finally she breathed again. She'd been experiencing the same thing for suns now. She thought her babe's head was resting low inside her. The grinding feeling seemed to come every time the child moved.

"Is it your time?" She Smiles gasped.

That brought her mind rudely back to the woman's presence. She tried to step around her.

"Wait!" She Smiles cried. "Please!"

The anger of seasons welled up sourly in Storm Trail's throat. "I have nothing to say to you."

"You were dying!" She had almost convinced herself of it.

Storm Trail looked at her blankly.

"In San An-tone-yo!" She Smiles went on. "If he thought you might live, he would have gone there to get you! He would never have left the Penateka without you. Please," she whispered again. "I cannot bear to have you hate me this way."

Storm Trail's heart spasmed. *She had told Raven she was dying?*

"You lied!" she spat.

"For him!"

"So you could have him!"

"So I could *save* him!" Then She Smiles's face crumpled. "It was partly that I thought he would come to me again . . . I did not know until I spoke to him that you, that he . . . that your babe was his. He wanted me once. If I got away from Kills In The Dark, perhaps we . . . perhaps he would want me again."

Storm Trail felt hurt shimmy through her, both in her heart and deep within her body. Her babe was moving again.

"And what of *me?*" she breathed, her skin blanching. "Did neither of you think of me?"

She Smiles's face changed. For a moment Storm Trail could not even remember the sweet friend she once had been.

"Look at you! Even as big as you are, you are beautiful. You would easily have found another!"

Storm Trail flinched. How like Yellow Fawn's accusation that was! And how unfair!

She turned away clumsily and headed up the bank. "I do not want to talk to you."

She Smiles's voice rang out again behind her. "He always wanted you! When he kissed me—"

"What?" Storm Trail turned back to her with an ungainly twist. *Tell me you are talking about before, about that time when I was a child.*

"He kissed me, but he . . . he could not play with me. His body wanted you. Please," she said again. "Do not hate me."

Storm Trail felt the blood drain out of her.

He had said he had not touched She Smiles, that he had not played with her. *He had lied to her.* Everything was so good between them now, so right . . . and it was all based upon a *lie.*

She began struggling down the bank, away from her. This time when She Smiles called out, she ignored her.

Now she understood why she had felt so compelled to avoid She Smiles all these moons. Maybe she had known. Maybe she had always guessed. He had left the Penateka to save his life. Had he taken She Smiles to amuse himself while he was gone?

Storm Trail choked. She was shaking, moving blindly. It was a long time before she realized that she had gone a very long way without collecting any more wood at all.

She looked up dully at the sky. The sun was gone now. The wind was chilling. She would have to go back.

She sat down on the bank instead, and that was when the pain changed.

It was not sharp and grinding and low this time. It started behind her, in the small of her back, and it moved to wrap around her belly, hot and heavy and spreading. "Three," she whispered helplessly. But it had been a lie. She had trusted him, gone back into his arms on a lie.

The pain passed but there would be another. She had seen enough women, enough ponies, birthing babes to know that. She had to go back, had to face him, and she could not bear it.

Ponies and women having their first babes took a very long time, she thought. She could stay where she was a moment longer. She hugged herself, shivering without a robe, but most of her cold came from inside.

She felt the first flutters of panic as the next tightening pain came again, bigger than the last one and certainly sooner than she would have expected. First babes did not come this quickly, she thought again frantically, then her pulse stalled.

This was not her first babe.

Everything was happening too fast. She knew what to do, but she was so cold, and there was no one to build a fire. She gasped as another pain hit her. She eased her weight down onto the bank again. A hole, she thought dismally. She had to start digging a hole for this babe to fall into when it came out of her.

That was when the rain started.

"Where is she?" Raven snarled. He was more furious than Nokoni or Naduah or even She Smiles had ever seen him. She Smiles began to cry.

"Tell us," Naduah urged more quietly. "What happened?"

"We talked about you," She Smiles wept, looking pleadingly at Raven. Raven felt his heart crash down to his toes.

Rain was hammering Mother Earth now in an icy downpour.

Naduah had said Storm Trail had gone for wood, but she had not come back. Raven looked at her robe, lying in a heap where she had left it that morning when it had been warm.

When she had not come back and the weather turned bad, Naduah had begun asking around for her. That was when she had brought She Smiles back to Raven's lodge. Now, hearing the rest of it, it was all he could do to keep from striking her.

"I will go find her," Naduah offered. "My grandmother is too old to travel, but I have helped her birth babes many times. I know what to do." For that matter, she was sure Storm Trail knew, too. She would not have been alarmed, except for the weather.

"No," Nokoni said sharply.

Raven met his friend's eyes. Nokoni would not see his own wife and his unborn child go out into this storm for anyone, and Raven did not blame him.

Raven glared at She Smiles. "How could you be so stupid, so cruel?" But even as his anger burned inside him, there was guilt, too.

"I will go," he said shortly. He began grabbing robes.

"Wait!" Naduah cried. "There are things you will need." She began racing around her lodge as much as she was able with her own child imminent. She took things out of parfleches and pushed them at him.

"Here, this is sage. Build a fire, burn it. It is for purifying a birth lodge, but it will work outside as well." She hesitated. She did not say it aloud, but they were all thinking it. How could a newborn babe survive in a storm such as this? "Bring the cord back. We will need that later, to tie in a tree so the babe has long life. Heat these rocks in the fire. When they cool enough to bear touching, you can place them against her back. Here." She showed him the spot. "That will help her, ease some of her pain and hurry the babe out."

"What else?" Raven growled.

"That is all," Naduah said helplessly.

He hurried out of the lodge, leaving She Smiles sobbing

pitifully behind him. His war stallion was tethered outside, but he had to go to the herd to get Storm Trail's favorite mare. He threw a rope over its head, and heard a muffled shout behind him.

Nokoni rode out of the storm toward him. The rain was changing to sleet now.

"This much I can do for you," Nokoni said. "You will be busy with your wife. I can build a fire."

They would have missed her if she had chosen that moment to lie down and rest. But Storm Trail had dug the hole she needed and had managed to find two more branches. She was planting them in the icy mud on either side of the hole when pain hit her again.

She finished quickly and grasped them to brace herself, to give her the leverage to push. She whimpered aloud, the wind snatching the sound away, just as it had done when she had tried to yell for someone back in the camp to come help her.

She could do this, she thought desperately. She had heard of women birthing with war bands. This was only rain, cold rain . . . and now a little bit of snow.

Fear wracked her anyway, because she had no soft robe or fur for the babe to fall upon when it left her body. There were no extra hands to catch it. Already snow was gathering in the hole she had dug. There was sloshy, icy water in there, too. She did not want her child to land in that. It would not kill it, but what a horrible welcoming into this world!

Pain hit her, arced, and ebbed.

She was not able to get her breath before the next one came.

She gritted her teeth and grabbed the branches and strained. The pressure between her legs was unbearable. She was looking down that way when strong white hands reached into her line of vision. She gasped and looked up. *Raven.*

She did not know how he had known to come and did not

care. She forgot that she was furious with him. She knew he would not let anything happen to them.

This time when the pain hit, she was able to concentrate on it. She let herself scream with it for the first time. Her voice ululated away on the storm.

"The head is coming," he said.

Cold, oh, spirits, it was so cold. The wind cut through her.

Then, impossibly, she felt the flickering heat of a fire beat against her back.

Was she dying? Was she in some sort of afterworld? Everything began to feel disoriented. She tried to turn around and look, but another pain gripped her, stopping her.

This time when she pushed she felt the child coming out, tearing her. She cried out. Raven caught the babe so that it would not fall into the icy wet hole.

Storm Trail rocked backward, falling into the freezing mud. It was all right now. The babe was not in the water. It would be fine.

She wanted to close her eyes and rest, but there was more to be done. She finally struggled up again to bite through the cord and tie it.

"Nokoni has built a fire," Raven said finally, hoarsely. "Can you walk just a little way, over there?"

"Wait."

It did not take her long to pass the afterbirth. He helped her up, and she moved stiffly to the warmth. She sat carefully, and Nokoni dropped another robe about her shoulders. Raven was standing a few feet from the fire, watching her uncertainly, still holding the babe. It looked to him as though there was a lot of blood, and that appalled him, but she did not seem alarmed.

Storm Trail held out her arms.

She wanted her child. She did not care if she ever touched

Raven again. But then she looked up into his tortured face and something broke inside her.

"Sit with us," she whispered.

He eased down beside her and gave her the babe. "It is a girl-child," he said, awed.

She was beautiful. Her hands were so tiny, so long-fingered and perfect. Her limbs were delicate. She cried angrily in the cold.

"I will warm you. Soon, I promise," Storm Trail whispered. She made sure everything worked, moved, was shaped as it should be. Then she began trembling with the miracle.

The babe did not look like Raven, like a white-eyes, as she had often wondered if it would. Her hair was midnight black, sleek and wet against her tiny perfect skull. Her eyes were squeezed closed in dismay at the wind, but once they peeked open and Storm Trail saw chips of onyx.

Raven watched them both and was helplessly, overwhelmingly, in love.

Nokoni left them alone.

"I will never forgive you," Storm Trail managed when he was gone.

"You have said that before." He wondered if his voice hitched, or if he imagined it.

"Never lie to me," she said hoarsely. "I can take anything but that. Always tell me the truth, even when I would kill you for it."

Raven nodded.

"Promise me," she said fiercely.

"Yes," he croaked. In that moment he would have promised to both of them his very soul.

"We should go," Nokoni said a very short time later.

The sleet had changed to a soft blanketing white. Storm Trail had wrapped the babe in one of the robes Raven had brought, but they were still very cold.

They doused the fire and mounted. Raven took the child from her. Storm Trail was uncomfortable enough not to protest. She would need all her strength to ride.

Raven looked down at his daughter, guiding his stallion with his knees. He knew that strong sons were every warrior's wish. For the first time in a long time, he wondered if a small part of his heart was still white, because he was elated with this girl-child, could not have asked for anything more. She was in her mother's image.

"Will you name her for us, friend?" he called out to Nokoni, who rode ahead.

"Yes, but I will need to think about it," Nokoni answered.

He would need to consult his spirit-protectors, Raven realized. He was so giddy with this child's birth, with finding them both alive and unharmed, that he was addled.

The ride away from the camp had seemed interminable. He was startled at how quickly they got back. They reached the lodges, and he was about to call out in his jubilation, to tell everyone of his new daughter, when he heard a strange strangled sound come from Storm Trail.

He looked at her sharply, thinking she was not strong enough to ride yet after all. She was staring at the tipis. Her mouth worked, but no more sound came out. She wore a look of horrified disbelief.

Raven followed her gaze. He did it just in time to catch sight of a white man ducking into Iron Shirt's lodge. And suddenly, in that moment, it occurred to him that he had not brought the babe's cord back to Naduah.

He refused to contemplate what one had to do with the other . . . because Naduah had said something about the cord promising long life.

Thirty-eight

Nokoni forcibly restrained him. "No! Stay here!"

They had gone directly to his lodge. Naduah was there, trembling fiercely, her face nearly as white as the snow outside. Storm Trail held her with one arm, her babe with the other, but her own eyes were wide and panicked.

"You have asked me many favors," Nokoni went on harshly.

"And now is the time you would ask a staggering one in return?"

"No, not staggering. But you owe me."

Raven could not argue with that.

Naduah had said that there was more than one white-eyes. Nokoni would not have them know that there were any of their own kind in this camp. It could only bring trouble, he said, if not now, then later. The few white children the Quohadi had adopted were all out of sight.

For Naduah, for their friendship, Raven let his air out. "So be it," he said shortly.

Nokoni relaxed. "I will go there myself and come back as soon as possible to tell you what is happening."

He ducked outside. Raven paced. Storm Trail watched him until she could no longer stand it.

"Stop!" she hissed finally.

"What?"

"Stop what you are doing to yourself, to *us*. Do you think of nothing but your own hatred of them? Why?" she demanded, unable to keep the question to herself any longer. "Why do you hate them so?"

He stared at her incredulously. "Do you have to ask me that?"

She left Naduah huddled by the fire and stood up to face him. "I hate them, too, with all my soul," she said fiercely. "And I still do not hate them as much as you do."

"You talk crazy," he muttered, but there was something lame in his voice.

"No." Now that she had started, she could not stop. "I think your hatred for them is wild, like fire."

Her words shook him badly. For one brief paralyzing moment, he thought of his vision quest dream, of that wildfire blazing over the prairie, leaving the charred flesh of animals in its wake. He wondered if there was a connection between that and this fury inside him now. He did not know, and he doubted if he could explain the rage that the white men ignited in him, even to her.

"Perhaps I only fear them," he said finally, "and I am loath to fear anything at all."

Storm Trail bit her lip. That she could understand.

Naduah roused herself. "We should eat," she said softly. "Nokoni could be over there all night."

"Yes," Storm Trail agreed, but not because she was hungry. She could not eat meat for four suns anyway after birthing her babe. But she thought Naduah badly needed something to do with her hands.

Raven started pacing again. As always, waiting was intolerable.

It was near dawn when Nokoni came back. Storm Trail and Raven slept in his lodge with Naduah, waiting for him.

Raven heard the soft tread of his friend's moccasins first. He snapped awake. "What happened?" he demanded. "What do they want?"

His voice roused Storm Trail. She nudged Naduah, and they sat up as well.

Nokoni settled before the dying fire and took his wife's hand in his own. "They want a council."

Storm Trail did not realize she had tightened her hold on her babe until the girl-child let out a small cry. "Here?"

"They came up the Quohadi crest to suggest another council?" Raven asked disbelievingly.

"No one travels in winter." Nokoni shook his head, and his voice was bemused. "We never even thought to watch the lowlands this moon."

"The *tejanos* travel all the time," Raven snarled.

"These men are *tosi-tivo,*" said Nokoni. "Those Aye-mer-i-cans you spoke of. They must be crazy, too."

Storm Trail groaned. Had they moved all the way here just so *different* white-eyes could find them?

"A council for what?" Raven demanded. "To get captives back again?"

Nokoni shook his head. "No. I do not think so. It is to give us . . ." He trailed off, struggling with the white-eyes phrase he had just learned. "In-dee-in pol-oh-cee."

The English words blasted into Raven's head. *Indian policy.*

"They said nothing of any captives we may already have," Nokoni went on. "But they want us to agree to return any that are taken in the future. And they want any ponies that our warriors steal from the white-eyes as well."

"That is insane!"

"Yes. But there is more. They say they talk true, that they tell us everything that will be discussed at this council. It remains only for our chiefs to go there and make some marks on a paper. All we have to do is stay behind a line they paint on Mother Earth, and they will give us presents whenever we ask."

Storm Trail gasped. "A line? How is such a thing possible?"

Nokoni shrugged as though the fine point were unimportant. "They say that we should recognize their white-eyes chief as our own . . . our Great Father." He shook his head. "I do not know what that is. They want us to trade with only the men they say."

"We never trade with white men," Raven snapped. "We steal from them."

Nokoni smiled thinly. "I thought it prudent not to mention that." He paused, glancing at Naduah. "My father said he would agree to all that, provided the *tosi-tivo* give us what those *tejanos* refused your Penateka when they first brought those bibles. The white men must stay on their side of the line as well."

"Will they do that?" Raven demanded.

"I do not know. You know them better than I."

Raven felt his heart chug painfully. "They will say they will, and then they will break their promise."

"Yes." Nokoni thought of what had happened to the other bands in San An-tone-yo. "They rarely speak true."

"Will Iron Shirt go?" Naduah spoke for the first time.

"Yes. He thinks to placate them, like children. They amuse him." Nokoni paused. "The white men say they have already been to your Penateka. Paya-yuca will go, though not Lost Coyote. The Wichitas and the Caddoes and even those people-eaters, the Tonkawas, will go as well and sign this paper talk."

"They have no choice," Raven spat. "The Wichitas, Caddoes and Tonkawas—even the Penateka—are already beaten."

No one argued with that. They all sat quietly, thinking. Finally Storm Trail spoke.

"If they could get to us up here, then they can go anywhere. There is nowhere safe from them," she whispered plaintively.

"There is a way," said Nokoni.

"What?" Naduah wailed.

"I begged my father not to go to this talk. He ignores my wishes, ignores my fear for my wife." His face hardened enough to frighten even Storm Trail, who knew him well and knew his inherent kindness. "Therefore I am leaving."

"Leaving?" Raven repeated blankly.

"The Quohadi."

"Where would you go? There is no band more isolated than this one."

"There will be now. I will make a new one. One of my own. I think there is only one way to keep these white-eyes away. That is what my spirit-protectors tell me, and I have been considering it for some time now. They remind me to listen to my name."

Nokoni, Raven thought. He Who Wanders.

"If we move constantly, they will never be able to catch up with us."

"All the Comanche move constantly," Raven said sharply.

"Not like we will."

Naduah was trembling again. "You would do this for me," she whispered. "But I cannot—"

Nokoni cut her off. "I do it for you, for our child, for all the children of all the People yet unborn. Anyone who wishes to go with us may come. I will welcome all. But we will never raid into Texas. I will condone no contact with those white men at all." He looked pointedly at Raven. "Will you come?"

Storm Trail held her breath.

"Yes," Raven said.

Storm Trail breathed again, feeling tears of relief spring to her eyes.

"Later," he added.

"Why?" Storm Trail demanded angrily. "Why can you not just give it up?"

"Later," he repeated, his face suddenly stony. "I cannot turn my back on those white men until I am satisfied with the blood I have taken from them."

"My father will agree to stop raiding them," Nokoni warned.

Raven shrugged. "Then let *him* stop. A Comanche man can speak only for himself. Your father cannot say what my war band will do. Iron Shirt's vows to the white-eyes do not bind me."

Nokoni sighed. "That is true."

"I have to do . . . something . . . first."

"What?" Storm Trail cried again.

"I do not know yet," Raven said pensively. "But I will know when I have done it."

Thirty-nine

The Quohadi camp had a desolate cold feeling without Naduah and Nokoni, and that cold ached in Storm Trail's heart. She wondered if Naduah had had her babe. Nokoni had not even waited long enough for his wife to birth it here. They had left, along with fifteen other men and their families, as soon as the white-eyes had departed and it was safe for Naduah to leave her lodge.

"Oh, friend," Storm Trail whispered into the wind, "where are you?"

Only Wind Bird answered her. She sat behind her, propped on the creek bank in her cradleboard. At least Nokoni had named her before he had left. He had done it in homage to Raven's spirit-protectors. Storm Trail only prayed that those spirits were as strong as Raven seemed to think they were. Every time he went into Tex-us, Storm Trail lived with a feeling of dull foreboding until he returned.

He was gone now, and even with Wind Bird's cheerful company, she had never felt so alone in her life. She had not made many other friends here. With Naduah, she had never felt the need.

She got the last of the roots she needed and stood up. Wind Bird chirped and gurgled at her. So beautiful, she thought again, amazed that someone so perfect had come out of her body. Then movement caught her eye and she looked up the canyon wall. More visitors had arrived.

They were *Penateka!* Storm Trail grabbed Wind Bird and

hurried for the trail they would come down on. There was
Eyes Down, and Star Line, and one of Lost Coyote's wives.
Her eyes flew over the others in disbelief—eight of them in
all.

Where was Lost Coyote? Why were there no men with
them?

Suddenly she knew that something had gone very wrong
again.

Johnny Moore was dying.

Thorn left the man's room over the saloon. He waited until
Jack Hays shut the door quietly behind him, then he drove his
fist into the wall.

"Jesus!" Hays burst out, startled.

Thorn rubbed his bleeding fist. It was as much anger as
grief that made him feel violent.

"Goddamnit. He knows. He knows and he can't tell me."

"Knows what?" Hays asked bemusedly.

"Who that trader was and where he got that Parker boy."

They went down the stairs. "Well, actually he isn't a boy
any longer, but nearly a man," Hays pointed out. "And Johnny
didn't get him. He more or less ended up with him."

Thorn knew he was right on both counts, but the latter, at
least, was salt in an open wound. Some lucky trader had stumbled upon John Parker in one of the northeastern 'Manche
bands, one of those relatively subdued now after their great
raid had come apart and Uncle Sam had begun holding carrots
of peace out to them. Raiding had tapered off to a low buzz—
just enough to warn a discriminating Texan that the hive was
still active.

Still a trader had managed to get in and out of one camp
with his hair, and he had turned over a few horses and blankets
and guns to get the Parker kid out with him. A tearful old
codger claiming to be his grandfather had surrendered him.
The trader had told Johnny Moore that the old guy had prac-

tically been grinning through his sobs. No one doubted that John Parker would turn tail and run back to the heathens as quickly as he could. The band would cleverly end up with John *and* the trader's bounty.

The trader didn't care. The ransom that Moore had arranged from the Parkers had more than exceeded the cost of the horses, blankets, and guns he had forfeited. *Thorn's* ransom.

They went outside and began trudging through the thick red mud in the streets. "I'm concerned about you, Matt," Hays said. "I'm not sure this is sane. You're obsessed with those Parker children."

"One Parker kid now," Thorn corrected darkly. "Only Cynthia Ann is left up there."

But he thought about what Hays had said. He had been searching for them for ten long years, come this spring. It had started out as a hunger for money, and by now he had gathered all the funds he needed to live comfortably in this new land. It had begun out of a need to perhaps buy his way home again, but he could no longer remember his wife's face, and he knew his children would not remember him. Now it was the god-damn principle of the thing. He had set a goal for himself and had encountered only failure. Cynthia Ann Parker was his last chance, and he was damned if he was going to give up until he found her.

They had reached their destination—an adobe-faced doctor's office on the main San Antonio avenue. Hays went in first and called out for the man, and the topic of the Parkers was forgotten. The medic was of Spanish and Pueblo extraction with dubious credentials, but it didn't matter. The government had supplied him with what Hays and Thorn needed.

"We need a couple of those cholera shots you're offering," Thorn told him.

"And pray God we're not too late," muttered Hays. "Poor Johnny."

* * *

Autumn was lush upon Nermenuh land. Raven rode hard,
but he still appreciated the luxuriant golden grasses as his stallion cut through them. They whispered and passed beneath
him in a blur. The air was good and thin, a little pungent with
the growth, musty with earth smells and dust. He heard a ci-
cada buzzing. The sun was white overhead, bleaching the sky.

Autumn was his favorite time. In autumn he could still roam,
but it was a bittersweet freedom because the season would
soon roll over into winter. The warmth of the air carried a
gentle reminder that he should enjoy it now because soon there
would again be snows.

One of his war band shouted from behind him. He looked
back without slowing his horse. It was Scout who had called
to him. The man was still with him all these years after the
magic gun fight, and he was now one of the best trackers
among all the People.

"What is it?" Raven called back to him.

"Penateka sign!"

They had just come up the scarp at the old place where
Kills In The Dark's ride had come to such a painful end. Why
had the Penateka moved even closer to the Balcones?

Raven reined in and looked at the faces all around him. "Do
you want to find them?" he asked his men. "We could sleep
here tonight." The Penateka men would want to see their kin,
he thought, and he would like to see Lost Coyote again as
well.

The Quohadi men shrugged. Several of the Penateka nodded.

"So be it." Raven pulled his stallion around. He began riding
in the direction Scout pointed.

They found the camp a short ride later. His war band came
to the high crest of ground overlooking the valley, and they
reined in. The Penateka were in one of the sloping grassy canyons that Raven remembered so well. But he had been wrong
all those many seasons ago. The white men could find them,
even when they camped down in one of these big swales.

Suddenly Raven's pulse hitched. *White-eyes.*

There were at least six of them in the Penateka camp. They had promised to stay away after that council last spring, but Raven had never believed that they would. One of his men made a move to go in anyway.

"Wait," Raven said. His instincts told him to be cautious.

He could not see all the way beneath the arbor, but Paya-yuca's huge legs were difficult to mistake. So was Kills In The Dark's pinched sharp face. *Kills In The Dark?* So the man had recovered, somehow, from his shame. He was like a refuse pile, Raven thought sourly. You could never get rid of it. You could only move away from it.

One of the white men jumped up and left the arbor. He went to the creek, ripping frantically at his trousers as he moved. He did not go to the place downstream where the people usually relieved themselves. He squatted as soon as he reached any semblance of privacy.

Dysentery? Raven wondered. Possibly, but a feeling coiled in the pit of his own gut, like an icy heavy snake.

"We will visit here the next time," he decided suddenly.

There were only a few murmured protests. They were not all that eager to go in while white men were in the camp.

They found a place to camp a healthy distance from the Penateka and their visiting white-eyes, and started out again early the next sun. They had barely traveled when something else caught Raven's attention.

"What cursed thing is this?" he wondered aloud, reining in.

Off to the west, vultures hovered. There were hundreds of them, but they were neatly organized, never straying too far north or south, as though the carrion they craved was placed in a straight line beneath them. Raven scowled. He had not come this way when they had ridden into Texas, but had cut east directly across the north country. He had noticed nothing like this there.

He kicked his stallion and swerved after the vultures. As the sun peaked, he found the first skeleton.

It was impossible to tell whether it had been a man or a woman. The birds had picked it bare of all flesh. It had not even been left in its entirety—a thigh bone was gone. A particularly enterprising wolf or coyote had carried it off, he thought, not willing to share with the rest of his pack.

Inexplicably Raven felt his gorge rise and his skin prickle. He had seen a great deal of death over the seasons, but this gave him a spooked feeling.

They went on along the line of birds and found an abandoned wagon. One wheel was sunken in drifting sand, as though it had been there for a while. Yet the wagon was still full of casks and sacks.

His men descended upon it. *"Get back!"* Raven shouted.

They jumped as though he had done the unthinkable and struck one of them. This time there was a chorus of complaints.

"Think!" he snapped. "What war band would take the people and leave this plunder?"

Raven saw them understand. Their eyes began to go wild. He felt it, too. This was too strange. Their *puha* was breaking.

He struggled to put common sense to it all. "No war band killed these people," he thought aloud. "It is *tejano* sickness. Leave the plunder and all that we got in the east as well. Kill all the ponies except those we need to ride."

A roar rose from the men, but it died as abruptly as it started. Raven was a leader who took everything he could from these white-eyes, no matter how insignificant. He made them suffer and had grown wealthy in the process. If he was ordering them to dump everything now, then something was seriously wrong.

A murky idea was forming at the back of Raven's mind. He thought of contamination now in Nermenuh terms, as evil white magic infecting everything, but he knew that they had to cleanse themselves of every tainted bit of it.

They mounted again and rode on fast, leaving the eerie death site and the slaughtered, stolen ponies. Raven noticed that some of the men scrubbed at their skin unconsciously.

What had killed those people? Then he had another, even more disturbing thought.

What were so many of them doing in Comancheria in the first place?

Storm Trail took the Penateka women to her lodge. Fear was a sour greasy feeling in her belly. They huddled at her cold hearth, and she was stricken by how old Star Line looked. Thick wings of white streaked down from the temples of her black hair.

It was chopped and butchered short in mourning again.

Lost Coyote. Storm Trail began trembling again before she even asked.

"What has happened?"

"They are all over," Eyes Down answered wretchedly. "And they brought sickness."

They. She did not have to ask who.

"They made a bargain, a pact to stay away!" she protested. "There was another council!"

Dove In The Night, Lost Coyote's third wife, looked up at her. "Yes, at a place on the northernmost reaches of our country. They call it Comanche Peak now, for us." Her voice was a sneer of contempt. "As though it has just now become ours."

Storm Trail shifted the heavy weight of Wind Bird's cradleboard against her back. "Iron Shirt went there," she said over Wind Bird's little voice. "They were going to draw a line on the earth."

Dove nodded. "Yes, they did that somehow. And we were not to cross it. Our warriors did not, for a while. They went back into Mex-ee-co for ponies. But the white-eyes were supposed to stay on their side, too, and that did not happen so we considered the peace broken.

"They came in wagons, streaming past our camps to go to somewhere west, looking for metal. Paya-yuca said they could pass unmolested if they gave us presents. They brought women and their own babes. They were not fighting men. They visited us, and they died with us. And then we started dying, too."

Storm Trail felt herself begin to sway. "How many?" she whispered. "Who?"

"My husband and Too Much. And Mountain, and Too Many Relatives, and Winter Song. So many . . ." Dove closed her eyes and shuddered. "It comes and gets in your guts. Only water comes out of you. Then you get lost in the spirit world— your body is here, but your mind goes somewhere else. Then you die."

Star Line spoke for the first time. "Not always."

"She had it," Dove explained, "and she got better. She was the only one. We do not know why it happened. Medicine Eagle had died by then, too, so there was no one to figure it out."

"We fled," Eyes Down picked up for her. "Your white warrior said that *tejanos* do not come here. We remembered that. He said if we wanted to get away from them, we should come to the Quohadi."

"Yes," Storm Trail murmured, then she closed her eyes. "No. Now they even come here sometimes."

Star Line gave a startling howl of terror, looking about as though she expected white men to mystically appear right there in the lodge. Storm Trail went to kneel beside her.

"You will be fine now," she crooned. "I will take care of you, and Raven will hunt for you. It will be fine now."

But even as she said it, she could no longer bring herself to believe it.

Raven came back two suns later.

Storm Trail heard the commotion of his arrival and ran outside to meet him. She hoped that he would not be long at the arbor. She needed to tell him of this strange new sickness. Then her heart plunged.

He brought no ponies, no plunder, no scalps. Though his

men had ridden out in hunting shirts and leggings, now they were near-naked. Their skin looked oddly reddened and raw, as though they had tried to wash it off their bodies. But they came right in. They had not lost everything to an enemy because they did not return in defeat and shame. And what enemy stole clothing?

She ran to Raven to take his horse.

"Do not touch it!"

She jumped back, flinching as though he had hit her. Suddenly anger burned through her.

"What is wrong with you?" she demanded. "You act like a crazy man!"

He scrubbed his hands over his face. Her anger dove coldly into new fear. "What is it?" she whispered. He looked so old, so tired and frightened. His face was one she almost did not know.

He didn't answer. He turned about instead to slash his stallion's throat. Storm Trail yelped and stumbled backward in shock and horror as the animal fell.

"What is happening?" she wailed again.

Still he did not answer. He went to the fire pit beside the arbor and began throwing his war equipment into the flames. Storm Trail gave a keening sound of terror. How could he do such a blasphemous thing to his spirit-protectors? They had blessed that shield, those arrows!

He saw her expression and finally spoke. "It is a more pure way of disposing of them than leaving everything abandoned on the prairie." Besides, he thought, if he had abandoned it, it could have infected others who came across it. He did not know how he knew that—he merely did.

The others were all gathering at the arbor now, staring in horror and amazement as Raven's warriors did the same things he had done.

"Is it the white-eyes sickness?" Storm Trail cried. "Is that it?"

He turned on her so abruptly she flinched away. "What do you know of it?"

"Eyes Down and Dove . . . they said the white-eyes brought it."

A terrible stillness came over him. "Eyes Down and Dove?"

She had never been truly honestly frightened of him before that moment. His face was deadly with rage.

"They are here," she whispered helplessly. "They fled the Penateka because everyone was dying."

Raven let out a strangled sound of helpless disbelief.

"What?" she demanded. "You told them to come here, that they would be safe here!"

He had. Bless his spirit-protectors, he had.

He looked around wildly and saw Eyes Down come out of his lodge. *His* lodge.

"Burn it," he choked. *It was not too late, surely it was not too late.* But he knew that despite all his own precautions, the Penateka had brought the *puha*-sickness here anyway.

"My lodge?" Storm Trail gasped. "Burn my *lodge?*"

"The lodge and everything inside it. Just do it. I will explain later, after we get out of here." He took her arms and looked down at their child. He could not find the words to tell her the utter horror of it all. He did not know if there was a word for epidemic in Nermenuh, and it was only a shadowy but certain idea in his mind anyway. He did not know how to explain something so evil and killing that it could jump from body to body, seemingly on a breath. He had come across more and more graves on the ride home. He had passed by a Tanima camp to find no one alive within it. The reek of death and feces had hung over the place like a vile cloud.

"We will go now," he said hoarsely. "We will travel awhile, make sure we—" He broke off. *Make sure we do not die, make sure we do not carry it.* "We will find Nokoni. It is time."

Sweet blessed relief filled Storm Trail at that. "I will tell Star Line and Eyes Down," she murmured, turning away.

"No!"

She looked back at him in confusion. "They came all this way to find us!"

Something spasmed across his face. "They cannot come, Fire Eyes."

"But—"

"Believe me. I told you I would never lie to you again."

Something wild came over her face. "They are *kin!*"

"I cannot help that!"

"Will you make me leave them again?"

"I did not make you the first time!" He took a breath, got control. He could not lock horns with her. "It was your choice then," he went on quietly, "and it must be mine now. I cannot give you an opinion this time. I am sorry."

In spite of himself he looked at the Penateka women who were gathering outside his lodge, staring at him. He met each gaze, telling himself that any one of them would have taken a knife to his throat after the council house massacre. But it did not assuage his guilt at leaving them to what would certainly be their own deaths.

He left Storm Trail and went to the arbor. Iron Shirt looked at him in arrogant disbelief as he explained to him what he had seen. "They said they would not come here. They gave me their word."

"But they *have* come. They are all over Comancheria. They are traveling across Nermenuh land, hundreds upon thousands of them."

"So what would you have us do, now that you and your men have left dead horses all over my camp?"

Raven felt an exhaustion as deep as his bones. His every instinct screamed at him to take Storm and Wind Bird and get out of here fast. Out of respect to this man who had taken him in, he had paused to warn him. Now the old buzzard would not listen.

At least he had tried.

"Move camp," he said. "You would have done it in a few suns anyway. Do it now."

Perhaps that would help, but as long as the Penateka were with them, he was pretty sure the Quohadi were in danger. But he could not bring himself to tell Iron Shirt that, could not bear to have it on his own conscience if the women were driven out, no matter what they might have done to him seasons ago.

"Do not go near anything those Penateka people have touched," he cautioned instead. "You should ask them to camp off just a little way for a while, by themselves."

He turned away, feeling too old for his twenty-six years.

Forty

Storm Trail rode silently, not looking at him. Raven hoped she was less angry than stunned. He did not speak either, because he needed to think.

He could not take this evil white *puha* to Nokoni and his followers. First he would find shelter for his own family, he decided, someplace where they could rest and wait to see if it struck any of them. He scrubbed a hand over his jaw. The one thing he tried not to think about as they came down off the Quohadi scarp was that he had only the magic gun now, with four precious bullets left.

They rode slowly west. Near dusk they found another rocky outcropping much like the butte they had lived upon with the Quohadi, but smaller. Raven scanned its walls as they skirted it, and he saw a shadow within a shadow on the face.

"Stop," he said. "Wait here."

Storm Trail obeyed without comment. She reined in and began crooning to their babe.

The rocky slope was banked by a litter of boulders. Raven climbed over them to the spot he had noticed. It was a cave, about halfway up.

It was perfect, but his skin went cold again as he realized why he liked it. If they should all take sick, no hungry animal was likely to find and molest them. If they died, their bones could rest here together with no one, nothing, ever likely to find them. It was, he thought, as good as a pile of rocks, if neither of them survived to bury the other.

He scrambled down again and jogged to their ponies. Storm had dismounted. She was kneeling on the ground with her back to him.

Suddenly she cried out. Her voice rose up to the sky, bouncing off the butte wall, a wail of agony, a scream of infernal fury.

Storm Trail heard him running for her. For a brief frozen moment that she knew she would remember for the rest of her life, she was excruciatingly and unnaturally aware of everything around her. Each sound was crystal clear, each smell perfect. She would remember it forever because it was the last priceless, precious moment of life being something worth living.

Then violent horror burst in on her. *No, no, no!* Not her babe, not her child!

She had taken Wind Bird from her cradleboard to change the padding tucked inside it. Now she stared at it, kept staring—no!—and her breath came in short hard pants of helpless denial. *Please, no!*

The padding was stained and foul with the babe's diarrhea.

It was mercifully fast for the little one. She was too young, too delicate to mount much of a fight. By the following darkfall she was gone.

Storm Trail's screams rang off the cave walls again when Wind Bird closed her eyes and shivered for the last time. Raven grabbed the babe from her. *No, Christ, no.* He had failed them. Unconscionable pain brought distant memory to the surface again, and he was neither white nor red in that moment, only a man, only a father.

Her knife. He remembered it and grabbed it from her before she could think of using it. He hurled it out of the mouth of the cave. It clattered down the rocks outside.

"Nooooo! No!"

She wailed the single word again and again. Raven made a

move to hold her, but she did not want comfort. She fought him viciously.

"Stop," he managed hoarsely. "Stop!"

But she would not. Her nails raked down his face. Her teeth found his arm, and all the while she sobbed, her face contorted with a grief he could not bear.

He wrestled with her, and after an eternity, she collapsed by the fire. She shook so badly he heard her teeth click together. He knelt cautiously and stroked a trembling hand over her hair.

How could she tell him? There were no words to say what was inside her, the gnawing loss, the incomprehensible helplessness. She did not know how she would go on, not without that child, that beautiful sweet babe. *Her child.*

When her crying subsided, he left her to take the little body outside. He protected her from animals beneath a too-tiny hill of rocks, then he sank down beside the mound.

He wanted to tell the babe that he had never loved another in quite the same way he had loved her. He wanted to tell her how he had felt when she had slid from her mother's womb into his hands. Three seasons old. He wanted to weep, needed it, and nothing would come. His throat was strangled and dry as sand.

Finally, dreading what he might find, he got up and went back to the cave.

The evil white *puha* struck Storm Trail next. He had known it would take at least one of them. They had not been able to protect themselves after it got into Wind Bird.

She was huddled at the back of the cave, crooning a Nermenuh lullaby that made his blood cold. She never looked at him. When her belly cramped for the first time and doubled her over, he went to her quickly and pulled her to her feet to help her to the water he'd found, but she fought him off.

"I can do it," she rasped, her voice raw from screaming.

He watched her from the mouth of the cave. She did not make it past the clearing where the horses stood.

Her bowels erupted suddenly and she sank to her knees and wept again with the shame of it. Raven ran for her and she tried to fight him off again, but this time he would not let her go.

"It is all right, all right. Come back. Come back to the cave."

He carried her back. By the time they got there, it seemed her mind had gone.

He thought at first that it was just grief, or perhaps she had fallen asleep in his arms. But when he put her down by the fire, he saw that her rest was somehow deeper than that, yet more shallow. Her cracked dry lips spoke in soundless words. He pinched her tentatively, but she did not rouse.

Not her, oh, spirits, do not take both of them.

He worked her soiled doeskin from her body and covered her with one of the robes. He was going to lose her, and he could no longer even imagine a world without her in it. Wind Bird, yes—spirits forgive him, but he could recall a time when the babe had not been with them. It would be the worst pain he had ever known to go on without her, but he could survive somehow. But he would not survive losing this woman.

With each dawn he carried her to the water and eased her down into it, washing the filth of her sickness away. Each time it got dark, he lay beside her in the cave for brief periods, watching her—as though by keeping his eyes on her, he could will her spirit and her mind back into her body. Her skin was like fiery parchment, without color. As the suns passed her ribs grew more and more gaunt. Each dawn he replaced the robe he had wrapped around her, taking the last one to the creek to wash it out. He needed to burn them—he knew that. If he did not, he would be next and there would be no one to care for her, to bury her. But there was nothing else with which to cover her, and if he lost her, then he realized he did not care if he died as well.

Finally her diarrhea stopped.

Raven was relieved, then terrified. It struck him that perhaps there were no more fluids left for her body to purge. He carried her to the creek again, far down it where he was sure it was not contaminated with her own excrement. He could not bring the water back to her. He had nothing with which to carry it.

Finally he went back to the cave to bring their pitiful belongings to the water. He wrapped her up again and sat beside her.

"Do not die. Do not go. You are the only thing in my life I never needed to escape from."

She murmured incoherently in her sleep, shaking her head back and forth, but she was only praying for her daughter, not answering him.

That was when he finally left her. He climbed down over the boulders again to the place where he had left Wind Bird. He had thought he would look for his spirit-raven, but in the end he only stared up at the night sky, toward a god he no longer knew.

"Who are you? *Curse you, what are you?* Are you white? Are you red? Whose side are you on?"

His voice echoed out over the rocks, escalating into a roar. He had the blood of so many men on his hands. Surely no god would listen to him.

"But she has done nothing!" he shouted angrily. "She has done nothing to deserve this. Take me, not her. Take *me!*"

There was no answer, just the eternal Comanche wind soughing over the rocks as though reminding him that it, at least, would live forever.

Raven glanced up at her face out of habit as he bathed her in the creek yet again. This time her eyes were open.

His heart slammed.

How many times had he killed men to have them look just like that, staring sightlessly at the sky? But Storm Trail was breathing, and after a stunning moment he realized that she was only watching him steadily, without expression.

"They took her," she whispered finally, flatly. Then she closed her eyes again and went back to sleep.

Raven carried her back to the cave. He had been forced to use his bullets to hunt, but eating had brought his own strength back and perhaps had kept her alive. Since realizing that he was starving her for liquids, he had been doggedly dribbling broth into her as well. He had managed to keep their rocky shelter reasonably clean, hauling water back and forth once he had a paunch with which to carry it. Now he gently put her down by the fire and waited.

At dawn she came around again.

He looked up sharply from their fire when he heard her move, and relief was airy and hollow in his chest. She licked her lips and spoke meticulously, as though learning words all over again.

"How long?" she asked, her voice parched. "How long since I lost her?"

"I do not know," he said hoarsely. "I lost track of the suns."

"You know." She said it as a statement of fact, without heat.

He forced himself to think it out. "About a moon now."

Her head moved infinitesimally as she nodded. "I saw her in the afterworld. She was crying for me." And then she went to sleep again.

Her words turned his blood cold, but he thought it was good that she slept. She would need to rest to recover her strength, but there was something unnatural about the way she did it, as though she were . . . escaping.

"Did it get you?" Storm Trail croaked the next time she woke. "Did it get you at all?"

Raven flinched, dribbling broth into her mouth. He had been waiting for the question, dreading it. "No."

"Why?"

He had thought about it. He'd had ample time and little else to do. *Because I did not come here until I had seen sixteen winters.* He knew somehow that that was it. During those first sixteen winters, somehow he must have picked up some kind of protection against it. It was a white-eyes disease, and his skin was white.

Guilt ravaged him.

Storm Trail sat up painfully, weakly, and inched her way closer to the cooking paunch. "I can feed myself."

He worried that she could not but allowed her to try, and she did it. He was no longer surprised by her strength and determination.

"Where did this come from?" she asked finally.

Her question took him off guard, and he had to struggle with his thoughts a moment. "I killed a boar."

"Do we have bullets left?"

"No. I used my knife." He forced himself to look into her eyes. "I am . . . sorry. For all of it. I tried to stop it." Such ineffectual words, saying so little. But he could not find better ones.

Storm Trail only looked away from him.

By the time the snows were deep upon Comancheria, she had regained her physical strength. Storm Trail thought about how Star Line had survived the sickness, too. For the first time in her life, she wondered if the spirits were not really just malicious nasty little creatures who liked to play cruel jokes. Star Line, too, had lost everyone dear to her, and still she lived on, a vacant-eyed survivor, a shell of the woman she had been. Storm Trail gave a shrill laugh at the irony of living once everything was gone.

Raven looked at her sharply. "What? What is funny?"

She shook her head. She could not tell him. She could not explain, and wondered how he could not know.

He was sitting on his bedding, a strange pile of mismatched hides. Some of them smelled. He had never been any good at tanning. Something tender tried to move inside her, then it died.

Storm Trail groaned quietly and lay down upon her own bedding. She felt him move closer to her. He put a hand on her shoulder. Her heart cringed.

"How do you feel?" he asked quietly.

"Tired. I want to sleep." She eased away from his touch. "Why do they keep taking them away from me?" she whispered soundlessly, her eyes burning again. "Why did you let them?"

He watched her lips but couldn't make out her last words.

Spring bloomed wildly, as it did in this north country. Raven thought it was as though the tremendous snows somehow soaked Mother Earth so deeply, they nourished dormant life to the fullest.

There was no life inside their cave.

Raven's heart ached as he stood in the lowlands with a doe slung over his shoulder. This was a new ache, different from the anguished pain of losing Wind Bird, but he had known it would be. It was just that he'd thought he would suffer it only if Storm Trail died.

Instead, only a part of her had gone.

After everything, he was losing her. He would give her her child back if he could, would give his own life up to return the babe to her. He would have died for either one of them, painfully, a thousand times, if the gods had only struck him in their stead. But he could not do that, the spirits would not take him, and now when Storm Trail spoke to him, she did not use her eyes. She was simply there, a quiet presence in their cave, a shadow moving beyond his line of vision.

Why?

He had not made love with her since she had recovered, and

that had been six moons ago. She never actively pulled away from him, but he felt her change under his hands whenever he touched her. It was as though her very flesh was shrinking away from his. He had never felt such agonizing frustrating loss, and he did not know what to do about it.

He got a better grip on the doe and made his way back up the boulders. She was sewing two rabbit hides together when he returned.

"You are getting good with that knife," she said flatly. "If I can gather enough of these, it will make a warm robe when the winds get cold again. Can you find more hares?"

His heart kicked. "This is only the first spring moon. The cold will not come back for a while."

Storm Trail shrugged one shoulder and went to drink from their water paunch.

"I think . . . I have seen no one pass by here in all the times I have hunted," he tried.

She made no response.

"Perhaps Nokoni and Naduah are all right," he went on. "They would probably not have had any contact with the white-eyes. I would like to wait another moon or two, just to be sure we do not encounter that white *puha* again when we leave here, but when summer comes, I think we can set out and look for them."

"That would be good," she said without inflection.

"Do you still want to find them?" *Talk to me.*

"Yes, of course."

"That is what we will plan, then."

"It is a good plan." *You hated those white-eyes more than you loved us!* Yes, she thought, oh, yes, Naduah and Nokoni would be all right, as they would be if only Raven had been willing to go with their friends.

But she did not say it aloud, any more than she would have left this cave and walked away from him, because none of it mattered anymore. None of it was important enough to expend the energy.

He left the cave again. Storm Trail curled up on her bedding, clutching the rabbit skins. They would have made a perfect robe for a toddler.

Forty-one

Summer was nearly gone again before they found any trace of Nokoni's band. Raven was not an expert tracker, and what little sign he did find seemed to indicate that his friend was as good as his word. He rarely stayed in any one place for more than a sun. His camps did not even leave enough marks upon Mother Earth to remain past a good rain.

Raven and Storm Trail rode as far west as they could go, then they turned south and went nearly as far as Mexico. As they turned east again, Raven's tension and misgivings increased. If they ran into white men, he had so little with which to defend them—his wits and his knife.

"What about that?" Storm Trail finally murmured, pointing to the side, and everything inside him stiffened. He looked her way sharply, expecting to see riders.

But there was only an ash pit on the far side of her pony. Raven dismounted to examine it, then rubbed at an ache behind his eyes.

"It is not them," he said finally. "There is nearly a moon's worth of refuse here."

For a brief moment Storm Trail sat up straighter on her mare, then her spine bent again. "We will never find them. No one could. *They* are safe."

Raven had started to mount again. He went still halfway up, feeling as though he had taken a bullet in the chest. In that moment he understood. He knew all she had not said, all she had been unable to say. Guilt exploded in him, screaming through his head, wrenching his gut . . . because she was right.

Sweet spirits, if he had gone with Nokoni when that man had left the Quohadi, Wind Bird would still be alive.

He had done this to them, to his child. He looked across his pony's back to her, pleading with her silently as he had never done before. *Forgive me.* But Storm Trail was looking down at her pony's mane, uncaring of anything.

Raven pulled himself clumsily astride. He rode east, not necessarily because he thought Nokoni had gone in that direction, but because his stallion's nose was already pointing that way.

They encountered the Penateka less than a sun later. Raven realized that it had been that band who had left the ashes.

He rode to the top of a rise and looked down at the camp. He saw perhaps fifteen lodges below. The sickness had all but destroyed the last of them.

He called back to Storm. "Stay here." She nodded without comment, without moving.

If by some stretch of the imagination the *puha*-thing was still active among the People, at least Raven was reasonably certain that he could withstand brief exposure to it. He left her and rode down into their swale. Kills In The Dark and Paya-yuca were both still alive. Perhaps the *puha*-thing spared all fools, he thought bitterly.

Paya-yuca met him and tried to usher him to the arbor. Kills In The Dark watched with a look of hatred that had not eased in the least over so many seasons.

Raven stood just outside the arbor, keeping one wary eye on the man. "I cannot sit," he explained. "We cannot stay."

"We?" Kills In The Dark demanded.

Raven realized that he did not trust him to know that Storm Trail waited alone outside the camp. He had failed her enormously. This was one small thing he could do to protect her.

"I have others," he said flatly. "They were afraid to come in because of the sickness."

He watched Kills In The Dark's eyes move speculatively up to the ridge beyond which Storm Trail waited.

"The sickness is gone," said Paya-yuca. "Bring them in. We have a little food."

"No, there is no time. We seek word of Nokoni. We would join him."

If the sickness had ever touched Paya-yuca, it had stolen none of his girth. The big man grunted as he sat down. "That is what they are calling them."

"What?"

"The Nokonis. That is what they call his band—Wanderers. No one has seen them in perhaps four moons now."

"Where were they then?"

"As far west as they could go. Some Yamparika ran across them by accident and mentioned it when we saw them."

"I thank you." He turned away, but Kills In The Dark stopped him.

"Is your wife with you?"

Raven nodded, his eyes narrowing on him.

"She should have been mine."

Raven felt his heart thump in disbelief. *"Yours?* You had the chance once, and you took She Smiles. You had another chance, and you lost all your horses."

"You always win," Kills In The Dark said with eerie calm.

"Because you are no competition," Raven snapped, disgusted, but he wondered, spirits help him, he wondered if she would have been better off with Kills In The Dark, if her children would at least be alive.

They found Nokoni and Naduah in the next moon. Storm Trail was sure it was some kind of miracle.

They were riding west again. By some quirk of fate and pure chance, the Nokonis were trailing a buffalo herd toward the east. The hunters went on, but Naduah and Nokoni waited for them.

Storm Trail dismounted and clutched Naduah. Something savaged Raven's heart. Her shoulders shook. She sobbed. She sobbed as she had not done with him in nearly a circle of seasons.

"Did you do it?" Nokoni asked finally.

Raven flinched. Was he asking if he had killed his own daughter? Then he understood that Nokoni was speaking of that unnameable *something,* the price of blood he had been driven to extract from the white-eyes at all costs, at such precious cost.

"No," he managed. "I stopped looking."

Nokoni nodded thoughtfully. "You are welcome here. You have been missed." He threw him his lance. "We should hunt. You can use that weapon. I will use my bow."

Nokoni gave a hunting cry and galloped off. Raven hesitated a moment, then went after him.

He did not think they would catch up with the herd, but it swerved around in a huge arc, heading westward again, and they were able to meet it as it came thundering back. Raven felled three of the beasts. But he could not, even in the deepest corner of his heart, find any of the joy in it that he had once known.

They camped where they had made their kills, though the area was not protected and there was only one place with scant groundwater. "It does not matter," explained Nokoni. "We will move as soon as this meat is dried. The water is enough to hold us for a short while."

They were sitting outside his lodge door. Naduah had made their fire there, and some of the meat sizzled over it.

There was no arbor. There was little wood, and no sense in using precious time to construct one for the short time they would be here. He and Nokoni were alone, although the camp moved about them, soft laughter sounding somewhere distant. Storm Trail and Naduah were inside the tipi.

Raven listened to the camp sounds, healthy *alive* sounds, and his heart pounded.

Nokoni studied his face. "Tell me how everything happened."

He had not thought he would be able to talk of it. But he got it out, each meticulous detail. The smells, the pain, the loss. And then he realized, with shimmering amazement and horror, that he was very close to weeping.

He choked. He could think of nothing worse than crying in the presence of another warrior, not even this man who had grown to be closer to him than a brother. Then Nokoni stood abruptly, striding several paces past the fire to give him privacy.

He spoke again over his shoulder. "Your wife blames you."

"I blame myself."

"As you should. But there is no going back."

There is no going forward. There was nothing waiting for him there but Storm Trail, estranged, distrusting him . . . hating him.

"Why?" asked Nokoni, repeating the question Storm Trail had once asked him. "Why do you hate them so much more than the rest of us?"

"I cannot understand why you do not hate them more."

Nokoni was quiet for a long time. "The Nermenuh have had many enemies over the generations," he explained finally. "Some of them I never met. I heard of them only when they were discussed over council fires when I was a child. The white men are but one more. They are more tenacious than most, but they are still just an enemy, and the Nermenuh have never been beaten by anyone because we are smarter. What I have done, for instance, has outwitted both the *tejanos* and *tosi-tivo.*"

From behind him, inside the lodge, Raven heard the laughing cry of Quanah, Nokoni and Naduah's son. He had been born nine suns after they had left the Quohadi camp, less than half a moon after Wind Bird.

Finally Raven wept.

The tears were scalding, bitter. When he stood up again, his legs felt shaky but he felt somehow purged. Hearing him move, Nokoni finally turned around.

"I think you should go to her, talk to her."

"She no longer sees me."

"She does. But she does not want you to know it."

"*I* would not forgive me under the circumstances."

"*You* do not have to." Nokoni paused. "What I have seen of the two of you is that neither one is the sort to give up. I think if she honestly could not forgive you, she would have died when she took the sickness. There would have been nothing left for her to fight back for. But she does live, and so she has not completely given up on you." He went to his lodge door and called in to Naduah. "Bring Quanah. We will walk."

When they were gone, moving off into the darkness, Raven looked for a long time at the tipi. There was no sound from within.

He shook his head. She had to know his grief, his shame, his regret. Or did she? Had she, too, thought that *he* should have known why she hated him, all those moons before he had finally figured it out?

He bent and ducked inside. He was not ready to face her, but his feet carried him as though with a will of their own.

She was sitting by the cold hearth, her knees drawn up. Her head was bent to rest upon them, her short glossy black hair hiding her face. He knew she heard him, but she did not look up.

"I cannot . . . live without you."

She seemed to spasm, her whole body tensing, then relaxing. It was not what he had meant to say.

Some part of him wanted to cling to his pride in spite of everything. Arrogant. That was what she had always called him. But he had humbled himself so much tonight, and the admission was so bald he could still hear it ringing in the air.

"Come back to me, please," he went on hoarsely. "Or if you cannot, tell me so, and I will go."

He had not meant to say that either, but it was out, and he knew in that moment that it was true. He would not torture either one of them this way much longer.

She did not answer.

"I was wrong. You were right," he burst out. "I should have let go of my hunger for their blood, if only for you. But . . . I did not know how to give it up. It was not horses, not plunder, not even hatred that kept me going after them. It was none of those things, just a . . . compulsion. And I grieve every sun for my choice."

"So do I," she said finally. *"Curse you!"*

He flinched and turned to go.

"Wait," she said hoarsely.

When he turned back, she was already on her feet. She was trembling. "I do not forgive you," she whispered. This time he knew that she meant it.

"But I know you kept me alive. I know I should thank you for it." There was not another living soul, she thought, who would have cared for her the way he had. Only Raven, her Raven. Ah, how that sinew had ended up binding them. She had forgiven him for She Smiles, but this . . .

"I cannot thank you," she went on desperately. "You should have let me die. I wish you had let me die."

"I could not do that to myself," he managed. And if that, too, was selfish, then so be it.

Storm Trail sighed and shuddered. "No, I do not suppose I could have let you die either, not even after I knew that your choice killed my daughter." She took a deep breath. "None of Nokoni's people died," she said flatly. "Not even one of them. But it was not just you, not just your choice that killed her. I blame myself as well."

"You?"

"I birthed her!" she cried vehemently. "In my hope, in my weakness, I gave the white-eyes something else to take away from me!" She took a step toward him. "I did not fight you hard enough! How many times in my life have I protested when something was not to my liking? But I stayed with you, waiting for you in that Quohadi camp, waiting for you to get over whatever it was that was driving you. *And it killed my child!*"

Her teeth snicked together with the tremors that ran through her. "What did you say once? Through every cruelty, we have both been to blame?" she asked, strangled. "When they take you, if they do not take me with you, then I will die by my own hand."

She closed the distance between them suddenly and pressed her cheek to his chest. She snaked her arms around his waist. Raven groaned. He did not deserve it, and he could not believe she had come back to him.

Death made living too precious, and Storm Trail needed life. She would not allow him to hold her for long. She turned her face up and rooted for his mouth.

They fumbled with each other, at their clothing. Her dress had seen too many washings, and it tore in his hands. He threw it aside and found her skin, so cold. He rubbed his hands over her frenziedly, warming her.

His tongue plunged past her teeth, seeking salvation, but when she met it she felt as though she was drinking life back into her own body. She tangled her fingers in his long thick hair and held on.

Raven, her own crazy white-eyes. Through all the good and all the bad it was him, his face, that had always been there.

His hands cupped her breasts, savoring the feel of them. He found her thighs and he lifted her, spreading them, impaling her. She groaned and tightened her legs around him, her arms around his neck, and she ground her mouth down on his.

Only then did they tumble back down to the earth, into the short grass Naduah had torn up to make a floor. He came down on top of her, her legs still tight around his hips, never losing the precious connection of flesh between them.

With the smells of life surrounding them, with the sweet scent of green and the dust of the soil, he plunged into her again and again, seeking oblivion. They grieved and touched. They ached and loved.

And neither one of them thought of the life they might be creating.

Forty-two

They did not see any more buffalo before the snows came, and the robe season of 1848 was one of the hungriest Storm Trail could remember. It seemed as though all the animals had gone to some afterworld and left the People forever. Or perhaps they were in an afterworld, Storm Trail thought wildly. Perhaps she really had died with that sickness and was only now realizing it, and the afterworld was a place where there was snow as far as the eye could see, where there was no sign of life other than their own.

She sat in her lodge with Raven, with Nokoni and Naduah and little Quanah, shivering a little as she thought of the unnaturalness of it. Raven looked her way and rubbed her forearm as though her cold was something he could warm.

"The buffalo do not like change," Nokoni was saying. "If there is even one small white-eyes building, they will not come within five days' travel of it. It is as though they sense its presence, and they know to stay away. I myself have never seen that happen, but I have heard of it."

"But there are no white-eyes buildings here!" Naduah protested.

"No," Nokoni agreed. "But they have put those metal trails up north."

Trains, Raven thought. That had been the newest *tosi-tivo* invasion, but their tracks had not come through Comancheria . . . yet.

"Do you think the herds are not coming south past those

rails?" he asked. "That the buffalo remain up north in Pawnee country?"

"That is what I am guessing. It is as though that smoke-belching beast has formed a barrier, a line over which the herds will not come to get back into our country. I want to travel south now when we move tomorrow. Maybe down there, far enough away from that metal line, we will find some herds."

Storm Trail shivered again. Six moons ago she would have asked him how they would get through the drifts. Now she knew that the Nokonis always found a way. The band traveled slowly, and they often rode miserably as sleet and ice assaulted them. But they traveled. Always they traveled. And they were all still alive.

That was the thin fragile desperation she clung to through a terror she had not even told Raven about. Through all its hardships, this way of living had so far preserved them, kept them whole. She had not seen a single white man since they had left the Quohadi, and she told herself she would not see one again as long as they stayed with Nokoni.

Suddenly a cold draft slid up her back, beneath her robe. The wind, she thought, it's just that endless wind. Naduah leaned over to feel Quanah's little fingers. They must have been cold, because she stood up. She left, carrying Quanah, waddling again. She had another babe in her, though this time she was rail-thin and the bulge of her child looked incongruous.

The men kept talking. Storm Trail's belly heaved suddenly, and she had to bite down hard on her lip, praying that the pain of it would make her forget everything else. But it did not, not this time. Her ploys and tricks to keep herself from thinking were working less and less as the moons wore on. She got up abruptly, making a move to go outside as well.

"Where are you going?" Raven asked, a thread of alarm winding through his voice.

"There is something I forgot to ask Naduah." *She had not*

forgotten, oh, no, never. But it was time now. Her own ideas were getting her nowhere. It was time to plead for help.

It was snowing when she went outside. Tiny stinging flakes bit into her cheeks and her exposed skin. She gathered her robe more tightly around herself and put her head down to push through the gales. There was a narrow path between their lodges where their feet had punched through the drifts.

Storm Trail ducked into Naduah's tipi without calling out first. Her friend would not have heard her voice anyway over the wind.

"Haitsi," Naduah said, surprised. She looked up as she tucked Quanah into his robes. "What is it?"

For a moment Storm Trail only stood, flexing her hands into fists beneath her robe, loosening them, flexing them again. She would have howled with the grief of it, if only Raven had not been so close by. She did not want him to hear this.

"Do you know of anything to make a babe go away?"

Naduah scowled, confused, then her face lit and she straightened. "Oh, friend," she breathed. "Have the spirits given you . . ." Then she trailed off as she understood what Storm Trail had said.

"This has nothing to do with the spirits!" Storm Trail cried. "It has everything to do with the white-eyes, and it is *evil!"*

Naduah's face drained of color. "Your babe?" she whispered. "Your babe is evil? But you cannot think that! Unless . . ." Naduah swayed. Had a *white* man put this new child in her friend? She was not thinking of Raven. She considered him no more white than she did herself.

But Storm Trail was shaking her head frantically. "Do not speak of it so!" she shrieked.

Why did this keep happening to her?

She lowered her voice. "You must not speak of it as though it were a child. You see, that is what I never do. My bleeding has just stopped. I tell myself that some badness, some new sickness has gotten into me again and plugged me up. That is all it is," she finished helplessly. "Just some badness."

Naduah began to cry.

"Before," Storm Trail went on, "I *believed.* I believed you and Raven when you said the white men would not find us. Do you not see? They did not find me, but they reached me. They sent their sickness to me, to my babe. Oh, sweet spirits, I believed and she died looking into my eyes! I cannot bear that ever again."

"No!" Naduah cried. "If you believed that, you would not have waited so long to come to me! You would not have given this child a chance!"

"I did not give it a chance!" Storm Trail wailed. "I beat myself with rocks! I have tried everything I can think of! It will not come out without your help! Your Quohadi grandmother was a healer. You must know of *something!*"

But Naduah stood firm. "You gave this child moons to grow!" She knew that, because now she understood why Storm Trail always had a robe around her lately. It wasn't just because of the cold. She was hiding what was happening to her body.

"Stop it!" Storm Trail cried, then she whipped around as the door flap rattled behind her.

Raven stood there, as white as she had ever seen him. "I knew," he managed. "I guessed. But you . . . you said nothing again, and I thought this was maybe just the way you got when you had a babe in you."

"Stop it!" she shrieked again. Her head pounded. Her belly twisted. If they spoke if it, if they made this babe real, then it would kill her just as much as Wind Bird's death to make it go away.

"This is the one thing I cannot live through," she went on wretchedly. "I cannot—*I will not*—keep giving them my children!"

Raven tried to touch her. She could not bear that now. Touching, loving, was what would tear her soul right from her body. Touching him made babes.

She shrank back from him violently, as she had done in those horrible moons in the cave. She pushed past him so fast that he had no time to react and grab her. He made a move to go after her, but Naduah stopped him.

"Wait!"

He looked back at her impatiently.

"Oh, friend, I think she speaks true. I fear that losing this babe would destroy her."

Raven's eyes narrowed. "What are you saying?"

"That . . . I think she is being torn in two. She cannot give another, but if she could easily kill her own child, then she would not have waited this long."

"I have to go to her," he repeated hoarsely.

"Yes, but . . . think, friend! How long have you guessed now?"

"Moons," he said quietly.

"She knew. She has been hiding it. And she has let it, and herself, live all this time."

He blanched. "Do you think she would take her own life over this?" He thought how she had been in the cave. Yes, he thought. Oh, sweet spirits, yes, she would. Nothing had ever changed her, destroyed her, as much as losing her child.

Naduah took a deep breath and prayed the spirits would not strike her dead for the blasphemy she was about to utter. "If she wants to make it go, I will try to help her," she whispered.

Raven's heart slammed. "Can you do that?"

"I know of something. Not to make a babe go away, but . . . if a babe cannot get out when its time comes, I know of a weed that can help a woman open up. Maybe . . . maybe it would work even if it is *not* the babe's time."

Raven thought he would vomit. "No."

Nokoni's voice came from behind him. "It is not your choice to make, my friend."

Raven whipped around. Nokoni stood just inside the door. "We are safe with you," he growled.

"Safer. We are never truly safe. Not from what she fears."

"If she wishes, I will try," Naduah repeated grimly. "I love her. But you must tell her . . . if the babe comes out . . ." She took a deep breath. "If the babe comes out, she must know that it will probably come out alive, and then die."

And that, Raven thought, was exactly what Storm Trail feared so desperately.

There was no way out. And he was terrified that it was going to destroy her this time, that she had come back to him only so he could lose her forever through another child.

He pushed past Nokoni. "I have to go to her."

He ducked outside into the storm. He picked up her tracks easily, small and fresh, heading toward the water hole. He followed them, walking at first, then he began running, an ungainly sprint through the drifts.

He bellowed back toward the lodges for help. Beside her footprints, in the snow, he saw dark splotches, like drips of death.

Blood.

He heard Nokoni and Naduah shouting behind him. He ran faster. *What had she done?*

He found her by the creek, sobbing, her knife in her hand. "I cannot do it!" she wailed.

He thought she was talking about birthing the babe. He dropped down to hold her, rocking with her. "I know. But it will be all right. We are a pair. We will see this through somehow. We will do it together."

"I cannot do it!" she wailed again. "I cannot kill it any more than I can let *them* do so!"

Relief blasted through him as he understood. He managed to get her up. He lifted her to carry her back to the camp. Then her next words made him stumble and go cold again.

"Do you not see? This is how they will finally destroy me!"

The wound Storm Trail had committed upon herself was shallow, above her babe, to the side of her navel. Naduah looked at it and breathed again.

"There is no way out," Storm Trail said quietly. A great,

deep resignation came to fill her, but it was not entirely cold. She was helpless. She had no way of fighting back against something such as this, something the spirits decried.

Naduah nodded, her heart breaking for her.

She was able to ride in the morning. Nokoni took them south, as he had planned. They traveled through another whole moon, encountering very little game.

Storm Trail felt a constant gnawing hunger. She ignored it. Hunger was so small in the overall scheme of things, so much smaller than her fear. But she did care about Naduah. Her friend looked pale and exhausted.

The snows were still on the ground, but Storm Trail took it upon herself to root beneath the drifts for any frozen growth she could find. She did it wherever they stopped, and finally on a sun when she came back to the camp with a particularly good harvest, she found Naduah hugging herself in pain.

"You are having your babe!" Until that moment Storm Trail had not appreciated how very much she really wanted her own, wanted him to live healthy and long.

She held Naduah's hand, squatting beside her, as the woman pushed. The babe was a boy-child, too tiny, so frail. As Storm Trail caught him, she trembled inside.

She held the babe and wept softly with Naduah with the joy of it, for a moment, only a moment. Then as she had been doing for moons, she forced her heart into grim acceptance and handed the child to his mother.

Nokoni asked Raven to name the boy-child, and Raven called him Pecan. Nokoni did not seem to mind. The babe's name would probably change anyway, when he grew old enough to make his vision quest. And both men had laughed when Storm Trail had told them that that was what he looked like.

Thunder Eyes came to them at the end of the spring moons, just as the air heated with summer.

They were riding, moving, wandering as always, when the first pain wrapped around Storm Trail again and squeezed. She had been expecting it for suns now. She had been feeling the grinding sensation for a while now, worse this time because this babe seemed so much larger.

Somehow she knew that this was a boy-child. It was not just that he was so big. She felt him somehow, felt his maleness inside her.

Raven finally glanced back to notice the change in her posture. He rode to her quickly.

"Get down. There is a place just over there where you can rest while I build a fire."

Storm Trail shook her head, surprised. "No. You can keep riding. Naduah is here. Naduah will help me."

But his face hardened in the stubborn determined way she had not seen in a very long time. "It should be me."

And then she understood.

He had not blamed her or hated her when she had tried halfheartedly to kill this child, but he still blamed himself for what had happened to Wind Bird. He would stand beside her with this child every bit of the way.

"I love you," she breathed softly.

She realized that until that moment, she had never said those precise words aloud. His face changed suddenly, as though his blood had rushed in and out of his head. She was amazed. She was with him, still with him, in spite of everything, and she had always thought that that said everything that needed to be said. She had told him she would die without him. She had thought that was enough.

Another pain hit her and she spoke around it. "Always I have loved you, even through the many times I wished I had never met you," she went on. She even managed a smile. "Oh, how peaceful my life would have been then!"

He grinned dazedly. "No. Even without me, you always found trouble on your own."

She thought about it. "You are right. And this should be us, together, bringing this babe out."

"Over here."

He took her reins, pulling her mare around to the place he had seen. As Naduah came back, Storm Trail waved her off.

Naduah hesitated, watching them leave, then she nodded almost to herself. Briefly she thought of how Storm Trail had said she had pummeled herself with rocks. *Spirits be with them,* she prayed. *Let this child have suffered no harm through her doubt.*

Raven remembered how she had planted branches the last time. He found some and dug them in on either side of a narrow crevice already worn into Mother Earth from the elements. Storm Trail had sage in one of her parfleches. He sprinkled it upon the fire he had built.

She loved him. Of course he had known it. He had known it when she had left her Penateka to ride with him to the Quohadi, and he had been sure of it when she came back to him after Wind Bird had died.

But hearing it weakened something inside him. He was not above needing the words. They warmed him, riveted him, like nothing else no other human being could have done.

He looked over at her. "How are you? Is it coming?"

She gasped and panted. "Slowly."

"Should you be here, over this hole?"

"Not yet. That is for when I need to push. Now there is only pain."

He nodded, wishing he could suffer it for her. As always she knew him too well. She watched his face and snorted.

"If you warriors were left to have babes, there would be no more Nermenuh at all. That is perhaps something the white-eyes have not tried yet—a magic spell to put our men in charge of birthing."

He chuckled softly. "I do not even like the blood," he admitted. He remembered how much of it there had been the last time. Having an enemy's blood on his hands had stopped disturbing him a very long time ago . . . but *her* blood frightened him badly.

He held her, murmuring to her as her womb tightened and eased, tightened and relaxed. As night fell, she finally moved over to the branches.

The urge to push was immense now, tearing through her, pressure building, giving her no choice. She gripped the branches and strained, and this time she felt herself tear almost immediately.

Raven made a strangled sound and reached again as he had done three circles of seasons ago. And this time the head that appeared was matted with damp, black curls.

He let his air out on a wordless exclamation of wonder as Storm Trail gathered her own breath, howled, and pushed. The boy-child did not slide out of her in one rush as Wind Bird had. Storm Trail had to strain again and again, bearing down. His shoulders eased out, then his chest, then finally, with a last screaming effort, Storm Trail pushed him from her womb and Raven caught him.

His throat closed with emotion. This time he did not forget the cord. He gripped the glistening length of it and took his knife to it.

"There." He handed the boy-child to her and placed a snippet of cord into the little pouch she had made for Wind Bird's so long ago. He'd found it in her parfleche and had ached to know that she had carried it all this time. He wondered if it was appropriate to put this babe's cord in it, and decided it was. This child was his second chance.

Storm Trail looked at her babe, and her heart stalled. His hair was black, but that was his only Nermenuh feature. It was curly, a cap of thick damp ringlets. She kissed his eyes to make him open them and knew what she would find before he did it.

They were blue-gray, the color of a stormy summer sky.

He chose that moment to scrunch up his face and howl in angry protest. Storm Trail laughed breathlessly. "He wants to go back inside."

Raven grinned. "Too late now."

"Yes, but I think this will be the last time he will give up on what he wants without a fight." The tiny mouth puckered and his eyes opened again. She had been too slow to give him her breast. *Oh, spirits,* she prayed, *let him always be able to fight and survive like we have.*

Trembling, she held him close to nurse him. "He is Thunder Eyes," she whispered.

Raven looked surprised. *"You* would name him? Can you do that?"

"It is done sometimes. And I want to name him for you, for the first thing I thought about you, the first time I saw you."

He was bemused. "What was that?"

She laughed breathlessly. "That you had eyes just like an ugly old storm cloud. They were not white all the way through like I told everyone they would be. That was the first time you bested me." Her face softened and her eyes got misty. "And I thought that maybe you were not crazy after all, the way our warriors said all the white men were."

He chuckled. "You have never admitted *that.*"

She smiled fleetingly. "I thought maybe you were just driven by the same feelings that always got me in trouble. I thought . . . maybe you were just like me. Maybe we were alike."

The babe nursed awhile. Raven took him from her. "I am," he said quietly. "We are."

Forty-three

Thorn was in pain.

It was not significant but nagging, no more than he could ignore. But as he crested the Comanche scarp, it occurred to him that he was getting too old for this. He was fifty-one now, well beyond the age when a man could comfortably travel by horseback across the vast reaches of a Texas that still, impossibly, was half-claimed by red men.

Fifteen years, he thought. It was fifteen years this month since the Parkers had been taken. Cynthia Ann had been eight. She would be twenty-three now, if she was still alive.

Logic told him that she was not. Too much time had passed without anyone ever catching wind of her existence. But John Parker had been adopted, and even Rachel Plummer had survived those brutal years of her captivity, so he tended to believe that Cynthia Ann had been young enough to be adopted as well. She was probably married to one of the savages by now, assuming they took wives in any conventional sense. Almost surely she would have been rutted upon, would probably have given birth to one or more half-breed maggots.

The poor child.

Thorn finally stopped, scanning the horizon. He would make camp, he decided, realizing that he was doing that much earlier than he would have fifteen years ago. He fell asleep dreaming about Cynthia Ann. In the morning he started up again, still in possession of his hair. By day's end he found the Penateka. He stopped on a hill overlooking the valley they were in, and he noted the stark difference between the band now, and as it had been all those years ago when he had brought them bibles. There were only a few lodges left now. This time the 'Manches seemed to be involved in some sort of funeral.

A big man was tied to a horse, and they were leading him out of the camp amid much wailing and caterwauling. Thorn recognized the guy, though he could not remember his name. *So his time has finally come. Good riddance, buddy.*

He waited awhile, less to honor their grief than through a judicious prudence. The Penateka seemed beaten, but rattlesnakes seemed inert, too, when they were sunning themselves on rocks.

A teary-eyed woman finally noticed him. She came to him and spoke in 'Manche and pidgin English and hand signs. A lot of the eastern bands could manage some semblance of communication these days without a translator.

"What do you want?" she asked. "Go away."

"I need to speak to your chief. I bring him gifts." He motioned to the packhorses he had brought along.

"We have no chief now." She wailed again. The sound scraped over Thorn's nerve endings.

"Is there no one to succeed him? No one who would take these presents and speak to me?"

She turned around and looked back at the camp vacantly. "That one, I guess."

She pointed to a pinched-face man. Thorn vaguely remembered seeing him before as well.

He went to him, leading the horses. "I bring gifts," he said simply. "You can have the horses. There are also kettles and cloth."

Kills In The Dark looked at the sorry animals with their bulging packs. "What do you want? Whenever you come here you want something."

There was no sense in denying that, Thorn thought. "I want information."

"About what?" He motioned, signed, and spoke in choppy

Comanche. Thorn responded in an English version of the same method.

"About that white man who lived with you once, long ago, when I first started coming here."

Something in the buck's eyes flared.

"He had long blond hair and blue eyes," Thorn went on. "He was a big man and he had a temper."

Kills In The Dark smiled slowly. "Do you come to take him back?"

Thorn hesitated. He decided not to tell the truth, that he wanted only to hold a knife to the buck's lying throat and force him to talk of Cynthia Ann. He remained convinced that the white savage knew where she was. But if he told this man that, they would probably hide the girl so well he'd never find her.

Thorn nodded.

Kills In The Dark's grin widened. "I would help you do that without payment, but you have already given it." He yelled something in an abusive tone, and three women rushed up to take Thorn's laden horses.

"I have not seen him now in three circles of seasons," he went on. "He was headed west to join the Nokonis. Go to the farthest reaches of our country there. Look for sign of very small camps that move frequently. That would be them. But if you wait, I think he will raid into Tex-us again. He will go back just to prove that he can. He is arrogant, that one. He thinks all he does is perfect, right. That will finally make him fall."

Thorn watched him turn away, but then the buck snapped his eyes back to him.

"If you ever get his hair, *I* will buy that from *you*," he added. "And if you bring me his woman, I will give you anything, anything at all. She should have been mine."

It was a good camp, Storm Trail thought, one of the prettiest places they had found in a long time. She was reluctant to leave it. She felt so happy here, so good, as though life was perfect and always would be.

The creek was deep and curving. The Nokonis were in the south country again, and the pecan trees that she remembered from her childhood grew in wild profusion along the banks. The circling line of the water formed them into a perfect arc. They clustered around a lush glade, protecting them on three sides. The water was cold and fresh.

She felt safe here, but she knew by now that Nokoni was less concerned with where they were than with where they had just been. If someone found the ashes from their last camp, they could perhaps track their hoofprints here.

Storm Trail sighed, lowering her lodge one more time. When she looked around again, Thunder Eyes was gone. She groaned.

Naduah laughed. "I suspect Quanah has something to do with this."

Both Thunder Eyes and Pecan were seeing their second springs, and they both adored Quanah. He was five now, and he took great delight in thinking up adventures to amuse them.

Storm Trail left her lodge where it had fallen in a heap about its poles. "I will find them."

"And I will finish up here," Naduah offered.

Storm Trail raked a hand through her hair. The water was the very best place to look, she decided. She was halfway around the bend of the creek when a hand snaked out of the growth and caught her by the elbow. She screamed reflexively, and Raven clapped a hand over her mouth as he dragged her back into the brush.

"What are you doing?" she gasped.

He looked down into her stricken face. The longer their lives remained peaceful, the more he tended to forget the fear that ran so deeply inside her.

His touched his mouth to her temple. "I am sorry," he said. "Look. I was watching them." And thinking that she would come along to collect the boys at any moment.

He pointed through the tangled vines that held the pecans captive. Storm Trail leaned up and peered that way.

Thunder Eyes was at the water, and he was indeed with Quanah and Pecan. Quanah had a toad, and Thunder Eyes was struggling to hold one of his own, though it was nearly his own size when it stretched out to its fullest length. He squeezed it so tightly the toad's eyes bulged.

"Oh, he will kill it!" She made a move to go to him.

Raven held her back. "And it will be his first lesson. Then he will learn to treat animals more gently."

"But it will break his heart!"

"You break mine time and time again, and it has not killed me yet."

She looked at him, genuinely indignant. "How do I break your heart?"

He kissed first one eye, then the other. "Just by looking at you, at how beautiful you are." His mouth captured hers. She bit his lip teasingly. He chuckled. "Yes—that, too."

"Nokoni wants to go," she whispered, wriggling closer to him in the brush.

"Do you think he will leave without us?"

"No."

"And Thunder Eyes is occupied. Do you realize how little time we have together since he was born?"

"Do you resent it?"

"Never. But I have learned to grab what I can."

"Yes," she murmured. "You are definitely grabbing."

He toppled her in the weeds. The thicket smelled like clover and plums. His hands held her hips and he came down atop her, the weight of him crushing her breasts, filling them with the old delicious ache.

She had never stopped wanting him. She marveled at how touching him was still so very good.

Her hair got caught in the scrubby growth of his beard—he needed to scrape it off. Her scent carried to him from the captured strands, something green like grass, something blue and clear like fresh water. Even after all this time, her scent aroused him like he would not have believed possible.

His hands slid to her waist, and now his hot mouth moved over her face . . . skimming her cheek, touching her jaw, the lobe of her ear, her forehead. She lost all sense of where they were and who might come along.

Raven hadn't forgotten, and it made what they were doing so much more delicious, so precious and special because they had to snatch the moment from the hands of time.

He scooped his hands beneath her, lifting her hips up to him. Growling, he took the hem of her doeskin in his teeth and tugged at it. She giggled as she had not done since she was a girl.

"Oh, my ferocious warrior!"

"Give me a moment. It will get better."

He used his hands to push her dress up the rest of the way. She was too thin—the buffalo were still agonizingly scarce—but he preferred not to see that. He did not want to notice that her hipbones were gaunt, and, as he pushed her dress higher still, that her ribs stood out. He had once promised her that he would always provide for her, and that was getting so very hard to do.

He bared her breasts and nuzzled them greedily, holding them captive for his tongue and his gentle teeth. Finally he brought his mouth back to hers. He kissed her deeply until she groaned against his lips. For a long time he took her breath in a leisurely oral coupling, sliding his tongue over her teeth, plunging it into all those dark secrets of her mouth, as though they had all the time in the world.

Then they heard Nokoni calling for them. Raven levered himself up for a brief moment to look out of the thicket. Thunder Eyes and the boys were gone.

"Do you want to stop?"

"No!" she gasped. "No."

He obliged her, kissing her once more. Then he lifted her breasts to his mouth again, and she reached for him beneath his breechclout. He was hard and warm . . . and he was right, they had so little time alone together these suns.

She stroked him and he gave a hoarse exclamation. "You *do* want to go back in a hurry."

"No."

"Keep that up and we will."

But she didn't stop, and he slid one hand down her belly to cup her, using the heel of his hand to make sensation rush and leap through her. She spread her legs wider and his finger slid into her.

He groaned again. She was always like this. After all these seasons she was still like this each time he touched her . . . wet, hot, ready.

He could not wait any longer.

He moved his hand and plunged himself into her even as Nokoni's voice got closer.

"We are . . . running . . . out of time," he managed.

"Want . . . to . . . stop?"

"No. Never."

She pressed her mouth against his chest as he rose over her, sliding into her, so sweetly pummeling her, over and over again. How she loved his skin, golden pale, so smooth and warm . . . and then she could not think at all because the sensation he had started within her was gathering, strengthening, on the brink of explosion.

He gasped and finished as they heard the one cry, the only words that could divert them. It was Quanah's voice this time.

"Buffalo!" the boy cried. "Father! I have found buffalo!"

Storm Trail went over the edge with Raven. She had no time to recover her breath before he scrambled out of the copse. She tugged her doeskin down and went after him.

Nokoni was on the other side of the creek. He raised a brow at them.

"I heard nothing," Raven managed.

"I would not think so."

For the first time in his memory, Raven felt himself coloring. And he knew that even if they were hungry, it was very good to be alive these suns.

"I meant . . . I heard no buffalo."

"No, I did not either," Nokoni admitted. "But Quanah knows what to look for. He must have seen something."

The men began following the sounds of the child's voice. "I will go back and finish packing," Storm Trail called out after them.

Her heart was thrumming. Buffalo. *Food*. Oh, spirits, she was so hungry.

She ran back to the camp. Naduah had already packed up both their lodges. They rode out quickly, cantering to catch up with the men, trailing their stallions behind them. The others were right on their heels. When they reached Nokoni and Raven, the men swung up on their horses and led the way.

They found the boys a short distance from the camp and lifted them onto their stallions as well. Quanah *had* found tracks, and the tracks were buffalo.

Their voices began to ring out happily. Behind Storm Trail, someone laughed. Her own belly rumbled. She felt saliva gather in her mouth. She swallowed hard. Naduah saw the reflex and laughed.

"Soon now. Soon."

Storm Trail nodded . . . but she did not smell them. Why did she not smell the herd?

She scowled, putting a finger up to test the wind. They were riding into it. The tracks led into it. She should have smelled them by now—that ripe gamy scent that filled the air to the very sky when so many of the beasts gathered.

Maybe it was a small herd, she thought. That would be all right. There were only twenty lodges of Nokonis.

Then she did smell something, and her heart plunged. It was not ripe and gamy. It was old, putrid, rotting. A short ride later they reached the herd and she understood why.

The men stopped abruptly, and the woman nearly galloped past them on the grassy knoll where they had reined in. They stared down in the direction the warriors were looking. Naduah shook her head, more in confusion than denial.

"I do not understand."

Raven did. He felt his gorge rise. Hundreds of buffalo carcasses laid below them, glistening white, inert.

"No," Storm Trail whispered. *"No."* The buffalo were already dead. Their hides were gone. Someone had taken their hides and had left the meat—all that precious meat—to go bad, and she was so hungry.

"Who would do this?" Naduah wailed.

Storm Trail laughed wildly. Who? It was who it always was. The white men were back, they were close, and once again they were pushing into her world to destroy it.

Nokoni was the first to speak.

"They wanted the hides for some reason, but had no use for the rest."

"No use for food?"

"They are not hungry," Raven snapped.

"Will we camp?" someone asked from behind them. "I am so tired."

Storm Trail felt everything drain out of her. It was not just their hunger, she thought, not just the hard ride they had taken to get here. It was the slow painful release of hope.

Raven moved Thunder Eyes onto his own pony, then he rode down to the fallen beasts, Nokoni following him. There were hundreds upon hundreds of the carcasses, and the smell coming off them was overpowering. Raven gagged.

They managed to see that the white men had been here quite a while ago. The glistening effect of the carcasses came from millions of squirming maggots.

"Go back," Nokoni coughed. They galloped to the crest again.

Nokoni glanced at Naduah. "This happened several suns ago, maybe as many as seven, ten. But the white-eyes have been here, have passed this way once. . . ." He trailed off at the enormity of that. *The white men had come this far west.*

They had come to kill the buffalo, and they had left them rotting.

"Where can we possibly go now?" Naduah wailed suddenly.

"North," said Raven.

"Why?" Nokoni asked hoarsely.

"Because there is only one place I can think of where they cannot get to us, at least not without us seeing them coming."

"The Quohadi scarp," Storm Trail whispered.

Nokoni looked as though he would protest.

"For a short while," Raven insisted. "We should go there and see if there is anything to eat. It is the safest place to stop long enough to think about this."

Finally, reluctantly, Nokoni nodded.

It took them a moon to reach the plateau. They did not see any white men or any more of the horrible wasted buffalo.

Raven understood quickly that Iron Shirt was angry with his son. Whatever had happened between them when Nokoni had asked him not to go to the Comanche Peak council must have been ugly. Raven had not realized it then because both Nokoni and his father were such private men, but now he saw that their estrangement was as cold, as aching, as his and Storm Trail's had once been.

They sat beneath the arbor with Iron Shirt's council, smoking while the women set up their lodges and called out their own greetings to old friends. Nokoni told stiffly of the skinned buffalo they had seen. Iron Shirt made no response.

"You think I lie about this?" Nokoni asked angrily.

"I have never seen such an oddity," Iron Shirt said, clearly trying to provoke him.

The Quohadi shaman, Turtle Dancing, broke in to dispel the tension. "But you have heard of it," he said, his voice slightly rebuking. "Our hunters have seen it as well."

"Where?" Raven demanded.

"Both to the north and to the east."

"What are they doing with the hides?" Nokoni asked, ignoring his father now, addressing the shaman.

But Raven had already figured that out. "Selling them. They must be selling them." He knew of only one thing that inspired reckless and crazy passion in white men—cold hard cash. Even he had once robbed the gentle Miss Myra to get some.

He squirmed uncomfortably. He had not thought of that old lady for a very long time. But since they had found those buffalo carcasses, his mind had gone stubbornly back to the white world again and again.

"Will you stay this time?" Iron Shirt asked his son.

"For a while," said Nokoni.

Iron Shirt looked away angrily. He had lowered his defenses for a moment, to try to bridge the gap between them, and he had been rebuffed.

"We must take Naduah where it is safe." Raven spoke the explanation his friend would not give. He earned a dark look from Nokoni for the effort.

Turtle Dancing shook his head. "I am not sure there is such a place any longer."

She Smiles was gone.

Storm Trail had looked around for her covertly as she and the other Nokoni squaws set up their lodges. She felt a strong sadness that her friend had gone to the afterworld, in spite of what had happened between them.

But Eyes Down was here. She approached Storm Trail, and she had a babe in her. Storm Trail hugged her briefly, and realized there was a coolness, a distance, in her now.

"Tell me all that has happened to you."

Eyes Down lifted her shoulders stiffly. "Scout's wife died with the sickness. He claimed me the following spring."

"Are you happy?"

A ghost of a smile touched her mouth. "When there is game, I eat well. He provides for me, and so I try to be kind to him.

It has never been this good for me before, ever." Abruptly she changed the subject. "She Smiles died with the sickness, as did all the Penateka women who shared her lodge. Star Line finally went, too, but not from that. I think her heart just gave up."

Storm Trail moaned softly. She finally turned away, wanting to be alone with her grief. Then she spotted Raven, and all her emotions washed away on a wave of something cold.

He had left the council at the arbor. He was standing nearby, and he was gazing steadily to the east.

He had that look of angry hunger on his face again.

Forty-four

Storm Trail could not bring herself to mention it to him, but it happened again and again as the suns passed. Each time, horror speared into her so deeply she could scarcely breathe. If he did what he was clearly thinking of, she knew it would be the end of them.

She had been willing to kill her own child to keep him from the white men, but now Raven would go back there, risking him willingly. She could not stand by his side if he did, but he made no immediate mention of it, and his silence was torment.

There was some scant game below the Quohadi scarp, just enough to keep starvation away, and he spent a great deal of time hunting. Then finally they saw buffalo.

When the first scouts rushed back from the plateau edge, hollering and shouting, Storm Trail jumped to her feet outside her lodge. They would be alive this time—they *had* to be alive. Naduah ran for her mare. Storm Trail was so excited that her hands and her thoughts would scarcely work.

"Thunder Eyes!" she yelled. "Get my pack ponies. Hurry!"

He toddled that way, old enough to know which ones she wanted. When they came trotting up to her lodge, Storm Trail grabbed him and swung him up on his own.

"Food, *Pia!*"

"Yes, babe, food," she whispered. "This time there will be food."

Naduah and Pecan had waited for them, though Quanah had

gone rushing ahead after the men. It was a small herd, nothing near the thundering masses that Storm Trail remembered from her childhood. The hunters had struck them by the time they reached the lowlands. A great dust rose as the earth rumbled.

She and Naduah and the children fell in behind the commotion. They looked for Nokoni's and Raven's arrows.

"We should work together!" Storm Trail called out. "It will go faster and be more fun!"

The first arrow they came to was Raven's. They dismounted and set to work. They did not do the butchering in any conventional sense. They started to, but then Storm Trail's belly cramped.

"Quickly," she urged. "We can finish getting the hide off later."

They stripped it only as far back as they had to, cutting through the sternum, reaching both their hands into the hot innards, searching and groping for those delicacies they craved. They shared, pushing the pieces into their mouths. Naduah closed her eyes in bliss. Storm Trail called out to Thunder Eyes to come eat.

He did not answer her.

"He has gone off to find his father," she muttered, mildly angry with him for one of the few times in his life. She always worried about him doing that. He could get hurt so easily.

She stood up, looking for him, and heard a scream from the direction of the distant herd. Her heart punched.

"A man has gotten hurt," she called back to Naduah, praying it was not Raven. He was always so crazy, took so many chances, and privately she thought he was getting too old to move like he used to, although she would never dare tell him so.

She started that way on foot, then she heard more howls and cries. She realized that they were from the women up ahead. Her pulse exploded.

"No," she whispered, backing up unsteadily. "No, please,

no, please, no. *Thunder Eyes!*" she screamed. White-eyes had found them again!

She finally saw him riding back toward her as fast as his little pony would go. She leaped upon her own mare. She was shaking too badly to ride. Reins, she had to get her reins, kick her pony—she finally managed to do it all, and she raced for her boy. She came up alongside him, reaching sideward to wrench him off his mount as he passed her.

Thunder Eyes screamed. She had hurt him—but better for her to do it than those guns. She jerked her own horse around in midgallop and they almost slid off its back, but she caught them, settled them again, and beat the mare faster, faster.

The white-eyes were galloping toward them, and the warriors raced to catch them. Then the men led them off, in a direction away from the Quohadi scarp.

Naduah gave a curdling howl of fear and swung up on her own horse with Pecan. They raced back for the plateau together, scrambling up the slope again. Smoke billowed up from the canyon the camp was in.

Fire. The camp was on fire. White-eyes were there, too.

Storm Trail swerved. "Another canyon."

They found a small hole, half the size of the one the camp had been in. They spilled down into it, the other women following them. Storm Trail galloped for a crevice at the back, a place that was cloaked in shadows. She pulled up there, dropping unsteadily off her horse. She swayed for a moment, clutching Thunder Eyes. For once in his little life, he did not struggle to get away from her kisses. He stared back up the canyon wall, his blue eyes huge with what he had seen.

They were safe. They were as safe as they *could* be, but where were Nokoni and Raven? Where was Quanah?

The men did not find them until dawn. Naduah and Storm Trail scrambled to their feet, clutching the children. Quanah was with them, as well as a handful of women from the Quohadi camp who had not gone out on the hunt. Naduah screamed and rushed for her firstborn, but Storm Trail could not make her feet move until she spotted Raven, then she nearly collapsed from relief.

He was riding behind the others. When the men stopped, he trotted on to reach her, sliding from his horse to gather both her and Thunder Eyes against his chest.

"It is all right," she whispered, stroking his face, his beloved face. "We are fine."

He sat wearily and she eased down beside him. Naduah and Nokoni, Quanah and Pecan joined them.

"They came in on us from the opposite side of the herd," Raven said woodenly. But there was a current of something else beneath his tone that stiffened her—a kind of anger and frustration she had not heard from him in a very long time.

Nokoni went on before she could think about it. "We managed to draw the fight off the other way, away from this scarp."

"Yes," Naduah murmured, stroking Quanah. "We saw that."

"It was not enough. My father and many of the older men did not join the hunt. When they heard the scouts screaming of trouble, they took up their bows. They, too, tried to draw the sol-jers away from the plateau."

Storm Trail's pulse skipped. "Sol-jers?" Not *tejanos,* not Rain-jers?

"Americans," Raven spat. *"Tosi-tivo.* They must have come down from the north."

Storm Trail groaned. If it was not one, then it was the other now.

"The sol-jers saw where my father's men had come from," Nokoni went on. "They followed his trail. That is how they found the camp. They got my father." He paused and his throat worked with pain. He had not gotten along with his father recently, but the grief of loss was still immense.

"All in all, we have twenty-three dead," Raven said, and the women who had gathered around them began wailing and howling.

Nokoni stood up and left them, to be alone to mourn. Storm Trail looked helplessly at Raven again, then her heart sank.

He was doing it again. He was gazing steadily up at the canyon rim, looking eastward.

"No!" she burst out before she could stop herself. "Please, Raven, *no!*"

He met her gaze, then his eyes slid away. "You do not understand," he said quietly.

"Then tell me! Everything is good for us now! How could you—"

He turned on her incredulously. "Good? We are hounded and hunted and hungry! There is no place we can go that they do not touch us!"

Storm Trail paled. She would not weep. She turned her head away, unable to look at him . . . and knew she was going to cry anyway.

"I do not know how to tell you," Raven went on more quietly. "If I could make you understand how this makes me feel, I would do it gladly."

"Curse you," she wept, getting to her feet. "You said when I birthed this babe, that we were together, a pair!"

He could not answer that. Guilt and anguish caught him by the throat. He had no voice at all, and still no words with which to tell her. "I am sorry," he managed finally.

"That is not enough!" How could he do this to her?

He flinched. "I would never force you to go along with my decision."

"I will not put Thunder Eyes to that danger!"

He knew, and that was what was torturing him, the only thing that had held him back this long. He had known it from the time she had allowed the babe to live. His eyes burned. "I know."

"You would go anyway? You would leave us?"

"I will come back."

"But I will not be in this Quohadi camp waiting for you!"

Nokoni finally returned. Fresh grief crossed his face as he

heard their conversation. "Do you speak of what I think?" he asked. "Are you going to raid east again?"

No one, not even Naduah, answered.

"You are my friend, closer even than a brother," Nokoni said tightly. "But I cannot allow you to ride out from my band, not if you go there."

"I respect your wishes," Raven said stiffly.

"I have thought this out," Nokoni went on, his voice dark, looking at the women. "When we wandered, we were hungry. We saw signs of white men. But we did not *see* white men. We came back here, and we were hungry, and they struck us. That tells me that my way was right. We must keep moving."

Raven looked at Storm Trail. Tears streamed down her cheeks, and it tore through something inside him.

"You should go with them," he said softly.

He knew a flare of desperate hope when she hesitated, but then she nodded. He swallowed carefully and closed his eyes.

"They have taken the buffalo," he said finally. "They have left no land unmolested. I will ride one more time, then I will find you. Then I will come home and be at peace."

Storm Trail turned away from him, stumbling and weeping in the darkness. She did not believe him.

No one went anywhere for another two suns. Some of the buffalo meat was salvageable, though it had sat on the carcasses overnight. They worked the least damaged and rotted of the skins as well, because they had lost everything else and they needed them desperately.

They were the longest, most agonizing suns of Storm Trail's life. She kept her hands busy, kept moving, trying desperately not to think, staying clear of Raven with agonized deliberation. But he came to her robe on the second night as they all camped outside.

He kneeled beside her to put a hand on her shoulder while she tried to sleep. She wanted to keep her eyes closed—had to keep them closed. She knew what he wanted. *She could not give him her blessing.* And she did not know how she would ever be able to say goodbye.

Of all the men she could have loved, she thought despairingly, why had the spirits sent her this one? Through all their seasons together, they had wept as much as they had laughed. Not a moment with him had ever been easy. They had torn each other's hearts out time and again.

And they had not stayed young forever, as she had once, in her arrogant youth, believed they might. As she rolled toward him, she felt so very old.

"I love you too much," she whispered.

"Hush." He held her to him as though he would never have the pleasure again. She could feel him trembling.

Storm Trail nodded against his chest. They had tried words. Words had failed them. The chasm between them was too deep this time.

He kissed her with exquisite slowness. He took her mouth again and again, and finally she could no longer feel him shaking. Perhaps because she was doing so as well now, and their tremors matched as they always had.

He smoothed her hair back from her forehead. It was just past her shoulders again, so thick, so shiny. He took a handful of it and pressed his face into it.

"I understand the wildfire now," he said softly. He would have to try to talk after all. He could not leave otherwise. "My dream," he explained.

"No," she moaned.

"I have to tell you. It is the closest I can come to why."

This time she was silent.

"I dreamed of fire consuming Comancheria," he said slowly. "Do you remember? It destroyed all the animals, but it never burned me. I am perhaps the only man who can stop what is happening to us."

She gave a strangled laugh. "You are so arrogant."

"Yes. But I must try, in case I am right."

"And if you are wrong?"

Then I will only destroy us.

He knew it, but he could not say it aloud. He kissed her again, and eased her down onto her back, sliding her doeskin up. He thought she would stop him, but he needed something to carry into the darkness with him.

Walk into the night. It was what the shamen called it when a man died of his own will. It was nothing so spectacular or noble as taking a gun to his head or dying in battle. It was a slow simple giving up.

He wondered if he would be doing that when he left this camp, if he would be losing her forever by succumbing to these demons he had no strength against. If he lost her, there would be no sense in fighting, in going on.

"Please," he said hoarsely. "Through all my life there has only been you. I need you now."

She grabbed his hair and pulled his face down to hers again. She kissed him fiercely, hard, wanting to hurt him.

They rolled together until she was on top of him. She grabbed his breechclout, fighting with it, trying to get it off him, until she could only sob in frustration. He took it off himself and pulled her back to him, sliding inside her.

They both went still, and she thought suddenly, wildly, that this would be the last time. They would not touch again, they would not love ever again. She began to cry harder.

They stayed that way until he could not stand it, until need throbbed. She seemed to sense it, and she began moving against him. He slid in and out of her, quietly, until her nails clawed bloody trails down his back and she arched her back in a silent cry.

He shuddered with his own release. He touched his mouth to her cheek lingeringly.

It was time.

Storm Trail closed her eyes as he pulled away from her. Cold air rushed at her. She was unwilling to watch him go, but it seemed that forever passed, and she did not hear his footsteps. She finally looked.

He was kneeling beside Thunder Eyes. She dug her teeth hard enough into her lip to draw blood. He touched the boy's forehead, straightened, and walked off into the night.

Forty-five

Autumn was cold, as though portending another harsh winter. As Raven reined in on a hilltop, a harsh wind pulled his exposed skin into gooseflesh.

Just the wind. Then he realized where he was.

He was as stunned and shaken as any of them as he called out a clipped order to his war band to stop. He looked down, and Scout came up alongside him and stared.

"This is where we got you," he said, surprised, "all those circles of seasons ago."

Raven nodded slowly. There was no sense in denying it. Scout never forgot a place, a track, his bearings.

The Rust Fort was still here.

He wondered wildly if they were the Rusts' kin down there, moving around within the newly bolstered walls. He had not thought of this place at all after those first circles of seasons, but lately a small insidious voice had begun pestering him. It had started with the abandoned, wasted buffalo carcasses. It had climaxed with the attack upon the Quohadi hunt. It whispered incessantly to him of Miss Myra and The Banker, of the Rusts and The Queen. And he knew that somehow, subconsciously, it had urged him back here.

Why?

He did not care if these people were Rusts, he decided. In fact, that seemed to make it . . . better.

The corn was still here, but the plot seemed smaller. Raven allowed that perhaps it seemed that way only because he had pushed through row upon row on that day in his memory, struggling to the place where he had left his gun, where he had found the weasel instead.

A smile touched his mouth, flickered, and was gone. He felt like crying. He kept studying the place instead.

The buildings were the same, in just the same configuration, but now he thought there was an extra one—a barn. A man was shoeing a horse outside its doors. No one moved in the corn this time, but he saw three women and two other men inside the fort.

"Go down," he said hoarsely, unknowingly repeating Wolf Dream's words from nearly twenty years before. "Take the women and any children you can find. Kill the men."

They galloped down.

Screams rose up from within the compound as they made their approach. More men spilled from the buildings and several of them managed to get to the gates. Raven counted them fast, with half his attention, satisfied that it was no more than his war band could handle.

They were pushing the gates closed as Raven reached them. He burst through them when there was barely enough space for his stallion to get through. He twisted around to holler back.

"Over the walls! Come over the walls!"

His men obeyed the crazy command though it could mean death. They had followed this white warrior off and on for seasons, and he had never led them astray before. Raven was wild, but the chances he took had never yet proved deadly.

Scout charged the wall first. He made it over the fence without being shot because Raven was riding through the white men inside, never allowing them to gather and form any kind of defense. They were too busy dodging his stallion's hooves to shoot accurately.

Raven leaped off his stallion and fell upon one of the white men. He plunged his knife into the *tejano*'s kidneys. Another white-eyes came down his own back. Raven spun with the deadly quickness that had always served him so well, his bloody knife still in his hand. He drove it into the man's belly and watched dispassionately as he fell backward, then he took his hair.

He left him and went into one of the buildings while his men disposed of the others. It drew him, beckoning him, and though the fight raged around him, he realized he was walking slowly, as though dreading what he would find inside. It was a cabin. It was the very place he had slept in seasons upon seasons ago.

He stepped over the threshold and finally understood what had been driving him, what had made him raid back into Texas again. There, on the bed, was a buffalo robe.

He began shaking with rage, with revulsion. He wondered if this was even the same bed as that he had slept on seventeen years ago.

A buffalo robe.

He roared a sound of anguish and went back outside without touching it, without touching anything. The killing was done. The women were lashed to the ponies. His warriors were ransacking the other buildings. There were no children this time.

He reached down and picked up the corpse at his feet, the first man he had killed. He shook him by the front of his bloody shirt.

"Why did you follow me? Why did you do what I did? Sweet Jesus, the same bitches *spawned* us!"

He dropped the man hard and went to the closed gate, pounding his fists against it when it would not yield. He finally got it open and he went back to remount his horse. He galloped through, back past the corn, to the hill.

"He was talking to a dead man," one of the warriors said uncertainly.

Scout frowned, then shrugged. "He has done crazier things since I have known him. Let us follow."

* * *

Thorn was tying his horse to the hitching rail outside the saloon. His hands were so immensely painful with arthritis now that he could barely handle the rope.

He had not found the Nokoni band before last year's snows. He had traveled all over the western country through the spring and summer seasons, and he had come up empty then as well. Now the wind blew with the cold wet threat of winter again.

He went inside and ordered a brandy. He took it to the fire and was warming his stiff hands there when a cowboy came banging through the saloon doors, calling Thorn's name. The bartender pointed the stranger his way.

"You still offering that bounty, sir?"

"Not a bounty!" Thorn shouted, smashing his glass to the hearth. Jesus, one of these fools was going to take that term literally and kill the white buck at first sight, before he had a chance to talk to him.

"I want him alive," he said more quietly.

The cowboy nodded. "Well, if you move fast, I reckon you just might get him."

Thorn's blood rushed painfully. "Where?"

"Don't know where he is, but I know where he *was*. He hit the Heidelman place just a short time ago. Left one guy there with his hair. He's still alive."

"How do you know it was the white buck?"

" 'Cause the guy says the savage what did this to him had long blond hair. Crazy as a March hare, too. Picked him up while he was lying there trying to die, and he shouted in his face. The guy said he was thinking for sure there was gonna go his scalp, but the savage just dropped him and took off. Reckon if he *had* scalped him, you woulda been out of luck."

"Yes," Thorn said quietly. He had not thought he possessed the energy, would not have thought it possible that he could have gotten back on his horse just now, but he pushed through the saloon doors and swung up into his saddle again.

He took out his billfold, pushed some money at the cowboy for the information, then he added ten dollars more. "Find

Hays," he instructed. "Jack Hays. Tell him to get as many men as he can and meet me at the Balcones trail. I'll be traveling slowly." There would be no help for that. "He can catch up with me if he rides hard."

He swung his horse away from the rail. This time, dear God, he was going to get the white bastard. He felt it as deeply as his aching bones.

Raven rode hard until he got up the scarp, as though demons were chasing him. Then he slowed gradually, first to a canter, then to a trot, before he finally reined in to a stop.

It was over, he realized dazedly. It was finally over.

Once again, Scout was the first to pull up at his side. "What is it?" he asked.

Now, finally, he could answer that question—but not as Scout meant it. He thought of how many times Storm and Nokoni had echoed those same words.

His mouth twisted. *Once I would have done anything, gone anywhere, defied anyone, to get what I needed.* Now he knew he would never have that elusive *something*. It was impossible, out of his reach. He could not flay the skin from his own bones.

"I am finished now," he said quietly. "I will go back to the Nokonis, to my wife and child. All of you who would like to come with me are welcome."

But he would not raid anymore, and they knew it. He would never again go into Texas; there were only ghosts and heartache there.

He shifted his weight on his mount. The small of his back hurt, and he was tired in a way he could never remember being after a ride. In the old Nermenuh world, the best of all worlds, he would begin thinking of retiring from the trail anyway, perhaps to sit on council, if they valued the wisdom of an old white man. He had seen thirty-four winters now.

The men talked for a while. In the end, roughly half of them decided to ride after Nokoni with him and spend some time raiding Mexico. The others would return to their families on the Quohadi scarp.

Scout was going back to the Quohadi. Raven jostled horses, riding close to each man to grasp his hand, to tell of his thanks. When he got back to Scout, he felt the most regret.

"Perhaps I will come later," the man said.

But from what Raven knew of Eyes Down, he did not think it likely. She had been free of Storm Trail's shadow for a while, and she would not be eager to move back into it.

Finally he split off from the others, feeling both a sorry weight against his chest and an immense lifting of tension. He and his men headed south.

When last he had seen them, the Nokonis had been in sorry need of lodges. Both instinct and common sense told him that his friend would take his people where it was warmest.

Jack Hays met Thorn near the scarp with seventeen men. One of them was Ben McCulloch.

"Have you picked up their sign?" McCulloch asked, the most expert tracker among them.

Thorn nodded and looked up at the sky. The clouds were low, bulging downward as though grotesquely pregnant. A harsh wind seemed to make them shift and roil. He had found the bastard's hoofprints, but they would not remain visible for long if it rained.

They moved quickly up the Balcones into Comancheria, following the sign. Thorn prayed as he hadn't done since he was a boy, beseeching his God to keep the rain away.

At dawn the tracks mangled.

"Pow-wow," McCulloch muttered, getting down to inspect them.

"What does that mean?" Thorn snapped.

"They stopped here to confer for some reason."

McCulloch walked a little farther ahead while they waited

for him. He came back, shaking his head. Thorn felt his pulse stall in dread.

"Eeny-meeny-miny-moe," McCulloch said. "Take your choice, boys."

In that moment Thorn purely hated Ben McCulloch. "What do you mean?"

"Looks to me like half of them split off and went south. The others went north. Do you know the tracks of your particular man?"

Thorn felt his head began to pound. "No," he said. *Jesus, not again.*

"Then I suggest you toss a coin," McCulloch said. "That's all I can tell you. Heads, we go south. Tails, we go north."

Another man muttered that he would just as soon go home. At least half of them had begun to doubt, in the last several years, that they would live long enough to see the end of this 'Manche war, even if they grew old and went in their sleep.

But Thorn took a coin out of his pocket. He prayed again, then he tweaked it with his thumb and sent it spiraling into the air.

Heads.

"Where'd you say that would lead us?" he asked tightly.

"South."

Forty-six

Raven rode well into Mexico before the skies opened up. He'd expected rain this far south, but it snowed.

If I had been born 'Manche, with that infernal superstition of theirs, I would call it an omen, he thought. The weather was just that odd. Before long, the short growth of his beard was frozen and crusted.

Then he gave a hoarse, glad cry. Directly ahead of him, on the horizon, he saw the glow of a fire.

He began galloping. He saw her as he approached, moving back up from the creek with a swollen paunch. A robe was pulled up over her head. It didn't matter. He would have known her scent if he was deaf, her voice if he was blind, her walk from the way her moccasins touched the earth beneath her.

He shouted for her, and Storm Trail looked up, then she swayed. *He had come home.* He had come back to her.

She dropped the paunch she carried, never feeling the icy water that spilled out over her moccasins. He dismounted and held his arms out to her, and she barreled into him, weeping.

"Your tears will freeze," he said hoarsely. Then he found her mouth and clung to it.

His lips were so cold. She fought to warm them.

"Thunder Eyes," he managed.

"With Naduah," she gasped. "In her lodge. Come, you are like ice."

She lifted her robe to allow him to slip beneath it with her, but he scooped her up in his arms instead. He carried her toward the two lonely tipis that sat near the outdoor fire.

"You left that for me," he realized. "The fire." There was no other reason the Nokonis might have one outside in this storm.

"I always did," she said simply. "I remembered how hard it was before to find this band."

"But this time I knew the kind of sign to look for."

They ducked inside, and Nokoni came to his feet with a sound of disbelief. Naduah cried out, and Thunder Eyes looked up from where he was playing with Pecan and Quanah. He squealed and ran for his father. Only then did Raven realize how desperately he had feared that the boy would not remember him.

"What did you bring?" Quanah demanded.

Raven sought Nokoni's eyes. "Scalps. A few horses."

Nokoni nodded. "Do you have enough?"

Storm Trail held her breath.

Raven nodded.

She moaned and sagged against him. *It was over.*

There was some food. Nokoni had found an antelope several suns before, and with water they stretched the last of it into a stew. They settled by the fire.

Storm Trail could not stop touching him. It would be all right now, she assured herself, skimming a hand along his strong thigh. He would stay home, and no white men would ever find them again.

Finally Raven put his horn bowl aside. He struggled for words. "I first came to Texas . . . just as the others came."

Slowly, one by one, the others stopped chewing.

"You . . . your people spared me my arrogant invasion of your wilderness."

"You are one of us!" Storm Trail protested, but he shook his head.

"No. My heart has been Nermenuh since the sun I got here, I think. But my skin . . . my cursed skin is white, will always

be white. I cannot change that. I am like them. I am the man
who wastes the buffalo, who strikes hunting parties with
women. I brought them here. Me, and men like me, the first
of us to come and set up homesteads in Texas and prove that
it could be done. They followed me. And *that* is what drove
me. The *shame."*

"No!" Naduah cried out. "It is no more your fault than it
is my own!"

Raven gave her a soft look. "It is different for you. You
were a child when you came to the Nermenuh. I remember
thinking about that once before, as though it were of great
importance. I remember wondering how much you remembered of that white world. You must have been a babe when
they brought you to Texas. Your father brought you. Your
mother did it. It was not your choice, as it was mine." *I stole
Miss Myra's money and came of my own volition.* "I had to
kill them, had to keep them from destroying us. It was my
responsibility. I had to try to turn back the tide that I had
started."

"And yet now you say you have given up," Nokoni said
slowly.

Raven's eyes were bleak. Storm Trail realized it hurt her to
look at him. "The tide is too vast. I can do nothing about it,
not even if I had a war band of a thousand. I cannot make a
difference."

Storm Trail put her head to his shoulder. Thunder Eyes came
to crawl into his lap.

Suddenly she wanted desperately to pull him out of the
lodge, to take him away somewhere where they could be alone.
She needed to touch him, to love him again, to reassure herself
he was back with her, unharmed. But the weather was howling,
and there were no other lodges to shield them from the storm,
to give them privacy.

She had nearly dozed off when she remembered something
else. It jolted her wide awake with a small cry.

For a moment—for one horrible moment—she remembered

the last time they had made love, before he had left on this last desperate raiding season. She remembered thinking then that it would be the last time they touched. She felt another sudden frenzied compulsion to love him again now, just to make that instinct impossible.

But of course they couldn't.

She finally eased down into her robe to sleep beside him.

The snow stopped just before dawn. As the sun came up, it glimmered off the drifts, turning them to sparkling white.

Storm Trail looked out at it while the others slept. With the new sun, her fears of the night seemed silly. They had been the work of her own demons, she realized. She had learned to expect trouble, to anticipate pain. But now there was a warm sweet feeling in the pit of her belly where the cold had once been.

She looked back over her shoulder at Raven. Thunder Eyes was safely asleep on the other side of his father. *My men,* she thought. Then Naduah stirred.

"Wait," her friend whispered. "I will go with you."

Storm Trail shook her head. "There is no need. I will bring water back. Stay warm for as long as you can."

Naduah nodded sleepily and closed her eyes again, and Storm Trail slipped outside.

Thorn watched the camp from behind a snow-covered hillock. When he saw the door flap of the tipi move, his heart nearly leaped out of his chest. But it was only an Indian squaw who came out, a real 'Manche with black hair, not blond.

"Goddamnit," he whispered. He knew, *knew,* that the white buck was in one of those two lodges. He was not one of those huddled miserably outside, and his tracks had led straight here. It had snowed rather than rained, and his trail had been ridiculously easy to follow . . . which convinced Thorn that fate was smiling on him this time, and it *was* the white bastard's trail.

"We can go in anyway and wipe them out," McCulloch suggested.

"No," argued Hays. "I'm reasonably certain we're in Mexico now, and that government hasn't taken too kindly to our troops coming in here."

"We're not American troops," McCulloch pointed out. "If you'll remember, us old Rangers ain't considered good enough for Uncle Sam's Army. We're too old and too used to whistling our own tunes." He chuckled.

"No," Thorn said quietly. "Let's wait a moment. Just . . . wait."

Naduah stretched last night's stew again with the water Storm Trail brought back. Raven and Nokoni waved it off, leaving it for the women and children.

One of the things Raven had brought back from this ride was oats. Horse seeds, Nokoni called them, shaking his head at such an imbecilic way to feed ponies. But they both considered it possible that other game might find the grain delectable as well. They would take it out from the camp, they decided, far enough that the animals would not pick up on human scent. They would spread it over the drifts, then they would wait to see what, if anything, approached to nibble upon the bounty.

"I want to go!" cried Quanah.

Nokoni smiled at him as he got to his feet. "That would be all right. Get the little bow I made you and bring your robe. I think we will be out there for a while and it will get cold."

Raven kissed Storm Trail lingeringly. "I will be back."

She smiled and touched his cheek. "And I will be waiting."

* * *

The door flap moved again. This time the white buck came out.

"Yes," Thorn whispered fiercely.

"Now?" McCulloch asked.

Thorn began to nod, then some instinct cautioned him. He shook his head again instead.

An Injun and a kid came out after the white savage. They got their horses and rode off. Thorn stiffened in an agony of indecision. Should he go after him? No, he decided, not yet. They could not be going far with a kid in tow. In the meantime he wanted to find out who else was in the tipis.

He didn't want to tangle with the white buck if he could avoid it. He had learned a certain healthy wariness of the bastard over the years. He would take him only if he had to, or if a sterling opportunity presented itself.

It was Cynthia Ann he wanted, and until he found out otherwise, he was assuming she was in one of those tipis. It was more than just a hunch. This band had been impossible to find through the years, and he wouldn't have done it now if the white buck hadn't led him here. It was the only place Cynthia Ann could have been all this time that no one had seen hide nor hair of her.

Thorn shifted the weight on his arthritic knees and waited some more.

Forty-seven

Naduah left the lodge, still yawning and stretching. She was nearly to the creek when she heard the sound.

It was not a war cry, not quite. It was the same, but different, as though someone was mimicking one. She did not think immediately of white-eyes because she knew they were in Mex-ee-co, but then she looked over at the east side of the camp and she saw white men.

She began backing up. She stepped into the crunchy ice of the creek and her moccasins plunged through it into the icy water beneath it. For a heart-stopping moment she was trapped there, struggling and floundering in it, and her blood was as cold as the water. Then she fought her way free, because she was Nerm, because she could not, would not, give up without a fight.

She managed to crash through the ice, back up the bank again. She ran, her legs flying. All that mattered was getting to Nokoni, but the snow slowed her down.

She felt a hand snag in her hair. It nearly tumbled her backward. She remained upright through pure will, turning on the white man wildly.

Thorn did not want to hit her. Jesus, she was a white woman, a Parker, the last Parker. He finally managed to knock her feet out from under her, dropping her down into the snow. He caught her arms above her head.

"Cynthia Ann!" he shouted.

Naduah froze, then she let out an ungodly wail.

The name whipped through her mind. She had forgotten it a long time ago, but now it was eerily familiar. They had come for her. They had finally found her.

"Run, Pecan, go to your father!" she shrieked. Her babe, her beloved boy, had just come out of the tipi to see what the commotion was about.

"Noooo!" she screamed as she saw white hands grab him before he could go for Nokoni.

"I am Nermenuh! I do not want to go! Do not make me go! *Nooooo!"*

Inside the lodge, Storm Trail went still as stone as the first sounds of fighting and howling and shouting came from outside. She knew them for what they were and could not believe it.

No—it could not be. Things were good now, and they were in Mex-ee-co, and Raven was back. Then Pecan ran outside and Thunder Eyes went after him.

"No!" she shouted. She darted after him, and into the arms of a white man.

Ben McCulloch caught her by the hair. "Easy there, easy. We don't want to hurt you. We just want your friend over there."

Naduah. She understood by his motions that they had come for Naduah, and for a single selfish and precious moment, Storm Trail shuddered and breathed. *They would not kill Thunder Eyes. They wanted Naduah.*

But she knew suddenly, as Raven and Nokoni had always known, that Naduah would not survive it if she went back now. They were not her people anymore, and it was not her world.

"No! *Naduah, run!"* Storm Trail screamed again, and this time she craned her head around to sink her teeth into the white-eyes hand that held her hair.

McCulloch swore. He twisted his grip on her hair. Hot pain sang over Storm Trail's scalp. She looked wildly for Naduah, then her heart stalled. She recognized the man who held her friend.

It was the man with the mustache, that man from San Antone-yo, the man with the bi-buls who had argued with Raven. *Not him, why him? He had helped her once!* "No," she wept, reaching for him. "Please, please, you would kill her. Leave her be. Let her go!"

For a moment hope surged through her, so hot and fast it was painful. He would recognize her, surely he would, and he would spare her again. But then his gaze slid away from her to Thunder Eyes. The boy was crouched wide-eyed in the snow just on the side of the tipi, watching them.

Storm Trail went wild again. But it was too late, and even as she fought, she knew it had been too late from the moment she had birthed him.

"There's another white kid," Thorn snapped, pointing to him. "Could be a Parker grandkid or something. Take him, too."

Storm Trail screamed. Thunder Eyes wailed in terror as one of the men grabbed him, a sound that cut through to her soul.

"Not my babe, not my boy! Please do not do this to him!"

They had him, oh, sweet spirits, they had him, and this was so much worse than killing him because she was his mother, he was her life, and they had *no right!*

But they were doing it, they were taking him away from her. Raven, Storm Trail thought wildly. Surely he would come back before it was too late . . . but then her heart froze into perfect ice.

Raven. And she knew in that singular heartbeat that they had followed him here. That was the only way they could have found them. His hunger, his guilt, his need, had finally destroyed them.

She kept fighting the man who held her, but her fury was different now. "Kill me!" she wept. "You stupid white coyote-scum, if you would take my child then *kill me!*" She aimed a knee at his groin. She tried again to sink her teeth into his hand. She spat in his face. She did not need to get free of him any longer. There was nothing left to get free for.

They had Thunder Eyes on the back of one of their ponies. He was reaching for her. She let loose with a curdling howl of agony.

Raven heard her as he sprinkled grain around the snow. There was only one thing on this earth that would make Storm cry out in that way.

Thunder Eyes.

He roared his own helpless response. "No! No, you bastards, *no!*"

Nokoni was already mounted and riding hard toward the camp. Raven leaped astride and followed him. As soon as they saw the camp, they knew at once that there was nothing they could do.

Nokoni's own scream of loss chilled Raven's blood, stopping it, even as his blood roared. Thunder Eyes and Pecan were lashed to ponies. A man had one arm locked hard around Naduah's neck. He dragged her backward, out of the camp, his eyes flinty and steady as he and the others trained their guns on the Nokonis. The other warriors stood staring in frustration, their weapons useless. If anyone went after the children, after Naduah, the white-eyes would kill one or more of their hostages.

Raven looked at Storm Trail. "Oh, Jesus, oh, spirits, no." No one held her, but she could not go after Thunder Eyes either, and the truth of that was agony in her eyes. One of the white men stood near the boy's horse, holding a gun to his temple, warning her away.

It had been his last ride.

But it did not matter, it had been one too many, and they had come home after him, had followed him here, and now they would take her child. Her voice was a wrenching, thumping litany.

"No, please, no, please, no, not my boy. No, please, no . . ."

Raven felt someone barrel into him from behind.

He put up no resistance when an arm caught him around the neck and he felt the cold kiss of steel at his throat. He twisted just enough to see who held him, and he was not surprised when he did.

"I win," said Thorn breathlessly.

"Kill her," Raven gasped.

"What?"

Raven searched for the English words. *"Kill her.* Kinder."

Thorn shook his head, either in confusion or refusal. "You'll hang in the town square, you bastard. You'll hang in one of the towns you tried to destroy. You'll hang for a traitor. I wasn't after you, but I'll be glad to take you."

Raven didn't try to figure out what he was saying. He didn't have to. He knew what they would do with him. He had known from the first time he had told the Penateka council of the new long guns. He could be hung for the life he had chosen.

He wondered if Storm Trail would see his heart in his eyes before they took him away. *I have loved you always.* But he had done to her the one thing she could not bear. He had cost her another child.

Suddenly she jerked and ran for Thunder Eyes despite the guns. His heart staggered. He had a moment, a breathless fraction of time when the man holding the gun on the boy could not decide whether to shoot him or her. Raven twisted fast, taking Thorn off guard. In the same motion he knocked the weapon from the man's other hand. It fell with a soft whispering thud through the snow, and he plunged his hand after it, bringing it up.

Her, then himself.

They would not kill Thunder Eyes unless they had to. He was young. He could change worlds and survive, just as Naduah had once done.

Her, then himself.

He pulled the trigger just as Thorn grabbed for his hand.

Thorn hit his wrist, driving his aim down. Storm Trail shrieked in pain, and Raven knew that the bullet had not taken her—*his final failure.* It had been low, wounding, but not fatal. He had succeeded only in keeping her from running for her son. He had not killed her. He had not spared her anything.

He roared a final sound of anguish. Thorn threw him face-down in the snow, and rope burned into his wrists as he bound them.

Part Four

Walk Into The Night

Forty-eight

The Prophet's abandoned dance camp seemed to hum about
her with remembered voices. Finally, forcefully, Storm Trail
shook them off.

She did not realize until she got back to her horse that she
still clutched Raven's feather. She opened her hand and the
wind caught it and lifted it, carrying it away. She groaned,
staring after it until she could no longer see it through her
tears.

He had shot her. She had seen him do it, had looked his
way in that last horrible moment as she had been running, and
she had seen him lift the gun. Then it had exploded, and she
had felt the ungodly pain. It filled her again now, as real as
it had been twenty circles of seasons ago. When she would
have gone for their child, when she would have died willingly
to save him, Raven had shot her.

Perhaps she would have understood if he had killed her.
Perhaps she could have looked down from the afterworld and
thanked him for sparing her these eternal winters of heartache.
But he had let her live, had let her go on forever, missing the
only thing she could not live without. And it had finally been
the one thing she could not forgive him for.

Thunder Eyes. Her child. *Why?*

She supposed that question had kept her alive all this time.
Perhaps she had known, had always known, that some sun she
would find out. She pulled herself astride—oh, how it hurt—
and sat for a moment. He would have gone with Quanah, she

decided. Nokoni was gone. He had looked endlessly through Tex-us for Naduah, and when he hadn't been able to find her, he had walked into the night. He had raided the white men one last time, and in that fight he had given his life.

Raven had killed him as well, she thought, as surely as if he had shot him, too.

But Quanah lived. *Twenty circles of seasons.* So much time had passed since that horrible fateful sun that she could not even imagine what the boy looked like now. She had left the band when Nokoni had died. She had gone back to her Penateka, to the remnants of her own people. And Quanah had led the last of the Nokonis back to the Quohadi scarp.

He was the Quohadi chief now, sitting in his grandfather's place. So much had changed since she was a girl. Quanah led their council, but he also fought.

She had not heard that he had died, so that was where she would go now. If Raven was not there, she thought Quanah might know where he had gone.

Raven sat astride, looking down at the nearly abandoned town of Adobe Walls. His heart ached as his mind tunneled and spiraled backward in time.

This had been Nokoni's country once, part of the remote western land that his friend had wandered. It had not been far from here that the white men had come and taken Naduah, when he himself had committed his own most heinous failure. Pain flashed through him, bright and hot. He knew Nokoni was gone now. He had found Quanah at Eeshatai's Sun Dance, and Quanah had told him.

He had asked him, too, what had become of his mother, his brother. Gone, Raven thought, all of them gone now. Naduah had been taken back to Saint Louis, to her *tejano* family there. Pecan, always frail, had succumbed to the harsh northern elements and had died that first winter. Naduah had lived only as long as her son had needed her. Without her boys, her husband, her beloved adopted world, she had walked into the night.

He had done that to her, Raven thought. He had killed her as surely as if he had shot her.

As for him, the white men had not hung him. They had been willing, and they had certainly been eager, but they waited one sun too long and they gave him one too many chances. He was a savage, after all. On the day they were to take him out to the square, Raven was finally able to lure his guard into his jail cell on a pretext of sickness. The guard had come in to tend to him . . . and the guard had died that day instead.

Raven had escaped to travel through shadows for many more long years, a man half-savage, half-white, a man with a mission. He had been wanted for the better part of ten years, then the Texans had forgotten him. Raven was without wealth now, at least in his own estimation. Funny, he thought, but after twenty years, some primal part of him still measured his own worth by the number of horses he owned. And he owned only the one he rode. But he had currency, plenty of currency, some of it stolen, some of it gambled for. Oh, yes, he had plenty of that.

He had used it to learn what had happened to Naduah, and the identity of every white man who had come to Nokoni's camp that sun. Of the nineteen white-eyes who had been there, twelve were dead by the time Raven had tracked them down. Texas did that to a man, even a Texas full of nicely subdued 'Manches. But he had found Ben McCulloch, who had directed him to Jack Hays. And Jack Hays had sent him to Matthew Thornberg.

Thorn had been sixty-eight years old when Raven finally found him, old enough to have long spent his cherished ransom money. He had told his triumphant tale of Cynthia Ann Parker too many times for anyone to care anymore. And he was old enough to admit with neither remorse nor regret that he had made a mistake with the blue-eyed boy.

He hadn't been a Parker. The Parkers hadn't wanted him. He hadn't been stolen from any Baptist fort on the frontier. No white family ever came forward to claim him. He was, quite simply, a 'Manche kid, a heathen with his white-savage father's blue eyes.

Thorn had finally turned him over to a childless family named Jeffers. And the Jeffers had quite successfully beaten the savage out of him. *Sweet spirits,* Raven thought, *he had been raised with bibles.* But he was alive. He would be twenty-four this spring, and he had enlisted with the United States Cavalry. Raven had heard it said that he was the best horseman the Army had ever known.

He would be, Raven thought with a twisted smile. The Cavalry very rarely enlisted 'Manches.

His last information about the young man had led him here, back up the scarp. It was no secret among the white men that Eeshatai would gather the last of the Nermenuh together with his Sun Dance, then they would attack Adobe Walls. It was an abandoned buffalo town. The hunters had come here to drink whiskey and to ship their bounty of hides back East, but they had stayed only until the last beast fell. Without the herds the town served no purpose, and the white men had wasted the last of nature's gift long ago.

Now there were only stragglers and low-lifes in the town. Raven did not think the Nermenuh realized that, or Eeshatai would not waste his efforts here. But he had not told Quanah, because in his heart he wanted the Nermenuh to have one last victory. Perhaps they would get it here, though probably not.

The white-eyes were sending in Cavalry, just in case. If Thunder Eyes was among them, then Raven would intercede. He would throw the battle to the white men then, though it would pain him deeply. But he had betrayed people before, and never with such good cause.

Finally, deliberately, he shook off thoughts and memories. He gathered his reins and rode down into the town.

Inbred caution made him roam around the perimeters first,

looking for familiar faces, for danger. Eventually he located the saloon.

It was in an old abandoned barn. The floor was dirt, and it smelled of whiskey and old urine. The bar was collapsed at one end, and the top canted dangerously toward one wall. The building was of wood, not adobe, and there were gaps between the planks where they had swelled and contracted with the elements. Wind snaked in through the slats, screaming and sighing. There were two men present—the bartender, and a lone haggard soul at one table, sitting far from the fire.

Raven went to a table near the hearth. After a moment the bartender came over to him.

"You see a barmaid around? You want something, from here on in you come up and ask for it, got it?"

"Whiskey," Raven said shortly. He would not drink it. He would nurse it . . . and wait.

The grizzled man brought it back to him. Raven held out one of his bills. "For the whiskey and for information."

The man's eyes narrowed suspiciously. "What d'you wanna know?"

"Has the Cavalry been through yet?"

The man seemed to relax, but then he eyed Raven's buckskins. He studied his hunting shirt, more 'Manche style than white. "What's it to ya?"

"About ten bucks." Raven held the bill just out of reach.

"We already know the Injuns is coming."

"And I know when. And how."

He had relearned his English well, though he had forgotten entirely too much Comanche in the process. What a strange lifetime, he thought, absently watching the man's eyes change.

The bartender snatched the bill from his hand. "Supposed to be here by nightfall."

"Coming up? Tonight?"

"No, the night just past. They're late. Guess they're not sure there's really anything to worry about. How many of those

'Manches you think there are left, anyway? Enough to be scared of?"

"Enough," Raven mused, drinking anyway in spite of his intentions. Even one was enough. He had always believed that . . . if only they could have gotten free of their horrible superstitions. Over the years, he thought, that had destroyed them as much as anything.

Dawn came. The barkeep sent him outside. Raven slept around the back of the building in a buffalo robe the man had given him. It was late afternoon before he opened again and Raven went back to the fire.

"You still here?" the bartender groused.

Raven didn't answer. "Whiskey," he said instead. He took it back to his table, and he waited some more.

The Cavalry came late that day.

He heard the hoofbeats outside, and Raven's blood ran cold, then hot. He remained seated, tense, watching as the soldiers came in. There was barely a scant handful of them. No, he thought, Uncle Sam didn't fear the 'Manches anymore.

Raven looked into each face, searched each pair of eyes.

His gaze moved to the man who had come in last. He was the right age, and he had black curls. Raven's throat went dry and his heart pounded. Those eyes . . . the young man had eyes the color of a thunderous summer sky.

Raven's heart broke.

He waited until the young man had bought the whiskey and took it to the others. There was laughter and ribbing that he was the youngest and as such the one who should serve the rest of them. He took it good-naturedly.

Raven stood up. His pulse reached a painful crescendo. He spoke the only name he was sure the young man would answer to. If he responded to it, then Raven's last doubt would be removed.

"Jeffers," he said hoarsely. "Silas Jeffers."

Silas turned sharply and squinted into the shadows to find him.

Raven felt weak. His search was over. *Twenty years.*

"Yeah," Silas said finally. "Who the hell are you? How do you know me?"

"I'm your father."

For a stunned moment the young man was silent, staring at him. Then he lunged for him angrily. Pandemonium erupted as Raven had known it would. Every soldier at the table launched himself to his feet.

Silas caught him by the front of his hunting shirt. The thin doeskin tore. He lifted him half off his feet. I'll be damned, Raven thought. He's taller than I am. And faster.

But Raven was only fifty-four years old. He wasn't quite dead yet. His joints were stiffer than they had once been, his reflexes not quite as fast, but now adrenaline powered him. He grabbed his son's wrist. Silas went for his knife. Raven grabbed that hand, too.

Once he would have managed to do it before the boy even thought of pulling the weapon, he thought ruefully. *Goddamnit, I'm old.* Silas got the knife, but at least Raven held him back from using it.

He twisted Silas's arm back with some more effort. He did not know how long he would be able to hold him this way. He managed to get the knife from his hand, and he held it to the boy's throat, moving around carefully as he did so that he could look into his eyes.

"Tell me one thing," he said affably. "If you're not my son, why do you think I didn't kill you just now?"

"You," Silas said finally, "are one crazy son of a bitch. And you smell."

Raven almost smiled. "I haven't had a good pair of buckskins since I lost your mother. She was the only one who could tan worth a damn."

Silas twisted, fought, but Raven held him. The soldiers were hanging back, wary, waiting. If they fought they would spill their whiskey, and Raven knew Cavalry pay was dear.

"Come on now, you've got to remember," he said softly.

Three years old. He had been three when Thorn and his men had taken him. Sweet spirits, there must be something about those early days that had stayed with him, Raven prayed.

"I don't need to hear it," he went on. Exertion was pulling at his breath. "You don't need to tell me. I'm nothing. *Nothing.* But there's a woman . . ." His throat closed.

"There's a woman," he tried again. "She's . . . beautiful. Her hair smells like springtime, and the freshest water you'll ever find. She's hot-tempered and she's wild and she'd try anything. When she walks, she swings her arms at her sides, like she's got somewhere wonderful and important to go. And when she thinks she's got you, she'll give you a sly sideways smile."

Silas was motionless.

"She'll be here shortly, with the Indians who are coming." He took a deep breath. *For her, the only thing I can give her now.* "I was at the dance where they got organized and made their plans. I left something there for her. She'll come here to find me, probably to kill me. But it won't be me she finds.

"They're going to attack here the dawn after the moon is full. Find her and call her name." Raven spoke slowly, very carefully, in Nermenuh. *"Storm Trail.* Or *Pia.* That means mother."

He let Silas go. He released his arm and dodged backward, dropping his knife at his feet at the same time. He turned his back on him. There was nothing else he could do now, and he waited for the blade to drive into his back.

He knew an angry man when he saw one, and Silas Jeffers had been rather unhappy.

Then again, he was his mother's son, Raven thought. He probably had too much courage to kill a man from behind.

"What the Christ was that all about?" one of the soldiers demanded.

Silas shook his head. "Crazy son of a bitch." *If you're not my son, why do you think I didn't kill you just now?* Well, he couldn't have managed it, Silas thought. He was an old goat . . . but fast, Silas allowed. Faster than he would have expected.

One of his friends came up beside him. "You want to go after him?"

But there's a woman. "No."

He didn't believe the crazy old codger. Except . . . he was relatively convinced that the codger had believed himself. There had been a look of such haunting pain, of such loss in his eyes, when he had spoken of that woman.

I am not half-savage, he thought. God help him, he *wasn't*. He pushed abruptly through the saloon doors and stepped outside.

The stranger was gone.

His eyes. His goddamned eyes. The haunted look . . . and the color.

"No," he said again, aloud, though there was no one now to hear him.

But he was adopted.

Christ, he knew that, and had never thought twice about it in recent years. The Jeffers family hadn't taken him in until he was seven years old. He had been stolen from somebody when he was a baby—from some nice white homesteaders long-dead by 'Manche lances. They were dead, and that was why no one had ever stepped forward to claim him, why the authorities had finally adopted him out.

His black hair was Mexican. His eyes were clearly German. That was what the Jeffers had told him.

But the *dreams.*

They had obsessed him as a kid, because if he had been captured, stolen, then why did they seem so sweet? The Jeffers had gotten angry with him when he had asked that, and he had learned quickly enough, after a couple of judicious lashes from Pa's switch, to stop asking. And the dreams had finally stopped coming as well. But they had been so good.

Not dreams, memories. There was one about a toad. He remembered that now, vaguely . . . toads, and other kids. But mostly there were impressions of a close dark place—*a tipi?*—filled with smells of wood smoke and leather and flowers—*like springtime*—and a woman's soft laughter, men's intense voices, gentle hands, and big strong hands, stroking his hair, lifting him.

Where the hell had that man gone?

It was best that he had gone of course. The most the dreams meant—and he was even willing to concede that they were actually memories—was that he had not been mistreated among the Indians, as Pa had always insisted he was. It sure as hell didn't mean that he was going to let them run rough-shod over Adobe Walls tonight.

Except the stranger had said the Indians wouldn't raid tonight. He had said it would happen with the dawn of the full moon. Silas looked up at the sky. Two or three more days then.

Silas felt something cold move inside him as he went back into the saloon. He had a sudden gut instinct that if the stranger had told the truth about that, then he had probably told the truth about everything.

Forty-nine

Raven saw the People arrive.

He had not meant to come back here. He had thought, when he left Adobe Walls, that he would leave Comancheria for the last time. But he had lived for this, it had carried him for twenty years, and he could not *not* know. And so he had ridden around the Nermenuh land for three days, loving it, aching for it, giving it his goodbyes.

It was a place where the wind had moaned his name when he had been young and so hungry for something more. Its rugged wilderness had inflamed him, its emptiness had comforted a spirit that could not be hemmed in. It was a place that had brought him love, a place he had fought so hard for that he had destroyed the woman who was a part of it.

He rode north, then south, looking out at the rippling grasses. Miraculously, perhaps, there were still corners, still valleys that remained untouched by the unconquerable white men. He found them for a last time, and it seemed to him that they waited silent and empty for the People to fill them again. They waited for their shouts and their laughter, their whooping war cries and their huge fires that leaped triumphantly for the sky.

His mouth twisted. *Such a special place, such a special time.*

Now he watched the moon go up, come down, and as light turned the eastern sky pink and gray, the great Nermenuh camp stirred again. Quanah moved his men into position, and Raven knew a fierce swell of pride that it would be Nokoni's son who led all the hopeful warriors of all the last tattered bands.

They began their approach to the town. Eeshatai galloped past him, dressed in only a breechclout, his pony resplendent with yellow paint signifying the sun. Quanah rode harder to catch up with the crazy prophet. Then behind and around them, the warriors charged.

They bore down on Adobe Walls, screeching and yiping. From somewhere behind him Raven heard the wild cries of their women, urging them on.

The Cavalry was waiting, and there were a few hunters in town as well. As Raven drew close with the others, he saw the long narrow barrels of Sharps buffalo guns poke out the ramshackle windows.

Jesus, he had forgotten they would have them.

The magic handguns were long forgotten now, surpassed by twenty years of something better. These guns could spit a bullet a mile.

The first warriors to reach the town were shot dead without ever having a chance to fight. The warriors began making terrified sounds of disbelief. Their medicine would break soon, Raven thought, his heart bleeding for them. That goddamned medicine, that *puha*.

Raven rode to catch up with them, shouting, but it was too late. The warriors had already split their ranks around the walls without finishing their charge, the charge that could have destroyed every man inside. They retreated to discuss the situation and Raven's heart tore in two—for them, for his people . . . and for his son, who was still surely inside those walls, a white man now.

The warriors charged again, but their old guns and their arrows would not shoot across a mile. They could not get close enough to do any damage.

Raven finally dismounted, watching the end play out, not caring if one of the bullets found him. The information he had given Silas had made no difference. The white-eyes had already known that the Indians were coming, and even five of those buffalo rifles would have done the job against spooky Comanche superstition.

Bullets spit into the ground around him and whined through the air, then he heard a different sound behind him.

He waited and felt his heart thunder.

"You could not kill me from behind nearly forty years ago, and you cannot do it now," he said softly, and he was amazed at how easily the Nermenuh tongue came back to him in that moment. It was as though he had never left, had never stopped speaking it after all. "Would you like me to turn around?"

He prayed that she would not ask it of him. He did not think he could look at her again without going mad with what he had lost and what he had cost them. But still there was no pain, no thrust of steel, no bullet. Finally he heard a horrible strangled sound.

He turned, caring more for her heartache than for his own.

She stood trembling, the knife raised in her hand. She was ready to let it fly. Her knuckles were white around the hilt. Her eyes were wild. Black, still so depthlessly black, and still sparking fire.

She was still beautiful, the young woman he remembered. He did not see the gray streaks in her hair. He did not see how thin and gaunt she was as her breasts heaved with frustration and desperation, nor the trace of sun wrinkles around her eyes. She finally rushed at him—he wondered if she meant to drive the knife in herself rather than hurling it. He caught her arm unwillingly, because he would die, he would do it gladly, but he needed to fill his eyes with her first. It had been so many years. He held her raised arm.

"I could have forgiven you for bringing the white-eyes!" she screamed.

"No." He shook his head, feeling sick. "No, you could never forgive that."

"Yes, some sun, in time! *Yes!* I could have. You were following the wind when you chased them, following your hungry heart, driven by a shame no one but you thought you should feel! *I could have forgiven that!* Even though I begged you not to go, I knew that you could do nothing else. But I cannot forgive you, will never forgive you, for shooting me, for driving me down when I would have grabbed my son back. *I would have died for that right!"*

Her knees gave out. She slid down, her arm angled upward painfully where he held it. He sank with her.

A bullet spit into the ground nearby and threw sod and grass over them.

"He would have died," he managed.

"No!" she screamed.

"If you had run for him, they would have shot him! I would not have seen you both destroyed!"

She began sobbing. It struck him then that all the tears he had ever seen her cry had been caused in some manner by him.

"Hate me for missing," he said hoarsely. "Hate me for missing that shot. I *meant* to kill you, to spare you. I wanted you to fall so you would not have to see. *I* wanted to die so I would not have to live with it. Because if neither one of us went after him, he'd live. *They would not kill a blue-eyed child!"* He dragged in a breath. "Hate me because they followed me there, because I must have led them to a place they should never have found. But do not hate me for saving his life."

She went so still in his hands that he thought she had been shot after all. And finally she truly looked into his eyes again.

"Why?" she gasped. *"Why?"*

He shook his head helplessly. He did not understand.

"Why did you have to come back?"

"To make it right."

She laughed shrilly and she began fighting him again. She twisted her knife hand free, but again, when she could have thrust it, she let it slide from her fingers instead.

His throat closed. He knew hope, and it was almost as painful as the despair he had lived with since he had lost her.

"I cannot do it," she wept. "Even now, I cannot. And that . . . is why . . . I hate you."

He pulled her to his chest as she cried. She did not fight him.

"Did you see anyone?" he managed. He already knew the answer. Silas had not found her. She would have said something. This entire conversation would have been different.

Another bullet came close. He felt its backlash of air past his cheek.

"Quanah," she answered, her breath halting.

Silas had not come to her. Thunder Eyes had not found her. He had not allowed himself to remember.

In that moment Raven could almost have picked her knife up and driven it into his heart himself. But she screamed suddenly, cringing back, as a warrior nearly galloped over them in retreat. He pulled her to her feet.

"Come."

"Where?"

"Back to your camp."

"I have nothing there. I could not even kill you. I have nothing left." But she had the answer, she thought. She finally understood why he had done what he had. She'd thought it would allow her to die. She knew he wanted it to allow her to live.

He held her tightly, forcing her to look into his eyes. "Because you did not kill me, you have everything left."

She shook her head and gasped. "You are so arrogant!"

"I have always loved you."

"Do not say that!"

"You are all there ever was. Come with me. Let me get you away from this place. Give me that much. Then if you want me to, I will go."

He had said that before.

She began stumbling after him. He found his horse, swung

up on it and lifted her ahead of him. She trembled violently as she let herself sink back against his chest.

She could not forgive him.

She could not believe him.

She began crying again. She still loved him.

Quanah caught up with them late in the afternoon. As soon as he reached the silent huddled camp, he looked for Raven.

"Haitsi, come walk with me."

They went a distance from the others. Quanah stood for a long time looking back at his ruined people.

"They beat Eeshatai to his death," he said finally.

Raven nodded. He was not surprised.

"We lost only nine, but there are many more wounded."

"It is not the numbers," Raven said, and Quanah groaned.

"No. It is new guns every time I blink. It is more white men with every sun I open my eyes."

"Would you give up then?"

"No," he said finally. "We are Nermenuh." He waited, breathing for a moment as though in pain. "How many of them are there? Did my father ever ask you that?"

"I do not think he ever really wanted to know." Raven closed his eyes. "There are a lot, *haitsi.* So many."

"Tell me what my father would do now."

Raven felt his throat close. *Oh, Nokoni, guide me, wherever you are, hear me and let me say the right thing. For him, and for you.* He opened his mouth without any true idea of what might come out, then peace spread through him, strange, aching, but all right.

It was as though he spoke Nokoni's voice.

"Hide," he answered. "Go to a place where they are least likely to look for you."

Quanah looked up at the sky. "Then what?"

He could not lie to him. "Then they will come looking for you."

Quanah nodded without much expression.

"There is a man named MacKenzie, leading their troops. He has heard of you and he wants you. You are the only strong chief left. If they get you, they have the Nermenuh. Kills In The Dark is inconsequential to them. He has only five Penateka lodges out there somewhere." Not even their eternal enemy, the white men, respected Kills In The Dark.

"Will they hang me?" Quanah asked.

"Do you care?"

Quanah smiled at his insight. "For my people, yes."

"Neither you nor your father ever signed a treaty, so you have broken no word." Raven wondered if that would matter and prayed to the spirits that it would. "I doubt if they will let you roam Comancheria at will, though. And they probably will not let you keep more than one wife."

Quanah gave a haunting replica of his father's grin. "So *you* go tell them that all but one of them will have to go."

Raven managed to laugh. Quanah took a deep breath.

"Then it is over," he said. "But they will have to come get me. I will never go to them in surrender."

An immense pain, an agony of regret, closed around Raven's heart. "No." It was a matter of pride, of principle.

"We will go to the big canyon. Palo Duro. A white man cannot find it until he happens right upon it."

Raven did not mention that he had once thought that about the Penateka canyons also.

Fifty

There was barely time for them to settle into Palo Duro. Quanah's wives put up his lodge, and Raven stopped Storm Trail as she was about to duck inside.

He touched only her elbow. "Come with me," he said quietly.

Her pulse scrambled with longing and the last denial she could muster. She looked back at him, and he found her eyes and held them.

"I want to be alone with you before they come," he went on.

No. Fear flared in her chest. She could not let herself believe anything he would say. Loving him was too dangerous, too painful. If she had learned nothing else through all their seasons together and apart, she had learned that.

But the white-eyes were coming. Again. And that was what decided her because there would always be white-eyes, and there were just some things she had learned she could not fight against.

He turned away and began walking out of the camp. Storm Trail took a shuddering breath and went after him.

He stopped in a switchback not far from the others. She slipped into it after him and hugged herself, feeling somehow safer hidden in its narrow rocky walls. Raven stared up at the night sky.

"Everything I did," he said finally, "I did for love of you."

She flinched. "Is this what you wanted? To give me excuses?"

"No, and I do not mean it as one. But we did not finish back there. It is important to me that you know."

A cold shaft of fear filled her. He was talking as though he was going to die when they went back. But then they were probably all going to die when the white men came this time, one way or the other.

"Even chasing after the white men that last time . . . you said I did it out of shame and hunger, but I did it because those men were destroying you."

A deep shudder went through her.

"Suvate, that is all." He turned to leave.

"Wait!"

He looked at her.

"Just . . . wait." She licked her lips. "I want to end it . . . with you."

He took a step closer to her and put his arms around her. Storm Trail went still, and his embrace tightened. She felt the urgency in him build as he shifted her weight, easing her down to the ground.

Then finally he kissed her again.

She gave a husky groan as his body covered hers, at the hard ridge of his flesh pressing against her through their clothing. She began kissing him back. *So long.* But she remembered his strange white-eyes custom well, and she met his tongue as he kept invading her mouth, hard and deep, relentlessly. Finally he moved his mouth to her breasts, biting the tip of one, then the other, so gently through her doeskin.

Through forty years he was the only lover she had ever known, the only one she needed.

"Can I take it off?" he asked, his voice deep and ragged, tugging at her dress.

Instead of responding, she met his urgent hands on her body, telling him with hungry strokes of her own. She pulled at his buckskins, then she wrinkled her nose.

They smelled.

She laughed for the first time in too many seasons, and too quickly it turned into tears.

He pushed her dress up, his mouth releasing her tight nipple only at the last moment to slide the tattered cloth up to her neck. She gave a low broken moan, but then his touch was back. His hands cupped the warm weight of her breasts in his palms. His touch shaped her ribs and her hips with the same kind of hunger that had driven him as long as she had known him. His fingers slid up between her legs, and she opened for him as she had always done.

He penetrated the waiting heat of her body, watching her face as though he would memorize it. And even as she gasped and arched, even as she reached out for him, she watched him, too. And then he plunged himself into her again.

It was like the first time and the last time, and her breath flew from her in pleasure and regret. His gaze stayed with her as the old sensation of tension coiled and rushed inside her, making it so much more intimate. She felt him stiffen as well, even as the first cries of horror and resignation came from back in the camp.

The white-eyes had come—for the last time.

So much finality, so many goodbyes.

He kissed her once again, lingeringly, deep, then his mouth skimmed over her eyes and her cheek. "Everything," he said again, "all of it, for love of you."

He helped her to her feet and watched her pull her clothing back into place, and he thought she did it like a cat who had just lapped up a bowl of cream she fully considered her due.

There were scattered sounds of gunfire now.

They left the switchback. The scene in the center of the canyon was both worse and better than Raven had feared. The soldiers came down over the rim—*Cavalry*—and the People waited for them stoically. Only a few warriors raised arms, and they were shot down.

The women did not keen this time, and that perhaps was

the worst thing of all, Raven thought—their total exhaustion of grief.

"What would you like to do?" Raven asked quietly.

"Do?"

"Do you just want to go to them?"

Storm Trail was shaking. "What will they do with us?"

He had sworn never to lie to her. "They will put you on a reservation."

She looked at him wildly. "A *what?*"

"It is land with fences. They will keep you inside, and make you live white. But they will feed you and they will clothe you and you will not have to worry that the buffalo are gone."

"No." She shook her head frantically. *"No."*

"Then we will run."

She stared at him, her jaw slack. "Will they let us?"

"No."

She understood slowly. They would shoot them for trying it. He watched the knowledge transform her face, watched her chin thrust out and come up, watched her eyes spark and her shoulders straighten, and he thought she looked nineteen again. He loved her more in that moment than in all the other years combined.

It was right, she thought. It was the only way it could all end, so many circles of seasons, beginning in Tex-us, ending in these last hidden reaches of Comancheria. They would die together.

"I am Comanche," she whispered. "I cannot give up. But . . . hold me."

"Always."

And then he saw Silas.

The boy, the man, was on a horse nearby, staring at them. His expression was strange, twisted. He had not called her name at the Adobe Walls fight, had not found her, but Raven was sure he understood who she was now.

Do it, he willed him with all his strength, all his *puha*. He called to his spirit-raven and he begged his old white-eyes god. He had never known hope was so agonizing.

Silas did nothing.

Raven cursed him and loved him and wept inside. He looked at Storm Trail. Her eyes skimmed over the young man without ever knowing he was Thunder Eyes, somehow, impossibly, not guessing, and Raven knew it was better that way.

"We should go now," he managed.

"Yes," she agreed bravely. "Which way?"

"I always loved the south, that Penateka land."

Raven whistled for his horse. The animal trotted to him out of the confusion. He swung up on him and pulled her astride, settling her in front of him. He held her as they galloped off, toward the canyon rim, and together they waited for the gunfire.

"Hey!" a soldier shouted.

"What?" Silas asked absently, his eyes on the man and woman who were escaping.

"They're running, for Christ sake! *Hit* them!"

"Let them go," he said flatly.

"Are you *crazy?*"

"The guy's white," he pointed out.

The other soldier squinted after the fleeing couple. No one else seemed to notice their flight. "Are you sure?"

"Very."

"Well, then, if he's white, I reckon he can live anywhere," the soldier said finally. "But her—she needs to be on a reservation. And if she won't go, we really ought to kill her."

The sudden intensity of Silas's rage stunned him. He did not know where it came from, and he had not expected it. But it boiled fast, rushing up in his blood.

And what would you see done with me?

He laughed harshly. He had inherited a white man's eyes. By a fluke of fate in the womb, he could live anywhere.

The other soldier raised his gun when Silas would not do it. Silas grabbed the weapon and pushed it down violently.

"Shoot her, and I guess you'd better shoot me next."

The soldier gaped at him. "Huh? Why?"

"She's my mother."

Epilogue

1876

The cabin stood in a timber break beside a full tumbling river. The grasslands stretched out before it, toward the great escarpment far to the east that had once guarded Nermenuh land. Some small rocky hills sat closer to the south, studded with scrubby cedar. Cottonwoods and mesquite tangled near the water, and thickets of plum and grapes were wild there.

The Penateka had always had the best of all the land.

Storm Trail stood on a low knoll with the cabin behind her and the vast reaches of Texas ahead of her. Far in the distance, a straggling line of Nermenuh made their way back to their reservation. She had made a personal vow to stand here, to wait for them, until it was finished.

Quanah had convinced the white men to allow the People to leave their reservation to hunt again. She smiled to herself. Quanah had turned out to be quite a politician. Raven said he could sell a drowning man a pair of stone boots. She wondered if it was his Parker blood. Texas, at least, considered him their own true son, even as they had once despised and slaughtered the Comanche he stood for.

The rations they gave the People were poor. The Nermenuh were, as they had been for so long now, hungry. And so

Quanah had gathered them together for one last magnificent hunt, like in the old days. Now they were returning.

Their ponies were not laden.

They had known of course that there were no buffalo left. She had known they would not find anything—but her heart was Nermenuh, and so she had hoped, prayed, against all odds. Perhaps there would be one small herd left somewhere, and the hunters would find it.

She heard the door of the cabin open. Footsteps came behind her. She looked about to see Raven, and she smiled.

"Are you all right?" He closed his strong arms around her from behind. Storm Trail leaned into him.

"I . . . hurt . . . in their place," she said in halting English, then she gave up on the twangy words she so detested. "My heart bleeds for them, and for the piece of myself that will always be them," she said in Comanche.

"I hurt, too," he said softly in English. Then he added in Comanche, "I bleed as well."

They watched for a while longer in silence, then he pulled her back toward the cabin. "Come inside. It is good there."

She gave him a wry look. It *was* good inside, but it was still a white-eyes house. She could not lie in their bed and look up through the smoke hole at the stars. It had corners, and corners bred dust and cobwebs with a quickness that boggled her mind. Its floor was hard, not gentle and giving as Mother Earth. But he had built it for her. He had built it for the white men, who would leave them alone on Nermenuh land as long as they pretended to be white.

Comancheria.

Raven stepped back to allow her to go through the door first. She looked around at those gathered by the big iron stove, and she finally smiled.

Thunder Eyes grinned back at her. She would never be able to call him Silas.

"Did they find any?" he asked.

She touched a hand to his head, to his thick black curls. "No."

"But you knew that—" he began.

"Yes."

"And you are sad anyway."

"I remember." She sat down beside the stove, and her face softened at his distress. "I am not sad. Not right this minute."

How could she be? He was Raven's most astonishing gift to her. She knew now that he had come back to Comancheria to find their son. For a long time he had thought he had failed her in that respect, too, but then, six months ago, after struggling with his own demons, Silas had ridden up to their door.

He sat on the floor, beside the chair that held his wife. The woman was young, beautiful, with snapping black eyes and a belly swollen with their babe. Her hair was fair. She was one of Quanah's people, the daughter of a stolen white child and a fierce Nermenuh warrior.

Raven made coffee. That was one good thing about this white world on Nermenuh land, Storm Trail thought. Once *toopah* had been a rare luxury.

The young woman put a hand to the child in her womb as the wind picked up outside. "It is a good night for stories," she said. "Tell us one, *Pia*. Tell us what you remember."

Raven settled down next to Storm Trail and watched her, waiting. When she spoke of the old days, he could always see it, smell it, feel it all over again. He loved her stories.

"Once," she began, "there were so many buffalo we moved camp every few suns when a new herd was spotted. Nermenuh was a spirit, you see, a way of life, as much as a people. It was freedom . . ." she gave a sly, sideways grin at Raven ". . . and it was arrogance. It meant chasing the wind. It was a *feeling,* but the people themselves . . . ah, the People. We held off the white men for forty long years."

Raven brought her more coffee and she paused to sip.

"Once—do you remember, Raven?—we raided all the way to the sea. . . ."

IF ROMANCE BE THE FRUIT OF LIFE—
READ ON—
BREATH-QUICKENING HISTORICALS FROM PINNACLE

WILDCAT (722, $4.99)
by Rochelle Wayne
No man alive could break Diana Preston's fiery spirit . . . until seductive Vince Gannon galloped onto Diana's sprawling family ranch. Vince, a man with dark secrets, would sweep her into his world of danger and desire. And Diana couldn't deny the powerful yearnings that branded her as his own, for all time!

THE HIGHWAY MAN (765, $4.50)
by Nadine Crenshaw
When a trumped-up murder charge forced beautiful Jane Fitzpatrick to flee her home, she was found and sheltered by the highwayman—a man as dark and dangerous as the secrets that haunted him. As their hiding place became a place of shared dreams—and soaring desires—Jane knew she'd found the love she'd been yearning for!

SILKEN SPURS (756, $4.99)
by Jane Archer
Beautiful Harmony Harper, leader of a notorious outlaw gang, rode the desert plains of New Mexico in search of justice and vengeance. Now she has captured powerful and privileged Thor Clarke-Jargon, who is everything Harmony has ever hated—and all she will ever want. And after Harmony has taken the handsome adventurer hostage, she herself has become a captive—of her own desires!

WYOMING ECSTASY (740, $4.50)
by Gina Robins
Feisty criminal investigator, July MacKenzie, solicits the partnership of the legendary half-breed gunslinger-detective Nacona Blue. After being turned down, July—never one to accept the meaning of the word no— finds a way to convince Nacona to be her partner . . . first in business— then in passion. Across the wilds of Wyoming, and always one step ahead of trouble, July surrenders to passion's searing demands!

Available wherever paperbacks are sold, or order direct from the Publisher. Send cover price plus 50¢ per copy for mailing and handling to Penguin USA, P.O. Box 999, c/o Dept. 17109, Bergenfield, NJ 07621. Residents of New York and Tennessee must include sales tax. DO NOT SEND CASH.

HISTORICAL ROMANCE FROM PINNACLE BOOKS

LOVE'S RAGING TIDE   (381, $4.50)
by Patricia Matthews

Melissa stood on the veranda and looked over the sweeping acres of Great Oaks that had been her family's home for two generations, and her eyes burned with anger and humiliation. Today her home would go beneath the auctioneer's hammer and be lost to her forever. Two men eagerly awaited the auction: Simon Crouse and Luke Devereaux. Both would try to have her, but they would have to contend with the anger and pride of girl turned woman . . .

CASTLE OF DREAMS   (334, $4.50)
by Flora M. Speer

Meredith would never forget the moment she first saw the baron of Afoncaer, with his armor glistening and blue eyes shining honest and true. Though she knew she should hate this Norman intruder, she could only admire the lean strength of his body, the golden hue of his face. And the innocent Welsh maiden realized that she had lost her heart to one she could only call enemy.

LOVE'S DARING DREAM   (372, $4.50)
by Patricia Matthews

Maggie's escape from the poverty of her family's bleak existence gives fire to her dream of happiness in the arms of a true, loving man. But the men she encounters on her tempestuous journey are men of wealth, greed, and lust. To survive in their world she must control her newly awakened desires, as her beautiful body threatens to betray her at every turn.

Available wherever paperbacks are sold, or order direct from the Publisher. Send cover price plus 50¢ per copy for mailing and handling to Penguin USA, P.O. Box 999, c/o Dept. 17109, Bergenfield, NJ 07621. Residents of New York and Tennessee must include sales tax. DO NOT SEND CASH.